SHADOWRUN:
IDENTITY: CRISIS

PHAEDRA WELDON

This is a work of fiction. Names, characters, places and incidents either are the products of the author's imagination or are used fictitiously, and any resemblance to actual persons, living or dead, business establishments, events or locales is entirely coincidental. The publisher does not have any control over and does not assume any responsibility for author or third-party Web sites or their content.

If you purchased this book without a cover you should be aware that this book is stolen property. It was reported as "unsold and destroyed" to the publisher and neither the author nor the publisher has received any payment for this "stripped book."

The scanning, uploading and distribution of this book via the Internet or via any other means without the permission of the publisher is illegal and punishable by law. Please purchase only authorized electronic editions, and do not participate in or encourage electronic piracy of copyrighted materials. Your support of the authors' rights is appreciated.

SHADOWRUN: IDENTITY: CRISIS
Cover art by Janny Wurts
Design by Matt Heerdt and David Kerber
Editing by John Helfers

©2020 The Topps Company, Inc. All Rights Reserved. Shadowrun & Matrix are registered trademarks and/or trademarks of The Topps Company, Inc., in the United States and/or other countries. Catalyst Game Labs and the Catalyst Game Labs logo are trademarks of InMediaRes Productions LLC. No part of this work may be reproduced, stored in a retrieval system, or transmitted in any form or by any means, without the prior permission in writing of the Copyright Owner, nor be otherwise circulated in any form other than that in which it is published.

Published by Catalyst Game Labs,
an imprint of InMediaRes Productions, LLC
7108 S. Pheasant Ridge Drive • Spokane, WA 99224

PROLOGUE

SOUTH BOSTON
UNKNOWN DATE
NEAR MIDNIGHT

In front of me, I saw a deserted alley.

Behind me was darkness.

My memories lived in that darkness, like a spirit not yet wishing to be seen as it hovered on the edge of manifesting in this world, or remaining safe in its own. It whispered to me as I looked up through the broken rooftops, above the glittering lights of Boston in the distance, north of where I found myself. Rain tapped my cheeks, my forehead, my bare shoulders as my cold feet scraped across the pitted and oily asphalt beneath them. The smell of the alley ahead was rich with decay, the foul odor of death and desperation.

Or was that *my* desperation I smelled? My sweat beneath the rain, beneath the night sky, beneath the ravaged ruins of the dark world I found myself in. I also smelled something I couldn't forget. The coppery scent of blood.

My blood.

I pressed my filthy hands against my ripped and shredded shirt on my chest to staunch the bleeding. It didn't hurt, but it should. My heart thundered against my palms as my head told me to keep moving, reasoned with my intellect, telling it that my chance of survival would be higher if I disappeared into the alley instead of remaining here in the open, along a deserted road between empty stores, their signs hanging by wires corroded by time and the elements.

Neon was the light to see by, its pink, green, and blue hum filling the spaces in the night as I caught my breath. I held something in my right hand. I could make out its silver surface, the soft blue and white glow of a screen and blood, sticky and full of hair on one of its corners. I'd taken this from someone, hadn't I? I had a half-formed memory of striking someone, but I couldn't see their face.

It was a commlink. Unlocked and untraceable.

I heard their boots beating the asphalt, the whisper of their communications in my ears, but I couldn't make out what they were saying. I shivered as I looked to my left, my right, and then dove headlong into the darkened alley in front of me.

I wasn't prepared for just how dark it was. The neon from the street didn't reach far enough inside, and I hissed as my battered feet caught on rocks and sharp objects. But I kept running because I knew on an instinctual level my life depended on it.

I wanted to puke. I wanted to rest. I wanted to find someplace warm.

But above all, I wanted to live.

Suddenly I could see down the narrow alley as everything turned an eerie shade of green. I stopped and blinked several times, putting a bloody hand to my face, to my cheeks below my eyes as a faint memory came to me. *Cybereyes...* At least that memory returned when I wanted it. I held up the commlink. My eyes had paired with it. I engaged the local grid to access RFID tags—that is, if anything in this foul place still had them.

A few things popped up on the augmented reality provided by the commlink, projected as an overlay on the scene in front of me. Manufacturers' tags, mostly. But I could see now, and I easily picked my way through even as I caught the shadow of something flying overhead. It cast enough shade through the green light for me to know someone or something had just jumped from one building to the other, across the alley.

Could they see me? I didn't know, so I stopped, looked around, and spotted a dark indention in one of the walls low to the ground. I slid inside and curled up before quietly pulling a piece of trash closer to cover me.

Their footfalls slowed, but I could see them coming. Three shapes. I knew there had been four before. I spotted the human girl and man, and the bulk of the troll with them. Most of them had cyber implants, upgrades that gleamed in my green vision.

The girl was looking around as if scanning. Probably had the same night vision I had, so I pushed myself as far into the hole as I could and held my breath. If she had infra-red to see my body heat, I was dead.

Abruptly, something landed inches away from me, but in front of them. Here was the fourth pursuer. I kept my breathing shallow as I watched the boots join the other three. I couldn't see his face. He stood with his back to my hiding place, but I did see a long, blond braid swing down to his lower back. The end was decorated with a large bead of some kind. "He came in here."

"Yeah, I know," the girl said, and I could see she had goggles on top of her head. Small sparkles followed her nose and jawline and a tag popped up that read *Josef's Tattoo and Piercings*, and gave me the address. I dismissed it.

"We saw him run in here, too." She lowered the weapon she kept balanced on her hip. "How is he still moving? I nailed him in the chest."

"Then obviously you missed," said the mystery man. His speech pattern, pronunciation, was very different than the other three. He wasn't from the slums. No, this one moved in loftier circles of society.

"We ain't got time for fight'n," the troll said, his deep voice low enough to feel it rumble against the asphalt beneath me. "If we don't find him and make sure he's dead, we don't get paid."

"Sloppy," said the male human. He raised his arm, and I could see a slim Fairlight Excalibur deck hanging over his shoulder. Pretty pricey piece of equipment. I knew this because my love of decking units resurfaced. The girl had a commlink on her wrist. None of their weapons or equipment had tags. Smart.

I assumed they were all SINless, just like me.

But I'd had a SIN, hadn't I? I knew I needed one to interact with this world, but I...

I couldn't *remember*.

I noticed a crossbow attached to the human's back. I knew about that. I didn't know how I knew, but I flexed my left hand and *remembered* having gripped a crossbow before. *Come on brain, if you can remember that, why can't you remember my name?*

"Yeah well, you do the killing next time, Mort," the girl said.

The human had a name. Mort.

"Killing is what you three get paid for. I'm just here to make sure you do it." The one with the braid turned, scanning the narrow corridor, and I held my breath again. "This alley runs for a quarter mile with two breaks. If he's bleeding like you say he is, he should be easy to track."

Mort pointed to the sky. "Not with this rain. It's already washing the blood away with the rest of the garbage."

"He's dead," The troll piped up. "Or he'll be dead soon. Ain't nobody in this part of town gonna help him. They'll kill 'im and rob 'im first. I say we done the job, and we go get paid."

"I'm not going back without some kind of proof. Clothing, lock of hair, a finger..." Mort said.

"That's disgusting, you know that?" The human female said.

The man with the braid moved back. "I'm going to circle around. You three can do what you want—as long as you find him." He disappeared, leaving the three of them standing in the cramped alley. I exhaled slowly, tried to quiet my anxiety. I was getting lightheaded due to loss of blood. Adrenaline and pure fear had kept me going so far, and now that I was still, I was dying faster.

I needed to move. But I couldn't if these three were still following me.

The logical thing to do would be to eliminate them. But I didn't have a weapon.

Something sung in my arms and legs, a power that surged straight into my toes. My muscles vibrated, subtly at first, as the memory in my body came alive and I realized I'd just loaded activesoft into my skill wires.

I had skillwires—why would I have those?

I glanced around the area where I hid. I spotted several objects that could be used for combat, a few as shields and a few as projectiles. Something in my head calculated the odds, coming up with the predictive analysis of certain movements and outcomes. The only variables were the opponents, since I hadn't seen them fight.

"I don't know about you two," the girl said. "But I'm betting he's in there, hiding somewhere. Aren't your cybereyes showing you anything, Peter?"

The troll answered. "I ain't got infrared, just tactical. And I ain't got a map downloaded for this side of town."

"There's the real threat," Mort said. "We're in Ancients territory. I'm surprised they haven't showed up yet."

"You want 'em to?" the girl said. "Stupid piece a drek. We don't need no ganger troubles. I say we go down the alley, and if we don't see him on the other end, we get the hell outta here. There's no way that soft piece of corporate drek survived my bullets."

Peter the troll moved out ahead of them, stomping past my position. I waited for a bit for the male and then the female to move past before creeping out of my hiding place. I wanted to be stealthy about it, but I was too wobbly on my feet and made a noise. The girl bringing up the rear heard it.

She whirled and started firing her pistol. I dropped straight down, but felt air split as the bullets flew over me. I launched up, grabbed the muzzle of the gun and shoved it up into her face. Her yell, as well as the spray of blood from her nose over my forearm and face, was my reward.

I didn't wait for her to fall or drop or die. I yanked the gun from her hands and turned it, aiming it at the troll's head. The wires hummed as I aimed and fired through the green light of my cybereyes. Peter the troll's head exploded like an overripe cantaloupe as it sprayed bone and brain matter all over the place.

A shot zinged past my right shoulder, just grazing the skin as I turned the gun on Mort the human and fired. The bullets struck his neck. I was aiming for his head. But my aim was off thanks to the stinging wound on my shoulder. He gurgled and choked and grabbed his throat to stop the blood, but I could see it cascade over his fingers like a waterfall.

Within two minutes all three lay at my feet, and I was on my hands and knees, puking my guts out.

Killing...was bad. I knew this. I didn't know my name, but I knew from somewhere in my head that this wasn't me. It *couldn't* be *me.* But I'd done it. I'd taken three lives in less time than it took me to make the decision to act.

The control from the wires eased back, and I started shaking. Bad shaking. This wasn't just the cold anymore. This was worse. I knew it was shock setting in. I was gonna die out here in this alley if I didn't get someplace warm, with medical supplies and a place to rest.

I had to move fast. There was still one more pursuer out there. The man with the braid.

The rain thickened and washed away whatever had been left in my stomach. I was driven to take what I needed and fast, because I didn't know where braid man was, and I was pretty sure him or someone else had heard those shots.

I went to the human male first. Mort was about my size and height. I wasn't exactly a small man. I was in decent shape. I stripped him of his weapons, deck, commlink and his coat and boots. The boots were a little big, but nothing I couldn't handle. The coat was long and had a hood, so I used that to hide my face. The bow and the pack of arrows I kept on the synthleather strap at my hip. I tucked the tech into a coat pocket and then stripped the other two bodies of everything I could find and carry, including weapons.

Once I had what I needed, I took off down the alley and turned onto the first street it intersected. There weren't any people around, not in this weather. I slipped into the doorway of what might have been an old electronics store, but had long since been raided, the windows broken and then boarded up, and then broken again.

The grungy, black-and-white tile floor clicked under my new boots as I trotted to the back of the place, toward where I assumed the office was.

There I stripped everything off and laid it neatly on a couch I was sure had been home to more than just vermin and other men's express. There wasn't much else in the room.

Dirty, crusty rags had been stuffed in a few holes in the wall. I didn't know whether they were there to keep out the light or weather. Water trickled from a sink faucet in the back bathroom, but it was brown with rust and possible pollutants. I yanked the stiff rags out and wetted them so I could wash off as best as I could. I avoided getting them near open wounds. The mirror had been smashed long ago, but I could just make out my face in the remaining shards. It somehow felt fitting that I saw myself, my eyes, my hair, all in the fragmented pieces of a mirror, just like the missing pieces of my memory. I was older than I thought. Mid-forties maybe. My face was swollen, bruised, and torn.

I had a hole in my chest, just below my ribs, where I was still bleeding from. I was too squeamish to reach in and find these bullets that little girl said she'd pumped into me. Why wasn't I dead? How was I still moving around?

After I asked myself that question, dizziness nearly dropped me to the floor. I felt another wave of it as I staggered back into the office.

I collapsed behind the desk and couldn't get back up. The water-stained ceiling, the smell of stale cigarettes, all of it twisted my stomach again as I turned on my side and curled up.

I was gonna die here, in some stranger's past. A man who couldn't remember his own past, but had fought hard for his future.

At least...that's what I was thinking when closed my eyes for what I thought would be the very last time.

PART ONE

CHAPTER 1

BOSTON
THURSDAY, FEBRUARY 28, 2075
(TWO MONTHS EARLIER)

"Come *on*, Oli. Just use the skillwires."

I narrowed my eyes over the sight of my crossbow, mentally calculating the wind, the distance, my height, the weight of the bolt, all without the help of a computer. I didn't bother answering Jericho. It was an old argument between us. Where he enjoyed the mental and physical abilities granted from using the delicate artificial nerves implanted beside his natural ones, I preferred using my own skills. It gave me a sense of accomplishment.

I inhaled, steadied my chest, and squeezed the trigger, keeping the stock perfectly still against my cheek. I felt the sharp slap of the wire, heard the *twing* it made when the tension was released, and kept my stance as I followed the flight of the bolt.

It struck the target two centimeters to the right of my calculated intent. In other words...I missed.

"Yes! Too bad you're such a straight up guy, chummer." Jericho's exuberance could be amusing at times. Right now? Downright irritating. "'Cause that makes four to two. You owe me meat. Not that soy-drek they pass off at the Beacon Street Cafe. I want the real thing."

"Do you have to use words like that?" I lowered the crossbow and checked my feet. I preferred to shoot wearing my old diving shoes. They were lightweight, allowing my feet to breathe, and the rubber gripped the asphalt floor of the shooting range well. Of course, I knew in a real life and death situation, these ideal conditions wouldn't exist. The target would move and return fire. The floor would more than likely be littered with debris, and I wouldn't be dressed in a comfortable t-shirt and swim skins.

"Like what? You mean chummer?" Jericho, a man a foot shorter than me and with less years against his stamina, shot me a grin as he placed his own crossbow in its case. "Or drek? Sorry...too much game play lately. I keep thinking I'm in *Dark City*."

"Yeah well, that kind of language is more for the SINless. Not us. It belongs in the game." I knew I sounded elitist in my head, but I'd worked hard, coming up from humble beginnings to the point when I could afford to spend time at well-polished bow ranges like this one. Stratos was one of three places in the whole UCAS where I could practice archery for the sheer pleasure of it.

"You need to lighten up, Oli," Jericho said as he draped a towel over his shoulder and put his hands on his hips. I set my crossbow into its form-foam compartment of the case. "Look, I know you're all into actually learning this stuff." He waved at the half-empty shooting area. "But with the skillwire you've got, you could buy some serious skillsoft for that thing and shoot just like Crisis."

"I don't want to shoot like Crisis." Crisis was the name of my character in a game Jericho and I liked to play called *Dark City*. I'd started the character in a different game when I was a kid, living in the south side of Boston. We didn't have tight Matrix access back then. Couldn't afford it. So I was always over at Jericho's playing, raising my stats and feeling a sense of accomplishment when my name posted on the high player boards.

Crisis became my alter ego in a way, through the rough years at school (I was tall for my age and always bigger than the other kids. I wasn't overweight, just...broad.), then my dad's death, and lastly, my grandmother. My grandfather was still alive, as far as I know, but I hadn't seen him in a decade. He'd never been around much when I was growing up, and practically not at all until his son died. Mom had retreated back to San Francisco, where she was born, to live with her sister.

It was sometime in those years when I found myself dependent on Crisis that I realized I preferred the online persona's life than my own. Crisis was sharp, skilled, quick-witted, smart and had more nuyen than he knew what to do with. And when I moved his stats over to *Dark City*, I found myself interested in changing up his style and his character.

In *Dark City*, Crisis was an assassin. And a damn good one. Quiet. Efficient. Lethal. And wanted by every law enforcement agency on the planet. I got so involved in the character and I let Jericho talk me into going in with him to get us both cyber modifications. I'd only go as far as skillwires, and I had to get the best. No half-assing it. Luckily the girl at customer service liked me and threw in cybereyes and her number. It was the biggest expense of my life, but at the time I thought it was worth it. And I got pretty good at using them and sprang for some language-softs as well. It was easier than actually learning them. Who had time for that?

Now, four years later and co-CEO of Andreas Martin Analysis Systems, AMAS for short, I played *Dark City* so infrequently that I couldn't even remember where I'd left the character when I logged out...which was about a month ago. I still used the projection-based knowsofts and the languasofts, but not the wires. It just...felt like cheating. Because when the software was gone, so was the ability and knowledge.

"Well, you should. Crisis is a badass. And you know..." Jericho leaned down as I shut the case. "They say there's a little of ourselves in our personas."

"Oh come on, Jer. Not that pseudo-religious Matrix crap." I stood and checked around the area. "Looks like we're good. Want that steak now?"

"Not tonight. Got an early morning."

"Too bad. Can't do it tomorrow. Got the company party, then Nicole and I are heading up to the mountains till Monday."

Jericho bounced on his feet. "You doing it up there?"

I gave him a look, since the way he'd said that sounded pornographic. "If you mean am I asking, yes I am. Ring's paid off and packed. We're meeting at eight, then taking the tram. Not risking the Honda on that kind of trip."

"Probably a good idea." Jericho picked up his bow case as I retrieved my own. "So..." he said as we started walking down the long path to the exit. The sky was just showing the early signs of dawn with brilliant hues in orange and pink. "When's the date?"

"For the wedding?"

"No, the acquisition."

I smiled at him. Jericho and I didn't work at the same place. He'd graduated from MIT&T, and then stayed around when they made him an offer he couldn't refuse. "End of the year."

"Wow...AMAS is going to be a part of NeoNET."

"Not really a part of. Just a R&D lab. The only reason they're interested is because of my project."

He looked at me sideways, his brows crossed over his nose. "So what's to stop them from just shutting the thing down? They'll own it after...when?"

"Deal finalizes December 13th. There's this big to-do planned in celebration."

"Yikes, that's like nine months from now."

"Yes. But they won't shut it down. Mason made sure in the contract. AMAS stays open as a subsidiary company. We keep working on what we're doing, but it's funded by NeoNET nuyen now."

"Sounds iffy to me," Jericho said.

I shrugged. "Nicole's going with me tomorrow night. You sure you don't want an invite?"

"Me? At a corp party? Uh-uh." Jericho laughed. "They'd make me wear shoes."

I had to laugh as well. He'd never liked shoes, even when we were young.

"Think you might reconsider and sell your parent's house? I mean, won't you move into an arcology?"

"No," I shook my head. "I still want to have it. It's on good land in a pretty okay neighborhood. Nicole likes it. She wants to upgrade it some, but thinks we should live there." I'd grown up in the suburbs, with the quiet and having neighbors I knew. My parents had been great at throwing block parties...but I doubted anyone did that any more. Not in that subdivision.

"You ever bring her here? Tell her about your elven archer fixation?"

We approached the office door and stepped inside. I checked the public board for my scores and was satisfied. Not Crisis's scores...but enough for me, the flesh and blood part of him. "I don't have an elven archer fixation."

Jericho snorted. "You do know you'd be better protected if you learned how to fire a gun."

"I know how to fire a gun. Without the wires."

"You know how to fire a *rifle*. That's like a crossbow. Good at long range."

"Are you after something?" I set my case on the floor by the front door.

"Well...you know that troll that likes to hang out in Dark City's cantina?"

"Yeah?" I shrugged my coat on as Jericho put his on. "Serilious."

"You know he's got that gang—"

"No."

"Oh come on. He's offered a lot of nuyen if we joined up with him. He wants you to be his rifleman."

"He wants a sniper."

"You're good at sniping." Jericho smiled. "In game."

"No. I don't like gangs in real life, and I sure as hell won't deal with them in a game. Now, am I giving you a ride?"

Jericho looked crestfallen, but nodded as he picked up his bow case. "Fine."

We stepped out into the brisk breeze as wind from Boston Harbor whipped a few loose papers and candy wrappers about. It wasn't the cleanest place, but it wasn't filthiest either.

But it was the only place I could pretend, for a little while, to be more than what I was.

CHAPTER 2

FRIDAY, MARCH 1, 2075

By the time Nicole and I arrived at AMAS, the party was in full swing. The lobby had been transformed into a gold-themed wonderland, complete with dance floor and bar. AR-projected doubloon-like coins fell continuously from the ceiling, giving the impression of raining money. I ducked when we walked in, then felt heat rise to my cheeks in embarrassment when Nicole laughed and I realized my mistake. When I looked again, my cybereyes projected a small window with information about the projection software used. When the company's ad started up in the peripheral of my vision, I dismissed it.

"Mason went all out for this," Nicole said as we strolled through the celebratory crowd. I recognized most of the faces. The ones I didn't, the tags picked up by my eyes gave me a constant feed of NeoNET personnel, their names, their rankings, earnings, and titles.

"I'll say. I saw the billing for this extravaganza. The salmon's real, farm-raised and imported from Chiba."

"And the Champagne?"

I winked at her. "The real stuff." We stopped on the other side of the dancing crowd and I stepped back to really look at her. I hadn't had a chance since picking her up outside her place in Beacon Hill. But now...taking in her silver gown that clung to her in all the right places, partially attached with paste and invisible fasteners, she was a goddess to me.

Nicole came from one hundred percent corp stock. Raised with a silver spoon in her mouth, she was the youngest of three children, born to one of the UCAS's top business and market analysts, Nathan O'Neal. I'd studied his texts all through college, and used his theories on economic growth and decline to create a few analysis programs myself.

Unfortunately, the latest one, a program we called *strip7*, hadn't worked. I'd worried my failures would cripple the company and jeopardize NeoNET's interest. According to Mason, it had quite the opposite reaction. They applauded my imagination and drive, and were more than interested in what we'd accomplished. Mason had made sure in the contracts that my team would be richly rewarded for their work.

"What're you looking at?"

"You." I leaned in and rubbed my nose to hers. She was magnificent. "I sometimes can't believe you fell for a guy like me."

She poked at my tie with her index finger, a silvery diamond outsparkling the glitter of the evening. I only hoped by tomorrow night, she'd accept my smaller, less extravagant offering of marriage. "You need to stop being so self-deprecating, Oliver. You're brilliant, good-looking, and you clean up nice, too."

I winked at her. "Bags packed?"

"I've been packed for weeks. I can't wait to spend three nights alone with you. No jobs, no rush, no worries."

To hear her say that meant the world to me. I just wished my dad could have met her and that my mother wanted to.

"Oliver!"

Nicole and I both turned to see my business partner, Mason Andreas, approaching. He looked incredible in his gold and black tuxedo. His dark hair had been slicked away from his face, making his high cheekbones look almost hawkish. Gold clamps decorated the pointed tips of his ears. As always, I felt under-dressed and ill-conceived next to him. Mason wasn't an elf, but a human like me, yet I understood why he had the augmentation done. In Boston, the bigger the point, the better.

I'd met Mason ten years ago, at a business conference in Seattle. I had a job as a rising software engineer, and at the time, thought I wanted to get into the security writing of decking units. I'd always distrusted the idea of PANs. Yes they claimed to be loaded with onboard security, but analysis on my part and a boatload of research had showed me that wasn't the case. There had been more PANs hacked in the past twenty years than any other common network in the UCAS.

Mason, my junior by about five years, had liked my theories, and my program and taken me in as an intern. At thirty-five, I thought I'd made it, being hired in by one of the up and coming businessmen of the time. That was just the start to bigger things.

And here we were, on the brink of moving Andreas Martin Analysis Systems toward a two-star rating.

We shook hands, and he kissed Nicole on the cheek. I didn't object too strenuously to this show of affection. After all, they had been engaged once, before I came to work for Mason. I never knew what happened between them, only that two years into my internship, they canceled their wedding and Mason threw himself further into the business. I'd never asked Nicole either. Wasn't my place.

Did I ever wonder if Mason held a grudge against me for dating his ex? At first, but after confronting him about it, and telling him I'd stop seeing her if it bothered him, his whole demeanor changed, and he promised me that Nicole and myself were free to do whatever we wanted, but not to let it get in the way of my work.

"My darling, you look as divine as ever."

"Why Mason—you're almost chipper!"

"I'll take that as a compliment." He glanced at me. "Would you mind if I take your young man with me to sign some papers?"

"You go ahead." She turned to me, grabbed my hand and squeezed it. "Get back to me."

"I will."

I watched her disappear into the crowd before Mason took my arm. "Come on. I set up the papers in my office."

We chatted about the party, about the upcoming acquisition and about mine and Nicole's weekend getaway as we strolled down the hall. Mason's office was at the end, a large, lavish spread with couches, wall vids, a real mahogany desk, and a sparkling view of Boston and the Charles River.

The paperwork lay on the desk. I went to take a look as Mason meandered to the wall opposite the view and opened a panel. The walls folded back and revealed an impressive bar, complete with a robotic server.

"Can I fix you a drink, Mr. Andreas?" the enhanced female voice asked. I watched as several arms, like that of a spider, moved up and down along tracks in front of vintage bottles of the finest liquors.

"Bourbon, neat," Mason said. "Anything for you, Oliver?"

"No. I'm fine."

"I really wish you'd reconsider and have at least one drink."

"You know why I don't touch the stuff." Alcoholism ran in my family, detected early in the genes. My dad refused to drink after he saw his dad die from it, and later scared me the hell away from it. He swore the gene was as prevalent in my genome as it had been in his own father's. Being a drunk wasn't my plan.

The contracts were printed on real paper, with what my cybereyes told was indelible ink. Once used, the print couldn't be erased or manipulated, which was good since Mason always chose to do his financial reports and personnel records on paper. He disliked digital footprints, and with all of his holdings recorded this way, only he had access to them. I wondered how NeoNET, the corp that brought us the Matrix, felt about this. I doubted they were going to keep copies of the contract off the digital highway.

They had been bound in hardcover, much like the old books my dad used to collect, and were now mine. Small markers had been set on the right edge of a few pages and as I flipped to them, I saw they pointed to where I needed to sign. "No one else has signed these."

"I know." Mason had his drink in hand as he stood on the opposite side of his desk. "The actual signing ceremony is Monday. How are we supposed to look all official and sign something if we already had?" He smiled and sipped his bourbon.

He had a point. The only reason I was signing early was because of my vacation with Nicole. Which...worried me a little. "Look," I said as I lowered the contract binder. "I can come back early. Nicole would understand because this is important. All of the officers should be there."

"Oliver," Mason said as he set his drink on the desk. "It's all right. You deserve this vacation and time away with Nicole. Please...take it. And be ready to come back to work refreshed on Tuesday, okay? The acquisition won't officially take place until December. This is all just a formality."

"Mr. Andreas?" A voice interrupted as the door opened. He hadn't actually closed it and there hadn't been a knock. Mason hated the sound of knocking.

Ecostuce Lew stood inside the door. Or that's what the AR tag said when I looked at him. NeoNET. Ork. Manager of Acquisitions and Sales. Southside division. Boston. I sort of recognized the name. It wasn't one to forget that easily. His profile picture for his public dossier didn't quite fit with the tall, thin, suited ork in the office. The picture on the projected tag was more robust, with a deeper green to his skin and smiling over his tusks.

The reality looked...frightened.

I set the binder on the desk as Mason strode to Ecostuce. They spoke in hushed voices, but I could still hear them. What surprised me was that they switched to Sperethiel, the elven language. Either the ork spoke Sperethiel better than English, which seemed unlikely, or was it possible that Mason didn't want me to know what they were talking about? Did he forget I had access to Sperethiel linguasoft? It was true I didn't have it loaded at the moment, since it rested on the company's server as part of a subscription, and if I accessed it at that moment, as CEO, he'd receive a warning I had loaded it. That would tell him I was listening in.

Not that I needed it. Sperethiel was the first language I'd learned when I started with the company, and discovered Mason Andreas loved all things elven.

"I told you not to interrupt. This is very important."

"I know sir, but you said to alert you the second MIT&T received the dump."

Mason sighed. *"I take it they received everything as agreed on?"*

"Yes sir..." Ecstuce hesitated, and I thought I saw him glance at me. I kept myself looking busy by flipping through the contract, even though I'd read it over a hundred times. But with the situation unfolding in front of me, a small part of me said to sit and read it *again*, but it was getting late, and I didn't want to be cooped up in Mason's office all night. Yet, I couldn't stop listening to their conversation. *"I-D needs confirmation."*

"They'll have it, and remind them that I'll give it. And not to move before they hear from me. Now get back to your room."

"But, sir..." and now the ork *sounded* frightened as his voice quivered. *"He wants to talk to you in private."*

"Liayah. *I'll call him in a few minutes.*"

The ork bowed and disappeared from the door. Mason turned to me and put on a smile. "Sorry about the interruption."

"No problem. Is there something you need to do?" I smiled and gestured to the contract, careful not to let on that I'd understood every word they'd said. "You don't have to babysit me, Mase."

"You're never going to stop calling me that, are you?"

I smiled. "No. But only because it irritates you. Look, I can sign these and leave them here."

Mason seemed to hesitate. What? Was he afraid I'll do something wrong? Like what? And why had his heart rate increased? I could see it on the profile dossier tags. "Are you sure?"

"I am. I'll just sign them and head back to Nicole."

"Okay. I'll see you back in the party." He picked up his drink and turned to leave.

"When do I get my copies of the contract?" It was a good question, and one I'd almost forgot to ask.

Mason looked back. "After it's all signed and done Monday evening." He nodded and left his office.

My own office was across the hall, down two doors. I grabbed the contract and tucked it under my arm before making my way down the hall to my door. I paused when I saw it was open. I knew I'd closed it and made sure it was locked before I went home.

The doors worked on a palm print and DNA database. Each door reacted to the office's occupant, and only that occupant. This made it easier for the sys-admin to keep up with who opened what office. The only way my office could be open was if *I* had left it like this. Unless someone had found a way to break in.

With the contract still tucked under my arm, I used my foot to push the door in just enough so my cybereyes could look into the dark. There were times I'd cursed myself for accepting that nice saleswoman's cybereyes offer, but then things like this happened and...not so upset about it anymore. There wasn't a way for me to actually learn to see in the dark, so it wasn't like I was cheating.

Nothing showed up with a tag, other than the usual items in the room, telling me their manufacturer, who sold them, date of creation, date of purchase.... I shut that streaming annoyance off as I entered, but I didn't shut the door. I left it just as it was. If I shut it, the connection between the frame and the actual lock would record on the mainframe.

I stopped just short of my desk and asked myself why I was thinking like that? What did it matter who knew I was in my office? It was my office. I didn't put that kind of paranoid thinking away as much as set it aside. I was still a little unnerved about the elven conversation, asking myself what MIT&T had to do with what dump? A dump of what? Data? And what was I-D? Was that someone's initials? A code? Or an actual identity?

Sighing, I kept the light off as I set the contract on my desk and placed my right hand on the second to the left wall panel below the picture frame behind my chair. A five-inch-by-five-inch drawer appeared and slid out from the wall. Inside it were several old style memory disks I kept information on. Mason had his quirks about paper documents. Well, I had my own when it came to my personal information. Like my dad, I kept it all close and safe and copied to any manner of disk I could find. Anything I worked on, I kept backups of. Including my present project and the software NeoNET was most interested in, *ghost7*.

After fishing the used and labeled chips out and sticking them in my pocket, I retrieved the last one I bought a week ago. I'd unwrapped it and formatted it already so it was ready to receive. Accessing the decking unit tucked into the inside left breast pocket of the jacket, I wirelessly connected to my own PAN. Once I had a clear connection, I opened the contract and scanned images of it with my eyes, uploading it all into the new chip.

Once there, I ran a comparison to the previous version of the contract I'd saved to my deck. After a few seconds, I found a few differences, but nothing major in the wording.

Nothing suspicious.

After everything was saved, I made sure the little drawer was empty and reset the lock on it. I told the room to turn on the lights and sat down at my desk to sign the contract. Once that was done, I made sure all my safety protocols were in place. Protocols that would delete my work if anything were to happen to me or to the company. *Ghost7* was a valuable, highly-volatile application that could cause some serious trouble if it got into the wrong hands. The last thing I wanted was for Mason to have to deal with that kind of fallout. Better to just get rid of everything if my codes were compromised.

"What're you doing in here?" Came Mason's voice from the door.

I'd just finished the signatures and closed the contract as he walked in. "I felt a little weird sitting at your desk without you in there." He seemed to accept that reason with a smile, so I handed him the contract. "Here it is."

"Good," Mason held the thing as if it were made of gold. "Now isn't it time you get back out there and show Nicole a good time?"

It was. We left together, and this time I made sure the door was shut and locked. Mason joined a group of suits as I swept Nicole into my arms. I kissed her and held her close as we danced, but no matter how much I tried, I couldn't shake the feeling that something wasn't right.

It wouldn't be too long before I discovered what.

SUNDAY, MARCH 3rd, 2075

Yesterday she said *yes*!

To me, down on one knee in front of the fireplace in our suite at the Emmerson Inn by the Sea.

We'd spent the day sightseeing, taking in the history of Salem in a way I'd never seen it. Nicole loved history, especially the old stories of the Salem Witch Trials. Given the way the world was now...it seemed odd to me that anyone would be hung for using magic.

Nicole's lineage could be traced from one of those founding families, or so she said. I hadn't bothered looking it up, because I didn't care if was true or not. She'd bewitched me, and I wanted nothing more than to share the rest of my life with her.

After showering, we settled on the couch in front of the fire. We had an 8:30 reservation at one of the finer restaurants in town, but she wasn't sure she wanted to go. The thought of staying in the room and ordering food in our bathrobes appealed to her. Snuggled on that couch together, my best-laid plans of wine, dinner, and dancing followed by a creative way for her to find the ring, all fell to the wayside when I got down on one knee, wearing nothing but the bathrobe, and asked her to be my wife.

After making love, we made that reservation for dinner, and the staff toasted us when she showed them the ring. It was one of the most magical nights of our lives.

Monday started too early with a knock at the door. I staggered to it in a pair of pajama bottoms, and found the manager of the Inn standing outside. "I'm so sorry to bother you, Mr. Martin, but I have an urgent matter to discuss with you."

I stepped into the hallway and closed the door partway so we wouldn't disturb Nicole, who was still sleeping. "What's wrong?"

"It's your SIN, sir," the manager said. I sort of remembered his name as Carlos...Clarence? He did look a little worried, with his bushy bows knitted together.

"What about it?"

"It...well, I don't know how to put this. I ran it through last night to establish the room's payment, and everything was fine then. But this morning we received a warning that a hold had been put on your SIN."

"A hold? By whom?"

"It was issued by the UCAS Intelligence Agency."

Now *I* was awake. "You're kidding."

"No sir. I contacted them personally, because I knew this had to be a mistake. We checked your record and your profile, and both came back with impeccable references, but I'm afraid the clerk I spoke to insisted the SIN I ran was...stolen."

"Huh. So, what does that mean?"

"Well sir, they wanted me to confirm the use of the SIN, but I told them it was a mistake, that I had simply had an operator malfunction. I've run into this sort of thing before, and confirming always brings more trouble than it's worth." He smiled at me, and I could see a hard copy of the final bill in his hand. I could also see through the paper where it had been stamped *PAID IN FULL, NUYEN TENDERED.*

Which translates to: *you pay the bill in cash, and I won't call the cops back.* "Just a second," I said as I stepped back inside, leaving the door cracked so he could see me. Luckily I always kept spare UCAS dollars and nuyen with me for emergencies, another habit from my father.

I brought my wallet to the door, and he showed me the bill. I gave him the exact payment, plus another 100¥ for his troubles. He gave me the bill, and I closed the door. Out of habit I scanned the hard copy of the receipt and stored it on my PAN.

"What's wrong?" Nicole said from behind me as she slipped her warm hands around my bare middle. She smelled of sleep and sex, a dangerous combination.

"I'm not sure." I tossed the paid receipt on the table to pack. "Apparently my SIN was reported stolen, so there's a hold on it." I faced her and cupped her face in my hands to kiss her lips. "I'm not sure how. I didn't report it."

Nicole looked more worried than I felt. She put her hands on my wrists. "I think you need to make a call, Oli. It's not good if something happens to your SIN." She winked. "I'll be waiting." With that she dropped her robe and walked with a definite purpose in mind to the bedroom.

Needless to say, concentrating on getting through the bureaucratic red tape of proving who I was and that I hadn't reported my SIN stolen, or hacked would be a better term, was a bit harder. Nicole had a way of scrambling my brains when she wanted to.

Carlos or Clarence answered my summons and was more than happy to get the person he spoke with at the UCAS Intelligence Agency back on the commlink. He transferred them to me, and I spent a few frustrating hours trying to get this misunderstanding straightened out. No, I didn't call to suspend its use. No, I haven't spoken to anyone at the UCASIA offices, except you. No, I don't know why this would happen. And after receiving a reference from Mason Andreas, I received a temporary SIN. Though this SIN had my information on it, it wouldn't allow me to purchase anything unless I connected it with my bank account. I tagged the new SIN and started to store it in my deck. Given that my original one been there when this alleged report of it being stolen happened, I decided not to keep the new one there, and instead downloaded it to a chip I kept in my luggage. Once there, off the grid and away from anyone's access but my own, I felt better. But I did upgrade the security on my commlink just to be safe.

The call and resulting stress killed our plans for the afternoon, but Nicole seemed okay with staying in, so we did a bit of driving along the coast after getting more sleep. We ate at a seaside hole-in-the-wall, and I had some of the best lobster I'd had in twenty years.

The rest of the stay was uneventful. The manager helped us take our luggage to the taxi and I tipped him again. He transferred his card to me, and told me to call him any time if we needed a place to stay in a pinch.

Back in Boston that night, we went our separate ways. Nicole had an early morning meeting, and I needed to go over any messages I would have received from the company. But the only ones were from Jericho, wanting to know if I'd gotten home yet, and was I going to have a ball and chain, or was I still part of the bachelor set?

I called him as I unpacked and sorted laundry. My apartment was small, but it was efficient and had a nice view of Boston Commons.

"I can't believe you asked her in your robe?" Jericho's laughter filled the living area.

I'd routed the call through the speakers and had it projected in the center of the room. I didn't feel like using the eyes. Sometimes I just got damn sick of having so much stuff pushed out in front of me, and I just wanted to see reality for a while.

"It was spur of the moment," I said as I made myself a soykaf and booted my personal mainframe. I might not have had any messages from AMAS, but I had several from *Dark City*. "And now we're engaged," I said as I scrolled through the messages from Jericho, who'd sent me Matrix shots of his persona kicking some Halloweener's ass in-game. "Hey Jer... I've got like six messages from Serilious. What is that?"

"No idea, *omae*."

"Jer...come on, man. Be honest with me. Did you tell him something, or promise we'd join the gang? I told you, I don't like dealing with gangs."

"Hey, pull back on the consternation, chummer," Jericho's animated persona, which looked like a spiky, green-haired elf with a left cyberarm, arched its brow in the holo. "I haven't talked to him since you left. Haven't even seen him in-game lately."

I opened the game server's missive area and checked the dates. The messages started Saturday night at just before midnight until ten minutes ago. And they all had the same header. *URGENT: YOUR ACCOUNT IS MISSING.*

My account?

I glanced at the chair where I usually sat while in the Matrix. "Jericho, meet me at the game entrance atrium."

"I'm there now."

"Okay...look on your friends list. Am I there?"

He paused. "Yeah. But you're not online."

"You're still seeing me, but these messages from Serilius all say my account's missing."

"Log in."

I headed to the chair where I got as comfortable as I could, given my stomach was twisting in knots just thinking someone could have also hacked my game account. I closed my eyes, took a deep, relaxing breath, and wirelessly logged into the *Dark City* mainframe.

The login was the first thing that made me catch my breath. It wasn't my usual preferenced one that I'd set my landing point parameters to. Gone was my chalet in the Alps with the roaring fire and spectacular view. Instead, I stared at an out-of-the-box standard landing with the directions and welcome for a brand new account.

New account? I hadn't created a new account.

"Son of a bitch," my every-guy persona said. I'd looked down to see the standard starter body and shoes. Moving my hand in the air, I dismissed the direction aid and manual as I called up Jericho's character.

He didn't answer my ping at first, then finally, "Look, I don't know you, but you're bothering me and I'm expecting an important call—"

"It's me!" I shouted. "It's Oliver."

The screen hovering in front of me cleared as Jericho's profile appeared. His persona looked me up and down and then laughed. "What the hell, chummer? Where's your stuff? Where's your..." He looked off-screen. "Oli, your original account is still showing as offline, and I would assume if the account was gone, you wouldn't show up at all."

"That's what I was thinking, but I logged in using the same password and name I always do."

"Oh, damn, that's not right. You should have come in as Crisis, not Oliver K. Martin."

I blinked. "What?"

"You didn't see it? It's your *name*. Oliver K. Martin."

I'd *never* signed into the Matrix under my business name. I'd always used Crisis, or my earlier persona name, MothMan. *Never* as Oliver. By default, new accounts kept financial information private, so others in the Matrix couldn't discover legal name and address.

But of course, there were always the hackers out to screw other people. At the moment, I was betting this was the work of one of those damn Technomancers.

"Dude, I think you need to talk to a System Administrator. Something's really wrong."

"Yeah..." I checked the message system. None of the messages from Serilious were listed. But why would they be? I was logged in as me, and those messages were for Crisis. "Let me get back to you, okay?"

"Sure. I'll be in the Barrens. If I see Serilious, I'll tell him what's happened."

"Thanks." I scrolled through the administrator directory and found HELP. Once there I was accosted by a rude, pink, Dongo-looking persona, then transferred to a more pleasant blonde, then transferred to a persona who looked like a mermaid.

She finally offered to help me, and put me on hold. The problem with the first three was a lack of information. All three of them hadn't been able to find any account listed under Crisis. I'd had this subscription for over eight years, and I found it impossible to believe a hacker had utterly obliterated my account.

As I waited, I opened a window and patched in my computer's mail system. It wasn't a standard function in the deck's software, but just a few rewrites of my own. I was 34 when Crash 2.0 took out the wired grid, and since I made my living back then designing and tinkering with cyberdecks, the whole disaster put me out of a job within a year, no thanks to NeoNET and the new Matrix. I was one of the lucky ones, not online when the system crashed. But I faced the chaos afterward, and rebuilt my life and my future.

But I never lost my affinity for decks, so when they came back again as the only way to jack into the Matrix instead of commlinks, I invested in them, but never got back into working on them full time. I bought a few and tore them open, modifying them just enough that I could use them my way, and grid administrators didn't throw warnings at me for using a modified deck.

I pulled up the messages from Serilious and opened the first one.

Empty.

I tried the second and third. They were all empty. No actual message. Just the header warning.

"Mr. Martin?" the admin said.

I redirected my attention to the hovering image. My persona never left the landing area. "Yes?"

"I really am sorry for all the trouble, but I think I may have found the problem. Your SIN was cancelled. It was reported stolen. Your account's not missing, it's just on hold."

The same glitch that made it impossible to pay the bed and breakfast was now causing this issue. And it wouldn't be the first, either. If I didn't get things updated soon, my utilities would be calling next, since all my billing came *through* my SIN.

I grabbed the chip where I'd stored the new SIN I'd gotten that morning. "Here's the updated one."

"Thank you." She smiled at me as the information transferred. *"One moment."*

I waited, double-checked all of the messages from Serilious, and thought if I could get logged back in, I'd go find the ganger myself.

"Mr. Martin?"

"Yes?"

"The SIN you gave us is listed as temporary, so I can't re-instate your account right now. You'll have to wait the required twenty-four hours for the approval process."

I forgot the new one was temporary. "Oh...well, I guess if those are the rules."

"We can set you up with our new premium package for your troubles. It comes with the latest starter equipment and software on the market, valued at twenty-five thousand nuyen."

"Yeah, I'll take it." Just in case this didn't work.

"Well, is there anything else, Mr. Martin?"

"Once it's approved, will I get a confirmation?"

"Yes you will."

"Thanks. Can I friend you? Just in case I change my mind about the starter package?"

"Of course. I'll friend you on your main account as well." She smiled. Her profile showed up on my friend list before she closed her window.

I took a deep breath and leaned back in my chair, breathing a sigh of relief. At least the reason I couldn't get into my account was a normal one, and not that it was hacked or stolen. I still didn't know what Serilius meant by it was removed. Even Jericho said it was right there in his friends list.

And even if it was hacked and someone took it, they really couldn't erase it. Nothing was ever truly erased from the Matrix. It was just hidden deeper, and in darker places. But by the time most things were found, hackers had already picked the accounts clean by using the IDs to steal other things, like nuyen and property.

That thought made me sit up straight.

I logged off the Matrix and into my savings through my commlink, since it was a secured direct connection not associated with a grid.

Everything looked normal. I checked all three accounts, including my dad's money, which he left to me along with the house. The house was still in my grandmother's name, Kristoph. I loved my grandmother, and my grandfather, even though I'd never really known him that well. They were my mom's parents, and close to both her and her husband. My online persona's name had been a sort of homage to her and her love of technology. An immigrant from Romania, I admired them both to start over in this day and age and make a life here in the UCAS.

Just because I was feeling a bit worried, I logged in under my dad's account. It was still active because I used it to pay the utility bills on the house and the outdoor maintenance. Having it all transferred into my name would have been too much of a hassle. Using his old account, I did a little online work and set up a dummy corporation under the name Yerger, the last name of my first heartbreak. I requested the name be added to the deed and sent in the required paperwork before I transferred the inheritance into the account as well. That way whoever hacked my Matrix account couldn't use it to access my parent's house or their nuyen.

My nuyen. Something I planned on using to take Nicole on the honeymoon of a lifetime.

Now that I was thoroughly freaked out, I transferred copies of my backups from Andreas Martin Analysis Systems into the Yerger account and encrypted their access, listing them as deed info on cactus farms. I still had my physical backups. Those I needed to physically hide. The only person I trusted was Jericho, next to Nicole. But I didn't want her involved in whatever the hell was going on.

I packaged the chips up and headed into Boston toward AMAS. I hit the local transit hub, rented a locker and stashed them inside. I'd used these lockers several times to protect things, since they weren't connected to the grid and didn't require a SIN to rent, just nuyen. I figured I'd send Jericho a message later, once my account was approved, to get the chips and stash them.

After that was done, I grabbed my commlink and called Nicole. She answered with her sexy, sleepy voice and told me to come over and bring a bag.

At that moment, all the crap and stress about my Matrix account faded away. I threw some things in a bag, locked everything up and headed to her place. I believed there was nothing the love of a good woman couldn't mend.

I was about to find out just how wrong I was.

CHAPTER 3

TUESDAY, MARCH 5, 2075

I had a few messages from Jericho when I woke the next morning. Nicole and I overslept, which was not a good thing to do on our first day back to our prospective jobs. She and I ran about with barely a word to each other. She finished before me, kissed me on the cheek, and ran out the door.

I packed my commlink and a few things into my bag as I left her place and took the elevator down. By the chronometer on my commlink, it was 7:35 a.m., and Boston was up and ready to start the day.

Since I was already running late, I figured a few more minutes wouldn't hurt, and stopped by my favorite coffee shop and waved at the troll kid behind the counter. Kid was an esthetic term. I'd known him for years, and watched him grow up. At the age of eighteen, he was already two heads taller than me. "Hey, Ted."

"Hey, Mister Martin. How's it going?" Ted grinned around his tusks and pushed his uniform hat on top of his head between his horns. "I've got your usual. Coffee with real milk." He set the cup on the counter as others lined up to order.

Ted's barista partner, a young human girl with pink hair and goggles hiding her eyes, took orders as she gabbed on her commlink with whom I assumed were her friends. It wasn't hard to guess her age just from the way she acted.

Twelve.

"Mr. Martin?" Ted motioned for me to step to the side and he leaned over the counter. The visual was ominous, but his eyes were always kind. "Uh, there's a problem with your SIN."

"Oh...right. Something happened to that one. Here," I lifted my wrist to where his commlink rested and transferred the information over from the temp SIN. I'd forgotten the shop had my other one on file.

Ted checked the projected screens in front of him and frowned. The he shrugged and shut off the display. "It's on the house, Mr. Martin. I know who you are."

"Ted? What's wrong?" There was something in his voice that alarmed me. That, and the way he started looking a little nervous.

Ted looked around and motioned for me to come all the way to the counter's edge, to the far end where the baristas stepped in and out. He lowered his voice, and I could see worry in his eyes. "The SIN you just gave me? It came up as stolen."

"What?" I blinked a few times, not sure what that meant. "But I just got it yesterday, after my SIN was put on hold. That was a temporary SIN."

"I don't know why, Mr. Martin. But the minute I ran that transaction, it flagged the SIN, which means the BMP will know. They're probably on their way now."

Which meant I couldn't stay—or I shouldn't. Having a SIN flagged as stolen was a serious offense, and given the run of luck I was having, it was likely I'd end up in jail until I could find a way to explain what happened. "Was my name involved?"

"I don't use names. I use nicknames for customers." He grinned. "I get a lot of would-be shadowrunners in here. They like to use handles, so I got in the habit."

I laughed. "Oh really? What's mine?"

"I call you MothMan, because you remind me of this player I used to know on the Matrix. He was a nice guy and was always nice to me. Taught me how to fight. And since you and your girlfriend are always nice to me, I figured I'd call you MothMan. You both never make fun of me."

Since I'd never confided in Ted that the character that taught him how to fight in a Matrix game was indeed me, under a previous character, his nicknaming me MothMan seemed a strange coincidence. I could never make fun of Ted. He was smart, had a wicked sense of humor, and he was just a kid.

I winked at him as I held up the drink. "I'll get it straightened out, okay? So I appreciate your help and your heads up."

"No problem...*omae*."

I winked again and said something that felt weird. "No problem, *chummer*."

As I left the coffee shop, two Boston Police vehicles floated down from the second-tier traffic lane and parked on the sidewalk. I held the door for them as I stepped out, then sipped my drink on the way to my office a block away.

When I waved my commlink at the executive door of Andreas Martin Analysis Systems, it didn't open and I slammed into the glass. I nearly dropped my cup. Instead I stood in front of the building in front of my reflection and stared.

"You okay?" said a voice to my right.

I turned to see one of the girls I always bumped into on my way up in the elevator. I didn't know her name, just her smile. "I'm...I'm not sure. My ID's not working."

"Oh no." She looked a little panicked as she waved her commlink over the sensor. The door opened. "Okay, mine's good. Go on in."

But I waited for her. After all my mother raised me to be a gentleman.

Once inside, however, two men in suits at the front desk strode past the nice woman to stand in front of me. "SIN," one of them said.

I wasn't sure what to do. I didn't recognize either of them, and the girl was already on her way down the hall to the elevators, chatting with another coworker.

"Sir, I'll have to see some form of SIN."

Ted said it flashed stolen. Would it do the same here? "I need to speak to Mason Andreas."

"I'm afraid Mr. Andreas is on vacation. I can't let you in without your identification. Is there a problem?"

"I'm not sure. I work here."

"Do you have your ID pin?"

The pin! I checked my coat and felt a bit relieved it was still there on the lapel. But, wasn't it supposed to open the door?

One of the suits saw it, and scanned it with his wrist commlink.

An alarm went off in the building and both men snapped into action. One grabbed my head and brought it down on the edge of the front desk. I instantly saw stars, and lost all control of my body. My coffee fell from my hands, and I felt it splash against my shoe as a sensation that echoed with the sudden pounding in my head. The other suit came up behind me and grabbed both of my wrists with lightning speed, binding them in cuffs tightly behind my back.

All of this happened in front of employees as they came and went in the AMAS building, a company I'd worked hard to build. I tried to tell them who I was, but my words slid from my tongue as I was jerked back up into an upright position seconds before I was pulled by my bound wrists down a corridor past the front desk.

I'd never been in this area of the building before. In fact, I'd never paid much attention to the lobby. My life was on the fifth floor, in my office and in the lab where I worked on predictive marketing analytics. I didn't even know there was a corridor like this in the building. But then again, I was the only one that knew, besides Mason, about Mason's secret stair escape in his office.

I'd lost my bag as well as my coffee, and what felt like my mind as I was half dragged down the blindingly white corridor. My knees collapsed from under me twice and I tried to tell them to slow down. Tried to tell them who I was. Tried to tell them to get Mason.

Even if my tongue couldn't work, I still had access to my commlink. They hadn't removed it or turned it off. Using my cybereyes connection, I sent a short message to Mason, Nicole and to Jericho, as well as one to Margaret, my lab assistant, with whom I was scheduled to meet with today.

Within seconds, both the messages to Mason and Margaret bounced back to me undeliverable. Jericho responded immediately with a curt <*Understood.*>

Nicole's answer didn't come immediately. In fact, I was tossed inside a room with no furniture, and left there as a pile of bleeding clothing in the corner before I got a response from her.

<*What's going on? I tried calling you at the office, but they said you don't work there??*

I opened my eyes as I sort of moved in and out of consciousness. My head throbbed, and my shoulders ached against the binders pinning my arms tight behind my back. I still wore my suit and coat, but somewhere along the way I'd lost my shoes. And I could see drops of blood on the white tile. My blood.

<*Oli? Talk to me! Where are you?*>

I finally summoned enough control to answer. <*I...don't know. White room. Head hurts.*>

<*Hang tight. Now I'm pissed off.*>

I lost all thought after that, and woke when something very cold and wet hit my face. I inhaled water and then snorted it out of my nose just as I was hauled to my feet. I wanted to puke right there on whoever's polished black shoes I was staring down at.

"What the hell did you do to him?" a male voice asked inches from my face. "Do you just like beating people up?"

"He resisted arrest."

I wanted to say I didn't resist anything, but my knees were giving way again. But this time two people caught me from either side and held me up.

The shoes moved back. "Well, we'll have to give him a good scan when we get him to the station. If he's got brain damage, you both are gonna have to come up with some better story that a wage-slave with no weapon and no historic proclivity to run deserved you slamming his face into the corner of a desk."

I heard him hiss as he pulled my face up with a hand under my chin. I wish I could say I recognized him or his voice, but I didn't. His face was just a blurred image with two dark spots for eyes and one for his mouth. "Jeez—you broke his nose."

"So what? We caught him."

"With a stolen SIN, not a bag full of weapons. Get him into the wagon and then book him."

Again I saw tile going by beneath me as I tried to keep up, but my socked feet just couldn't. I was roughly tossed into the back of a van and left on the floor to jostle around as it hit every pothole in Boston. I was pretty sure I dozed again, or maybe passed out, because the next thing I remembered was being dragged into a cell where the binders were removed and I was stripped of my coat. That's when they saw the commlink and took it, too.

I curled up on a cot and pulled my knees up to my chest.

"They really did a number on you," A deep voice said somewhere close to me.

I braced myself, expecting to get hit or roughed up in some new way here.

"What'd you do?"

When I was sure this new voice wasn't going to slam my face into something else or drag me across the cell, I opened my eyes. My sight was coming back, though blurry on the left side. I was pretty sure if I could think clearer I'd be more than a bit scared. I'd be out of my mind with panic and freaking out.

I looked into the face of a dark-skinned ork. His features were handsome. Strong. And the tusks protruding from his lower jaw weren't as large as some I'd seen. They were neatly cut back and didn't interfere with his speech. His skin had markings on it, tattoos that could only be seen in the light. And at that moment, I wasn't in the best shape to see anything.

"I...I don't know."

"You don't look like a runner." He leaned in close, and I couldn't tell if he was sitting or kneeling. "And you don't smell like one. That's an expensive brand of aftershave."

"Not a runner," I managed though I wasn't really clear on what a runner was.

"That I can see for myself. So either you pissed your boss off, or you've been framed for something."

"Neither." I closed my eyes. I wanted him to stop talking to me. I wanted him to just go away. I was in pain. And it was getting worse.

"Then tell me something, Aftershave," the ork said, his voice was close now. I opened my eyes again, and we were nose to nose. "Why are you on this side of the bars? Shouldn't you know some wicked brain moves to get yourself out of here?"

I didn't have a clue about what he was talking about. So I ignored him.

But he didn't ignore me. He just kept asking me questions, picking at why I was there and I was honest when I said I didn't know. "Said...my SIN was stolen."

"Yes," the ork said as he leaned back. "It was stolen, but not by you. You're the victim here, Aftershave. What you need to figure out pretty quick is...are you going to stay the victim?"

"Martin?" Came a louder voice. "Oliver Martin?"

I almost didn't answer because I thought it was a dream. A voice said, "He's over here. I think he's dying."

"He better not be!" A woman's voice said. "You get him out of there right now, Sergeant. And I swear if he's been beaten, I'll have your jobs. Do I make myself clear?"

"Yes ma'am. Salvo? Berman? Got get Mr. Martin and his things and get him signed over to Miss O'Neal."

O'Neal. That was Nicole's name.

I lifted my head as the bars moved and I was hoisted up once again. And again, I wanted to puke. I was redressed in my coat and given my commlink back, and when I saw Nicole's worried face, and Jericho's behind hers, I cried.

I couldn't stop myself.

I rode in the back of Nicole's car to her apartment as Jericho drove. The two of them knew each other from the same school, and even though their paths never crossed socially, they got along pretty well. But then, that was just Nicole, and one of the reasons I loved her so much. Status and position didn't seem to mean much to her. Only courtesy—and how you treated your fellow man and metahuman—was important.

Once we were in her apartment, she had Jericho take me into the bathroom and remove my clothes. He put me under a warm shower, holding me up as she got her personal autodoc ready.

After the shower, Jericho helped me inside. I lay back on the soft cushions as the temperature adjusted itself to my body and lots of little tiny mechanical arms started working on my bruised and broken soul.

When I opened my eyes now and then, I could see Nicole and Jericho talking just outside the glass of the doc and I wondered, in my fuzzy state, what they were arguing about.

CHAPTER 4

WEDNESDAY, MARCH 6, 2075

I woke up disoriented as hell. I pushed and beat at the glass shell as my arms pulled wires and tubes away from my skin. "Hey!" I yelled.

Eventually Nicole appeared and put her hand on the glass. Within seconds it pressurized and opened. I was naked inside the machine, still sore and very, *very* confused. "Nicole—"

She put a finger to my lips. She was wearing her nightgown, and her hair was tousled. "I didn't expect you to wake so soon."

"What...what happened? Where am I? What time is it?"

She leaned down and kissed my forehead before she stepped back and started removing the electrodes from my chest, shoulders, face, and arms. "I'll answer in reverse. It's four a.m., Wednesday morning. You're in my arcology suite, and as for what happened, we're still trying to straighten that one out."

I digested each piece of the puzzle, but couldn't put them together. "It's...It's Wednesday?"

"Morning. Very early, yes."

"I've been in this thing..." I looked around at it, at the blood smear where my head had lain.

"For nearly twelve hours. Jericho and I got you in it about three or four yesterday afternoon. It took us four hours to find you, after we figured out which station you'd been taken to."

Station. I put my hand to my face. My nose was sore, but it wasn't bloody.

"Your face was smashed against an immovable object. You had a concussion, and a pretty bad one. It didn't help that they never got you any medical attention." She put her fingers on my forearm. "It was as if they wanted you to die."

"What's...what's going on? Why did they do that? My temporary SIN didn't work out front, nor did my ID pin, then..." Things started coming back to me. "Then these guys at the front I'd never seen before wanted to see my SIN, and then..." That's when the pain started, and my memories were fuzzy.

"They literally attacked you, Oliver. I've already lodged a formal complaint against them and put in a few messages to my father. I can't believe they were that rough with you. People have trouble with SINs all the time, but that's no way to treat one of the owners of the company!"

Something she said to me came back. "You...called and they said..."

Nicole had a pained expression on her face. "They said you didn't work there. That you *never* worked there."

"At AMAS? How can they say that? I helped *make* that company! That's where the Martin in the name comes from!"

"I know! I've sent messages to Mason, giving him a detailed message on what they did to you, plus images from the auto-doc and a readout of what it had to do to heal you. But he hasn't gotten back to me yet." She leaned into me, and I put my arms around her. Her soft warmth felt reassuring. "The whole time you've been in the doc, I've fielded calls from the Boston Police. They want to know where you are because I bailed you out of jail."

"That means I'm on bail. Why do they want to know where I am?"

She pulled back to look up at me. "They won't tell me. Whenever I ask questions, they disconnect. Jericho's freaked out. He started doing a bit of investigation himself. We both suspect this started Monday morning with your SIN. Remember the inn?"

"Yeah...but the agency gave me a temporary one." I didn't mention what had happened in the game, and the nice lady in customer service.

"Jericho found out your SIN wasn't stolen at all. It had a hold put on it."

"Well, yeah...that's what that guy at the agency said, but then he issued me a temporary one."

"I know, but why?" She searched my face, a confused look on hers. "If your SIN is suspended, why give you a temporary one before they find out why the original isn't working?"

I sat up straighter. I felt better—not wholly ready to take on the world yet, but close. "Who exactly can put a hold on a SIN besides the UCAS Intelligence Agency?"

"I don't think it's a question of who can, but who *did.* Jericho couldn't get that far. Hacking isn't really his forte. And then, as of Monday night, your *temporary* SIN was reported stolen."

"I didn't report that."

"I know. We can't find who did. Your original is still good, it's still there, but just on hold. Like a...*pending* status. I spent an hour on the comm with the agency, who insist you never contacted them, and they never issued you a temporary SIN. Apparently, the only temp SINs they issue are criminal ones."

I pushed her back gently, and removed more of the electrodes as I slipped out of the autodoc. I wasn't a big fan of the contraptions. Always looked like a pill-shaped coffin in my opinion. It was a bit scary to get inside one and be at the mercy of the thing's programming. I mean, think about it; if it gets programmed to take you apart piece by piece, all it has to do is inject you with a sedative to keep you quiet, and start hacking away.

I touched my nose. "It's still crooked."

"Gives you a little more character." She smiled. "You're avoiding."

"I'm trying to put it all together and not panic. If they're claiming I didn't talk to anyone at their offices, who did I speak with?"

"Did you use their listed number?"

I hesitated and then gave a long sigh. "I didn't exactly call them. That guy at the Inn did, remember?"

"Well," Nicole pursed her beautiful lips, making them form a bow I wanted to kiss. "I sent all the information you received for the temp SIN to this new agent, and he swears they're all forged documents. They in turn alerted the BMP. I think we should hand over that guy at the Inn, too. I have to go in tomorrow morning and give a full report on everything that happened. But since it happened to you, you need to go with me and file a formal report."

"No. No freakin' way am I going back into a judicial facility. Not after what just happened to me. Something wrong's going on, Nicole. And I have to find out what it is and right now, I don't trust the BMP. Whatever this is, they're in on it."

Nicole gave me an eye roll. "Oh please...you sound just like Jericho."

I narrowed my eyes. "What do you mean?"

"He started on his conspiracy theory stuff." Nicole shrugged. "He claimed that the only way your ID pin wouldn't work was if someone went into AMAS's security node and changed it. And the only one with that kind of clearance would be Mason Andreas or you." She chewed on her lip a second. "Though, I am a little curious as to why Mason hasn't returned mine or my dad's calls since this started."

The doorbell rang. As Nicole went to answer it, I rummaged in my bag I'd used the night before and pulled out a pair of lounging pants. They were better than nothing. I spotted the chips I'd saved my AMAS data and contract to in the bottom of the bag.

I heard Jericho's voice as I entered the living room, and he looked visibly relieved to see me standing.

"Dude." He gave me a short hug, which was normal for Jericho, before he stepped back. "You look a hundred percent better."

"I guess they slammed my head into that desk harder than I thought?"

Jericho looked at Nicole with a frown. "You didn't tell him?"

She glared at him. "I didn't want him to worry."

"What?" I looked between the two of them. *"What?"*

"You weren't just slammed into the desk. They beat the crap out of you, but after that first slam, you probably don't remember it." Jericho's hands, down at his sides, clenched into fists. "I was so pissed when I saw you. Not as mad as Nicole, though. That station's gonna have ringing ears for weeks after the dressing down she gave them."

I slowly shook my head. "What the hell did they do that for? I mean, after that initial kiss to the desk, I wasn't even able to stand on my own in the first place."

"They gave me some ridiculous story that you resisted arrest and fought them."

I honestly couldn't remember if I resisted anything. I had a vague memory of protesting. But to beat me so bad I needed a doc?

"Keep going," Jericho prodded.

Nicole grabbed my hand. "Remember how I said I couldn't find you? I wasn't kidding. I called every police station within a hundred-kilometer radius, but no one had heard of Oliver Martin. So I went to AMAS and confronted two women in the lobby, who had no idea what I was talking about. Luckily, I found a nice lady who said she helped you get into the building, and told me there were two larger men working the security desk that morning. Two men she'd never seen before, but she recognized their numbers on their badges." She squeezed my hand. "That's how we found where they took you."

"Oli, they took you to some rundown, little used building in Bunker Hill," Jericho said. "There wasn't even a sign outside that said it was the Boston Metro Police. If it weren't for Nicole's dad's influence, you'd still be there. Nicole posted bail on a contingency that she brings you back for the actual bail hearing, which is the day after tomorrow, Friday. She argued you needed medical attention, and you would probably die in there and if you did, as your fiancé, she would sue."

I smiled at Nicole. "I love you. I can't believe your dad helped you."

"I love you too. And that's one of the reasons he helped. He likes you. Thinks you're good for me. And he was a little pissed at Mason not answering his calls." She kissed my cheek. "I know I should have taken you to a hospital, but after what we went through to find you—I just didn't trust anyone. So I paid them, and we brought you here."

"And I'm glad you did. But, why would they continuously call you to see where I was? That's still not making sense." I looked down at myself and sighed. I was covered in fading bruises on my arms, and a few deep cuts. "I need to run by my apartment and grab some clothes. I don't remember much, but I do remember that I was stripped down to nothing." When I looked up at Nicole, she had an odd look on her face. Jericho did, too. "What?"

She glanced at Jericho.

He shrugged when he returned my look. "I already went over to your apartment to get more clothing...only it's not your apartment anymore. Some guy's living there with his girlfriend. Said he's been living there for eight years."

"Eight years? He's living..." I moved toward the door. "This is insane. Take me over there. I have to see for myself."

But Jericho put his hand on my arm. "I did see it, Oli. Your stuff's gone. He was really happy to show us. Even eager. I went all over that place, and it's like you were never there. Even the dents in the wall in the spare bedroom, the ones I put there when we were moving in the shelves? Gone."

"But...that's impossible. I was just there last..." I had to rethink that. "I was just there Monday night."

"I know. I also bribed them not to tell anyone I came looking for you."

He had my attention again. "Why'd you do that?"

This time Nicole answered. "Because for once I'm sure Jericho's not totally off in conspiracy land. Something's going on here. Oliver. That's *your* place. Someone else is living there, your stuff is gone, your SIN's reported stolen, but it's not your SIN, it's the replacement you were given, and no one can access your original."

"Where's my commlink?" I walked back into the back bedroom where the doc was located. It retracted into the wall as I walked in. "Where is it? I remember he gave it back to me."

They followed me in, but Jericho shook his head. "Oh, they gave the shell back to you, Oliver. Not the node. It's just a dead machine right now. It's on the table in the kitchen."

I went to the kitchen and found my commlink in several pieces. She was right. The node had been removed. That meant the receipt for the Inn was gone, since I'd never transferred it off the commlink node. "What...in the hell is going on?"

"I don't know," Jericho said. "But if I were you, I'd find an encrypted network and sign into your accounts and check them. Because it seems to me that someone's trying to erase you."

CHAPTER 5

WEDNESDAY, MARCH 6 - THURSDAY, MARCH 7, 2075

I spent the rest of the evening with Jericho and Nicole, going over what steps I should take next to figure out what was going on. Moving around town unaccompanied was a bad idea, according to Jericho. And I was surprised to see Nicole agree with him. Usually those two were at odds with one another, with Nicole protesting Jericho's more paranoid view of the world. Their differences made sense to me, since Nicole was born into a wealthy family, while Jer and I weren't. We'd seen things she didn't have the background to understand. But meeting Nicole on the street, no one would know she was the daughter of a business tycoon.

What we worked out seemed a bit extreme, even to me. But looking at the damage to my face in the mirror, even though it was mending nicely thanks to Nicole's auto-doc, I was willing to take measures to protect myself.

First up, we needed to find out who I had spoken with Monday evening. Jericho was pretty sure it wasn't someone from the UCAS Intelligence Agency, or if it was, they were an inside man. So I contacted the Immerson Inn By the Sea and spoke to a woman named Rachael. Imagine my surprise when she greeted me with anger and contempt for skipping out on my bill and giving them a false name. Nicole had to take over the conversation and calm the woman down. I knew her name, since I'd made the reservation with her. But I'd given her my name, not a false one.

Jericho and I stepped out onto Nicole's balcony as she masterfully handled the woman, then hung up. She joined us outside afterward. "Wow..." was her first comment.

"What's going on?" Jericho asked.

"Well apparently she had you down as renting the room under the name Oliver Maddox, not Martin. And she had an address that traced into South Boston, and not your apartment."

"But she said I skipped out on the bill. I scanned a copy of that bill—only it was on the node on my commlink."

"I kept the hard copy. Don't look at me like that. How many times have Jericho and I told you to keep some kind of paper trail? I scanned it and sent it to her. She had to admit it was a legitimate bill, and it was addressed correctly, where her records weren't. But the nuyen you gave that guy to pay for the bill never went into the account. So I sent it to her using my own SIN. As for the person who came to our door that night—she doesn't know who that was. She had an emergency that night, and was called to the hospital, so she ordered a temp to come in and just watch things while she was gone. He was already gone when she got back, and it seemed her emergency had been a crank call."

"Oh come on, Nicole," Jericho said. "You're telling us that wasn't a set up?"

"I won't say anything because of what it looks like." Her irritated expression just made her look all the more beautiful to me. "But it does look like someone set Rachael up to be away from the Inn, then came to our door to tell us your SIN wasn't working, then put you on the phone with a complete stranger."

"While I thought I was speaking with the intelligence agency..." I groaned. "And gave them everything they'd need to actually hack my SIN."

"That's what it looks like. And this temporary SIN you were given probably belonged to the criminal you spoke to." She put her hand on her head. "Man, what a mess."

"Yeah but," Jericho said with his hand on his chin. "That doesn't explain what happened at AMAS. It made sense that his SIN was flagged as stolen, because the asshole that did this probably reported it stolen, but that wouldn't have anything to do with Oliver's lapel pin not getting him into the building."

"True," Nicole started pacing the length of her balcony, her arms folded over her chest. "Nor would it have anything to do with the way these new security people acted—" She held up her finger, "—which I checked on, Oliver. No one's seen them since your 'arrest.' Both the regulars called in sick and these two showed up, arrested you, and then vanished."

"Holy hell... you think any of this is connected?"

"I don't know. But now we have some of the answers to what happened at the Inn. Oliver, you should check your accounts."

The second part of our plan was to see what was really out there in the Matrix. Jericho had brought in one of his older model decks so I could sign in with one of his many accounts. I suggested not checking any of the accounts in Nicole's arcology apartment, for safety's sake, because it really was starting to feel like someone was out to get me.

Nicole volunteered to look into the third thing on our list, finding Mason Andreas. She left the apartment with promises to be home early for dinner and more promises to be with her father all day to use his contacts. Apparently Mr. O'Neal was just as disgusted with what had happened to me at AMAS as I was. Even he'd been told I no longer worked there, which prompted him to drop by unannounced to see Mr. Andreas, who wasn't in. Mr. O'Neal had taken a few pieces of the company stationery that still had my name on the masthead, and the receptionist insisted Mr. Martin still worked there.

I had a day before my court hearing, thanks to Nicole paying my bail, and the constant harassing calls from the BMP had worried her enough to call in and make sure my bail was in good standing. It was. After that, she left and Jericho left, the latter having to get to work at MIT&T.

I made the decision not to log in until the next day. I didn't want to tell either of them I was too scared to do it myself, and was relieved when Jericho volunteered to take the next morning off and help get me set up.

I picked a small cafe Jericho and I were familiar with, and the two of us set up a table there early the next morning. Nicole went to work, vowing she'd have Mason Andreas's attention by the end of the day or know the reason why he was dark, and Jericho left me with everything I needed before he took off for his job.

The deck was in good shape, but Jericho was known for taking care of his things. The account I used was Nantucket36. I didn't know why he'd named it that, and I didn't ask. The profile for the account was set up as a female with an address in the harbor. I logged into the Matrix and started my morning activity.

First up was to take a look at my accounts. I figured if I logged into them, anyone watching them would know I was checking. So...the best way to see them was as an administrator for the bank. Since Jericho used the same institution I did, he had a spoofing algorithm already set up, since he liked to look at his accounts from the admin side.

Yeah, a different kind of weird. It's Jericho. I just don't ask anymore.

The password worked, no red flags, and within minutes I filed through several accounts as if looking for something, and saw all of mine were closed

This revelation chilled me to my core. My bank accounts were *closed.* All the money in them gone. Not transferred, but withdrawn. I couldn't look into who'd withdrawn it because again, I didn't want to get caught. Anyone else monitoring those accounts would see this fake admin name and investigate. People closed and cleared out accounts all the time. Why take a second look?

Fighting back growing nausea, I checked the account under Yerger. That account looked to be intact, as well as all the other accounts I'd attached to it. All the nuyen was there.

Whoever had done this didn't know about that account.

I logged out and backed away into the decking unit's landing area. If they hadn't bothered that account, then I was pretty sure they didn't know about the house, since it was in my grandmother's name. I did a public record search on property over a large area and spotted Yerger, which had originally been Kristoph. I did a bit of hacking to see if I could discover it'd been changed. Everything looked fine.

I checked my Matrix mail, the one I kept with the same address I used for *Dark City*. I gasped when I found over twenty messages from Serilious. They were forwarded notices from the game. I clicked on the most recent one.

Crisis,

Log in as soon as you can and switch the account payment source to something more secure. Someone's been trying to access your game account, and we've been able to stop them, but they're getting better.

S

The message was time stamped two hours ago.

We? We've been able to stop them? Was Serilious part of an admin team and I never knew it? It was rumored that the staff of *Dark City* had alt characters they played in as NPCs so they could watch and listen to game play. Using a sleezy character like Serilious was brilliant, if this was true.

Looking around the cafe, making sure no one was looking at me funny, I signed into the account, hoping it wasn't suspended anymore. *Ding!* The relief that washed over me was like a nice spring rain. My account was Crisis once again—

Wait...if the account was off the probationary period, that meant my SIN wasn't suspended, didn't it?

Before I could log out of the game and check, my message cue lit up and Serilious's icon showed up under admin. I opened it and Serilious's texts showed up with the game generated voice.

<*You're alive!*>

I hesitated. <*Do I know you?*>

<*Not officially. But the how and why I seem so interested isn't important now. I've hidden your account for the moment. Whoever is trying to break in is on now. Go into your preferences and change the owner's name. Get rid of Oliver Martin and set the payments to a different account if you have one that hasn't been hacked.*>

I put my hands flat in the table. The only way he'd know my name was if he really was an admin and had access. So how was someone else doing this?

<*Oliver, do it now. If I keep hiding your account, I'm going to get fired. That'll piss me off. You won't like me pissed off.*>

Not sure I like you right now. I did as he said, though I felt a bit irritated. I hadn't asked him to do this. Yeah, I was happy he did, but threatening me over something he'd done on his own? I definitely didn't like him. Screw him when he's angry.

I logged into the preferences and quickly changed the payment and owner info from me to the Yerger account. Once it was accepted, I turned back to the window. <*Done.*>

<*I see. Good work.*>

<*How did you know to hide my account?*>

There was a long pause before: <*I'm good at spotting phishing. After over fifteen attempts to access your account, I hid it to see what this bastard would do. He's still online, but not active at the moment.*>

<*Why would you do this for me?*>

<I've been watching you for a while. I like players who build their characters. I read your game journals. Your...assassin has a very interesting history.>

Now I just felt embarrassed. Really embarrassed. I didn't think anyone read those game journals because no one knew I played this game but Jericho.

<I always wondered...the skill with which you play in game... do you practice IRL?>

<I do. But I don't see how–>

Something flickered in his window before it disappeared. A second later, I heard the screech of wheels, and one of the other kids jumped out of his seat and yelled, "It's GOD!"

GOD was the Grid Overwatch Division, an entity set up by the corporations to monitor hacks in the Matrix. It was supposed to cut down on cybercrime and hopefully bottleneck the flow of information. That meant stifling information the corps didn't want released. But as far as I could see, what they'd created instead was a better underground network by forcing kids like these to be on the lookout.

And warn others.

Before the black suits were even out of their windowless vans outside, the cafe cleared out. I powered down my deck and moved with the others, following through a side door hidden from view, doing as the others said.

The door led down a flight of old, wooden, and damn scary stairs illuminated by a single flickering light at the bottom. The train of escapees moved around the stairway to another door behind it and filed through. That's when the lights went out and whispers started, instructions to hold hands. I joined the chain and we carefully picked our way through the dark down what felt like a narrow concrete tunnel. I brushed the walls a few times. They were cold and wet and the smell of water intensified. Were we nearing the harbor? I was another salmon swimming along downstream with the others to the only destination I wanted.

Freedom.

I knew they were looking for me. I had a feeling in my gut that I was the target. But as I moved along, I couldn't for the life of me think of what I'd done to trigger any alarms.

The darkness ended, and we were once again in a semi-lighted corridor. It was damp and smelled foul as we moved beneath pipes and beside more long forgotten concrete walls.

I had the feeling most of the others in that café had been down those tunnels several times before. It was a wonder GOD never found them. Had this been an escape route created for countless non-conformists throughout the decades, or had the owners of the coffee cafe chosen their location because it was part of its own underground railroad?

CHAPTER 6

ANDREAS MARTIN ANALYSIS SYSTEMS
BOSTON
THURSDAY, MARCH 7, 2075

In a rare display of loss of self-control, Mason Andreas raked his arms across his desk, knocking everything to the floor. He accompanied the futile act with a bellow reminiscent of his father's. He had always hidden from that sound, because it heralded the beatings he and his mother were sure to receive that evening. And now, hearing it from his own throat disgusted him. He had vowed not to be as physically cruel as his father had been. Instead, he'd simply taken the inherited cruelty and manifested it in a need to control everything and everyone. And if one cannot control others directly, they could be manipulated.

Except for Oliver Martin. No matter how much he'd studied his friend these past years, Mason hadn't been able to pin the man down. He still didn't know Oliver's passions, other than Nicole, nor did he really know the man's history. There was literally nothing in the Matrix on him except a few games, all linked to Oliver's Matrix account.

Knowing someone, their secrets, their most intimate details...that was power. Information that could be used to pull the strings of the puppet. Mason knew this all too well. Not because of his abusive father, but because of the abrasive partnership he'd formed, voluntarily, with NeoNET. Specifically, with Apollonius Turk, the liaisons manager for NeoNET and the East Coast's premiere bastard.

Mason had never been very good with finances. That and his insane need to gamble had brought him to the very edge of ruin. He'd nearly cleaned out his family's coffers, nuyen that had been built on the backs of the wageslaves for decades, handed to him with pride by his father, with the understanding that Mason would bring his family's riches, name and standing to even greater heights.

And then the old bastard died. And Mason...well, he had no idea how to *make* nuyen, only spend it. And then he'd found Oliver Martin. Brilliant. Trusting. And full of ideas that made little to no sense to Martin, but they made nuyen, and they held the promise of more. Mason's financial struggles had reached into the deep pockets of AMAS, unknown to Oliver.

Mason would lose the company before Oliver's work could be completed and sold and Mason would be homeless, nameless, and...SINless.

Enter that bastard, Apollonius Turk. He brought solutions to the table for Mason, a means to finance Oliver's work and make AMAS into a household name. The acquisition would free up Mason to continue his lifestyle, and keep his family's standing.

But the contract came with too many strings, too many provisos written to benefit Turk. Strings that would leave Mason rotting in jail for embezzlement if conditions weren't met. The acquisition and hereto after funding of AMAS would only happen after the delivery of *Ghost-7* and all the research, notes, and accompanying intel on the software. If these things weren't handed over, it granted Apollonius, not NeoNET, the right to take everything. Meaning all of Andreas Martin Analysis Systems as well as Mason's holdings.

If the program wasn't delivered as requested on the closing date.

The techs from NeoNET had already set up their own supervisors and analysts in the company's lab, as if they knew or sensed Mason would fail.

And he was going to fail because of Oliver Martin. *Cheeky bastard.*

Too bad the bastard didn't have any family Mason could throw under the bus. Apollonius wanted to bring Nicole in for questioning, and nattered about it every day, at every meeting. But Mason wasn't going to let that happen. Nicole wasn't for sale or barter. She was his. Would be his again, once they were finished.

But before Mason could carry out his own plans, they had to find the program. His people had taken everything Oliver had ever had. Apartment, accounts, savings, 401K. All emptied into the coffers of Mason Andreas. And none of it contained any clue as to where the bastard could have hidden *Ghost-7*. It had taken an entire day to find the hidden panel in Oliver's office, but even it was empty.

Mason had nothing.

The tech who stood witness to Mason's little temper tantrum, an ork named George Spinoza, remained quiet, pressed against the wall next to the door. If Mason hadn't locked it, he was sure the guy would have bolted. George's report on not finding anything on Oliver's node, home node, commlinks, or deck, was what had set Mason off.

After taking two deep breaths, Mason moved away from his desk. "Pick that stuff up."

George nearly tripped over himself to do the boss's bidding. And he just kept talking as Mason looked out his office window, down at Boston. "—Not my fault. I tried everything I know, ran every scrubber I have, but Mr. Martin never did his work on the company nodes, and not in his company commlinks. I mean... please, Mr. Andreas. Just...don't let anyone know that was me."

"Was you?" Mason glanced back at the ork.

"On the commlink that night?" George, a handful of desk items on his arms, paused. "I've never broken the law before, and I'm pretty sure impersonating an agency agent is a bad thing. I can't go to jail, Mr. Andreas. I only did it because I was told to."

"Yes..." Mason slowly nodded. "And in that conversation, did you let anything slip? Did you make a mistake that led us to where we are now?"

Mason already knew George hadn't made any mistakes. He'd listened to the phone recording himself, and never heard a waver or quiver in the ork's voice. George had presented himself with charm and grace. Just like a good little drone should. But he also knew incessant questioning could cause George to admit his guilt, and if he did that, Mason would have a possible problem on his hand.

George's face went blank for a second, his tusk-rimmed lower jaw dropping a few millimeters. "No...no I did it all on the script, Mr. Andreas. I did exactly what you wanted me to do."

Mason looked away.

"Really, Mr. Andreas," George replaced items on the desk. Mason could see the ork's reflection in the glass. "Oliver Martin had a squeaky clean record until you erased it—"

Mason moved fast, drawing on his own skills at melee fighting, something he'd had to learn as a child growing up in South Boston. He landed a solid right cross to the ork's left jaw, and then brought his knee into George's groin. George dropped what things he still had in his hand as he grabbed his crotch and went down on the floor, hissing and huffing, unable to breathe.

"Never...*ever*...say that out loud again, do you understand me? *You* were the one that erased Oliver's identity. *You* were the one that made it appear he had never worked here."

George made sounds, but they didn't sound like words. So Mason kicked him in the side and George moaned again. "Say it!"

But the ork couldn't, and Mason knew it. Didn't matter. Mason had his reasons why Oliver had to disappear. For good. Because instead of made up stats on corporations, Mason had fed the program *real* stats on *real* corps to discover their weaknesses. The program had then given him the steps necessary to stabilize them and grow them into viable assets. But when Mason showed the results to Apollonius Turk, he'd reversed the use of the application with horrible results, then he had applied the recommended outcome to the same companies.

Instead of thriving and rising to the top of their industries, within six months, all three of those corps had declared bankruptcy.

Mason doubted anyone would notice that all three of them were companies similar to Andreas Martin Analysis Systems, developing software along the same lines. Turk felt it was imperative that if they were going to run tests on the program, that it should be done on their competition. Thus, all obstacles to achieving his dreams were destroyed.

Mason just hadn't counted on Oliver being both cautious and brilliant enough to catch what was being done with the tests. So now no one could find the prototype. *Ghost-7* was gone. Without it, there was no acquisition, no position at NeoNET, and no future for AMAS. To file the paten, trademark and copyright, they had to have the original.

Unfortunately Oliver had already filed the patent for the engine of the application. The fact couldn't be erased. Unless they showed they owned his original.

Watching George try and stand, Mason wished it was Oliver in front of him. Then he could kick the drek out of him to get the prototype back. Oliver's being alive was what bothered Mason the most. The bastard had been supposed to die at the hands of his men in the BMP. Resisting arrest was the cover story. And then, with Oliver dead, he could reinstate the man's identity with the one he wanted to show the world. The one where Oliver was a criminal, a thief. Discredit him enough so that even Nicole wouldn't want to keep his memory.

But they'd screwed that up, too. Oliver had survived, and noble Nicole had to butt in. There was no telling what she was thinking now, and she wasn't under any obligation to talk to him. And since Oliver's bail was paid by a creditable person, and the hearing was set, there wasn't much Mason could do legally. So he'd reinstated Oliver's identity with the company, as well as his accounts, which would go back online by evening. There wasn't much he could do about Oliver's apartment. All of his things had been sold or burned.

But Apollonius Turk wasn't going to give up that easily. He still had men out there looking for the bastard, and if they found him, they'd bring him in.

Very quietly.

His comm buzzed, and he engaged his AR. It was his contact in the Grid Overwatch Division. "Yes."

"The target surfaced in a coffee shop over near the college, but by the time we got there, the place was cleaned out. Not even a barista. They saw us coming and scattered."

Mason clenched his jaw, and considered kicking George again as the ork finally got to his feet, though he remained hunched over. "Find him." He waved at George to go.

But when the ork opened the door, Apollonius Turk and his bodyguards stood in George's way. "My, my, good sir. You look simply dreadful. Why don't you let Max here take you back to your office?"

Mason's eyes widened as the troll manhandled the silent and cowering George out of the office. Apollonius and Maxine stepped inside.

Apollonius smiled, revealing brilliant white teeth. "Change of direction, Mason. Change of direction."

CHAPTER 7

The tunnel dumped us out into the Commons, and I followed students and patrons as they scattered in all directions, blending in with the other students. I stuck out like a sore thumb, and quickly ducked into a nearby campus clothing store.

I used nuyen to buy a new set of clothes and left the old ones. After walking for several blocks and reassuring myself that I hadn't been followed, I headed to a sporting goods store that still used magnets for anti-theft. They had the usual warning signs, and my AR lit up with warnings not to go inside. I paid a kid to walk through the door with my deck and bring it back to me. Surprisingly, he did, and once I knew it was wiped, I took it apart and scattered the pieces in trashcans everywhere. I didn't know for sure they'd come to the coffee shop because of me, but in case I was the target, I wanted to eliminate whatever device they'd tracked me down with. I'd have to repay Jericho for it later.

I pulled the hood of the jacket over my head, and crossed the bridge into Cambridge. From there I went to Somerville, and took a train to Everett. Unfortunately, the ticket took the last of my handy nuyen. Unlike a SIN or credstick, tracing nuyen wasn't possible. Though Nicole had given me a stick loaded with more than 5K that morning, I wanted to save it for an emergency only. I needed another decking unit or commlink to get in touch with Nicole and Jericho, and I knew just where there were a few spares.

It was close to six in the evening before I reached my dad's old house in Everett. It wasn't exactly a short distance from the train station. The yard looked like it needed a trim, but the bushes and trees were in good shape. The lawn service was on a monthly auto-pay account as part of a patron service my dad had set up before he passed away. Another thing I'd switched to a different name and account.

I walked the neighborhood for half an hour before I was sure the house hadn't been compromised, and then I just felt embarrassed for thinking like that. Here I was, reverting to game thinking as Crisis instead of living in the real world. But... my real world was starting to look a lot like *Dark City* lately.

Trotting across the street and around to the back door, I manually punched in the code. If there was one thing I prided myself on, it was my memory. Not quite eidetic, but close. I could memorize numbers and crunch them in my head. Well, most numbers. I'd hit a few limits over the years, and had to use my comm as an aid.

The house smelled musty and unused when the door opened. Another good sign that no one had been there. Shifting everything over to the Yerger name had been a good idea, though I'd thought it was sort of silly at the time. Now, as I stood in the kitchen and checked the fridge and automatic delivery...I patted myself on the back.

I prepared a meal first. Hard to think on an empty stomach. I took it to my workroom in the basement and ate as I pulled out my old equipment. The commlinks there and the few decking units I'd toyed with were old. Outdated, but nothing I couldn't fix up. It was going to take newer parts, though.

That's where I hesitated. Normally I'd just jump in the Matrix and order them. Boom, same-day drone delivery. But given my present state of crazy...that just seemed wrong. And I sure as hell didn't want a drone anywhere near the house.

Here's where my thinking like Crisis had to end. I didn't know where to get the parts I needed, cheap and fast. I knew there were black market areas, places that bartered as well as sold. I had a lot of good stuff I was sure would work as a trade.

It was long after eight, and dark, and I was pretty sure Nicole and Jericho were both worried about me. And I was really sure the vids were posting up lots of illegal recordings of the event at the coffee shop. I needed information. Craved it.

After I cleaned the kitchen and showered, I checked the bedrooms for clothing. After Dad died, Mom and I pretty much left things as they were. She couldn't bring herself to store his stuff. Neither could I. My sister, on the other hand, wanted to sell it all and take the nuyen. Luckily she was working for Renraku in Europe, and had pretty much disconnected herself from the rest of us. I wasn't even sure I'd told anyone I had a sister.

When I stepped into the closet to grab a box off the floor, the wood beneath my feet popped. I jumped back and then knelt down to remove several slats to reveal a plastic bag. Of course my imagination took off everywhere, thinking what if my dad was into something illegal and this was his stash? Or this might be someone's head buried under here.

That's Crisis thinking again.

But as I hoisted the bag out of the hole, the shape and *clank* of metallic things inside assured me it wasn't a head. Unless it was cyberware.

When I looked in the bag I sat back on my ass, unsure what to think. Inside were two carefully wrapped Solstice presents. The paper was aged, but had kept pretty well, just a little mold on it here and there. Bright red and green, with silver foil deer bounding across.

One was tagged for me, the other for my sister.

Was...what was this? Were these gifts my dad had hid from us and then forgot about? I couldn't remember any discussions between my parents over gifts. No arguments. Nothing. Did Mom even know these were down here?

I carefully opened mine, and was hit with an overwhelming feeling of nostalgia. Dad had died five years ago, when he was mugged late at night after picking up something for my mom. Something she needed for dinner that night. The BMP said the shooter had been a chip-head, still soaring from a bad experience from a bad BTL chip. The clerk at the Stuffer Shack said the guy had shouted, "Death to all Leaf eaters!" and shot my dad.

My dad wasn't an elf. My dad was human. Just as human as me.

I closed my eyes when I thought about the date of his death. December 2nd, 2069. Dad had never given us Solstice gifts before. That was Mom's thing. Was this something he'd done before he died?

Blinking a bit as raw emotions welled, mingling with the stress and anger and frustration of the past few days, I noted the name on the box. *NeoNET*.

It was a decking unit. New. Never opened. I ripped the paper back on my sister's as well. The same kind there as well. He'd bought these, knowing the decks were coming back, wanting to give us something of himself.

My dad had spent his whole life making these things, before the Crash changed everything, and wireless was the answer.

Had dad gone back to work back then? I couldn't remember, because I'd been hard at work on *Ghost-7* and making my own name. I think...

I think my sis and I had canceled coming home for Solstice that year.

And then he had died.

It was a soul-crushing guilt I'd learned to carry, but sitting there on that floor, I didn't have the strength anymore. Tears dropped on the matte black metallic packaging as I opened the box and pulled out a Hermes Chariot. Not top of the line, but more than doable. The thing was seven years old, and would probably need a lot of firmware upgrades, maybe some hardware...

But I had my solution. *Two* of them.

I spent several hours that night working the decks to get them compatible with the local grid. One I would use for communication, keep it simple and linked it to the Matrix and my game login. The other one, intended for my sister, I outfitted for hacking. It wasn't everything and a bag of chips. Not yet. But I made big plans to get where I could start hacking my way back into Andreas Martin Analysis Systems and find out who had erased me from my company.

I fully intended on getting my identity back. Even without Mason's help.

Getting comfortable in my dad's old recliner, I settled in and dove into the Matrix. Downloading the game took a few minutes, but once the login came up, I was in and blasted with over twenty messages from Serilious.

Each of them sounded increasingly panicked, but he never gave away my real name, where I'd been, or if I'd been involved in that raid at the coffee shop.

The instant message window of the game popped up. I moved my character to a rooftop and put up an AFK sign before I answered.

<*You keep hounding me. Why?*>

<*You're okay. Good. I was afraid GOD had you.*>

I hesitated at first, but responded. <*You knew about the raid?*>

<*Only a split second before it happened. GOD's agents are good about their encrypted communication. Have you seen the vids?*>

<*No. Been offline.*>

<*Good choice. Luckily your name isn't mentioned in the raid, just that GOD had word of a shadowrunner in the vicinity, hacking their system.*>

<*I was* not *doing that!*>

<*Calm down, boyo. You need to get it straight right now. Whoever's out to get you–and all of their allies–will lie to find you and make you disappear.*>

I turned my character's head as I looked down at people walking below. <*How do you know all this? Who are you?*> I sort of assumed they were Irish descent, given the use of "boyo," but I wasn't sure.

<*I'm an interested party who knows another interested party. Neither of us are fond of NeoNET.*>

<*I don't work for NeoNET.*>

<*No, but you appear to be a key figure in a company they are desperate to own. Or, they want something your company has. Would you know anything about that?*>

I didn't like the question. This person, this Serilious, seemed to know a lot about me, and I knew nothing about them. <*I'm just an analyst. That's all.*>

Several minutes passed before he responded. <*Suit yourself. But listen to me. They can't find you at the moment. Your bail hearing is set for tomorrow morning. I suggest that you stay out of sight until then, and make sure you hire security to get to the courthouse.*>

<*You think they'll try and kill me or something?*>

<*Worse.*> Another long pause. <*I just added this account to the Gold Membership, which means the company will protect all your privacy. I've also tweaked a few things so no one will link this to Oliver Martin.*>

Now I knew this was an admin. But why were they so interested in me?

<Once your bail hearing is over, you need to hide with us.>

<What? Why are you doing this? I don't even know you.>

<Like I said. We're interested in keeping you alive. As to why,> —and again, a pause like before— *<There's been a hit put out on you, Oliver Martin, from a very well-known Mr. Johnson. Your enemy wants you alive. But if they catch you, and they will if you don't have our help, you won't remain alive for long.>*

My frustration with this impossible situation reached a head. I wanted to shout at this stranger, demand they tell me who they were since they knew so much about me, but before I could even start I received a missive from Serilious. *<Read it.>*

I opened it and watched as it scanned clean. *<What is it?>*

<Your obituary. It's scheduled to run Saturday morning.>

CHAPTER 8

ANDREAS MARTIN ANALYSIS SYSTEMS
BOSTON
THURSDAY, MARCH 7, 2075

Mason stood beside his desk, watching Apollonius as he approached the window and Maxine took up a spot at the door. He was pretty sure the troll was there to keep people out—and to keep Mason in.

"What tipped Martin off to GOD's arrival at the Moonshine Cafe?"

Apollonius's words caught Mason completely off guard. He'd just learned of Oliver's escape not five minutes ago. How could this man already know? Unless... "You told GOD to raid the cafe."

"*I* didn't tell them. No one tells GOD what to do, Mason." Apollonius turned and smiled his beautiful smile at Mason, the frame of the Boston skyline an impressive background around him. "I merely suggested there were questionable individuals in the cafe."

"Were you having him followed?"

"Yes. It was easy. I'm surprised you didn't think of this yourself. It was obvious to me that Mr. Martin was with Miss Nicole, since she paid his bail. I've had the arcology under surveillance since I learned Martin survived."

"The...whole arcology?"

Apollonius shrugged. "The entrance and exits, both known and unknown." He smiled again, but Mason didn't like the expression now. "Nothing happens in this city without me knowing, if I am interested in it. And I am very interested in bringing Mr. Martin in, Mason. He holds the knowledge of

Ghost-7. Either its design or the prototype. He's an asset you—and I— cannot afford to lose."

But Mason wasn't past processing the fact that Apollonius had that kind of influence with the Grid Oversight Division. Hell...Mason had people he relied on to feed him information, but Apollonius actually gave orders. Was he really that powerful? Most residents of Boston didn't even know his name. Mason wasn't even sure NeoNET really knew who he was either, only that he had a reputation for delivering what he promised. And now, Mason was slowly understanding that the kind of power Apollonius wielded wasn't obvious. It was dark and invisible and deadly.

"You haven't answered my question. What—or who—tipped Martin off?"

Mason swallowed. "I don't know. I know it wasn't my contact at the Division."

Apollonius nodded. He looked satisfied, but Mason knew that wasn't always the case. "Martin's signature on the Matrix wasn't visible, per se. The only reason GOD found him was because my spies picked up his physical trail when he came into the Commons. The Agents' onsite takedown was flawless, but on their arrival, the café was empty, with maybe a single patron inside, two baristas. No sign of Martin.

"I've looked at his record, Mason. Oliver Martin is a whiz at market analysis, he has the golden touch at knowing what companies, what tools, what products will succeed or fail. He had a passing interest in decks, but there is no information as to whether or not he improved this proclivity, so let me be very clear here. In a nutshell—Oliver Martin is unremarkable. So," Apollonius had moved toward Mason while he was speaking, until he was leaning over the desk, his aquiline nose only inches from Mason's. "Let me be *perfectly* clear—what or who tipped him off, or the entire cafe to that matter, that GOD was coming?"

Mason felt sweat trickle down his back, as well as his forehead. "Maybe it's someone he knows and we don't?"

"His best friend works in advertising."

"Oliver and I didn't associate much outside of the company."

"Because he stole your fiancée, Nicole O'Neal."

It didn't matter how afraid of Apollonius he was, the mention of Nicole again woke his defense mechanism. "Don't drag Nicole into this."

"She's already a part of it, Mason. When she paid that bastard's bail, she made herself a target. However...I'll overlook her, as long as you cooperate."

"Cooperate?" Mason's temper and irritation flared even stronger than his fear. "Cooperate is all I've done."

"As of now, I will be overseeing the retrieval of Oliver Martin and his interrogation to find the prototype. I will also have access to Nicole O'Neal, but—" Apollonius held up that finger once again as he straightened and moved back, "I give you my word that I won't harm her. You have to understand, Mason, the way to someone like Oliver Martin is through those he cares for. And since he doesn't have any family we can use, Nicole is the only leverage we have."

"He has a sister."

"Yes, we found her. But she and Martin have been estranged for quite a while, having had no contact with her brother since their parents's death. She also didn't return for their funerals. She works for Renraku. We'll hold her as our last resort."

This conversation made Mason nervous. "What do you mean you're taking over the retrieval?"

Apollonius narrowed his eyes and Mason took a step back. "Is there something wrong with my use of language, Mason? Getting Oliver Martin back is the priority for me. He's become a problem. I handle problems. He wouldn't be a problem if you'd handled him from the moment he realized what was being done with his invention. But you didn't do anything, instead resorting to your own ridiculous quest to remove Martin's identity and steal the company from him as some sick revenge for taking your girl." He brought his left arm over his chest and propped his right elbow on top of it as he ran the index finger of that and across his lower lip. "I'm right, aren't I?"

Mason just stared at the bastard. Yes, he was right. But he wasn't going to give Apollonius the pleasure of acknowledging it.

"If you had just stayed out of my way, none of this would have happened." Apollonius pursed his lips. "Martin's hearing is tomorrow?"

"Yes."

"And he'll show up?"

"If Oliver Martin is one thing, it's a law-abiding citizen. He would never purposefully break the law."

"I saw his dossier. The man's clean. Not a single infraction, until you deleted his ID." Apollonius abruptly turned and headed to the door, which Maxine opened for him. "Pull your people off of Oliver Martin, Mason. I'll contact you when I have the prototype."

Maxine nodded to Mason before she closed the door. He nearly collapsed on the desk, but managed to make it to his chair to plop into. He really wasn't sure why his heart was pounding so fast, or so hard. No, that wasn't true. He knew *exactly* why. Because he was truly afraid of Apollonius Turk, more than he'd ever been afraid of anyone. This man could make Oliver disappear if he wanted. And Nicole.

And me.

He activated his AR and called all of the investigators and private handlers off Oliver Martin except one. He kept the most expensive one. The one whose experience in surveillance rivaled the others. That one he kept on Nicole's apartment with the express order that if anything happened to her, Mason would put a bounty on the elf's head so high he wouldn't be able to move.

After that, Mason remained in his chair and looked out the window over Boston. He hoped Apollonius Turk found the prototype. Otherwise, he feared *he'd* end up on the other end of Turk's interrogation methods, and that was a position Mason refused to put himself in.

It was past eleven o'clock, dark outside, and Oliver wasn't back yet.

Nicole O'Neal watched the surveillance cars drive away outside the arcology. Her apartment was located on the outside wall, and gave her a stunning view of Boston Harbor in the distance. The daughter of a wealthy and powerful family, she knew what to look for when it came to corporate and clandestine dirty tricks, so she'd picked out the cars easily enough and ran their registration once they showed up hours after she brought Oliver home. They were all private and well bonded, and a little more hacking showed they were all paid by the same account. She didn't need a forensic accountant to tell her the account belonged to Mason Andreas. That much was a given. Her father had warned her when she and Mason were engaged that the man she believed she loved was nothing but a phony and a crook, and the only reason he wanted to marry Nicole was to be brought into the O'Neal family.

At first, Nicole hadn't believed any of it. Mason was sweet and sincere and very caring.

Until she met Oliver, and her heart had become a fickle bitch. It wanted Oliver. Tall, rugged, handsome, and so endearingly shy...what woman wouldn't fall for him? The only regret she'd had after breaking off the engagement with Mason was that she had ever said yes in the first place. He seemed okay with hers and Oliver's relationship, but Nicole had also seen Mason's temper. She knew what he was capable of.

So it wasn't a stretch to believe Mason was the one behind this whole identity crisis and Oliver's subsequent arrest and assault. The fact it had taken her so long to find Oliver in the system, along with their reluctance to let him go, it all spelled a conspiracy of some kind.

But why? Oliver seemed to be as confused as she was. Why was Mason so bent on destroying him? Was it her? The engagement? Was this Mason's way of getting revenge against her, by destroying what she loved?

Or was there something else? Something she wasn't seeing?

The door announced a visitor. She checked the AR feed on her commlink and saw Jericho's familiar face. She let him in as she closed all the windows and shuttered the apartment against snooping devices. This was something her father had installed in her security system, and didn't come standard for most of the units.

Jericho was the one to discover something was wrong on Tuesday morning, when he'd tried sending a message to Oliver for lunch. The missive came back with a message announcing the receiving account didn't exist. Jericho had tried repeatedly to contact Oliver, but when everything had failed, he'd called Nicole.

She felt she owed him a great deal for that, fearing if they hadn't tracked Oliver down, he might have disappeared without a trace.

"Hey," Jericho said as he set a dark bag on the couch. Looking around, he frowned. "Where's Oliver?"

"I don't know."

"He didn't come home from Moonshine Cafe?"

"No. And he hasn't sent me any messages either."

"Drek," Jericho said as he shrugged his jacket off. "We need to find him as soon as possible."

Nicole approached Jericho. "What's wrong?"

He turned on the trideo player and turned the volume up, then motioned her into her bedroom and pulled up his commlink's AR. She opened hers as well and watched as he led her through a set of complicated routines.

Abruptly, an account showed up. "That's Oliver's ID!"

"Yeah. It appeared online about an hour ago. Fully intact, with no warnings or liens against it. Except for this." Jericho moved a few windows away and projected a VR image into the space in front of the two of them. Nicole recognized the local information hub, a spinning house of market reports, news stories, and people pieces. Using his finger, he turned the information around, and she recognized a hack he used to get into the hub's office database. "Jer—"

He didn't respond, just skimmed through thousands of data files until he found one and opened it. The date was set for Sunday, and the header—

Nicole's knees went weak. Jericho put his hand on her shoulder and said her name. But her eyes were already scanning the generic obituary of Oliver Martin. There were holes in the piece, blanks left to fill in before finalization. "How...?"

"I already contacted the writer on this. He's a level one journalist working for peanuts to get through school. He said he just gets the requests and overlays the templates for information. This one he said was submitted by an anonymous source."

"Anonymous? How can an obituary be unknown?"

Jericho said in a calm voice, "It's always submitted that way in the beginning, in case it gets pulled. Someone submitted this one four days ago, Nicole."

She looked at Jericho's brown eyes as her mind registered what that meant. "Four days... We were on our vacation."

"Uh-huh. It's like I suspected. This was all planned, Nicole. Someone's trying to utterly destroy Oliver."

"But why?"

"I think it's got something to do with that thing he was working on." He started to touch his commlink and then pulled his hand away.

"What's wrong?"

"Nothing. I just thought better of something. Either way, we have to get Oliver back into protection, or someone's going to kill him."

"That's just impossible, Jericho." Nicole dismissed her AR and took a few steps back. "Think about what you're saying and how it's not making sense."

"Yeah. I know. Which is why this is freaking me out, Nicole. Oliver's just an analyst, he's a market researcher who works for a company who creates marketing tools. It's not a glamorous job, but it does roll in the high stacks. You still trying to contact Mason Andreas?"

"Yes but he hasn't answered me." Nicole swallowed. "I think he's behind this, but it's not about Oli's job—it's all about revenge."

"Same difference." Jericho shrugged. "Either way, Oli's life is in danger. We might not know why, but we know when, and that's between now and Sunday. That's three days."

"His bail hearing's in the morning," Nicole said.

"Then he'll either get hit then or before it." Jericho looked around the room. "You got a couch I can rest on?"

"Rest?"

"Yeah," Jericho removed his outer jacket and retrieved a set of deck wires from the pocket. "If he's at another café, that means he's half-diving, he's looking around the Matrix. I need to dive in and find him and get him back here."

Nicole pointed to the sofa in her bedroom. "Set up there."

Jericho set his jacket on the sofa's arm, retrieved his black bag, and pulled out a deck. He set it beside him on the couch and plugged the wires into the unit, then into the data jack at his temple. "If something happens, pull me out. If I find anything, I'll tell you."

Nicole nodded and watched as Jericho leaned back and closed his eyes.

She stood in the center of the room, feeling helpless. Oliver was out there trying to find his identity, now it was back online and there was an obituary ready to be published. Jericho was looking for Oliver. Nicole did the only thing she knew to do and pulled up her AR again.

"Yes hi, Davina. Is Dad in?"

CHAPTER 9

BOSTON
FRIDAY, MARCH 8, 2075
1:00 A.M.

Serilius would only meet up in-game to talk. Still at my parents' house and still logged in, I headed over the rooftops of Boston toward the harbor where the NPCs were usually found. The usual NPCs that meandered around the area—muggers, chip heads, and Mr. Johnsons—were all conspicuously missing.

In-game, Crisis was an elf, and a very skilled one. Dark hair, tall and thin, and high on the stealth points. His crit hits were off the charts, as that was the only skill I leveled up first and I hadn't spent enough time switching out skills, since I liked Crisis the way he was. In stealth mode, he was invisible to everyone.

I climbed down an old fire escape and then jumped the rest of the way, landing with no sound on the oily asphalt. Creeping along the alley to the opening, I spotted the character just outside the bar Rancheros. Serilious was big, a massive troll, with a high level and stats that made me hesitate. If this was a trap, he could kill my character pretty quick.

But then, it was just a character and a game. What was I worried about?

"We can talk in the open. This area of the node is on maintenance. I've changed your status to NPC." His voice was deep, but pleasant, and did have a slight Irish lilt to his speech.

"How did you do that?" And he'd made me a NPC?

Serilious' shoulders slumped. "You want to discuss game mechanics, boyo, or do you want to protect your life?"

Good point.

I stepped out from the alley's shadows and approached the hulking troll who'd been turned away from me. He spun to face me as I approached and I had to squelch the instinctive reaction to draw weapons and disappear again. "How did you find that obituary?"

"I'm a knowledge dealer. I'm good at my job."

"In game. But you found that out of game."

"Aye."

I pursed my lips. "How do I know you're not the one who put it there?"

Serilious looked out over the scenery. "You don't. So you're going to need to trust me."

I narrowed my character's eyes. "Why? I don't know you, or at least I don't think I do."

Now he looked directly at me. "We've never met out of game. But when I play as NPCs, I can watch characters and learn about their players. You caught my eye. Especially when odd things started happening to your account. Which brings me to why we needed to meet here and we're keeping this in private dialogue."

The troll abruptly punched the ground, which cracked and released a violet bubble that rose up around us. He'd activated a magic spell in the game, one that made both of us nonexistent.

I raised my brows. "You don't trust this node?"

"I don't trust anything. Especially not when it comes to the level of crackery your enemy's coming after you with. First off, do you know why you were targeted?"

"Not really. I can speculate."

"Do you suspect who?"

"My business partner came to mind, but I can't figure what he'd gain by erasing my identity."

"Are you friends? Do you owe him nuyen?" Serilious asked.

"Yes, and no I don't owe him anything." These questions made me revisit the idea of *Ghost-7* again, and my suspicion that this was all about that prototype and the weird conversation Mason had had in Elvish. But I didn't want to mention it to this stranger. For all I knew, this could be the same person who'd been deleting me.

"Your ID is live again, you know this." Serilious tilted his head at me.

"Yeah I saw it, but I didn't want to access it."

"Smart. I think it's bait. So here's what you need to do." The troll pointed a thick claw at my face. "Stop poking the bear, junior. Don't do anything else. Disappear for a while. New identity, which I can give you if you want. I can also arrange passage for you out of Boston to a safe place where you can't be found."

"Out of Boston?" I frowned. "I can't leave here. I live here. My friends are here, my job, and my fiancée. I can't just up and disappear."

"What's all that mean if you're dead?"

"Are you that certain I'm in that dire of a situation?"

The troll shrugged. "I've seen all kinds in this game, which makes it easy for me to spot a worthy candidate. And you're it. You're not a criminal, but someone's making you out to be. So the best thing you can do is not be there for them to destroy. Don't let them win."

"You're talking about walking away from my life, aren't you?"

"Boyo, don't you get it?—it's not *your* life anymore. Someone's messing with it, and they're playing hardcore. This has corp drek written all over it, so I suggest you consider what it is you want. Whoever you pissed off is gunning to destroy you, by either killing your identity, destroying your reputation, or your life. Or all three, which is what I vote for."

I took a deep breath in both worlds and ran fingers through my hair. "I can't just walk away."

"Then take a short break. Either way, disappear. Come with me. I can help you."

"I don't even know who you are. Have we ever met IRL?"

"Not yet. But you have met an associate of mine. But you won't remember."

An icon flashed on the upper left corner, which meant I had out of game mail. It could be Nicole or Jericho trying to contact me.

Serilious continued, "Look, I had to take a chance letting you know. And it makes sense that you don't trust me. You should log off now. Don't stay online too long in any one place unless you know the connection is GOD free. So take this."

Another flash of the mail icon, only this one was in red, which meant an in-game message from an Admin. "What is it?"

"The name of the bastard who told you that your SIN was suspended. The tool who lied to you. That's his entire dossier.

You look him up, get answers. Maybe then you'll trust me. And if you do, just contact me ingame and the offer's open. As long as you're alive. But once you're dead..." The troll shrugged. "It's off."

I nodded and thanked him before I teleported my character back to my game house. I transferred Serilious's message to my commlink's node and logged off.

There were more than ten messages waiting for me, including the one from Serilious. I stared at the sender addresses, all the same. It was an address I'd used consistently for years.

It was Mason Andreas's private contact.

I opened the first one.

Oliver!

What's going on? I've been in Tír Tairngire since the signing on Monday. My assistant says someone hacked into the personnel node. Please contact me as soon as you get this.

M

The message was repeated on each missive. Was it really Mason? Was this really all just the work of a hacker, looking for personnel information and not a personal attack on me? I wanted to believe this. I needed to. Because if it was true, then my life could return to normal, and the arrest and everything that had happened could be expunged, and I could go back to my normal life.

My heart wanted to respond immediately. But my mind, that little part of me I'd listened to off and on during my life, the cautious piece of me—the one that'd gotten his ass beat a couple days hours ago—said not to. Or if I did, that I needed to be cautious about it.

I sat on the couch, staring at the window of my AR, all of Mason's missives opened. I'd sort of forgotten about Serilious. And what about him? Why was this perfect stranger—someone I'd only run into in a game—so interested in me outside of it? How did he know so much about me?

A new idea occurred to me; all of this could have been caused by this associate of Serilious's? He had access to my personal information. He could see who I was, what my future was like. He might even know who my fiancée is, and given her position, what if he planned on kidnapping her next as part of some terroristic plot to control me?

I couldn't remember a time in my life when I'd been so indecisive. Calling and talking to Jericho was my first response, but wouldn't Serilious know that? And he knew Jericho's in-game character. He had to know we were friends.

No, I didn't want to drag my best friend into this any further.

I closed the AR and disconnected before taking another shower, then changed into some of my old clothes. The style was more college freshman than professional, and I had to admit I felt a bit more comfortable like that.

I grabbed the commlink and my deck (and hid the second one) and took the train back across the river and settled into a local twenty-four-hour antique bookstore near the college. There I ordered a soycaf, set up my work area on a table in the back, and blended in. I hadn't shaved in two days, so a thin beard had started around my chin. I thought it made me look very different.

First, I used the open connection to return the missives. Luckily, the message would only have the identifier for the coffee shop and not the exact commlink. I could get away quick if I needed to.

The response was instantaneous, as if Mason had been waiting for me to call. I set up AR window on the local node and accepted the incoming missive, keeping it text only.

<*Oliver! I'm so glad you returned my message. But why can't I see you? Why aren't we on a voice call?*>

I wanted to talk to him. I always wanted to because I'd trusted him. And though he said he'd been in Tír Tairngire all this time, I still felt a bit...cautious. <*Long story.*>

<*How do I know it's really you?*>

<*Ask me a question.*>

<*What is my given name?*>

I smiled at that one. Mason Andreas had worked hard at keeping his first name a secret, not that I thought it was a bad name. It just wasn't something he was proud of. <*Aubrey.*>

Mason's avatar appeared, an elven warrior that sort of resembled him. <*Okay. It's you. Now, tell me from the beginning–what happened?*>

So I did, but I used a much more abbreviated method, hitting on the highlights. I left out any reference to *Ghost-7*, because I still wasn't sure this wasn't all about the prototype. I was pretty happy when Mason didn't ask about it.

<*Good Heavens, Oliver. This is terrible. I heard when I got back, and we've made sure everything's been returned to normal.*>

That explained why my SIN was back and working...but I still didn't want to try it out <*Do you have any idea why someone would attack me like this? And for what reason? I mean, what's the point? I don't have a life anyone would want, and I'm not wealthy.*>

<*But you will be, Oliver, once this acquisition is complete. I spoke with Apollonius Turk when I found out what'd happened. He told me to communicate with you how important it is to keep an eye out. He himself has been the victim of kidnapping attempts, as well as extortion.*>

Drek. I winced at the thought. <*So you think they did it to work in some way to extort nuyen?*>

<*Could be. Are you all right?*>

<*I'm a bit banged up, but fine overall.*>

<*Are you with Nicole? I've tried calling her, but she hasn't returned my messages.*>

<*No, I'm not with her. She had some things to do.*> That wasn't exactly the truth but I wanted to leave her out of this as much as possible, for her own protection.

<*Maybe you should stay at home.*>

I explained to him that I no longer had a home, and appreciated his colorful metaphors in response. <*I will get that taken care of, Oliver. I promise. Just come in tomorrow so we can get everything straightened out.*>

<*I will, but after court. I have a hearing in nine hours and can't miss it.*>

<*That's right. The arrest. Why don't I meet you there with our lawyers, early, and we can get everything ready? File a dismissal, since this was all a misunderstanding in the first place.*>

<*Sounds good. What time? My hearing's at eleven.*>

<*Let's meet at eight. You know how these paper pushers are.*>

<*I will. I'll meet you at the courthouse.*>

There was a slight lag in his response. <*Let's pick a less public place. How about that hole-in-the-wall breakfast place you like over on Charles Street? My treat.*>

<*Thanks Mason. I knew you'd know what to do.*>

<*I'm glad you called, Oliver. We'll get everything straightened out tomorrow.*>

I disconnected and logged off, feeling the best I'd felt since...Sunday night. Mason would take care of things. I thought about calling Nicole and letting her know that Mason was handling everything, but after looking at the time, I didn't want to wake her. I would surprise her later today, once the arrest was dismissed and everything would be okay again. I would just head back to the house where I knew I was safe, grab some sleep, and meet Mason in the morning.

CHAPTER 10

Mason sat back in his chair and shifted the view in his AR. Apollonius's persona looked exactly like the real thing, which only fueled the rumors of him being a very vain man. "Was that to your liking?"

"That was very well done, Mason. I didn't know you could lie so convincingly. Then again, it was all in text. If he heard your voice, I'm sure you would fail."

Mason chose to ignore the remark. No one knew Oliver the way he did. They'd been friends for nearly ten years, but it just occurred to him to use what he knew—and that friendship—to his advantage. There was a way to salvage his plan, and even use Apollonius in the process, thus making the man happy. "I recommend not being seen at first. Allow me to lull him into a false sense of security. Then you can take him."

"I appreciate the forethought. I'll keep it under advisement."

"Apollonius," Mason sat forward and used what his secretary called his executive tone. "You tasked me with finding the prototype. Only Oliver knows where that is. The way I see it, this makes him a valuable asset. The more cooperative he is, the higher the odds at retrieving that information."

Now he waited for the response. Apollonius had a hair trigger, one Mason had seen and experienced on more than one occasion, and it'd taken him a while to sift through the exterior to see where he could push the right buttons. Mason's problem was that Apollonius' buttons kept changing minute to minute.

"I see your point, Mason. Very well. My people will be waiting in the back in case he chooses not to trust you." Apollonius disconnected without another word.

Mason didn't have time to gloat privately, as his AR buzzed again. This time the name on the caller alarmed him.

Nathan O'Neal. Nicole's father and CEO of one of the city's largest banking institutions. Since Oliver's arrest, Mason had fielded many calls from O'Neal. He didn't want to talk to the man, but he had to keep their association in good standing. Especially since he'd been quietly buying up shares in one of O'Neal's privately-owned businesses, Commons, Inc. a research company used by most all of the businesses in Boston as a means to get the low-down on possible clients, tenants, employees, etc. For some reason, Apollonius wanted the company.

Mason shut off the protocols and accepted the visual communication. "Good evening, Nathan. It seems an odd hour, doesn't it?"

"Yes, Mason, it does. It's about time you answered. But when it comes to my daughter..." Nathan was in his late seventies. A human with dark hair, just graying at the temples, and a handsome face. This was where Nicole got her good looks. She had her father's sky-blue eyes. "It seems something's happened with Oliver, and I need to know what you're going to do about it."

Really? As if I'm his to command? But Mason put on a pleasant face and smiled. "Fortunately, I have good news about that. Oliver's SIN has been reinstated, and his identity returned. We found the person responsible, and will be bringing him to justice. In fact, I've already spoken to Oliver this evening, and we'll be clearing up the matter tomorrow."

Great and obvious relief colored Nathan O'Neal's face. His shoulders lowered. "That is excellent news. Have you told Nicole yet?"

Mason noted the man had never seemed to like him while he and Nicole had been engaged. In fact, if the roles were reversed, he doubted Nathan O'Neal would give a rat's ass if Mason were in trouble. "Not yet. Would you like to do the honors?"

"I would...and thank you. I appreciate all your help."

"Any time, Nathan." Mason disconnected and scowled. He knew Nathan O'Neal had worked behind the scenes to destroy his and Nicole's engagement. He was aware of the black file her father amassed against him, which included his past crimes.

All petty, but not something he wanted Nicole or anyone else to know. At least not until this acquisition was finished.

Or...maybe not at all. He opened up his Ghost file, the one he'd started when his lab team started quietly using *Ghost-7* to get rid of their competition. It was all labeled as field testing work, but Mason had figured, why not use real targets and clear a path?

Once they had *Ghost-7* back, another test would have to be run to make sure nothing had been tampered with. *Commons, Inc.* was next on the list. He didn't give a damn if Apollonius took it over or not.

"Who keeps trying to reach you?" Jericho said as he pulled the wires from his datajack and yawned. It was way past one in the morning.

Nicole touched her commlink and checked. "Daddy. But I don't have time right now to go over again what's happened." She looked at Jericho. "Nothing?"

"Just that he spoke with a friend in a game."

"Friend?"

"Yeah, an admin that plays a NPC. Non player character."

Nicole smiled. "I wish I understood games."

"It's not hard. But, this NPC player said he spoke to Oliver a couple of hours ago, and he was safe. It might be he's laying low till the court date in a few hours. Protecting you."

Nicole felt her cheeks grow warm. "I'm worried, Jericho."

"Me too." He put his deck and paraphernalia away before standing up. "I need to get going. What time's the hearing?"

"Eleven." She checked her chronometer and sighed. "About nine and a half hours from now."

He stepped closer and put a hand on her shoulder. "I'll be there to show support. And to be a character witness if I have to be."

That made her laugh. "I'm sure he'll appreciate it, Jer."

"You going to be okay?"

"Once I know Oli's safe, I'll be just fine." She saw him out and locked all her doors. Walking over to the window, she looked up and down the street. No unmarked cars.

Her AR buzzed again. Still her father. Better to answer now, or he would show up at her door next. "Hey Daddy, what's up?"

"Nicole, where's Oliver?"

"I don't know. He went out this morning. A friend spoke to him, said he was okay."

Her father used a few colorful metaphors.

"What is it?"

"Nicole, you need to find him. I just got off the phone with Mason Andreas."

"That's wonderful! Did he clear all this up?" Her heart beat fast against her chest.

"Well he says he tried to. But I don't trust him. I'm sure he's up to something, and Oliver's in the center."

"That's ridiculous. Is he going to get Oliver out of this mess?" It took a bit of coaxing but her dad finally spilled the conversation. And after listening to it, she couldn't figure out why her father didn't trust Mason.

"It's just a feeling I have, Nikki. You have to trust *me*."

"Daddy, you've always thought Mason was a bad man. And all he's done is good. Now he's going to help Oliver. When are you just going to admit that you're wrong and stop meddling in my life?"

She disconnected and threw her commlink into the couch. Either way, no matter how angry she was at that moment, she felt relief wash over her. Mason was going to help Oliver fix everything. Of course Mason would do that. He and Oliver were friends.

She needed to let Jericho know. But it was late and she felt she could sleep now that she knew everything was going to go back to normal, and she and Oliver could finally get married.

CHAPTER 11

BOSTON
FRIDAY, MARCH 8, 2075
8:00 A.M.

I woke early, feeling better than I had since the party at AMAS last Friday night. It was hard for me to realize it was Friday now, and I hadn't been able to work, or check on the prototype's field tests. There were still two of them running.

After a long hot shower, some clean clothes, shoes and a shave, I looked decent again. I looked and felt like me. And by the afternoon, I would be me again, and I could put this all behind me. It would be a long time before I could forget it, but as my mother would say, conflict builds character.

I didn't want or need any more character. I was done with it. I wanted my life, my job, and my career back.

Which meant I needed to retrieve the prototype from the locker. Unfortunately, I hadn't had time to send Jericho the locker code. I had to get out there and expose myself to get the chips back. For now they were safe. I'd only paid for a month's rent. After that, I had no idea what would happen to anything in that locker.

It might be a good idea to send Jericho a message, just in case.

I got to the designated place early and looked around. No Mason yet. I ordered a soycaf and grabbed a table in the back, taking the chair that faced the door so I could see him come in. I logged into my Hermes, the one with the false name on it, and sent a quick, encrypted missive to Jericho, telling him about the locker and giving him the code to open it. Once I had the prototype, I could get it back on AMAS's research node and finish up the finals before we handed it over to NeoNET in December.

Before I logged out, I saw Serilious's message still waiting for me to answer it. I reached out to tap it open. The dossier came up, the one belonging to the criminal Serilious said I spoke to on Saturday night. The one that suspended my SIN.

My heart leaped into my throat when I recognized the name and the face of one of AMAS's top researchers. In fact, I'd worked with him since the beginning on the *Ghost-7* project, spent a lot of time with him, and even showed him some of my preliminary notes.

George Spinoza.

Included with George's AMAS file were law enforcement reports. A few were from Knight Errant, but there were over a dozen from Lone Star. None were violent crimes. They were all complaints and pending suits against George Spinoza for theft of personal information, as well as selling corporate secrets. This guy had all of this on his record, and Mason hired him anyway? Or was it possible these complaints were invisible to Mason?

Or worse, had Serilious fabricated them in order to pin this crime on an innocent man's shoulders?

A call came in, and I recognized Serilious's icon. Looking around the restaurant, seeing other patrons on their commlinks, busy with their own personal conversations, I answered. "You had the file tagged so you'd know when I opened it."

Serilious's voice came through loud and clear, exactly as it sounded in game. This gave me no clue as to who he was in the real world. *"Yes I did. It took you long enough."* There was a pause. *"Why are you still in the city?"*

That made me sit up and look around. Great, was this crazy person following me? "Look, I appreciate you trying to help me, or thinking you could, but it's all fixed now."

"Fixed?"

"Yeah. I talked with Mason last night. He's been out of the UCAS with his wife so he didn't know this had happened to me."

"Bullshit, boyo," Serilious snapped. *"That cocksucker's lying to you. You know how I know this? Because he never left town. He's been in Boston since you were arrested, helping that crazy-ass person NeoNET hired as your liaison to find you."*

"You just don't know when to stop, do you? First you try and frame George and make me think he engineered my identity being stolen, and now you want me to believe Mason's a part of this, too?"

"Yeah, I do. You need proof? Check into it yourself, omae. *You're good with a deck. And it's not illegal to check travel records. And those files I sent you on Spinoza are real. That tech might come off as harmless, but he's not. He'll laugh nervously just before he stabs you from behind because he got paid."* The icon looked fierce and pissed off. "Don't *meet with Mason Andreas, and especially not with Apollonius Turk, Oliver. Get out of there. Do your research. They went to a lot of trouble to screw with you this past week. Do you even know why?"*

That's where the sticking part was. I didn't really know why, but I had a hard suspicion.

"Drek...Oliver, you need to get out of there. Now!" The connection vanished.

I sat in stunned silence. It occurred to me that Serilious hadn't asked for anything. Not really. Not even payment for helping me. So what was he after? What vendetta could he have against Mason, or Spinoza?

I checked the chronometer on my AR before I pulled the wires from my deck out of my pocket and shoved them into the jack at my temple. Hacking with commlinks had become pretty much impossible over the past decade. Decks were the only way to dig up the real information. The stuff I needed to see.

I am not a hacker. I know the basics and have rudimentary skills, the kind everyone learns and uses in school, either to change grades or cheat what systems we can. I knew the basics about the weapon, but wasn't even close to an expert in using it. Checking the validity of the reports on Spinoza was easy enough. They were real. Even checking on flight records for specific individuals was easy, and just like Serilious said—Mason hadn't flown anywhere in the past week.

Why had he lied to me? And was he *still* lying to me? Did he know Spinoza was the one that had destroyed my identity? That he had impersonated an Intelligence agent? The impersonation alone was a criminal offense, and if reported, the guy would get a lifetime in prison.

I went over the information again, double-checking what I could, and by the time I finished, I wanted to be anywhere but in that restaurant. Alone. Waiting for someone I wasn't sure I could really trust. Here I was, putting my trust in someone I didn't know over someone I thought I knew. I saved everything and disconnected.

That's when I saw Mason enter the restaurant. The maitre'd approached him, and I ducked beneath the chair. I watched their legs and as they walked to the right, I crept along to the left. I managed to slip into the restroom area and saw a back door.

"Oliver."

Mason's tone stopped me in my tracks. I didn't realize he'd seen me bolt. I lowered my shoulders, but didn't turn to face him. "Why, Mason?"

"It's just business, Oliver."

I half-turned and narrowed my eyes at him. "My life is just business? What has it got to do with—"

"The complaint you filed, the report on the dangers of *Ghost-7*. When I realized you had more of a conscience than me, it became obvious you were going to get in the way of the future."

"You mean *your* future. You were the one that approved the use of real companies in the tests."

"Yes."

"You brought down three of AMAS's competitors using it, Mason. What you did—"

"Was legal. I insured our success, Oliver. And I proved your application was everything you wanted it to be."

I put my hand to my chest. "I never wanted it to put people out of work or cause heartache. *Ghost-7* was built to help a business analyze its own shortcomings. It was written to give smaller businesses a fighting chance, not to destroy the competition."

Mason slowly shook his head. He stood in the center of the arch, cutting off my only access into the dining area. Everything inside me screamed to run. *Run! Get away!*

My muscles caught fire as the skillwires hummed. My skillsoft subscription opened, and I downloaded an actionsoft I'd been holding in the queue. I was ready to fight my way out of that restaurant.

"Oliver—"

"I know about George, Mason. I know he was the one I talked to on the phone Monday morning. He managed to make me SINless. And he wouldn't have done that on his own." I felt my chest tighten. "Not without your approval."

"Where's the prototype?"

"It's exactly where it's always been," I heard myself say, marking up a bravado I didn't feel. "Out of your reach."

My old friend, the man I went into business with, sighed as the exit behind me opened.

When I turned, the only thing I saw was the large fist of a troll as it struck me across the face.

It was also the last thing I saw, and felt, before my world went dark.

So much for the skillwires Jericho always wanted me to use.

PART TWO

Two months later

CHAPTER 12

AMAS HEADQUARTERS
NEWBURY STREET, BOSTON
THURSDAY, MAY 2, 2075
MID-MORNING

Mason stared out the window of his twenty-fourth-floor office. The floor-to-ceiling glass walls gave him a panoramic view of the Boston skyline. It was dark outside, and the lights of the city reflected the stars above. He thought of Nicole, and of course that thought brought Oliver's face with it once again. The look of betrayal when Maxine came through that back door.

He thought of Nicole again. She wasn't forgetting Oliver like he assumed she would. Oliver Martin no longer existed in the world. At least not in the way he went out. She wasn't going to forget Oliver, and she wasn't going to drop it. Two months since his disappearance, she still remained stubbornly loyal to him, still believed he'd come home. And until he and Apollonius had the prototype in their hands again, Oliver would have to remain missing.

A knock at the door roused Mason from his memories. He turned. "Come."

The door opened and Apollonius stepped in, flanked by his two faithful bodyguards. Max and Maxine, male and female trolls, both quiet and very attentive and very visibly armed. Apollonius had told him early on in their negotiations that his life had been threatened on more than one occasion, and he felt much more at ease with the two of them close by. "Mason..."

Mason's nerves bristled as he strode toward Apollonius. "You didn't have to come here."

Apollonius glided closer. "I tried calling, but your secretary said you weren't taking calls."

Mason scowled. "I'll have to have a word with her." He realized a moment later he'd turned off his own PAN and commlink, making it difficult to contact him. "What can I do for you?"

"I have some...bad news, Mason," Apollonius put his hands behind his back as he turned to face the view of Boston's skyline alongside Mason. "I'm afraid your friend...is dead."

Mason's reaction came from his gut as he turned to his left and faced Apollonius's profile. "*Dead?* What—what the hell happened? You were just supposed to extract the information from him, not kill him."

Apollonius didn't turn from the window and despite his anger, Mason was again awed by the man's beauty. "We did try. We kept him quiet, safe, and secure within our facilities for nearly two months. He was interrogated daily."

"Did he die there?"

"No," Apollonius shook his head before turning to fix Mason with his fierce eyes. "Somehow, he managed to escape. Unfortunately, our retrieval team was a bit more...zealous in their drive to take him back into custody."

"Zealous?" Mason balled his hands into fists. Yes, he was angry at what Oliver did, but he never really wanted him dead. Just disgraced. Demoted. Removed from his wealth and position. It was something he'd intended on doing to Oliver himself later on—a part of Mason's constant need for more. For control. "How could you let this happen—"

Mason wasn't prepared for the hit. Didn't see it coming. So when he found himself on his ass, staring up into the angry visage of Apollonius Turk, his anger transitioned into fear. He tasted blood and ran his tongue along the inside of his lower—now split—lip. The entire left side of his face burned as he moved his lower jaw back and forth.

"You should have informed me how dangerous your friend was, Mason. I now have six dead interviewers to deal with, not to mention..." He didn't finish. Instead, Apollonius stepped back and redirected his attention back to the window.

Mason pulled a handkerchief from his pocket, dabbing at the blood around his nose as he spit out what had pooled in his mouth. He got up on his own, with no aid from Apollonius and straightened his suit. *What did he mean, he had six dead interviewers? And what has that got to do with Oliver?* He wanted to ask, but he also didn't want to get hit again.

"You'll have to make this right, Mason," Apollonius's voice was low and held a bit of warning in it. He looked completely composed, and Mason checked the man's knuckles. Not a scratch on them. *Did he hit me? Or was it one of the trolls?* The latter seemed unlikely, since they were standing on the other side of the room. Trolls were more tanks than stealth, in his opinion.

Not wanting to ruffle Apollonius's ire any higher, Mason didn't ask how, but waited silently.

Apollonius smiled. "Knight Errant will look the other way on the deaths. So will the BMP. When we're done spinning our story, a good part of South Boston will be under siege by law enforcement as they look for the criminals who raided our facility and killed our people." Now the smile finally reached the man's eyes. "We give them their proper impetus, they give us what we want."

Impetus? Mason looked away, back out at the twinkling night skyline. So Apollonius had lost people in Oliver's escape. *He plans on blaming others for the tragedy. His reputation remains intact, and others in South Boston will die.*

Finally. "What is it you want from me?"

"I want *Ghost-7*, Mason. That is the only reason NeoNET's even dealing with your little company. That software is theirs. They paid for it. And now your incompetence at keeping your people in line have taken it from them. You have forty-eight hours to get the software back," Apollonius looked at Mason. "Or I will bring *you* in for an interview."

Mason had to fight not to take a step back to show his revulsion. "You expect me to produce a piece of software in forty-eight hours that you couldn't extract from its creator in two months? I'll need more time than that."

He felt Apollonius's stare, but continued to look out the window. If he intended on hitting Mason again, he'd just take it, but there was no way he was going to get bullied into an impossible task and have this bastard take everything away from him.

Then, "You have two months. That gives us four months to get it up and running for NeoNET. The deal closes in December, Mason. The prototype must be in place by then."

"You'll have it by then." Mason wasn't sure how he was going to discover where Oliver had hidden the damn thing. Being honest with himself, he'd let their friendship fall away, thinking of Oliver as just a worker beneath him. An asset. Nothing more. Now he regretted that attitude because he wasn't as sharp as he could be—as he should be—to match Apollonius's manipulation abilities. To put it simply, Mason didn't know much about Oliver's personal life. "We'll need to have a funeral."

"A memorial would be better," Apollonius also looked back at the window. "I'm afraid the body isn't in...any condition for viewing."

Mason tried to feel guilt. Or even remorse. Sadness. But he was reaching for nothing in an empty room where he knew his conscience had died a long time ago. "Let me make the arrangements. This will get me in close with his fiancée... former fiancée."

"That was my thought from the beginning, Mason. But I kept my promise not to touch the girl as long as we had the creator. But with him dead... You were once engaged to her, weren't you?"

Mason glanced sharply at the immaculate elf.

"Miss O'Neal should be the place to start. She'll know his most intimate thoughts, and if she won't tell you what you want to hear..." Apollonius did that odd smile again. "We'll take over and invite her in for an interview."

Having Nicole at the mercy of Turk with the probability of her ending up like Oliver wasn't something Mason would allow. Finally, it was time to broach the subject. "What if... what if he never confided in Nicole? What if we can't find the software?"

Apollonius held up his hand. "Our people have assured me we can salvage the project and get it back on track—but it could take years to duplicate Mr. Martin's work. I'm afraid your deal would be completed, and Andreas Martin Analysis Systems would go the way of the transistor radio."

Mason chose to file the not-so-veiled threat away. "How would you salvage the project?"

"I've made a few arrangements with my contact at MIT&T. They have a few specialty techs who are good at reverse engineering something. I'm assured they can replicate it, though it would greatly speed things up if we could find Mr. Martin's original program specs."

"But Oliver cleaned everything off the nodes."

"Not everything," Apollonius faced Mason. "We still have the end result."

"You mean they're going to look at what the software did to BaseBach Auditors and work backward?"

Apollonius nodded.

Mason rubbed his face, wincing when he aggravated his growing bruises.

"Alas," Apollonius continued. "If we had his notes, his designs, anything he could have used in the creation, it could speed the process along. You're sure he never kept his work on any of your nodes?"

"I am. If Oliver was anything, he was into secrecy. He liked keeping everything in one place so he always knew where it was. He just didn't tell anyone else where that place was." Oliver never kept a single work hour on AMAS's network nodes, always paranoid someone would steal his work. And now that caution would be the end of everything for Mason. Just as it had been the end of Oliver.

Mason put a finger to his lips. "I have a few things to take care of before I break the news to Nicole."

"To take care of?"

"A bit of...housekeeping I've kept in reserve in case Oliver's story ever made it to the media." Mason didn't want to use Nicole—he loved her. Had always loved her. Since the day he first met her. And she had been his—until she met Oliver. "Give me a few days to make arrangements for Oliver's memorial. Closed casket. Maybe a cremation."

"He has only a sister, correct?"

"I learned from Nicole that Oliver's mother's still alive. She's living in Tír Tairngire." He closed his eyes and sighed as he realized the enormity of what he needed to do in order to smooth over Oliver's death.

Apollonius nodded as he turned and headed toward the door. "Keep me in the loop on what you tell her and we will work tirelessly to back you up. Alert me the moment you have anything of Mr. Martin's that deals directly with *Ghost-7*."

Mason nodded, but remained silent as Apollonius left.

Alone again with his thoughts and the Boston skyline, he ran through the ways he could break the news of Oliver's death to Nicole. Beautiful, sweet, elegant Nicole. A human with a pedigree like no other. Tall, beautiful, smart, and once—five years ago—his fiancée. She would need comforting, someone who would know how she felt. And who better than the man she considered Oliver's best friend?

A day ago, he didn't think he'd ever have a chance with her again, not with her attention so focused on Oliver. But all of that had changed with Oliver's death.

He had two goals now for December, still seven months away. To recreate Oliver's greatest achievement in statistical market analysis—and to win back Nicole's heart.

CHAPTER 13

SOUTH BOSTON
MONDAY, MAY 6, 2075

I never expected to open my eyes again. And when I did, I never thought I'd be looking into a set of sky-blue eyes. I blinked a few times. The irises were all wrong. They weren't round like a human's, but slitted like a cat's, or an elf's. But they were different. And they were accented by silver white lashes and brows.

The eyes smiled as the young woman pulled back from my face, and I saw her tiny pugged nose and full lipped mouth. I also spotted long canines, four of them, two on each side, as well as the fall of silvery white hair that rained down on either side of her petite face and pooled on my bare chest.

No...not completely bare. I felt something tight around it, and lifted my head enough to see it was wrapped in bandages.

"You," said the girl with the very sharp teeth. "Are pre-*tee*."

She had an accent I couldn't identify. Nor could I figure out *what* she was. I didn't think she was a vampire. Nor did I suspect she was an elf, because the ears poking up through her hair were more like a wolf's. Her skin was slightly tanned and flawlessly smooth.

I laid my head back down and took a second to look around where I was. I was still in the office I thought I'd died in. But I wasn't behind the desk anymore. In fact, I didn't see the desk at all. The entire room had been cleaned out, and I was on a mattress on the floor.

The girl moved over me and I braced myself, thinking she was gonna jump on me, and I was gonna feel pain. What I felt was stiffness in my muscles. And sore. I was sore all over my body.

She didn't land on me though. She did stand and sashay to the other side of the room. She wore an interesting outfit, a sort of blend between erotic dancer and rock climber. Her boots were tan, and made of soft-looking leather. And the tan pants she wore covered her thick thighs and nicely rounded ass. I'd noticed her ample cleavage and flat stomach because she wasn't wearing a top. The only thing covering her breasts was her long hair.

But that's when I saw the tail. A long, slightly banded, silver and white fox tail.

She was a shapeshifter.

She came back holding a cup and knelt down beside me. I'd heard about shapeshifters, but I'd always thought they were wild and uneducated and kept to themselves. Obviously, I realized as she urged me with her long-nailed hands to try and sit up, I was terribly mistaken.

The cup held water. Clean. Cool. With the hint of something in it.

"It's got some medicine in it. Something herbal she likes to make. Kills headaches in seconds, and I figured you were going to wake with one hell of a brain banger."

I hadn't been expecting a male voice. I nearly choked on the water when I heard it, but she hadn't opened her mouth. She didn't even flinch.

But I did when a tall, dark-skinned ork stepped through the office door and looked down at me. He was as menacing as he was calm, both reflected in his tone. His head was shaved bare, and I could just make out dark tattoos covering every inch of it. His tusks were trimmed and filed down, and he wore what looked like old military fatigues like my grandfather—

I froze and looked away. My grandfather? Was that a memory? Was it a truth? Had my grandfather worn clothing like that? The knee-high laced boots, the gray and black pants tucked into the tops, the t-shirt and jacket...

Was this...*my* memory?

"Variant," the shapeshifter said. "He sick, no?"

"No," Variant the ork said as he stepped closer and put his hand on her head. "I think he's having a moment."

She put her hand on mine. I hadn't realized I was shaking until I felt her warmth. She smiled at me and I saw the teeth. I took in a deep breath and winced. Still sore.

"Breathing like that's gonna hurt for a while," Variant said. "But it'll be good for you if you keep doing it. Strengthen those muscles."

"Where...?" My own voice sounded like a croak, so I cleared my throat as the shapeshifter tried to push me to drink more water by touching my hands on the cup. "Where am I?"

"You're in exactly the place Loki found you. Which is her den."

"Her den?"

"In case you haven't noticed, she's a lupine shapeshifter. Fennic Fox, to be precise."

That explained the white hair, ears, and tail.

"She came to me and said there was a dead man in her den."

"But this isn't a den."

Variant smirked, which looked interesting around his tusks. "And you aren't dead."

But I should be. I knew that. I finished the water, which made Loki happy. She took the cup and bounded off, almost on all fours, as she left the room.

That left me alone with a strange ork named Variant.

He offered me his hand. "Orlando Variant."

I took his hand and returned his strong grip, but I shook my head. "I'm afraid I, ah...I don't know my name."

"Interesting." He sat on the ground beside the mattress and crossed his legs. "We found you with some gear. Gear I recognized."

Uh-oh. The three who were trying to kill me were friends of the ork! I put my hands down and felt the wires humming, software downloaded.

No...it *tried* to download, but failed.

"Friend," Variant said. "I need you to calm down. Your skillsofts have been deactivated, as has most of the gear in your head. Especially your jack."

"What? Why?"

"Because you were downloading subscription skillsofts that made you trackable. And the last thing I want is for anyone to find you. At least, not yet."

I put my hand to my head and looked at him. My cybereyes didn't read any tags, which meant there weren't any to read. But it made sense. I understood how the skillsofts worked, I just couldn't remember why I had them.

Wait... I looked at him. "A subscription? Was it my subscription? Did it give my name?"

"Unfortunately, no," Variant said. "The subscription service has very good security to prevent hacking into it. So the closest my decker could get was that it was a company script, and you were a number assigned to access it. Nothing after that. But every time you accessed it, that number was tagged."

"Someone...had tagged me?"

"Yes. Now, let's start this conversation over so we can both benefit, hm?" He shifted his position just as Loki came back into the room. She had a bag filled with snacks and packaged foods, the kind easily found in a shack. "You need to eat, and Loki's claimed you as her cub, so...eat."

"Claimed me...cub?"

He shook his head. "Just go with it. I do."

Loki offered me a banana and an apple, and I ate both before I knew I was hungry. But once I started, I couldn't stop eating. Her tail lashed back and forth and she jumped on all fours a few times before she tore into plastic-encased muffin and devoured it, grinning at me with food in her mouth.

"You say you can't remember your name," Variant began. "But you remember you have skillsofts."

I nodded before finishing the water. "I know I'm human, that you're an ork, that this is Boston....it is still Boston, right?"

Variant slowly nodded. "Last time I checked."

"I know about...gear. About things. Decks and cybereyes," I pointed at my own. "I just don't remember who I am. My name, my family, what I do...what I did..." With that I looked down at the bandages encasing my chest.

"You were shot with a modified machine pistol. I recognize the wound. Got a nasty graze on your shoulder as well. But what's most curious about you are the number of wounds, old and new."

"Number?"

"Your entire body shows signs of trauma. You've been abused, left to heal, abused again, and then again, left to heal." He tapped his own temple. "I can't even imagine what kind of damage they did to this."

I stared at him. "You said you recognized the gear I had."

"Yes I did. But don't worry. They weren't any friends of mine. Just local drek who considered themselves bounty hunters." Variant pursed his lips around his tucks. "Which does give us a clue to add to the other ones."

"Other clues?"

Loki moved in close and sniffed my neck. "You have pain. It echoes all around."

I gave the somewhat beautiful creature a blink. "My pain echoes?"

"She means you've experienced a lot of physical pain recently. Not just the wounds. Pain before that." He pointed at me. "What I said before. You've been tortured."

I wasn't prepared to hear that. "Tortured?" Images of being hung from the ceiling of a dungeon and flogged came to mind, along with being burned with hot pokers.

"It's not like that," Variant said with a small smirk. "I personally can't tell. But Loki said you have mana scars. And the only way you got those was if someone tried to extract information from your mind. You've got more than a few physical scars." He nodded at me. "Look at your wrists and your ankles, and once you get those bandages off, you're gonna be really freaked out at your chest."

I did, and what I saw surprised me. Mostly because I hadn't noticed them before. Both of my wrists were bruised. Fresh bands of black and blue bruises around each of them. My ankles showed the same.

"Now look at the inside of your arms. We didn't see them till Loki cleaned the blood off. You've got injection marks."

Variant was right. The inside of my forearms were covered with welts where needles had been slipped in. "I—"

"I know. You don't remember. So tell me what you do remember."

I told him about the moment I believed I woke up on the streets. About being chased and about the three chasing me. After I described what I did to them—I had to put my hand on my stomach when I remembered throwing up, afraid I'd do it again. But telling it didn't have the same reaction, and my stomach didn't seem to notice.

"Looking at you," Variant said. "I'd say you were lying. But I saw what you did to these bastards, and it's exactly as you describe them. You were using the wires. Now that they're deactivated..." He put his hand to his chin in a thoughtful pose. "I'm thinking with the nuyen I can get from the gear you stole, we might be able to grab a few skillsoft downloads. They're not gonna be as smooth as what you're used to, but no more subscriptions for now. Not unless you want whomever's after you to find you again."

I didn't say anything. I didn't know what to say. Whoever I was, or am, or could be, seemed to know things didn't come free. "So, what's in it for you?"

The ork threw his head back and let out a nefarious laugh. Once he finished, he glared at me. "You, for now. That wiring is good for long range. And the crossbow you had can be adapted for you. I've been looking for a sniper. One I can train to take my place so I can be more involved on our runs." He nodded at me. "Until you pay back the time and nuyen I spend on you, your ass is mine, chummer."

Loki leaned in close and purred in my ear. Her skin was soft and she smelled like leather and wildflowers. "Cub."

Right.

"Now," Variant said as he stood. "First thing we gotta do," he put his hands on his hips. "Find out who you are, and why someone tortured you and wants you dead."

"I'd like to know that myself," I pushed Loki's pile of foodstuff to the side and attempted to stand. But when the room swayed, so did I. Loki, though small, caught me and put me back on the mat.

"Not yet," Variant said. "Loki'll stay with you while I call in a few favors. Also need to figure out what to call you. I'll let you decide on that."

He walked to the door to the office, then turned back to me. "Welcome to world of the shadowrunner, mister nobody."

CHAPTER 14

SOUTH BOSTON
THURSDAY, MAY 9, 2075
EVENING

It was dark when I felt something warm cover my mouth. I started to fight back, but heard the soft, accented whisper of Loki in my ear. "Company."

We were still in the same office I'd collapsed in. Or rather, Loki's self-proclaimed den. A few days had passed since the ork's visit, but she had remained with me the whole time. She talked very little about herself, but asked hundreds of questions about me. Unfortunately, there were so very few I could answer.

My stomach churned, now confronted with the arrival of this company, along with the growing hunger for food other than the cheap snacks the shapeshifter seemed to live on. I nodded, and she took that to mean I understood. I still wasn't connected through a commlink, so messaging was out of the question.

It was dark, and the place smelled of mildew. The rain had stopped sometime after I fell asleep, which made listening a bit easier. I could see her outline from the flashing neon lights filtering in through the grimy windows. Her ears were perked forward and turned and twitched like a fox's. I held my breath and concentrated on the outside as well. And then, just there, I heard what could be the shuffle of a boot, and the *shush* of leather against concrete.

Loki held up her hand, pretty confident I could see it, before she slowly and noiselessly, reached into a bag slung over her left shoulder and resting on her right hip. She pulled out two chips and handed them to me. I recognized them as skillsofts created to fit into a skilljack. But the light was too dim for me to see if anything about them said what they were. I couldn't tell if they were action, lingua, or know.

She touched my arm and gestured for me to load them, then pointed to the crossbow and the quiver of bolts I'd stolen off my attacker a few days ago. I slowly nodded. I understood she wanted me to fight, and she was handing me the skillsofts to use. Given what I remembered in the alley, I'd had to access a few to escape with my life, but I was still wounded.

I slowly dropped my hands to the quiver and slipped it over my shoulder as I caught another noise above us. Once I slid my fingers around the crossbow's grip, I experienced a second of disorientation. A memory of comfort. I'd taken the weapon from my foe because it felt right to have. And now, holding it in my left hand...it felt like home.

Loki made an aim and shoot gesture, then pointed to the door and then up. I didn't know the hand signals, but they were pretty easy to interpret. She slipped a lethal-looking weapon from her hip holster and held it up. The pink neon from outside made her sharper canines look red tinged as she smiled at me.

Making sure I was still dressed in the stolen clothes (and wishing I could wash them and myself several times), I crept along the floor to the door. Loki grabbed my arm and pointed to the chips in my hand.

Right.

The skills.

I paused and loaded one. The jack hummed at the base of my skull, apparently happy to have been fed something inside its empty memory. The skill copied, and I removed the chip. The new skill appeared on my very limited AR as a new disk with the word *BRAWL* across it.

A brawl skill?

I loaded the second and a new icon popped up: *CHUMMER SWAY*.

What the hell was this? And where did she get these skills? I assumed they were pirated, or stolen. Whatever they were, I was pretty sure they were homemade.

I turned to point at the chips, but Loki wasn't there. I was alone in the office. I shoved them into the pocket of my pants, then grabbed the long leather coat on my way out of the office. I paused in a dark alcove long enough to put it on, which helped a bit with the cold, re-strapped the quiver to my hip, and fixed the crossbow to the back of the coat. The former owner had sewn in a magnet which corresponded with the one on the bow. Just swing it back and *click*, into place. I grabbed it over my shoulder and it released. I didn't know who I'd killed to get this, but I appreciated their ingenuity.

I also found the guy's wrist commlink in the inner pocket. I'd just assumed Variant had already sold what I'd stolen. Apparently not.

Once the commlink was in place, it wasn't hard to find a local connection. But free access was heavily monitored by GOD, so I spoofed an ID, the first one that came to mind, and created a new persona named Crisis—it seemed like the perfect name, given our present situation. There I accessed a few public archives and found out exactly where I was and in what building. There was a chance the intruders could see me as well, but only accurately if they knew my handle. Infrared would give them a better target, so finding a place well shielded would be better so I looked for a staircase and found one. Up I went.

With my hands unburdened, I half-wished Loki had left me a hand weapon. Crossbows are good for long range—which given the direction she'd pointed, might be what she wanted me to do. Get to higher ground and a get an eagle eye look at our company.

As I headed through a second story window and onto a rusted fire-escape, it suddenly dawned on me to question how I'd known to do all that. The commlink, the spoofing, the whole putting together a plan. Had I done this in the past? Was this what I normally did? Was me knowing this stuff the reason someone tried to kill me?

Was I a thief? I knew I wasn't a runner. But there was something oddly familiar as I leaped from one fire escape to the other. Of course, my wound didn't help with my agility, and I landed with a less than quiet noise onto the other set of steps. I quickly—as quickly as I could move, since I was now gasping in agony—slipped into the unlocked door of the taller empty building. Squatters, BTL users, chipheads...all of them lined the hall as I choked through the stench of smoke, vomit, and urine and half-ran, half-limped to the opposite inside staircase. Once there, I took in a few deep breaths, then started the climb up to the roof.

The door was unlocked, no surprise there, so I slipped out and hid in a nearby shadow and waited. I caught a brush of something through the lens of my cybereyes. I wasn't sure at first if it was real or some sort of hiccup. I triangulated the movement and gave my targeting a wider birth as I pulled the crossbow from my back.

Even without activesoft or wires, my muscles responded as if they knew what to do as my hand retrieved a bolt. I nocked it into the channel and slowly pulled the string back as the targeting computer in my eyes gave me a place to aim for. Yet... there was a puff of breath to the right so I waited, even as the target flashed red.

Several seconds passed as I warred with myself. *Do I go with my instinct or do I go with the computer?* Just as I had to make a decision, the same glint appeared in line with where my gut told me to aim.

I released the bolt. It sliced through the air with an audible *shwip* that ended with the grunt and cry of its target.

He or she'd been wearing some kind of reflective suit, a cloaking material or something that made them nearly invisible in the darkness and rain. But it couldn't stop the rain from striking the suit's still physical body underneath.

They became visible as they collapsed on the roof. I didn't know what part of them I'd struck, nor was I sure it was a critical hit, or if they were playing dead. Instead, I remained where I was and waited another three seconds.

It was in those three seconds I found my humanity again. I...hadn't realized I'd lost it until then. As I watched the figure lay still, I saw in my limited memories the bodies of the three I'd killed when I woke into this nightmare. I stared at a spot near my foot and brought my hands up so I could see them. That event put blood on my hands. Real blood. Three bodies. Dead...

And I killed them.

Me.

I knew in my rational mind that I had fought for my life. If I hadn't killed them...they would have killed me. The only thought was that I had had no choice if I wanted to live. But why me? Why had they been after me?

Why was this individual now prone in front of me after *me* too?

What had I done that warranted such a desire to see me dead? The ease I'd used to kill those three—was that it? Had I killed someone they loved? Had I robbed them? Had I—

I put my hand to my forehead. *What have I done? What did I do? The ones before had chased me. I knew their intent. But this one...he'd made no move, and I'd played judge, jury, and executioner.*

Why am I even now thinking on such a base instinctual level as to plot the death of this figure I didn't even know?

I looked again at the fallen figure. If they lived, would they talk to me? Give me answers? Some kind of stability? If I gave them back their life...would they give me back mine? Somewhere in the back of my mind I knew the answer was no, but another part of me, the one unwilling to accept this was the sum of what I was, held...hope.

I silenced the song of the wires and brushed aside the BRAWL skillsoft that had moved into my vision on my AR, waiting to be activated, demanding to be used. Crouching over, I kept to the shadows as I ran to them and knew they were dead. That brief hope vanished like the reflection in a once still pond, disturbed by a stone. I grabbed their boot and pulled them out of the eye of anyone watching from another roof. Survival Me was still there, watching the shadows, sniffing the air, listening in the dark.

Emotional me slid down on his ass and wept in silence.

My target was an elf. He'd shaved his head, which drew attention to his finely pointed ears. His scalp had been tattooed with an "A" in the back, and he had night vision goggles on his eyes.

I checked his pockets and retrieved a few weapons and found a stash of softs, which I also appropriated. I wasn't sure I wanted to use them, but maybe Variant could make back some of his nuyen.

That's when someone made a noise behind me. The wires hummed as I ducked and painfully rolled away from them. I doubled back and swung my legs around to knock them off their feet. Within seconds I landed a solid hit to their jaw and had my stolen weapon in their face.

It was another elf. This one female, with a green mohawk and half a face of chrome. She smiled up at me, which was just damn creepy, but she didn't go for a weapon. In fact, she didn't have one in either of her hands.

And it looked as if my strike hadn't even touched her, even as my knuckles screamed in pain.

"So you're the chummer this piece of drek was chasing."

Frowning, I stood back and cooled the wires, but kept the gun trained on her and my finger on the trigger. "Say again?"

"This bastard's been hanging around Loki's den. Not that I have any loyalty to the furball, but I do respect that she keeps to herself and cleans up the vermin." The elf slowly dusted herself off as she got to her feet and rubbed at her jaw. "So, why is a decorated assassin following you?"

I made a face and glanced at the lifeless body. "This elf's a decorated assassin? How does that work? There's a place that gives awards for killing?"

She laughed, and it was pleasant enough. She wore a skintight leather suit with a utility belt, vest and a stock of ammo and guns plastered all over her body. Truth was, given the RIFD tags and specs that flagged on them, she could've killed me at any moment. "His name was Heise. That's what he said he was. A decorated assassin. Did private work for corps. Not really a runner, but he's been known to gather intel for a few of the local teams." She pointed to the body. "You mind if I grab what's left?"

I shook my head and lowered the weapon. She knelt down and did a thorough job on the body, ending it with yanking off his leather jacket, belt, boots and pants. "I have a friend who'll dig these. That's only if you don't need them?"

I sized the elf up. She was a lot thinner than me, though I figured we were the same height. "No. Take'm."

"Thanks." She pulled a small wad of material from her back pocket and flicked it into the air. The wad became a backpack, and she shoved all the items inside. "What're you called?"

I opened my mouth. There was that question again. Loki called me cub but...that wasn't appropriate.

"What is it, chummer? You got a problem with names? I'm Vertigo, in case that helps."

It was imperative I have a name, or at least something others could use for now. Something I thought I could remember an answer to. I thought about the account I'd created to sign in to the local grid. "Crisis."

"Seriously? Your name is *Crisis*?" She looked skeptical as she hefted the bag on her shoulder.

"Your name is *Vertigo*?" I gave her the same level of skeptical sarcasm.

"*Touché*, Crisis. You do good work. Especially with that crossbow. If you're as good with a rifle, I might have some work for you."

My AR opened as she sent me a calling card. I accepted it and the software in my eyes scanned it. The information was clean. It gave me ways to find her if I needed anything. I also spotted a very familiar symbol in the lower corner. I blinked away the display and looked at her. "You're an Ancient?"

"Indeed."

Something exploded behind me, and we both turned to see a flash of blue light.

"I'd say Loki found the other one."

I looked back at Vertigo as she said, "There were two of 'em, watching the den. I noticed and watched them, thinking I could get in on some action. Beat me to it, Crisis." She hefted the backpack. "Better get down there to Loki. She's good a slinging a spell, but if she runs low on mana, she'll revert to natural form. She'll need you."

I looked back as another flash of blue light hit. When I turned to ask Vertigo a question, she was gone. I retrieved my bolt from the guy's neck, sheathed it, and climbed back down the stairs to get to Loki.

The one attacking Loki was easy to spot and even easier to take out. Loki became a fennec fox, just as Variant said she was, and climbed on my back as I bent over the second attacker and took what I wanted. Weapons mostly, power packs, nuyen, a commlink, and another pair of night vision goggles.

Once I was finished, and several others had come out to see what the commotion had been, I faded back into the shadows with Loki in the hood of the coat. She licked the back of my neck as I moved away from the dead assassins and deeper into the barrens of South Boston.

I was Crisis for now. I'd killed five of those who'd crossed my path, and I had a purpose.

Learning what—and who—I'd been before I made myself into who I am now.

CHAPTER 15

SOUTH BOSTON
FRIDAY, MAY 10, 2075

Mason stood outside Nicole O'Neal's door, a dour expression on his face. He was there to deliver the bad news after making sure no media outlets had discovered the Andreas Martin Analysis Systems's CEO's death. So far none had, and it wasn't surprising. Mason had made sure to keep Oliver's name and face out of the media as much as possible. He wanted himself to be the public face, the name everyone would know when he moved into the offices at NeoNET.

The press releases were ready. Now it was time for his greatest performance as he took a deep breath and pressed the ringer on her apartment door. He was sure her apartment's preferences would tell her it was him, having read his SIN on his commlink. Now it would be up to her to open the door.

After what felt like an eternity, but in reality was closer to five minutes, the door slid open and Nicole stood in the door's frame. She looked as beautiful as ever. Her dark hair fell over her shoulders, cascading down to a suit of rich brown with tan piping. Her nails, visible when she crossed her arms over her chest at him, were glossy and brown, and the engagement ring Oliver gave her sparkled on her left ring finger.

"Mason...you got a lot of nerve showing up here."

"Nicole." He braced himself, already knowing her greeting had set her tone with him. "I know my presence gives you cause for alarm, but I assure you I'm alone. And I...have some very bad news."

Her confidence and demeanor broke at that moment as she lowered her arms and stepped forward. "Is it Oliver? Did you find him? I haven't given up hope—"

"Nicole—"

"Because if you've done something to him, I swear I'll alert every news vid in Boston and tell them what you did—"

"Nicole," Mason said with a stern voice. "Please, may I come in?"

"No."

"Very well." He let his arms fall to his sides. "I regret to inform you that Oliver's body was found early this morning in Boston Harbor. It looks..." He saw her expression shift from anger to shock, and had to take in a breath to finish the lie. "The coroner said he'd been shot several times before he went in. And he'd been in the river for over a day."

Nicole didn't move for a few seconds, then. "No..." Her voice was just above a whisper.

"I'm so sorry."

"You're lying, Mason. It's all a damn lie. *You* took his identity from him, so there's no way the Boston Police would have called you with an identification."

She had him there. But he was prepared. "Nicole...if you'll let me in, I can give you the full story. Everything we've uncovered in the last twenty-four hours."

He watched hesitation play over her face until she finally stepped back and he entered. The place was as nice as he remembered, with designer furniture and a view of the harbor.

He stopped in the living room and waited for her. Nicole pointed to a chair. "You have five minutes before I call the authorities."

"I will be as quick as possible." Mason sat in one of the side chairs and took another deep breath. Lies like this took concentration, enough so that he could remember them and not be tripped up later. He called up his AR and retrieved the file he'd prepared with the paper trails, solid evidence conveniently manufactured with Turk's skill, and some eyewitness testimonies guaranteed to make Nicole doubt her former fiancé's intentions.

He sent them to her and he watched as her focus shifted and she brushed the air in front of her to download the file. "That folder contains everything we found. Names, dates, vid feeds, all provided by Lone Star operatives. They uncovered the truth about what Oliver's been up to since your vacation." He gave a dramatic pause. "I'm afraid Oliver was the one that engineered the whole identity crisis."

He waited, watched her expression, and wasn't disappointed as she went over the evidence.

"Mason..."

"Please, Nicole. Just hear me out." He could see she was teetering between holding it together and falling apart. What he needed to do was push her where he wanted her to go. Look carefully at the communications, funds transfers, including a fake ID he created the day you came back."

Mason watched her pull up her own AR so she could examine the attachments. "Oliver had been working on a highly secret, very volatile piece of software that analyzed market stability. It analyzes a company from the ground floor up and finds its weaknesses, not just in its departments, but in its employees. I can't say much about the software, but it was something revolutionary."

She sniffed. Nicole's eyes were wet as tears fell over her cheeks. "I knew he was working on something called *Ghost-7*."

"He told you?"

"Oliver didn't tell me what it was, just that it was the heart of the deal you brokered with NeoNET."

"Yes, it was the key piece that NeoNET wanted to further develop, to hopefully sell as a tool to improve commerce and efficiency in the corps." Mason hid his irritation that Oliver had shared *any* information about *Ghost-7* with Nicole, no matter how limited. "The evidence I gave you proves Oliver had a plan in motion to frame Andreas Martin Analysis Systems in *Ghost-7's* mishandling. He engineered his ID wipe, his imprisonment, all of it in order to smear AMAS's name while he secretly stole *Ghost-7* and made arrangements to sell it to a group of shadowrunners."

Nicole moved her hand in the air to sort the papers. He knew she was looking at the texts between Oliver and a few well-known names in the shadow world, names he'd been given by Apollonius Turk, who apparently had his own shadowrunner contacts. The names were those of suppressives other runners wanted out of the way, so by putting a bounty on their heads, he was not only helping the BMP, but NeoNET's contacts.

"As you can see, he moved money out of his account, but we haven't been able to trace where to. He also paid some people to go in and clean out his apartment, as well as hired actors to move in and pretend to have lived there for years."

"No..."

"Yes. I'm afraid so. It's all there. Receipts, contacts, even his call to the Intelligence Agency to put his own SIN on hold the same day he claimed to call them and demand to know why it wasn't working." Mason shifted on the couch, getting himself ready. "I'm sorry all this came to light on the same day they found his body. But we're pretty sure the shadowrunners killed him."

Nicole shook her head as she went through the information. Mason waited patiently, not sure if he should add to Oliver's alleged guilt.

Finally, she closed her AR. "Get out."

"Nicole—"

"Leave. Now."

Unsure if he'd succeeded in procuring her cooperation, Mason stood and headed to the door. He paused a few seconds before he touched the panel and Nicole finally said, "I want to see him."

Damn. He licked his lips and turned. She was still on the sofa facing the windows. "I'm afraid there's not much to see. Just...a torso and a leg or two." It'd taken them a few hours to find someone that matched Oliver's height and build, but less time to create the corpse. "I can give you the morgue's address—"

"No. Just...go."

He wanted to be there when she broke down, to hold her in his arms and tell her everything would be okay. It would cement him in her good graces. But Nicole O'Neal was a delicate flower, and would take time to cultivate. The knowledge Oliver had spoken about *Ghost-7* was enough to give him hope that she might know where he'd hidden it. It also made it his imperative that Turk would never know this so he could protect her from him. If she had that knowledge, it was Mason's, and no one else's.

He made it to the lift before her door opened and she came running to stop him. Mason hid his smile beneath a mask of sadness as he brushed a tear away from her cheek. Her voice quavered when she spoke. "Please...come back and tell me everything you know."

“Of course,” he said as he followed her back to her door. He shut it, and made sure it was locked. He was in, and Mason knew if he worked her the right way, he would stay in for the rest of her life.

CHAPTER 16

SOUTH BOSTON
MONDAY, JUNE 3, 2075

Variant Orlando, goblinized at the age of twenty-two, former physics teacher turned extractor for hire for the local gangs in South Boston, sat at his desk in his office. He "owned" a former theater, laying claim to it with blood and a lot of favors. The lower floor he'd turned into a runner bar called The Slaughtered Donkey. There, he catered to local runners and Johnsons seeking a safe place to do business. He had handshake agreements with all parties. Only one gang had dared attempt to drive him out of South Boston.

Now no one remembers their name.

He brought in regular performers, some comedians, and the occasional name on the trideos. He took a cut of successful runs, small in comparison, and he arranged revenge runs for those whose Johnsons proved less than reputable. Variant Orlando was formidable.

But what he wanted most in this world was revenge. And he'd worked long and hard to bring that revenge to fruition.

And after thirty long years, that time was close.

It stood in front of him, in the center of a ring of chairs, in the form of a mark he'd carefully watched. Of course, this wasn't exactly how'd he'd planned on using the human. Variant's arch enemy had just made things a whole lot easier. But there was still time. Time was on his side.

Time...and a seething anger.

They were in Variant's private office on the second floor. A month had passed since Loki had found their mark bleeding in her den, and the man named Crisis had proven himself loyal.

He followed orders, and shared with Variant when other hired runners argued against them. But what surprised Variant most of all was Crisis's accuracy with his crossbow, and now the rifle Loki had stolen for him. He was proving to be one hell of a sniper and scout, and seemed most at ease when Variant gave him a target and a few days to return the intel. Crisis was thorough.

And quiet.

Sometimes a little too quiet.

On Variant's left sat Pearl, an olive-skinned beauty. Elf and technomancer, and the one who friended Variant after his goblination when no one else would. Pearl was their face, their intel gatherer.

On Variant's right sat Loki, watching her adopted cub with pride. He hadn't questioned the relationship between Crisis and Loki, just as long as Crisis protected his adopted daughter. And so far, he had.

On Loki's right sat the three gang representatives. Vertigo, from the Ancients. Cleeve, from the Spikes, and Sheldon representing the Cutters. It was rare that the three of them were in the same room without inciting a brawl, but Variant had his troll bouncers at the ready. Five of them. All hellacious spell slingers.

Finally, when the room grew quiet and all eyes turned to him, Variant stood and faced Crisis. The human didn't look like the same man found bleeding in that office. He'd put on a few pounds and started bulking up, yet still maintained a lithe figure. His hair was short and still gray and white at the temples. It was Crisis's face that changed the most. It was hardening. Lines had deepened, and Variant knew in another six months Crisis wouldn't physically resemble the half-dead wageslave he'd been when Loki had found him.

But inside? There was something going sour in there. Variant could tell. And he would have to address that soon, before it rotted Crisis from the inside.

"Ladies and gentlemen, elves, trolls, dwarves, and orcs..." He looked around the room. "It is with great honor I called you all here to witness the addition of our newest member. You've all met him, worked with him, and he's pledged to uphold the standards set by me and the gang representatives present."

Everyone nodded. Except for Cleeve. But then, he never looked happy about anything.

Variant continued. "He will be added to our roster for hire, a valuable asset to future runs, and a deadly weapon against tyranny."

Several nods and "hear, hear" from some.

Until Cleeve pushed his chair back and stood. "I'd like to challenge this stranger."

"Challenges are not allowed at these ceremonies." Variant glanced at his people and gave the silent signal. *Be ready*. "This is merely a formality for introduction."

"I wasn't given the opportunity to vet this human," Cleeve said as he strolled into the center of the circle and started walked around Crisis. To Crisis's credit, he didn't flinch or look at Cleeve.

"Your leader was, and an approval was given."

"Well, chummer, we all know my brother's a bit of a twit," Cleeve laughed. No one else did. Variant noticed tense muscles and narrowed eyes directed at the Spikes member.

"I'm sure your brother will appreciate learning how you really feel," Crisis said, still not facing Cleeve.

"Oh yeah?" Cleeve whirled and stared at Crisis's back, his hands down at his side. "Well you'll never get the opportunity to tell 'em!"

Variant felt he was too slow to react. He sensed Cleeve's hostility toward Crisis, and had no idea why the Spikes leader would send the psychopath as their representative.

Until he watched in amazement as Crisis's still form blurred. That was the best word he could come up with. The man, dressed in his leather gear, his crossbow and rifle crossed across his back, his quiver at his side and his long knives tucked at the small of his back, *blurred* as he drew those knives and within seconds had them crossed at Cleeve's throat in an X formation. All Crisis had to do was pull them apart. Slice and dice.

Silence, as thick and palpable as being underwater, filled Variant's office. Until Loki purred, and then laughed. Everyone started laughing. Everyone except Variant, and Cleeve and Crisis.

Vertigo stood and moved around the two combatants, transfixed in the center of the room. "You doubt Crisis's abilities, or his loyalties, Cleeve? You? Or the decision of your leader? It won't be Crisis that delivers your conduct or your words to him. It will be me."

Variant held up his hands. "Please, be seated. Cleeve, are you finished?"

The ork hadn't moved, his eyes locked with Crisis's. Finally he gave an almost imperceptible nod and Crisis stepped back, lowering his knives. That's when Cleeve moved and grabbed at his own knife, a short dagger hidden in his sleeve.

Variant and Loki shouted out, but there was no need.

Crisis ducked, twisted, and brought both blades around to neatly cut into Cleeve's middle. He didn't cut his torso in half completely, but slashed through enough that the ork was dead before he hit the floor.

Damn.

<*You know Charique knew this would happen.*> This was Pearl's text, and her white wolf avatar appeared in Variant's AR.

<*Yes I did. He's been wanting to get rid of Cleeve for some time. And he's made sure I was the one that did it. Sorry son of a bitch.*>

Crisis stood back and held his blades down at his sides. "I'm sorry, Var. It was...instinct."

And the wires. Variant knew that much. He and Pearl had fully outfitted Crisis with everything he'd need to hone his skills in all three softs. Active, language, and knowledge. Crisis was fast becoming their intel gatherer scout.

"It was a fair fight," Vertigo said as she kicked at Cleeve's lifeless, bleeding corpse. "He asked for it." She pulled a rag from her bag and handed it to Crisis. "Wipe your blades." He did, and she took the cloth back, packing it in some plastic container. Variant could only wonder what sort of magic she was brewing at Cleeve's expense.

Variant held up his hand. "If we're quite through? Good. Crisis—" The man turned to face him. "It is with honor that we welcome you into our shadowteam for a probationary period of two months. After which...well...we'll cross that bridge when we come to it. Welcome, Crisis!"

Everyone cheered and congratulated him, and Variant watched his face as they did. In two months he hadn't seen Crisis smile but once, and that was his reaction to Loki naming him her cub. Since then, the man had worked hard to prove himself a viable killer, and he'd made a local name for himself. The name Crisis was on several wanted databases...but there was no face, no DNA. Just the name.

A half hour later, it was just Pearl and Variant in his office as the others retired downstairs to listen to music and continue the celebration. She helped put the chairs back in their briefing position near a vid projector where he went over Johnson jobs with the team.

Eventually she joined him at his desk and leaned against it as he sat down. “Cleeve’s sister isn’t going to let what just happened go.”

Variant grated his lower jaw. He needed to trim his tusks again. “I didn’t know Cleeve’s sister even cared.”

“They were mutual friends, I think. I’d had a few reports of them harassing some local, smaller gangs. It’ll just give her a stronger reason to go after Crisis.” She looked at him with her expressive dark eyes. Pearl was beautiful, and he’d told her as much, but he was also aware of her own feelings toward him. She found him...ugly. And maybe he was, with his dark skin, his tusks, his shaved head and tattoos. But the outward appearance bore little resemblance to the man inside, the one that craved contact...and love.

But only after revenge. “Crisis’s past is buried deep. You altered the BMP reports and SIN files on him to fit someone else. Even if he were ever caught and his DNA tested, no one would ever know his real identity.”

“What if *he* does?” She crossed her arms over her chest. “What if one day he remembers?”

“I’m counting on it,” Variant said as he leaned back in his high backed chair. “I’ve been waiting so long to find the perfect person to bring down Apollonius Turk. Crisis is it. He was tagged as the man’s enemy in a way that left no room for his survival.” He sighed. “If you hadn’t of told me about his archery skills, or if I hadn’t seen what they did to him in that cell...it’s all divine providence, Pearl. I was meant to rescue him, to save him from his own ignorance and build him into someone who could seek revenge and take back his life.”

Pearl shifted where she sat. “Var...I understand what you’re doing, and why you’re doing it. You think he’s the key. But how can he be if you don’t even know why they wanted him dead so bad. I mean...why go through so much trouble to destroy this man’s identity? Why torture him the way they did?”

"My guess is he knows something. Something they were desperate to either keep quiet, or something they wanted back. He was running, Pearl. My guess is he still has whatever it is."

"And you think it's enough to hurt Turk."

"I think it's enough to make him sit up and admit to what he did to my wife." He admired the silver jack in her temple, the one that didn't really connect to anything. So many technomancers had followed the advice on GiTmo, the Ghost In The Machine Online board Pearl and he subscribed to. In the beginning, there hadn't been much out there for technomancers, until this board showed up. And for a time it had to travel from commlink to commlink, always moving so as not to be caught. Only recently did it become stable enough for more and more technomancers to find and get advice, seek help, and find others of their kind. GiTmo had found a home, one even GOD couldn't touch.

Variant would support them in any way he could. Because it was GiTmo who had told him where his wife had been taken. And it was a group of technomancers and sympathizers that tried to rescue her from NeoNET's tower...only to find that she'd died while undergoing experiments. Her capture and incarceration had been engineered by none other than Apollonius Turk...another name GiTmo had provided him.

"Var, you know I'll stand behind you on this. But knowing and understanding what you just said...don't you think it's unfair and cruel to use him like this? He had a life. Why not give it back to him?"

"I *am* going to give it back to him," Variant declared. "But I have to fix it first. Oliver Martin's profile reads that he stole from his own company, from Mason Andreas himself. That he falsified attempts to remove his identity, and then was killed by the same shadowrunner team he tried to hire. I need the truth."

"You need that truth for more than just Crisis. You need it to prove you picked the right patsy." She slid off the desk. "I'll keep searching for those answers."

"You try contacting that info broker of yours? Red something?"

"His name's Rick Lang, but everyone calls him Red. I've left him messages since I heard he was back. Rumor is he's got some easy street gig watching a CEO's girl. If he doesn't answer me, I'll go down other avenues if I have to. Just remember, Var, that Apollonius sold your wife the moment he discovered what she was. Don't sell this poor guy just get your revenge."

He understood her compassion, and her caution. But what she didn't seem to understand was that as he was now, there was no more Oliver Martin. That man was changed, molded into the very game character he'd made in *Dark City*. Even if he discovered who he'd been...he doubted there would be any going back.

Pearl started to the door. "Pearl."

"Yes?" She turned to face him.

"Did you ever remove the account?"

She smiled at the question. "I'm good at my day job, Var. Have a good night, boyo."

He watched her walk out of the room, enjoying the sway of her hips and the twitch of her ass. Then he relaxed back into the chair. No...he knew Crisis could never go back to what he had. He could only move forward, or he could die trying. Variant knew this from the moment he'd chosen the innocent wageslave. The exacting of revenge, of making those more guilty of sins pay for their crimes, required sacrifice.

And sometimes the innocent suffered along the way.

PART THREE

November, 2075

CHAPTER 17

SOUTH BOSTON
THURSDAY, OCTOBER 31, 2075

Seven months.

Seven months since I first woke to this life. Since running down that street in the dark. Seven months since my first kills.

I wasn't afraid anymore. Not like I'd been. I knew I could handle myself in most situations. I could improvise. Though most of the jobs now were gathering physical intel. Watching the mark, casing the location, and reporting back. I found vantage points for a clean shot if needed, or better places to work from the shadows. It had all become routine. The name Crisis was on everyone's watch list, but all they had was Loki's artwork. A symbol she liked to scrawl everywhere we went.

A daisy. A freak'n daisy.

And I think I was happy.

I just...wasn't sure.

What wasn't routine, and what I tried to ignore at first, were the nightmares. They started out slow, just something that would wake me up early in the morning, or right after I'd fall asleep. Several times, though, I woke certain there were people in the room with me. Large, shadowed figures with sharp knives and salt, and if they touched me, it burned. There were needles and questions...questions I could never make out and had no answers to.

They grew in frequency a few months after I started my probation period with Var's team. Luckily I kept them pretty much hidden, not talking about them, until they kept me awake at night. I was inundated with the overwhelming certainty I was being harassed and chased and I wasn't...

I wasn't real. That I wasn't doing the right thing.

It was October 31st, and we were setting the pick up for a new job. The Johnson had contacted Variant two weeks prior. He wanted some piece of something a company had hidden deep inside a secured node in what looked like an abandoned building. Variant had created a name for himself as the one to retrieve the irretrievable. Having looked at the known schematics of the node, I had to agree with Pearl that this might be the run to end all runs.

My job was to scout ahead and get a feel for the guard's rotation. Who they had hired, and then who the hired guns had hired. My initial scouting established this so-called abandoned building was anything but. There was all kinds of *Nope* involved with it.

Knight Errant had this job secured, but it looked as if they had a few independent contractors on the streets and in a nearby Stuffer Shack. On my last night of surveillance, I noticed the same chrome-enhanced guy had been in a burger dive behind the building every night I went in for a soycaf.

My cybereyes stored the images, which I fed to Pearl. We planned the heist down to the minute. I had my role memorized and timed, running through it several times. We got into positions, had our encrypted channels open, and showtime arrived.

The first of the hired hands showed up on schedule, and I watched through my scope as I made him disappear. Hired hand two vanished, and then three. Four didn't show, and I gave the signal to hold.

I yawned a few times from my perch atop a neighboring building, nothing but a shadow to all but the sharpest, most expensive infra-red scanner. It was that yawn and my tired eyes that nearly missed hired hand four. He came in from a different direction, a cup in his hand. I recognized the stroll... but there was something different.

<Var...I think something's not right.>

<We don't have time for maybes, Crisis.>

<It's not a maybe. The fourth hand came in from a different direction this time. Why change procedure after seven days?>

There was silence on the channel as we all watched the fourth hand. He went to his usual corner and looked around. Looking through the scope I saw him reach into his pocket. I set my rifle down and pulled out my crossbow, again looking through the scope. He had a box in his hand. I relayed this to the group. <*I think it's a deck.*>

<*A deck? Pearl?*>

<*On it.*>

I nocked a sedative-loaded arrow as I watched hired hand four. My cybereyes scanned him from top to bottom and caught something very familiar, and very wrong. < *That's not a hired hand. It's Knight Errant!*>

<*Pause everyone. Let's see what he's up to.*>

I kept my arrow aimed, my hand ready to squeeze the trigger...a wave of dizziness made things blurry, and I had to lower the crossbow before I fell from where I was. I saw Variant's texts across the AR projected for my cybereyes, but the dizziness...

I wasn't seeing the streets below anymore. Or at least not the real streets. Everything looked rendered, suddenly. And I wasn't me. I wasn't really me and I was talking to—

"Crisis!"

I snapped out of my fog and brought the crossbow and scope back up. All hell was breaking loose down below. Two Knight Errant armored trucks had arrived, and the occupants were fanning out.

<*You want me to take them all out? I'll give away our presence.*>

<*wHhAT hApPen yINg?*> Loki didn't use the messaging system much, preferring direct contact.

<*I got it!*> Pearl's text was a green line of goodness on the AR. <*We'll rendezvous.*>

<*Crisis, you get her home.*>

<*Yes sir.*>

And I did. I holstered my crossbow and rifle before climbing down and pinpointed her signal on the AR map. She was still in position. The Knight Errant officers were covering the surrounding buildings.

I moved behind my building and slipped down a fire escape, then into a sub-basement toward Pearl. She was moving now, coming along the tunnel in front of me. I pressed myself into a shadow and waited, making sure it was just her. When she ran past I waited, hands on my knives, the wires in my muscles singing. A few beats, nothing on the scans.

I ran after her, and caught up with her near the entrance. We ducked down a side tunnel to a connecting basement. I opened the door, and the two of us went inside. I shut the door and locked it. It was an abandoned safe behind the Stuffer Shack. The building had once been a bank.

We hunched down in the dark, waiting.

I became aware of her against me. Her smell. A familiar scent. Something like flowers. I saw soft pillows and a woman's nude hip as I blinked several times...

"Crisis?" she whispered.

I blinked again and looked at the AR. The KE officers were above us. I put my finger to my lips and made the signal to hold.

She held tighter.

Oliver...are you okay? You look upset...

Oliver?

Pearl put her hand on my face, her skin cool against mine. "Hey," she whispered. "You okay?"

I nodded, and changed the subject after checking the map and making sure the KE were moving away. "What happened?"

"There were a few ICs on the node. Our intel said nothing about them, so I triggered one, but *after* I'd retrieved the intel."

"Where's it at? The intel."

"My sprite took it for me. She'll hide it for me until I need it. Don't worry, no one will find it in the Matrix."

"Your sprite is a girl?"

"She is for me."

I never pretended to understand technomancers or their abilities.

She shifted her position. "Crisis...you disappeared on me for a moment there. You looked...well, it's hard to see in here, but I swear you looked a little freaked out."

"I...it's nothing."

"Trust, Crisis. Trust me. Trust Variant."

I wanted to trust them, but something...*something* inside said not to. At least not yet. It warned me that what I was experiencing was secret. It was personal. But it wasn't mine. Or it wasn't anymore. "Just tired, is all. I'm not sleeping well."

"What kind of not sleeping? Nightmares?"

"I...I keep having dreams of being...hurt. There are fists and baseball bats and nails and knives." I absently put my hand on the gunshot scars on my chest.

"You need to tell Variant about these nightmares."

"I don't want to disappoint him."

She smiled at me. "I don't think he'll be disappointed at all."

THE SLAUGHTERED DONKEY
NOVEMBER 4TH, MONDAY

"He's remembering the torture."

Variant looked away from the report he'd been reading on his AR and focused on Pearl. She'd arrived with Crisis three hours after the job. Variant had been a little worried, but he also had faith in his new member. Crisis had appeared a little shaky, but his instincts at routine and examination were a boon. "Oh?"

"He blanked last night. I think it's coming back to him." She put her hands on his desk. "I think we need to tell him."

"Not yet."

"What exactly are you waiting for?"

Leaning back, he reached up to tap the documents he'd been reading, sending them to her. She straightened and waved her hands as she recalled them. "What is this?"

"I consider myself a good coordinator. I'm a good fighter. And I used to be a damn good schoolteacher. And I didn't get this way by looking the other way. I make a habit of making notes on everything and everyone we extract, steal, or deliver to our clients. This is a document I found while scanning the intel you brought back an hour ago." He smirked around his tusks. "Look at the signature at the bottom."

He watched her eyes track down and then widen. "Oliver Martin. What is this?"

"It's a message I found buried inside the metadata. I don't know how it got there or why, but apparently whatever this package is, it's got something to do with Crisis."

He watched as she read the document while standing up. When she was finished, she dismissed her AR and stared wide eyed at him. "This is a proposal, Variant. For something that just can't...this kind of thing isn't possible, is it?"

"You mean the software mentioned? I'm not a market analyst. I have no clue what makes one company better than another. What I am impressed with is the level of detail he went into on how it works, and how it can be abused."

She took a step back. "You think this is why they were after him."

"I think it pertains to that. The information in this packet isn't software. It's not an application. It's an idea."

"You opened it?"

"Of course I did. I told you, I keep track of everything." He recalled his AR and moved it over to a holoscreen for convenience. Pearl took a seat on the other side of his desk and watched. "This is a folder of notes. I couldn't tell you what the notes mean, because they're written in some dialect of Chinese I don't have the language soft for."

"But Oliver would."

"Yes. I think he worked in this language. I think he was as paranoid as I am. It's what makes him a good member of this team."

"So this could be his work."

"Could be. Only Oliver Martin could verify it."

Pearl licked her lips. "I never ask this, and normally I'd be very insulted, but...who is this Johnson?"

"A man named George Spinoza. I checked him out once I identified a thumbprint." Variant pulled up the man's dossier. "He once worked for Andreas Martin Analysis Systems, under Mason Andreas. He was a tech in their development department. And here's where it gets interesting. According to open records with AMAS, George Spinoza filed an affidavit claiming that Oliver Martin stole something from the lab, something very important, belonging to the company. A day or so after the filing is when Oliver's identity showed back up."

"I remember that."

"I know it was Spinoza who engineered that, and I'm willing to bet it was on Andreas's order. Then, the day Oliver disappeared and didn't show up for his hearing, Spinoza disappeared as well. Andreas told the BMP the two were probably working together."

Pearl stared at him. "Exactly how do you know all this?"

"It helps to have a hacker with a suspicious mind on a secret payroll. The black file we found, and that's what I'm calling the bullshit information the UCAS Intelligence Agency came up with, shows this detailed downward spiral of Oliver Martin." He moved the documents to her AR and made a rude noise. "They claimed he'd been planning on stealing this prototype called *Ghost-7* all along, and was in the process of framing

Mason Andreas when he was caught. Unfortunately, his fiancée, Nicole O'Neal, unwittingly helped Oliver escape, and he's been missing ever since. Until they allegedly discovered his body in the harbor May 8th."

Her mouth opened, then closed. "So this information about Oliver has been out there all this time, and we didn't see it?"

"No." He smiled and moved the documents back to the packet. "What I just told you I read in copies of missives between Mason Andreas and George Spinoza. Apparently the little shit kept copies of everything Andreas said, down to messages specifically detailing how to frame and destroy Oliver Martin. Andreas came up with the plan and Spinoza executed it."

"You mean this bastard's a whistle blower?"

"In a twisted, sort of evil way...yeah. My belief is he did this because he didn't trust Mason Andreas, and he witnessed first-hand what happened to Oliver Martin. Somehow, this little packet of Oh Shit was lost and Spinoza, AKA, Mr. Johnson, hired us to find it." Variant chuckled. "My guess is this bastard has no idea it was Oliver who helped in the retrieval."

"Now how would someone who took meticulous notes with that level of paranoia lose something so valuable?" Pearl rubbed her chin with her index finger.

"My suspicion is Spinoza dumped this file somewhere to keep it safe, then lost access to it."

"So," Pearl cleared up her AR. "Why was Knight Errant there?"

Variant shrugged. "If I were to wager a guess, Spinoza dumped it in with something Knight Errant would kill to protect. Double security. To a point even he couldn't get to it. But my question is, does anyone else know this file exists?"

She stood then, and stepped toward the door.

"Where are you going?"

"To locate this Spinoza and find that out." She paused as he stood and joined her at the door. "Variant, those KE officers came close to finding Crisis and I. That node wasn't anything special, and yet I found serious IC on it. We need to know why before we hand this over. And we have to tell Crisis. He needs to know who he was, before he can really be who he is."

He smiled at her, around his tusks. "I know, Pearl. But I think whatever this *Ghost-7* is, it's the key to bringing Apollonius down. And right now, that's the most important thing. It's what I've been working for all these years."

"And what about Crisis? Doesn't he get a say in any of this?"

Variant didn't answer. Pearl's words ignited irritation fueled by guilt. He couldn't consider anyone else right now. The only thing he saw in front of him was the revenge he'd wanted for decades.

CHAPTER 18

BOSTON
TUESDAY, NOVEMBER 5, 2075

I returned to my hovel a block away from The Slaughtered Donkey and took a long shower, letting the cold water wake me from whatever dream I was drowning in. I kept seeing images, faces—I smelled perfume, and recognized the scent of fresh coffee. Real coffee.

As far as I knew, I'd never had real coffee. Real coffee meant real milk, not soy. The coffee was real—as far as I knew. I couldn't remember ever having it with real milk because it was so expensive, but I swear I could taste it, or what I thought was it. Sleep should have been a high priority, but instead I got dressed, ignoring the bed that had betrayed me.

Loki came into our place—ours because I was her pup, after all—and into my room. She sniffed me, made a face and then licked my cheek. "Pup is confused. There is much lost in here—" she touched my head, "—you must find it."

"You mean my past."

"Yessss." Loki put her arms around my chest. I wrapped mine around her shoulders and felt her purring against my body. I found comfort in her touch, in her scent, her presence, because she had been the first to show me kindness. The first friend I made in this new world.

"Loki...I need to try something."

She pushed back from me and canted her head to the side. "Try something?"

From her expression I realized she was thinking I wanted to try something bad. I held up my hands. "No...no. What I mean is...I want to try real coffee."

Loki's expression wrinkled up. "Why you want that? Bitter and yucky."

"I...I just want to try one. I want to walk around a while and just think."

"This is good. I go with you."

"No...no, I want to do it alone. Oh, please don't look at me like that. I promise after I take this walk, you and I will have a walk. Maybe down at the harbor."

The promise seemed to perk her right up. She insisted I keep my commlink on and my connection with her open. I agreed and changed into casual wear, a long way from my usual leathers and protective gear. I felt naked without my crossbow or rifle, but I did strap two daggers to my calves in case I was jumped. And there were the softs if I needed them, always ready and willing. I wasn't worried about being recognized as Crisis, this low priority news vigilante. The only recording anyone had of me was a dark figure. Might or might not be me. Pearl and I both thought it was Variant.

I took one of the few trains that still ran near South Boston to the Commons. I don't know why I picked there, other than I just went where my instincts—or someone else's instincts—wanted me to go.

When I arrived, I shoved my hands into my pockets, pulled the hood of my coat over my head and just walked. The autumn leaves were nearly gone, some holding onto the branches of trees through sheer determination. It hadn't rained or snowed in nearly two weeks, so the fallen leaves were dry, and kicked up in little rustling bursts with each footfall.

I watched the students, I watched the passersby, I guessed at their lives, what they did, if they were married...and in my little made up stories, they all had pasts.

They all had a purpose.

They all had...history.

I didn't think I was being morose or overburdened with emotion. My head ached behind my eyes, so I turned down a particular street. Ahead was the sign for a coffee and bakery shop, so I stopped and breathed in the aroma. Loki may say coffee tasted bitter, but it smelled heavenly. And it stirred something in me. Something I still couldn't see, or touch, or know just yet.

Couples, singles, students, businessmen and women—they came and went through the door as I stood there, swimming in a sea of what-might-have-beens stitched together with the unsettling feeling of what...had been.

"Hey, you okay?"

It took a few seconds before I realized the male voice was talking to me. I blinked at him as I silently scolded myself for letting anyone—especially a young troll dressed as a barista—sneak up on me. But as I watched him, I got an image of him speaking again, like an echo of another time and place. His hair had been shorter then, and he hadn't grown the van dyke.

"Sorry...I was lost in thought."

"I'll say." He held the door open. "Wanna come in and get a soycaf?"

"Sure." I followed him, and was instantly assaulted by the stronger smell. But I also recognized the tang of sugar, the homey essence of steamed soy milk and the mind opening feeling that I *had* been here before. Not just stepping into a coffee shop, but *this* particular one.

I walked up to the counter as the troll came around and looked at me expectantly. "I'm uh...not sure what to order. I mean I don't want a soycaf. I want a real coffee."

"Soycaf is real coffee, it's just the milk's not from cows. But we do have some. It might not taste like what you're used to. Look, you kind of remind me of someone, so why don't I make you what they used to drink?"

"I remind you of someone?"

The kid nodded and started at the machine. "Executive type. But you'd never know it without the suit. He always came in for a morning coffee, *real* milk," he shrugged. "Sometimes he'd take goat's milk, watched the paper, and overtipped me."

None of that felt familiar. "What...what is it about me that reminds you of him?"

"Your face. But he was much rounder. You know...well-fed guy."

"And I look—?"

The kid grinned around his tusks "You look well-seasoned. That's what my dad calls it. Means you've experienced life, and it's left an impression on you." He continued to work, and I heard the milk steaming. "So, you live around here?"

But I wasn't ready to let this fat executive person go. "So what...what happened to this guy?"

He shrugged. "I don't know. He came in one morning, and looked really upset. Wasn't as neat and trimmed, you know? And his SIN had an alert on it. Which just didn't make sense to me."

"You mean it was stolen?"

"That's what it said, but I knew the guy. Used the same account for years, and no problem. So for it to flag as stolen seemed like a system error to me, so I erased it and gave him the coffee for free." With that he set the cup on the counter. "Just like this one. It's on the house."

"You can do that?"

"Of course. I'm the owner."

Wow. I nodded, picked up the hot container and sipped it. Loki was right about the coffee—without the soycaf, the flavor shined through. The real milk only enhanced that flavor.

I loved it. "Nice."

"Good."

"So you've always owned this place?"

"No. Not till about five months ago. I received an anonymous donation with the paper work already filled out. All legit. So I took the deal, and now it's mine."

That made no sense. "Who was this donor?"

He put his hands on the counter and leaned to me. "I have no idea," he said in a low voice. "All I have to do is send in the trid recordings every night."

"Recordings?"

He pointed at the ceiling, to the small bubbles I hadn't noticed before. "Right there."

I looked directly at the closest and sipped my coffee with real milk. "Interesting. So the person that sold it wants the feeds...why not just have them auto-sent?"

"Beats me. He said he wants them hand-delivered. These cameras aren't even on the grid. No one can access them but me." He smirked. "I got customers behind you."

That was the second time I'd allowed someone to sneak up behind me. He reached over the counter. "Nice to meet you. I'm Ted, by the way."

I already knew this because his name flagged in the store's tag in my AR. I shook his hand anyway. "Cri—Chris."

"Nice to meet you, Chris." He turned his attention to the two men behind me.

I had my coffee. Learned there was a guy that I sort of looked like that came in here, and yet nothing came back to me. Nothing jumped out that gave me a clue as to why I had the headaches, and why I vaguely remembered this coffee shop, and why I was having these dreams of a woman and a man with pointed ears—

"It's always the pretty ones that marry wrong, isn't it?"

The voice was to my left, but he wasn't speaking to me. He was addressing his companion, another young human. Both were dressed casually. A bit better quality than what I owned, but less than what a few of the executives wore, holding coffees.

His friend answered with a laugh. "Yeah, but which one do you mean? The girl or the elf?"

"Oh come on, we all know that guy's not a real elf."

"Oh, then how come you know that?"

"'Cause my mom works for Andreas Martin Analysis Systems, and says Mason Andreas's a poser. He just likes *looking* like one. And besides, everyone knows it's just another one of those corporate mergers."

Andreas Martin Analysis Systems.

Mason...

Andreas...

A...M...A...S

Each time these names were spoken, a bell rang somewhere in the distance, as if heralding the coming of something very important. Something I'd been waiting for.

I looked at them, and then tracked where they were looking. The shop's trideo was playing a news program, and on it were shots of two people answering questions outside of some night club.

My gaze slid off the blond-haired man with pointed ears and locked onto the woman. Her raven hair was pulled back from her face and as he asked her a question, she smiled for the camera.

I lost all sense of where I was as I beheld the face from my dreams. The one hovering over me, smiling that smile at me, her dark curls framing her face and tickling my cheek.

I smelled her perfume. Jasmine Rose. Something created just for her.

She was the inspiration.

Images flashed by on the screen in my mind as I saw her over and over. Frowning. Laughing. Crying. I saw her angry, yelling, smirking...at me. In every picture she was looking directly at me. And then I saw her through some kind of glass, and I couldn't reach her. I remembered pain...the same kind of numbing pain I'd dreamed about.

"Hey...Chris?"

The stabbing pain behind my eyes. She put her hand on that glass and said, "I love you," to me.

"Chris—"

To *me!*

"Hey, can somebody help me?" Ted's voice echoed in the dark as the real coffee slipped from my fingers and everything went dark.

I don't know how long it was before I came back. I didn't know where I went, but I'd brought something back with me.

"He's awake now," Variant said as he leaned into my field of vision. "Hey...Chris...you okay?"

I stared at him, willing him to see the answers in my eyes. And I believe he did. He turned to someone I couldn't see. "We'll get him home. I can clean up the mess."

"No no...it's okay," Ted was saying. "I thought maybe he was sick or something, the way he'd started shaking. And he seemed very disoriented."

"Yeah. He's had a pretty rough couple of weeks. Just getting over something," Variant helped me up on my feet and the crowd that had gathered moved away. Pearl appeared at Var's right, and I focused on her.

She leaned in close to me. "You remembered something."

I slowly nodded, and grabbed her shoulders as I took her into my arms. She was one of the ones who had taken me in, who had patched me up, who had given me a new life when my previous one had been stolen.

I owed her. And Variant. And my precious Loki.

Because you see, what I brought back with me from that white blindness of oblivion was *Me.*

"My name is Oliver Martin," I whispered in her ear. "Mason Andreas took everything from me."

She tensed against me, and I felt Variant's hand on my shoulder. "It's time to have that talk now."

I pulled away from Pearl and looked him in the eye. "It's long past that time." I could see the trid playing behind him, and beheld the repeat of the news cycle, and her face and

Mason's, announcing their engagement and the date of their wedding.

December 21, 2075.

Nicole O'Neal was marrying Mason Andreas.

My fiancée was with the man who had killed me.

"Yeah," I said as I dragged my gaze back over to him. "And after that talk, I want to hire your team to get my life back and kill that son of a bitch."

CHAPTER 19

TUESDAY, NOVEMBER 6, 2075
EARLY MORNING

I don't remember when Variant gave me the sedative, but when I awoke, I was in his apartment above The Slaughtered Donkey.

My memories were still there, but fuzzy. I knew I was Oliver, I knew Mason had taken my life from me, I knew I'd been tortured for what felt like years and I remembered...

Nicole.

I didn't want to cry or break down in front of her, but apparently I had no choice, as who I was had to deal with who I am.

The two separate Olivers.

No...Oliver and Crisis.

Crisis. I couldn't believe I'd named myself after my game character.

Or did I? Now even my present memories seemed to be sketchy.

The door opened as I sat up. Pearl came in with a tray of food. It smelled wonderful. Variant followed her, and then Loki ran inside and jumped on me, tackling me back to the bed.

"Cub! You awake!" She hugged and licked me, and I held her close, stroking her beautiful main of snow-colored hair.

"Loki, come on. Let the man eat. He's been out for a while."

Loki let me go, but stayed on the bed as Pearl set the tray beside me. I handed Loki a piece of what looked like real meat, and she purred happily as she rubbed against me. My stomach growled as I bit into spiced potatoes and delighted in the food. "Where'd you score this?"

"Don't worry about that," Variant said as he pulled up a chair and Pearl settled against a wall, her arms over her chest. Something about her eyes looked funny, and I realized she was online in her weird technomancer way. "Just eat while I talk."

"Is this the talk you mentioned at the shop?"

"Yes."

I chewed a minute, swallowed. "You already knew who I was, didn't you?"

"I didn't know who you were when I first met you. I knew who you were when Loki found you."

"That doesn't make sense."

He leaned forward, his elbows on his knees. "Crisis—"

"Oliver."

"Crisis is who you are now. It's who you're going to have to be." He sighed. "Oliver Martin is dead."

I didn't remember that, and nearly choked on another bite of potato. Loki beat my back and I put my hand on her shoulder so she'd stop. I grabbed the bottle of water and drank half of it. "What?"

"The persona who was Oliver Martin was declared dead over five months ago."

I dug into those memories. My anger was fresh and still raw when I thought of Mason. But when I thought of Apollonius Turk it turned to rage. Flashes of blood, pain, the gleam of a knife, the blow of a fist. "Turk...Turk was the one that..." but I couldn't finish the declaration.

"Apollonius Turk has a reputation. One I have first-hand knowledge of. He's sort of a one-man show when it comes to fixers. You need a job done, he handles it. And someone in NeoNET hired him to make the acquisition of Andreas Martin Analysis Systems go smooth. When I discovered this little-known fact, I had to ask myself—why would a corporation like NeoNET hire a fixer to oversee something as cut and dry as an acquisition? The fact didn't fit the situation. If someone hires Turk, that means there's a problem they don't want surfacing. And Turk only works for the corps. So that meant there was a problem." Variant nodded at me. "Like you."

I wiped my hands on a napkin, then my lips. "Why me? Why did he do that to me? Why...why did he come after *me*?"

"We were hoping you could tell us."

Again I was drowning in a lake of images, some from a past I was slowly learning, others from my present. "I—I'm not sure. He wanted something."

Variant straightened up. "Does the name *Ghost-7* ring a bell?"

It rang all my bells. I pitched forward with my hands on my head as more images came forward. Nothing was in order that I could recognize and nothing...nothing made sense.

Except...

In an instant, Variant and Loki were at my side, and helped me back onto the bed. "The doc who took a look at you, the one that patched you up in Loki's den—he said you lost your memories because of a serious shock to the system. I guessed that shock was the torture, maybe drugs, or even when you escaped and were shot. Do you remember escaping?"

"Some of it..." My voice sounded odd in my ears. It didn't sound like me. Not anymore. "I remember...a dark room. A single light. I couldn't move, and they kept hitting and punching, asking me...'where is the prototype?'"

"Now we're getting somewhere." Variant stepped back. "Was it *Ghost-7*?"

I found myself nodding. "They lost the prototype. It was the thing NeoNET wanted from us. From AMAS." I remembered the news, the images of Mason. "Nicole..." I looked at Variant. "I have to tell Nicole."

But he held out his hand. "That's not a good idea. Not yet. She's getting married to Andreas, and as far as we can tell, she bought the whole story he fed her."

"Whole story?"

Pearl stepped forward and handed me my commlink. I put it on and activated the AR as I received files from her. "This is what's out there for Oliver Martin. This is what the world believes, *if* they search your name."

I read it. Every page of it, but I felt myself growing distant from it. I had who I was tentatively resting in my mind, but this didn't mix with what I knew.

Everything pointed to me stealing the plans and prototype to a new software, developed by the bright minds at AMAS. A software that would revolutionize the ability to develop a successful company. This software, once released to the public, would give smaller businesses and corporations a fighting chance against the conglomerates that ruled the world. *Ghost-7* would have heralded a new age of commerce.

But Oliver Martin stole it and tried to sell it to shadowrunners, more than likely to overseas investors, and was killed in South Boston by a shadowrunner team, possibly the one who helped him fake his ID being switched, and then orchestrated his disappearance. Until what was left of his body showed up in Boston Harbor. He was identified by his DNA.

The project was shut down and NeoNET, being the gracious corporation they were, honored their agreement to back more research and development by AMAS, in order to possibly rebuild the software one day.

"This—This is all wrong," I muttered.

"We were hoping as much," Variant sat back in his chair. "Care to enlighten us?"

So I did. As best as I could. "Mason and I started the company with an idea. This general description of the application's merits is...was...our mission statement. This is what we wanted to accomplish with this software. I was good at seeing patterns. It's why I like chess. It's why I like the crossbow."

"I don't get that one."

"It's all long range. It takes a different set of skills to aim at a target so far away. You have to factor in distance, weather, wind...even my ability. It's the same science of thinking I used to create *Ghost-7*."

"So it's really supposed to give companies a fighting chance?" Pearl sounded surprised. "Because that would be nice, but I don't see NeoNET sharing their profits with anyone."

"And you'd be right." It came back now, every damn painful moment of it. "When we were ready for field tests, Mason took over that area, wanting to be more involved. He was always good at being the face—the outward appearance of the company, even though the science was beyond him. And he had the capital to invest. At that time...Nicole and I started seeing each other romantically. She was originally engaged to him when we met."

Pearl winced. "Ouch."

"You okay?" Loki said. She'd already finished the rest of my meal for me, and was now licking her hands clean.

"I'm fine, little one." Pearl smiled.

"Yeah." I swallowed. "So you see why I was so eager to let him help. I felt guilty. A few months passed, and I was reading something in the coffee shop—the one you found me in. By the way, how *did* you find me there?"

"Loki followed you." Variant said.

I looked at her and she beamed with pride, then frowned. "Need to teach you better ways to be invisible. Stomp like bear."

"Keep going," Variant prodded.

"I'd been so enamored with Nicole that I hadn't paid much attention to anything else. Until I read about three very important business closings. Bankruptcy in each of them."

"That doesn't sound odd."

"It does when all three were direct competitors of AMAS." I put my hands on opposite arms and hugged myself. "I downloaded every statistical report out there and studied them. And every one of them went down the exact same way, using the exact same method."

"Which was?" Pearl asked.

"*Ghost-7*."

"What made you think that?" Variant put his hands on his knees. "All kinds of things could make a business fail. Lack of interest in the product, which was just bad research. Drek investments. Downturn of the market. A flood of similar products from overseas, sold cheaper."

I gave him a half-smile. "You know your economics."

"You could say that."

Pearl had told me once that Variant had been a teacher before his goblinization. I'd just assumed it was language or social studies. But apparently I was wrong. "You're right, of course. None of those things were present at the time of the downturn. And that's not how *Ghost-7* works."

I could see they weren't following, and I couldn't blame them. So I got up off the bed and started pacing...like I once did. "In analytics, I study statistics. Those aren't just numbers, but variables, much like the ones you just gave me. All kinds of things happened to make it fall. For instance," I stopped and looked at all three of them. "Trees in the forest. Or rocks along a hillside, even better. They don't move on their own, they need some kind of outside force to cause change. That could be weather, cars, earthquakes, people, natural catastrophe—

but in each of those instances, the old saying that a chain is only as strong as its weakest link proved true."

Again, I lost them. Crickets.

"Imagine the rocks on the hillside. An earthquake happens. A few dislodge and roll down hill and take out the weaker ones. It rains, and some are washed down with the same result. These are those every day pitfalls. Like the bad market, bad research, or lousy product. But sometimes there are catastrophic occurrences that no one sees coming. A black swan event. Those happen because something capitalizes on attacking that weakest link, which then starts the avalanche of doom."

"Crisis—"

"Wait," Pearl put up a hand. "You're not talking about the company and market and weather. You're talking about the people."

I nodded. "Yes."

"Huh?" Variant looked confused.

"Let me try," Pearl said. "Forget the rocks and landslide. But think about a corporation. A lot of times it's a bad decision that destroys a company. Yes, we see the bad investment, but where did the decision to make the investment come from? Many times—and I've seen this over and over—it comes from higher up in the company, or someone with a bit of power who told someone else to make the call. So the person that made the call gets shit-canned, but, the one who made the bad decision is still there."

I pointed at her. "Right. That is exactly what *Ghost-7* was designed to find. It doesn't look at markets and products—it looks at people. At their evaluations, at their life's decisions, at their grades, their relationships. The software burrows down on who in the company as it is, is capable of making bad decisions. Who is the lynchpin?"

"Oh, hell," Variant said.

"Exactly. And as part of those field tests, I gave Mason a standard questionnaire that was made to look like an employee form. Like an admissions test. It asked questions on decision making, which was fed into the software along with everything else."

"I don't like where this is going."

"Neither did I, especially when I visited those companies as they were shutting down and discovered those same damn questions had been added to their employee forms three months earlier. And in each company, a lynchpin was discovered."

"Wait," Pearl shook her head. "That doesn't make sense. If they found the lynchpin, then the companies should have improved."

"Oh, fragging hell," Variant said as he stood and took a step back. "They fucking did it backward."

I nodded. "They reversed it. They made the field tests show them who would make the company flourish, who was the best at what they did."

They both looked at me. "And?" Pearl said.

"What did they do?" Variant took a step forward. "Crisis, what did you find out? What happened to those employees?"

I looked at Loki sitting on the bed, now licking the empty plate. "They disappeared a month before the companies went out of business." I looked at Variant and Pearl. "No one knows what happened to them."

CHAPTER 20

The truth of why I'd been taken and tortured seemed almost... anti-climactic to me. For months, I'd sort of built up this other identity of myself as an international spy or businessman, carrying the secrets to global peace, or something equally as dumb. And though the reality was just as noble in the eyes of Loki and everyone else, I still felt like a complete ass for building the damn software. The parts of my memory that weren't returning as easy were the ones that would tell me whether or not I had any conscience thought about the repercussions of what I was doing.

But then maybe I didn't have any, and that's why I couldn't remember them.

Everyone else on the team were as surprised and shocked to hear about what I'd worked on. What I'd created. Variant wanted to know if it was possible for me to write the same kind of program as a wyrm he could use to analyze a company's security system.

I couldn't. Not without the basic information on the latest security systems on the market. And the last time I checked, those companies guarded their secrets quite nicely.

It was during this team meeting that I learned a lot more about Variant's past. For some reason, it had never occurred to me to investigate him. I guess I hadn't wanted to bite the hand that had healed and fed me.

I always knew Variant hated NeoNET. And given his present financial condition, I figured his violent emotions toward them had to do with investments.

I was wrong. I was so damn wrong.

Before his goblinization, Variant's wife had worked for NeoNET in one of their R&D departments. He'd been a teacher, just as he said he was. And then the goblinization happened, and he was summarily let go from his job, since the initial attack had occurred in the middle of class, and frightened some of the students.

After it was clear what happened to him, Var fell into a deep depression. Their friends stopped coming by, the neighbors never spoke, and he couldn't get another teaching job. His wife worked harder to keep the bills paid, taking on more projects with NeoNET than she should have. Variant finally got a job as a dock worker with a crew of orks and took up fishing, trading, and made a lot of contacts over the next few years.

But then something happened in his wife's lab, some accident that NeoNET officials, especially one named Apollonius Turk, insisted was the work of technomancers. The autopsy showed Annette had also been pregnant. He lost both his child and his wife in the accident.

"So, because they hired this Turk guy, you knew there had been a problem?" I asked as the others broke for food and Variant remained in his chair. I moved to sit beside him.

"Yeah. Not many people knew Turk's background. But I did. Just his presence alone set off alarm bells, and I knew the story about technomancers was just that—a story to hide what really happened. See, Annette's work was *about* technomancers. Trying to comprehend how they connected to the Matrix with their minds. She really wanted to understand them."

I recalled some information I remembered reading on technomancers. Something I'd researched when I met Pearl. "The TM groups say NeoNET takes TMs off the street and experiments on them. If this was true—"

"You'd think knowing that would destroy NeoNET's reputation. Oh it tainted it, but it's like they're covered in Teflon. Nothing sticks. So they continue to operate, technomancers continue to disappear, and innocent people continue to die."

Pearl approached us with sandwiches. She handed me one, since Loki had devoured the first plate of food she'd brought me. "Being a technomancer myself, I can understand the desire to expose NeoNET and all its atrocities. But sometimes brandishing a big stick isn't the way to do it."

Unwrapping my food, I looked up at her. "You're more into subterfuge. Sneaking in the back door."

"Or in right under their noses. No one expects their death to come through the front door." She smiled at me before handing Variant his sandwich. When he didn't take it because he was brooding, she set it on his desk. "At first, their tactics were strong-arming. After all, that's how they'd been handled. But I think in time they'll come to realize we have a power that others can't wrap their head around. And the little we reveal about ourselves, the better we are to defend ourselves against persecution."

There were times when Pearl just scared the hell out of me. I sensed there was a lot more to her than just a knock-out body and a killer face. "So, what do you think really happened?"

"We don't know," Variant said, though his eyes were focused on something—or someone—else. "I just know she died. My child died. And I wasn't even given the courtesy to bury them."

"Huh?"

Pearl spoke up. "Apollonius Turk insisted they had to get rid of the bodies. Variant didn't have anything to bury." She looked at her own sandwich. "It was a low blow. What was even lower was when they refused to pay a settlement."

"No settlement?" My years in corporate came to the front. "What about her contract? She worked in a lab. There are specific riders to protect the company as well as the families of the employee." Of course, most of those riders were always written with a gag order in mind, settlements always came with conditions attached.

She shrugged. "Their policies are very specific. One would assume they cover all injuries in the lab, but they don't. There's nothing there for the intrusion of a third-party faction, armed and dangerous. Which is how they filed it, and Variant was denied."

"On a technicality."

"A made-up one." I noticed Variant's hands clenching and unclenching into fists. "Technomancers never stormed that lab. Something else happened. Something they've kept hidden. It's something I've worked hard to discover. It all burns down to one truth. Apollonius Turk knows the truth of what happened to my wife."

A lot of things clicked into place at that moment. "And you think I'm the one to help you discover it?" I snorted. "That's a lot of faith to invest in someone Loki found dying in an abandoned building."

There was a subtle look between the two of them, Variant and Pearl. I wasn't as gifted at understanding the nuances of relationships, but after years in the corps' eat or be eaten atmosphere, I was pretty good at reading some things. It took a few seconds before I understood the looks they gave one another. I especially focused on Pearl's expression. "You knew I was coming."

She refocused on me, but didn't say anything.

I took a step forward. "You both knew this was going to happen to me. You knew I was going to be in this situation."

"No." Variant looked at me, faced me with his full gaze. I didn't read deceit or suspicion in his eyes, but I did see a small bit of worry. Or was that resignation? "I honestly didn't know who you were...nor did I care...until you were put in the same cell as me."

"Same cell?" I kept my eyes locked on Variant as I searched through swiss cheese memories that came and went. Some in bright colors, others in monochromatic brown. I narrowed my eyes. "When I was arrested just inside AMAS."

Variant said, "I don't know the cause, I just knew when they dumped you on the floor, you weren't a criminal. Your soft hands, no scars, and what remained of your clothing. What I gathered from the guard, a contact that'd taken me years to cultivate, I learned your name. And I also learned he had no idea why they'd been given the order to beat you." He leaned his head to the side. "You weren't supposed to leave that cell alive."

I tried to remember those moments, but they were as hazy now as they were then. "There was a voice."

"That was me. I messaged Pearl a visual and a name. She came back with a stolen SIN, and a warrant for your arrest. You had stolen the SIN from the real Oliver Martin."

"No..."

"We know a set up when we see it." Pearl spoke up. "Yours was obvious. I looked your history up in places people like Mason Andreas and Apollonius Turk can't imagine, and they gave me the name of your fiancée."

"Nicole," I felt something thunder inside my chest. "She... she said she couldn't find me at first. But she didn't say how she did."

"I made sure it was anonymous." Pearl looked sad. "She made it possible for you to survive, but then the creators of your demise had to change their tactics. So I made it my business to watch you, boyo."

Boyo.

The only person that had ever called me boyo was... *"Serilious?!"*

She smiled. "I do have a day job, Crisis. Imagine my surprise when I realized the man that interested Variant was none other than the best assassin in *Dark City*. I'd already been watching your character. Mostly because our game personas are like our alter egos. We do things in imaginary settings we would never do in the real waking world." Pearl's smile faded. "I saw what was coming, and when I couldn't get you to follow directions, we tried to stop Turk from taking you."

"But we were too late." Variant put his hands in his hips. "You were gone for two months. They ran stories on you, about how you'd been caught stealing files from AMAS, intent on destroying NeoNET." He snorted. "I have to admit, the lies they told were pretty impressive, but I'd already met you. I assumed you were no runner."

I swallowed and looked at the floor for a few seconds as the memories of waking in that alley resurfaced...but nothing before it. "How...how did I get out of there? Away from where ever I was?"

Variant smiled. "It took every minute of a month and a half to find you. And then two more weeks to figure out how to get you out. Where they held you might have been in Ancient territory, but it was well hidden and beefed in high-level security."

Pearl snorted. "But even the best make mistakes. They get slack. And they get bored."

I looked from one to the other. Months with the two of them, studying their habits and decisions put a look of shock on my face. "You infiltrated their security."

"That's what took two weeks after we found you. We weren't even sure you were alive in there. But..." Variant shrugged. "Pearl can be persuasive, and guards too long posted over a tortured corp kisser crave a bit of excitement."

Another pause. I said, "They let me go."

Pearl cleared her throat. "They arranged your escape. And I arranged the reactivation of the skillwires. Loaded in a one-time use skillsoft of a prison break. You'd been drugged with serum that all it took was me giving you a whispered order and you were free."

I closed my eyes, searching my memories. "I don't remember any of it."

"You won't," Varian said. "The drugs prevent it."

"You got away," Pearl said as she rubbed at the back of her neck. "Variant saw what you did. But he was ducking detection himself and the one leading the charge against you found him. Once he finished fighting, you were gone."

I looked at Variant. "The one with the braid."

"Yeah," Variant looked put out. "Punk ass—had a mask on—and he got away. But not before I put a little hurt on his ass."

Pearl continued. "We weren't sure where you went, until Loki found you. Told us the story about how you killed those hunters, the assassins hired by Turk to bring you back, or kill you."

She stepped forward until she was in front of me. "Crisis was and is a part of you. He's your alter ego. And now you will have to make the choice, whether to be Oliver Martin again, or carry on as Crisis. Either way, there is a moral imperative to take back what was yours."

This was too much. It pressed on my shoulders like dead weight as I stumbled back and sat down in a chair. All of this. I'd been used by a man I considered my best friend...and I'd been used by a man I looked up to like a mentor.

Who was I supposed to trust?

This wasn't a decision I could make lightly, and it wasn't something to make quickly.

"Crisis," Variant said, and he and Pearl were standing in front of me, blocking my escape. "Do you know where this prototype is? Hey look at me, if you still want us to kill Turk—"

"Stop," I got up, and he let me shove him out of the way. "I can't talk about this right now. I need to think."

"There's no time for thinking. We have to know if you took the prototype. Do you have access to it? Crisis...if you have it you can—"

"Stop!" I whirled on him as the wires in my muscles sung. I didn't remember striking him. In fact, I didn't remember hitting either of them. But they were feet from me, their noses bloody and my knuckles stinging. The softskill had acted. A hair trigger. Pulled by my anger.

I hated that I'd struck Pearl. She didn't deserve that. Not at all.

But I didn't want to be used anymore. I didn't want them telling me what to do. I turned, grabbed my jacket, crossbow and quiver, picked up my rifle at the door, and stalked out.

It was time I went out on my own and discovered my own truths. Decide my own way. And not be used like a goddamn puppet.

Like a character in a game.

The problem was, I didn't know where to start. But as I left *The Slaughtered Donkey*, a name came to me. A name I associated with trust and friendship.

Jericho.

CHAPTER 21

BOSTON
FRIDAY, NOVEMBER 8, 2075

I made sure I wasn't being followed this time as I exited my hovel two days after I left Variant's office. I showered, dressed in civilian clothing on the outside, but beneath I wore the leathers that had protected me from enemy fire time and again. I kept my crossbow in a viola case on my back, and slipped my arrows into a satchel at my side. I hoped I looked like any other music student out for an evening walk.

I ran a quick search for Jericho's name, as well as the online personas I knew about. Nothing turned up, which was odd. Normally I could always find him by one of his names. To find nothing set off my first alarm.

Discovering he no longer lived in the same place was the second. Then I discovered he no longer worked at MIT&T.

Either Mason and Apollonius had gotten to Jericho, or he was hiding. And Jericho was very, very good at disappearing. If he didn't want to be found, he wouldn't.

Except...when he gamed. Jericho was addicted to *Dark City*, a place where he could be more than what he was. Having exhausted all other avenues, I figured logging into the game for a quick search wouldn't hurt. But should I do it as Crisis? My account was still there, according to Pearl, and I was an admin. She'd given me the new password. But if I did log into the account, I was pretty sure it would send Pearl an alert as well. And I didn't want to talk to any of them right now.

I found an out of the way place to set up my deck, slip into the grid just like every other law-abiding citizen, and created a new account with *Dark City* using a clean SIN. My account name would be...I looked again at the registered name on the account. Takamoto Daisuke? Wow...where exactly did Variant get these things?

There were a few upgrades to the character creation interface, but most of it was the same. I rolled up a character pretty fast, a female archer, and named her Nicole Oliver. Once I was in, I repeated a few quests to level up to a comfortable and fightable number.

Two hours passed. I checked the world outside the game. No one staring at me. In fact, I was one of many online, most of which were playing games.

Back in, I visited all of Jericho's old haunts. I checked names to see if his old account was online, but it wasn't there. I could only assume he'd deleted it for the same reason he disappeared. I didn't know if it had anything to do with what happened to me.

Just when I felt like logging out and heading home to face Variant, I caught sight of a shadow to my right and behind me. I kept walking down the street but angled my camera for a better look when I stopped the persona at the merchant area. From there I could get a better look around.

The shadow didn't move, and I thought maybe it was just my paranoia bleeding through. And then it did move. It was a slender man, dressed in black. Even his hood was black. I didn't recognize the moves, but it was obvious he was watching my persona.

I didn't think it was possible for anyone to find me in this game. After all, I hadn't played it in nearly eight months, and I never played a female. Besides, everyone thought I was dead, right? At least the principal players.

So who was this mook? I checked his level when he wasn't paying attention. Damn. At his level, he could one-shot my character without breathing hard. So a fight was out of the question. How was I going to engage? I needed to know who was behind the character.

I thought of someone. I placed the character into rest mode and moved into support. With her name at my fingertips, I asked for the same person who helped me all those months ago. I didn't tell her who I was but I recognized her persona icon when it came over the game's internal message system.

<Welcome to Dark City support. This is Angie. How can I help you?>

Taking a deep breath, I gave her an awful story about escaping an abusive husband and playing this game with my kid, but there was a player stalking me, and I was terrified it was the husband. I understood if she couldn't help me but anything that could let me know if I needed to log off and call the BMP would be helpful.

Angie was sympathetic and did a bit more than I hoped. A NPC activated nearby, rezzing in as a BMP cop and approached me as if we were engaged.

<Miss Oliver,> Angie texted. *<I see the one you're talking about. And though I can't give you their exact information, I can tell you they've been a player a very long time. Their account is a gold account, and this particular character is three months old. He doesn't have anything written up in the history, and his rep for admin status is untarnished.>*

<Thank you so much. So, it looks like he's interested?> You know...make it believable I'm a single mom. Looking for romance maybe.

<If he's stalking you in-game, I doubt it's for anything malicious. He might just be shy. I can tell you this much. He's a male in real life, and he's single, and he's just returned to the game.>

<I can't get a name, can I?>

<Just the character name, which is Jax. Anything else I can help you with?>

I thanked her and kept an eye on Jax. Nothing about what she said told me it was Jericho, but who else could it be? Why would anyone even bother to track a game character—especially a noob—unless they were either curious or a pervert? And if this turned out to be a perv, I would probably kick their ass the first chance I got. I had to pause as that thought washed over me—so different than how I used to think. There was a time when the only way I could kick someone's ass was in-game. But now I knew I could really do it.

Standing around letting the shadow follow me wasn't getting anywhere. So I headed to a place I knew was deserted, a rooftop Jericho and I used to hide out on and talk when we didn't want to face the real world and weren't in the mood to play the game.

I climbed to the top and sat in the exact same spot I sat in as Crisis.

And I waited.

It didn't take long before the shadow turned up. Only this time Jax didn't stay in the shadows, but stood in front of me in the open. The character didn't look that different from his previous one. Tall, red-headed, slender elf with an arsenal to impress any gun nut. But I knew there was more than just firearms. Jericho liked to look incompetent—it always put people off their guard.

But not me.

"You can't stay here," his character said in a voice I didn't recognize.

I activated my own voice and chose an appropriate female one. "I don't see your name on this rooftop."

"Leave. Now."

"Make me."

I knew his moves. We'd spared often enough. He turned as if to go and I braced myself, slipping my knife from the sheath at my hip and reaching around to grab the small pistol at my back. I had a crossbow, but I kept it hidden for now. I had to make sure.

I counted to four, and as always, he jumped and lunged backward at me. And if I were someone who'd never seen that tactic, he'd have landed either on top of me and commenced pummeling me with overjuiced hits, or he'd have landed in front of me or behind me and filled me full of lead.

But I wasn't there when he landed. And he was obviously confused by this. When he turned to find my pistol in his face, the muzzle between his eyes just above the bridge of his nose, he stopped. I had my opportunity at that moment. I could have continued the fight. Showed him what I'd learned in the past five months, but I felt I was running out of time. I knew Variant and the others would come looking for me if I didn't report back. I'd gone from one set of masters, Mason and the company, to Apollonius and his torture, to Variant and his crushing certainty I was the one who could help him exact revenge for his wife.

For now, I would remain with Variant. At least they'd fessed up to using me.

I removed the voice mod and spoke in my voice, which I'm sure looked odd coming from the woman in front of him. "I'm flattered you saved my spot all this time Jer, but you really need to learn some new moves."

The character's face looked blank for a few seconds before my message icon flashed. I left the characters standing there, mine with her gun pressed against Jax's forehead and opened the mail. It was from Jax.

<*This isn't fragging funny.*>

So I answered him.

<*No, it's not. So why are you hiding in* Dark City*? Why aren't you at your apartment?*>

There was a long pause. Long enough that I got a little worried I'd scared him off. I was just about to log off the game when the message <*RL. Now.*> appeared.

Jax vanished. So I logged off as well.

I put my deck away, retracted the wires, and sat back to enjoy my now cold soycaf. Since he didn't give me a location, I knew he was coming to me. He'd taken that long pause to trace my IP, so he knew where I'd logged in from. I hadn't bothered hiding it. This is what I wanted. And why I'd sat in the back in the dimmer part of the place.

A half-hour passed before I saw him near the front. He hadn't changed physically. Still small and thin and wearing the nicest wageslave clothing with the highest price tag. Though I did notice a gold pin on his lapel as he went up on his tiptoes and scanned the tables. Dressed as I was, given the cut of my hair and the two-day growth on my face, I doubted he'd even recognize me.

I was right. His eyes moved over me and to the next table. So I raised my hand and waved. Simple. But effective. He looked back at me.

And froze.

At that moment, I wasn't sure if he was going to collapse or bolt. I sort of thought he'd do both, so I stood and walked over to him. His gaze tracked my appearance from my head to my boots and then back up again as I grabbed his upper arm and led him back to my table in the shadows.

When he didn't sit, I leaned in close. "Jericho, sit down."

He sat.

I returned to my chair, and we stared at each other for a few seconds before he said, "You...You look like Crisis. Only you're real."

"I am Crisis. For now."

He swallowed. "It's really you. You're not dead."

"Despite the news about my demise at the hands of what...a shadowrunner team?...I am very much alive. It wasn't runners who nearly killed me, Jericho."

He held up his hand. "Not here. I believe it's you, and I'm trying really, really hard not to break down right here. Just give me a minute." He got up and turned away. I sipped my soycaf. Then when he turned back around, he stared at me. "Tell me that what Mason told Nicole is a lie."

"Sit down. You make me nervous, and you're blocking my view." Which he was. I was happy to see Jericho, and though the old me would have given him a big bear bro hug, this me, Crisis, was a bit more standoffish. Never give one's enemy the impression there's a soul on the planet that means anything to you. Once you do that, their life is forfeit. That was Variant's best advice to me.

Jericho finally sat back down. "You didn't answer."

"Because I don't know what he told her. It must have been a doozy, since she's shacking up with him. Or it might be the drek I've been reading on the Matrix."

"Oh. That." Jericho looked around. "Can we go somewhere more private?"

My privacy was still active, but I realized Jericho wasn't going to relax until we were somewhere he trusted. "Commons?"

"Yeah."

"We go together," I said, not wanting him to get away from me. I hadn't really shaken the idea, the ridiculous thought, that Jericho was working for or had been working for Mason or Apollonius, so I was going to swim on the side of caution.

We left the bar in single file, me behind him, and walked the two blocks to a bench we used to sit on before things got so drekked up. Now he turned to me and jabbed a finger at me. "Look at you! You *did* become a shadowrunner!"

I grabbed his hand and slammed it down on the bench between us. The wires sang, ready for action and I put my face up against his. "I know you always feel more comfortable in the open, Jericho, because you think we can't be bugged here. But there are drones that can pick up a whisper a quarter of a mile away. So I suggest you keep it down. Clear?"

Fear flickered across his face, and I felt responsible. But he recovered quickly. "I'm sorry, Oli—Crisis. I just thought you were...dead. We both did."

"Both?"

"Nicole and I. I mean, when you didn't show up for the court date, and Mason was there with corroborating evidence that you'd been the one to screw up your identity and tried to frame him to make it look like he had, and that you'd emptied your accounts that morning and disappeared, leaving her to pay all that money..." He shrugged. "We didn't want to believe him. Nicole did eventually, given Mason's evidence. It was all so complete, so...damning. I just refused. We had a fight, and I haven't talked to her since."

"You two haven't communicated at all?"

"No." He looked sad. Like a lost child. "After a while she was ready to believe that shit, but I...I knew you. I knew you loved her and your job, and I also knew you were scared about that prototype you were working on." He snapped his fingers. "Is that it? Was it about that?"

"Yes it was—"

"Did you really steal it? They said you wiped the company's nodes, taking the payroll with you."

That son of a bitch. "No, I didn't steal it. No, I didn't take any nuyen. I was kidnapped."

Jericho sat back. "Kidnapped? That morning?"

"Yes. Look, I'll tell you all about it later. Right now, I need to know if you ever went to the locker at the train station and got the bag out of it?"

"The what?"

"I sent you a message right before I disappeared. Did you get it?"

He looked down as if scanning the memories. "I remember something popping up in my inbox in *Dark City*. It said it was from admin, and had a string of numbers." Jericho looked at me. "But yeah, I went to the locker and got the bag out. It had chips in it and a copy of the AMAS contract."

I felt a wave of relief wash over me. "Please tell me you still have all of it?"

Jericho looked worried. "Is it important?"

"Jericho—what did you do with the chips?"

He sort of fidgeted in his seat. "For two months Nicole and I worked together, looking for you. I gave her the bag and showed her the message. She said she stored everything in a safe place because it had to be important. When they told Nicole they'd found your body and everything they claimed about you was true, like I said, I refused to believe it. I couldn't swallow it. And for a while Nicole refused to believe it as well. Eventually she resigned herself to believing you'd done it all to yourself as some elaborate plan and I refused to give in. We parted ways."

"Are you saying Nicole has the chip? Why did you give it her?"

"I thought you were *dead*!"

I felt my heart cave into my chest. Jericho of all people...I thought for sure he'd have kept a back-up of it, even if he lost the original. I held up a hand to ease his protesting. "Okay...do you know if Nicole still has it?"

"I don't." His frowned turned into a mischievous smile. "But we can ask her."

"She'll talk to you?"

"Noooo..." He kept smiling that smile, and it was starting to make me nervous. "But I know where we can talk to her without her fiancé around."

CHAPTER 22

BOSTON HARBOR
FRIDAY, NOVEMBER 8, 2075
AFTERNOON

Nicole stared numbly at the rows and rows of wedding gowns hanging in front of her. After only an hour at this, the sea of white was starting to look like a snowbank, and she was snowblind. One dress looked like the other, and no matter how technology changed over the decades, it seemed the tradition of picking the wedding dress didn't.

Mason was smart to duck out of this ritual, claiming he had duties to perform and a meeting with Apollonius Turk. But he was always meeting with Apollonius these days. With the approach of the acquisition looming just a few weeks away, all their attention was focused on making this new prototype work as well as Oliver's had.

Oliver...

She schooled her features into a mask she knew gave away no thoughts or emotions of what was behind it, yet conveyed to the world that of an accepting, well-educated bride, debutante, and heir. She didn't want anyone to see how she really felt. To see how, as that deadline approached, her thoughts returned to her betrayer as often as breathing. Nicole never wanted to believe Oliver was capable of the deception Mason showed her, but the evidence...especially Oliver's last effort to use his program to destroy her father's private company—

It was unforgivable.

And yet, why was it when her thoughts did return to her sweet, gentle Oliver, those were the words and emotions that surfaced first? Her love for him, her need for his support, his words, his warmth beside her in bed—these were the thoughts that came minutes before the memory of betrayal, and of being left alone that day in court. She remembered how disappointed her father looked when his nuyen was wasted on Oliver's bail, and then the devastation wrought on Nathan O'Neal's face when he lost Commons, Inc., and Mason revealed that it was the work of Oliver's prototype.

No.

Stop.

No more thinking about Oliver.

Mason had been there to pick up the pieces. He had been there for her even after she dumped him for Oliver—

"Miss?"

The voice shocked her out of her thoughts, and she made sure to arrange her expression into a smile. "Yes?" she said before she turned to face the attendant. She hadn't noticed the deeper voice, or the scent of aftershave, until she found herself looking into the face of Jericho.

The mask slipped when he winked at her. "Miss O'Neal, have you chosen a dress?"

She sputtered just a bit as she looked at the open door to the lobby. He wasn't locking her in the room with him, and he wasn't threatening her. But then, why think such things? Jericho had never done anything aggressive in his life, no matter what Mason accused him of. In fact, the only thing Jericho had ever done wrong, in her eyes, was to stay loyal to and supportive of Oliver. And for that, she'd punished him.

Heat rose to her cheeks as she looked away and grabbed the nearest gown. It was a floofy thing, with lots of satin ruffles and sequins, and not something she would normally choose. She couldn't believe Jericho actually worked at the boutique, which meant he was there to talk to her. But why here? And how did he know where she was?

Nicole was also aware of the surveillance cameras, there to protect the gowns. If she said or did anything odd, she was sure Max, the troll Apollonius had assigned to watch out for her, would see it. Ah, but not in the changing rooms. No cameras in there, and she could claim privacy.

"Ah, zat is a Cherie Nostalgia Unlimited," Jericho said in a fake French accent. And a really bad one. She also knew he'd just made up the designer name as well, but only because she could see the real designer's RFID tag through her AR. "Please follow *moi*."

Nicole had a hard time keeping the smirk off her face as he grabbed the dress, in a very non-attendant fashion, wrinkling the satin, and then followed him through the lobby, past Max to one of the back rooms. Jericho stepped inside the room for a few seconds, then stepped out and pointed to her commlink. "I'm afraid zat is not allowed..."

This brought Max up close and personal. But Jericho put up a hand. "Ooh! Broody men. 'ow 'andsome, but it's for the zecurity of zee designer. There iz no oder way in or out. Please, do you wish to enter the ladeez boodwah?"

Max looked a bit embarrassed, and declined entering the women's changing room. Nicole smiled as she removed her commlink and handed it to the troll, frowned at Jericho, and stepped into the room. She was surprised Jericho came in behind her, or that Max allowed him to do so. But she was pretty sure he gave the troll the idea he preferred men.

Once the door closed and the lights dimmed, she turned to see Jericho lock it and pull out a small circular device. He put it on the door above the lock. "We don't have a lot of time, Nicky."

Nicky. Only Jericho had ever called her that. She'd never liked it, but at that moment, it was wonderful. But of course she still gave him her indignant look, so she pointed at him as he checked each of the mirrors with his commlink. "What the hell are you doing, Jer? Because you are *not* a wedding attendant."

Jericho made a face. "No I'm not. I'm here because a situation has come up, and I need your help."

"Mine?" She put her hand to her chest.

He stepped from the mirror, and she noticed he was actually dressed in the shop's uniform. She pointed to his clothing.

"Borrowed, and don't ask how. Oh and you need to strip down and put that dress on."

"What?"

"You want your big-ass handler out there to barge in if you don't come out and show the owner the gown? You can be damn sure Apollonius is watching this drek to make sure you choose a suitable one." He turned away toward a wall without a mirror. "I promise not to look. But just keep picking ugly dresses."

Nicole understood what to do. And it was Jericho, after all. The only man who had never made a pass at her. So she proceeded to undress so she could put on the satin monstrosity she'd chosen. "You called Max my handler."

"Mm-hmm."

"Why?"

"We don't have time for stupid, Nicole. I know what Apollonius Turk is capable of. I know what power he has. And I know how he wields it. Me voluntarily disappearing precluded my involuntary disappearance."

Nicole stopped as she took the gown off the hangar. "What? Mr. Turk doesn't do that kind of stuff. Damn, you sound like the trideos. All of them think the man's some kind of monster."

"Because he *is*." Jericho sighed as Nicole dropped the dress and, wearing little more than a bra, panties, and high heels, stepped into the center of it. She needed a real attendant to help her get it zipped or buttoned or whatever it did. But Jericho would have to do. "But that's not why I needed to talk to you without Mason around."

Ah. It wasn't just Apollonius he didn't trust. "Okay."

"Do you remember the stuff I gave you? Oliver's stuff?"

"Before you disappeared?"

"Nicole, we can have that conversation later. Besides, I'm not the one that abandoned Oliver—"

She turned and looked at his back, the dress heavy on her shoulders. "Now you wait just a damn minute," she hissed, aware she didn't want to bring her attendant—her *handler*—into the dressing room. "*You're* the one that went off the rails and refused to believe irrefutable evidence that Oliver was cheating the company. He stole *Ghost-7*, Jer. I showed you what Mason showed me."

"Yeah. You did. And I didn't believe it. I *know* Oliver, Nicole." Jericho turned and faced her, and she noticed his eyes didn't rake over her half-naked appearance. She focused on his expression, his body language, his tone. "Oliver was betrayed, kidnapped, and beaten, and we were all led to believe he was dead, that he'd sold the prototype to a shadow team that killed him. Seriously..." he shook his head and then shrugged. "So where is this program he sold? Why hasn't someone used it?"

He took a step toward her. "Because that never happened, Nicole."

"Oliver wasn't kidnapped..." She took a step back in the dress, the satin around her rustling uneasily. "He skipped the hearing to sell the prototype."

"No, he didn't."

"Yes, he *did,*" she hissed. Her eyes stung where she held back tears. She couldn't do this right now. Remembering her love while wearing a wedding dress for someone else. *This isn't fair!*

"He was taken from a cafe near the courthouse. Taken by Apollonius's bodyguards, and Mason was the one that set him up."

No.

"He was taken from there to a secret location where he was tortured, day after day, while they tried to find where he'd hidden the prototype."

She shook her head.

"The days blended into night, until I couldn't think anymore, but the only thing, the only light that kept me together, was knowing you needed my protection from those bastards. And then I escaped." The voice changed, deepened, and she put her hands to her face as she stared at an unmoving Jericho. A Jericho who wasn't talking anymore. "I don't know what they did to my mind, Nicole. I lost myself for a while. But now I'm back."

Nicole spun around and the gown's skirt and train sailed out behind her.

He was there. Alive. Standing in the farthest area of the room. He looked older, somehow. Different. His hair was short, and he had few days growth on his face. He wore a leather coat that hung to his thighs. His hands were covered in fingerless gloves, and she spotted a commlink on his wrist. At his back was a crossbow and a rifle.

Saying he was different wasn't just about his physical appearance. There was something to his shoulders, his stance. He stood taller, his shoulders back and his eyes were alive in a way she'd never seen before.

He took a step toward her, and she stumbled back. He stopped. "Nicole."

"You...You died." She hesitated, unsure if she should run, or stand her ground. Fight or flight. She wanted to believe the man in front of her was Oliver. She needed to believe he was as innocent as Jericho believed.

She took a step forward, then another, her right hand out. The ghost of Oliver didn't move. In fact, she knew he was focused on her and his features softened as she poked his chest with her finger. He was solid, real, and hard as brick beneath the coat.

Nicole didn't jump when he reached up and covered her hand with his own and pressed it flat against his chest. "I think a part of me did die. I don't know exactly what they did to me in that hole, but it was enough to erase who I'd been for a while, so I could become what I am now."

Whatever he was, he was different. "And now...you're not Oliver anymore?"

"Mason and Apollonius forced me to grow up, Nicole. They made me what I am today."

Someone banged on the door. "Miss O'Neal?"

Jericho stepped forward. "Let me zip you up."

She allowed it and then looked at herself in the mirror. "I look like..."

"Meringue," Oliver finished, and she smiled.

He smiled. Nothing could cover that dazzling smile of his. "I'm fine!" she yelled back. "Not sure this is the right dress."

"You have to go show them, pick another, and come back," Jericho said. "If you come back and you don't tell them we're here, then Oliver and I will know you trust us."

It was a hell of a risk they were taking. Nicole knew it would take just a word from her and the place would be locked down, and they would be arrested by Knight Errant. But she already knew her decision before picked up the skirt and headed to the door. "Better put that bad accent back on, Jer."

"It's not that bad...is it?" He grabbed up her train as Oliver disappeared again.

"It's drek, Jer," she said as the door opened, and she and Jericho marched out to show off the worst dress ever.

Once the faces were made, and Apollonius's secretary was standing there. *Who called her?* Nicole assumed Max had, and that was fine. At least the secretary would carry on the ruse about finding a dress. She thought it was hideous. Nicole agreed it was hideous, and chose two more dresses, and they went back into the changing room.

Nicole felt her heart rise into her chest when she saw Max come out of the dressing room, then she and Jericho stepped in and shut the door. He put the device over the doorknob again before Oliver appeared and took the dresses from him.

When he turned to face her again she ran to him and this time she didn't poke him. She wrapped her arms around his chest and she felt the comfortable sensation she'd longed to know again as his strong arms enveloped her.

"Nicole," Oliver said gently. "As wonderful as it is to see you, and know you trust us, you have to change dresses. We can't let them come in here."

"Oh, damn," she sighed as she stepped back, a chill making her shiver as his warmth vanished. Jericho came behind her and unzipped the dress. "I thought they'd see you."

"Oliver's gained a few skills," Jericho said as he helped her step out of the dress.

Where Jericho never blinked at her half-nakedness, she caught Oliver's appreciative gaze and waited for it to come level with her own. He blushed red and looked away. "Sorry."

"No, no. I always enjoyed the way you looked at me." She pointed to his commlink. "How much time do we have?"

"Not much," he said as he blinked, and she knew he was accessing his AR. "I should leave after this fitting."

"Leave to where?"

"Nicole," Oliver stepped forward. "Jericho gave you some things of mine. Things I'd left with him. One was a bag of data chips."

"Yes...I remember him giving them to me. He said you sent him a message how to get into a locker after you disappeared. I was mad and hurt—and I kept them for a while. I tried to see what was on them, but I couldn't open them. They were encrypted."

"What did you do with them?" Jericho said.

Nicole had to think back as Jericho brought her the second dress. "I had them saved to my apartment node and then destroyed the actual chips."

"Are those files still there?" Oliver asked.

"No," she stepped into the dress and Jericho helped bring it up to her shoulders. "Everything in my apartment was transferred to Mason's place when I moved."

"So the actual node is in Mason's house?" Oliver narrowed his eyes.

"No. He downloaded everything from my node, including the security protocols and handed them to Apollonius, since he would be handling access in the house."

Jericho and Oliver looked at each other. "Apollonius has the information from the node?" Jericho said.

"No—yes, he does. But the weird thing was they downloaded it all into a node at MIT&T."

MIT&T! The conversation in Elvish. "Why?" Oliver asked.

"I'm not sure. My father was angry about it, though. Said there was financial information on my node that he'd stored there, and he wanted it back." She narrowed her eyes at Oliver. "Mason said father lost his company because of *Ghost-7*. That you used it to destroy him."

"Your father lost Commons, Inc.?"

"Yes. But with Mason's help, he was able to save the rest of the businesses. It was bought by someone named Eponius Kurt." Her shoulders lowered as she straightened up. "Dad's not stupid though. A little digging and it was obvious that Apollonius Turk bought the company before bankruptcy." She looked at Oliver again. "Answer my question, Oliver. You didn't make that happen, did you? With *Ghost-7*?"

"No, Nicole," Oliver said as he stepped close to her. She looked up and he took her breath away. He was ruggedly handsome now. Stern, almost, but she could still see her Oliver in his face. "I don't even have access to *Ghost-7*."

"Mason said you stole it."

"No. I copied everything to chips, and then hid them in a locker—"

She felt her cheeks grow hot again when she realized she was in a wedding gown. "That was on those chips? *Ghost-7*?"

"Yeah. I never stole it, I just didn't want NeoNET getting their hands on it yet. There were...there were things about it that I didn't like, things I questioned."

She lowered her head. "I am so sorry. You risked your life to protect your work and I literally gave it all to Apollonius Turk."

Jericho laughed. "Yeah be he apparently doesn't know he has it. I'm betting it's still on that node as some superfluous file no one can identify."

Oliver looked past her to Jericho. "You know what I have to do, and what I need."

He nodded. "I'll find out. How will I contact you?"

"I'll contact you," Oliver looked back down at her. "Thank you. I just wanted you to know I never betrayed you."

And with that, someone pounded on the door again. Nicole turned to yell at them to stop that, and when she looked back, Oliver was gone. She turned to face Jericho. "What's he going to do?"

"Something stupid." Jericho turned her back around so he could button up her dress. It was a tad big, and just as ugly as the first one. "He's gonna break into MIT&T."

CHAPTER 23

MIT&T
BOSTON
SATURDAY, NOVEMBER 9, 2075

The MIT&T video lab was located in the Weisner Building on the corner of Amherst and Ames, just a few blocks over from the harbor. The sun set at its usual early time, it being December, but we'd already decided where I would be.

Vertigo and her people, Chaz and Liza, a set of twin elves, agreed that scaling the wall was the best point of entry. We had the schematics uploaded to the group, and Variant made sure we had our positions marked.

He also hired a local rigger, a dwarf named Sherry, whom he trusted to get us out of the area, fast.

Three buildings formed a sort of triangular courtyard. The Weisner, the Spell Building, formerly known as the Mudd building, and the Division of Health, Sciences, and Magic. I was able to do a small amount of reconnaissance before the sun started setting, and Variant's assessment was right. The courtyard was poorly-lit, with only three lamps. And the campus security drones made their passes in increments of twenty minutes. They appeared to be on a loop, according to Loki, who spent most of the afternoon watching them.

We each approached the Weisner Building from a different direction at a different time. I was scheduled earliest and first, along with Sherry, before the doors were locked and secured.

I slipped in through a back entrance with Loki in fox shape on my shoulder, and kept to the stairs, making sure I avoided any cameras flagged in the plans. I'd already checked the lab's schedule for tonight. The place would be closed and empty, with no events, lectures, or parties scheduled.

The roof of the Media Lab was a miasma of shapes and levels. The side facing Ames Street had walls that looked like risers. On the corner and the Amherst Street side was a roof terrace just outside a conference room. Walls of windows separated the two. A rounded V-shaped roof covered the area from the weather. I'd been inside that building a great deal in my youth. Attending talks in the lecture hall on the opposite side. I knew where the blank spots were for the drones, since the rotation on the sixth floor was limited, so setting up a few cables for climbing was easy. Especially since the silver cables blended right in with the iron grid-work on the Ames Street side.

Variant had argued with changing the exit strategy from the entrance, but given the city's use of drones, I liked the idea of the exit cables being beside a roof that obstructed the view of a group of shadowrunners escaping.

I spotted Sherry's GMC stepvan, then reported my position to Variant and gave the team the coordinates of the escape cables. Loki changed her shape, dressed, and grabbed her tools out of my bag before she climbed a few of those block walls to check on Chaz and Liza and their progress on the climb up and in. I could see everyone's approach and made sure no one could see me in the shadows cast by the setting sun.

Overall, I wasn't happy about this plan. It felt a bit over the top to me. But Variant had something in mind. I just hoped there wouldn't be mistakes due to the addition of Vertigo and her people. This should be a clean snatch and vanish...not some opening for a personal vendetta.

Not that I didn't have one. I just preferred to work in the shadows. Strike when no one was expecting it.

I joined Loki on the far side of the Media Lab building, opposite of Amherst Street. We crouched in the shadows, and at the designated time I lined up my first bolt as the drone came around the corner of the building. The wires in my muscles sung as I squeezed the trigger, and the arrowhead landed on target against the disk-shaped flying saucer. It wobbled a second before I got the all clear that Jericho's feed was synced up. He'd created a loop for each of the three drones, specific to their path around the building. Each one recorded with a randomizer for passing cars and students. It wouldn't fool the human or metahuman eye for long if they were paying attention, as the same thing would eventually show up again and again, but it should last long enough to get the job done.

The second and third drones were compromised in the same way, and we waited to get the all clear from Jericho.

<*You got maybe twenty minutes. The loops are ten minutes long, and once someone spots the repeat of something, they'll start snooping.*>

<*Thanks Jer,*> I answered and headed back to the cords hanging over the building. Two were already moving as the team ascended. I chanced a look over the side and spotted Variant and Pearl on one, then Vertigo and Chaz on the other. <*Where's Liza?*>

Vertigo waited until she was topside with us before answering verbally. "I'm not sure. She's not caught, though. Chaz would know it."

I looked at Chaz. He was an exceptionally tall elf, with a shaved, tattooed head and a few chrome enhancements. Because of the shadows I couldn't read his face, but I read his body language. He wasn't worried about his missing twin.

And that worried *me.*

I texted Variant on our private channel. <*I don't like not knowing where Liza is. Twin here isn't anxious about her. That tells me he knows she's doing something else.*>

<*I agree, but we don't have time. If they screw up this mission, we leave them. Got it?*>

I didn't like it, but I agreed with it. We were all operating as a team because we needed to if we were to going to survive this. Hitting a node in MIT&T didn't seem like such a big deal, but given this was technology and thaumaturgy? It worried the hell out of me. I wasn't exactly gifted with magic, nor did I really understand it. But I had a healthy respect for it.

Loki stepped forward and sniffed the air. "We move now."

We crouched low and followed Pearl over the multi-height roof and landed on the open terrace in front of the conference room and the wall of windows. She stood in front of it, her hands moving in front of her. Within seconds, the door popped open and we paused. No alarms.

Variant went in first, followed by Vertigo. Chaz, Loki, and I remained outside.

<*Chris, you have to come with us,*> Pearl said in group.

<*Me? Why me?*>

<Because I need you to show me what I'm looking for.>

Drek.

<Come on. Loki and Chaz will be okay as lookouts.> He meant that Loki would be okay with Chaz. Truthfully—I would be afraid for Chaz if he tried anything that irritated or angered the little fox. I'd seen her temper when unleashed.

I set my crossbow on my back, grabbed my pistol, and followed them in. They were already past the reception space. I moved quickly down the hall past the kitchen to the stars in the back. Within minutes they were two floors down, with Pearl ahead of them, and me bringing up the rear behind everybody.

I didn't like this closed-in space. I was used to being on rooftops or in alleys where the sky was always there. Enclosed made me nervous. It also activated my melee skillsoft, which made me even more jumpy.

<Cameras are connected to Jericho's switch. We've got less than twenty minutes.>

I brought up the rear as we descended to the bottom of floor three. We paused at the bottom door as Pearl held up her hand. Again we made it through to the next level to floor two, and each time she left the door unlocked as Jericho made sure the security system believed otherwise.

Once in the basement node room, the wireframe map appeared in front of me, overlaid on my cybereyes. The door itself didn't look like much. Just another door with a lock knob. Once it opened and popped toward Pearl, she reached a hand out to me. "Come on."

"Go on. Vert and I will stand out here." Variant checked his chronometer. "We've got thirteen minutes."

I moved past him and the Ancient and put my hand in hers. There was an odd sensation that traveled up my arm to my neck and into my head as I stumbled after her.

We stopped just inside the door, where my vision played tricks on me. I saw dozens of boxes in a large room. It looked like someone's basement, or what my parents' garage used to look like. "This can't be right."

"You're not seeing the reality, Chris. This is the inside of the building's mainframe. All those boxes are nodes, and each one stores different things."

"Mainframe, but how—" and then I saw Serilious in all his ugly glory. We were in the Matrix, sort of. But she was pulling me along with her. Looking down, I saw I was my Crisis persona, in tight black leather, crossed swords, and pointed ears.

She pulled me along behind her, and I swore I could smell soured socks and mildew, as if we were really inside a basement or a cellar. "The node we're looking for isn't on the mainframe. So what we need to do is look at the room with both eyes. Use my eyes, the basement view, and use your eyes, the reality of your cybereyes. The one node that doesn't look like a box of junk is the one we want."

I had no understanding of the mechanics of what she wanted, but it seemed simple enough. So with my hand still in hers, I unfocused on the spread of boxes in front of me and tried to concentrate in my cybereyes. The sudden shift was disorienting. So was Sherry's icon popping up in my AR.

<Sorry guys, but I had to move the van. There's something interesting happening on the Ames side. A huge troll and a bunch of suits just got out of a limo and they're heading inside the building. I don't think they saw the cables.>

Troll and a bunch of suits? *<Sherry, can you send us a shot of them?>*

<Not now.> Variant's persona popped up. *<Get busy!>*

I made a note of where she moved the car too, across Amherst but parked on Ames, before I refocused on the double-vision. Well, not so much double-vision, but triple. I had my normal sight, which showed me a pretty large room with six-foot and ten-foot nodes in even rows. The room was sort of dark, with the red hue of an exit light to my left. Then, when I looked at it with my cybervision, I could see the grid overlay with named nodes. And when I added in what Pearl saw and the boxes appeared...

And there it was. In the back to the right. A six-foot node with no grid marker and no box image. I pulled her to it and stopped as she put her other hand on it and closed her eyes.

Abruptly I was in an office building with her, walking behind as she passed room upon room of open doors. I looked in as many as I could, but they were empty, or had very little in them, other than a desk or sometimes a bed or another door. Eventually I looked into a room after we made a right turn, and saw a terminal locker just like the one I'd left the original missive in. I stopped and pulled her back and pointed.

She stepped in, her hand still in mine as she put her free hand on the locker. It opened and inside was a letter. She picked it up and handed it to me. <*Is this it?*>

<*It...It's a letter.*>

<*In here it's a letter. Touch it and you'll know if it's yours. You'll see what's inside. I can't.*>

I gingerly took the envelope from her, but it was empty. I checked twice. Someone had taken the information from this node and erased all trace of it, but left the envelope, the packet that once had the information, right where it should be. <*It's not here.*>

Suddenly we weren't in the abandoned office building anymore, but standing in the middle of what looked like the north pole. Something told me this wasn't real, that it was just part of the software, the environment, but that didn't explain why I was suddenly very damn cold.

Serilious donned a fur coat. "This is bad."

"Y-Y-Yeah..."

"Chris, you're a game character. Grab a coat from your inventory."

Inventory? I checked and actually found my bag. There I rummaged through and put on a thick, floor-length fur. Not exactly fashionable, but effective. "Why are we in the north pole? We still on the off-grid node?"

"Yes. And someone installed IC on it."

That...made no sense. Why would anyone put that kind of protection software on an off-grid node? I said as much.

"I don't know. But I can't find the door out. And as long as you're holding my hand, you can't get out either."

Drek.

Snow started falling fast as she took off at a run in the direction of a shack. I ran after, all the while thinking there was someone or something behind me. So when I stopped to look, my jaw dropped and I stumbled back in the ankle deep snow.

It was a good fourteen feet in the air, the size of an arcology, and covered in white fur. And it had teeth as big as me. I screamed like a little girl. I had never seen anything so big or so real in any game I'd ever played.

<*Run Chris! That's Black Ice!*>

Serilious was beside me, pulling me to my feet. We both started running to the shack with that thing lumbering behind us. We were nearly there when I chanced a look back and stumbled. It roared, I roared, and then I closed my eyes. I was pushed aside by something and then silence. Just the ticking of snow around me. When I opened my eyes, I could see Vertigo standing in front of me, facing away. There was no sign of the gigantic snow thing.

"Vertigo!" I shouted as I scrambled to my feet. "Let's go!"

But when I touched her, she didn't move. I moved to stand in front of her, but she was as still as a statue, and as hard. I stumbled back in horror as I realized she was covered in a thin layer of ice.

"Chris!" Serilious' voice echoed around the snow.

I screamed at Vertigo and started hitting her, trying to break the ice. Some of it cracked, but some of it seemed to get thicker.

"Chris, look at me!"

And then her eyes moved and she looked at me and I saw a frozen tear as it dropped from her cheek.

Someone hit me, hard, and I reacted because of the wires. I struck and they struck back and then I was being held down on the ground with lots of people talking to me.

"—Calm down!—"

"—Damn it, he broke my nose!—"

"—You got her?—"

"—Yeah, but you need to wake him up!—"

"—I swear I'm gonna kill that bitch!—"

I blinked to clear the fog and looked up into the faces of Loki and Variant, with Vertigo on my right. Above them stood Chaz and in his arms was—Vertigo. She wasn't moving. "I thought...where's Pearl?"

"I'm right here," Pearl leaned over Variant's head. She was pale and she looked devastatingly tired, but she was alive. "I started to charge in front of the IC, but Vertigo showed up and pushed me out of the way. I'm afraid it got her instead of me."

"How did she—?" Then I saw the wires coming out of Vertigo's datajack. She'd actually jacked into the node itself. But why?

Chaz said. "We have to get out of here."

I was on my feet, though unsteady, in minutes. "What the fuck happened?"

"IC," Pearl said. "Your friend Jericho tried to stop it, but he didn't have access to the node."

"How...why did..." But I was still shaking.

Variant said as stood, "It was taking you too long, so she went in manually just as Jericho warned us an IC protocol had been activated. Right now, we've got to get out of here. Loki and Chaz had to join us when the drones switched their movements. I can only guess the loop's been discovered."

"Are we trapped? I heard Sherry say there was a troll and suits," I said.

Loki took my hand and I put my arm on her shoulders. She was shivering. "Loki?"

"She cast a cloaking spell," Chaz said. "That allowed us to get down here. But it won't last much longer, so she's a little tired. You know how big spells wear her out."

Variant motioned for everyone to follow him to the door into the node room. Once outside, he turned to face Chaz. "You need to come clean with me, Chaz, right now, because if Vertigo doesn't make it, I'm not having the Ancients blame me."

Pearl put her hand on Var's arm. "Not now. We've got to get out of here. Jericho's made a passage for us to go through to get to the GMC."

Jericho's persona popped up. <*Everyone okay?*>

<*No,*> Variant replied. <*Give us the map.*>

A new wireframe map showed up on my AR, and I overlaid it to the actual building. <*Oh hell, Jer. We have to get back to the roof?*>

<*I'm afraid so. The only way back out is straight up. Everything has been locked down. They're aware of a breach, they just haven't figured out how and where yet. You're going to have to get back to the cables at the terrace. Once you're down, I can get you. But you're gonna have to do it fast before they call in backup...crap, they called Knight Errant.*>

<*We're on our way.*> Variant looked at Pearl. "You up for some more hacking?"

"Damn right I am. Sons of bitches." She put a hand on Chaz's arm, then one on the unmoving Vertigo before she headed back to the stairs.

Loki jumped on my back, over my bow and held on as we ascended the stairs and I hoped like 'effing hell we could get to the roof office with little interference.

<*Oh hell...whose drones are* those?> Came the message from Jericho.

So much for hoping.

CHAPTER 24

SATURDAY, NOVEMBER 9, 2075
LATE EVENING

"Nicole—"

"Dad," she placed her elbows on the table, a very unladylike thing to do. But dinner was finished, the dishes cleared away, and dessert was coming. She clutched her soycaf in both hands, the warmth from the ceramic reassuring. Her wine was half-empty, and her father's coffee long gone. "Remember when you said marrying Mason was a bad idea?"

Nathan O'Neal had been checking his AR for messages. His eyes refocused on her, through the images in front of him, and he blinked. She watched as he shut down his AR and leaned forward. "Say...say that again?"

"You're not funny."

"I'm not trying to be, especially when it sounds like my daughter might be coming to her senses." He looked from his left to his right before he leaned his own elbows on the table and lowered his voice. "Do you finally believe me?"

"Daddy I've always believed you about Mason. I just didn't have a choice."

"What—you're not pregnant, are you?"

Nicole shuddered. "No. I—I know what he did to your company. I mean, I know how he did it."

"You what?"

"Listen to me," she put her hand on his and spoke in a lower voice as well. "I know he sabotaged Common, Inc. so he could take it over."

Nathan's voice was harsh. "Then you need to tell me how he did it. That bastard actually threatened to take my other companies if—"

She leaned forward. "If what?"

"Nothing. I told him no. And so far nothing's happened."

Nicole's shoulders slumped. "This...this is all my fault then, isn't it?"

"No," Nathan squeezed her hand. "It's not. Oliver's betrayal was just too much for you—"

"Oliver didn't betray me or you, or Andreas Martin, Dad." Nicole stopped herself right there. Actually telling him that Oliver was still alive wouldn't do anyone any good. Her father was a just man, and if he still believed Oliver was guilty, he'd feel compelled to turn him in. So maybe it was better to start slow and just save his reputation. "Oliver didn't show up that morning because he was kidnapped."

"What?"

"It's true. I have the proof, and I want you to see it." Meaning Oliver, just not now. "He was kidnapped and drugged and tortured by Turk. And he was killed by one of Turk's assassins."

Nathan started to lean back, then stopped. "That doesn't make any sense. Why would Apollonius Turk do that?"

"Because he believed Oliver had the prototype in his possession."

"He said Oliver sold it."

"He didn't, Dad," Nicole said. "And he never stole it. Yes he downloaded it before the trip we took north, the one where he asked me to marry him. But he did it to keep it safe, not to steal it. There's a lot to tell you, and this really isn't the place. Just... believe me when I say Oliver Martin was not the man Mason painted him to be."

"Nicole, I've seen the evidence the Boston Metro Police had on this guy. His ties to shadowrunners? Are you sure he didn't steal it like they said he did?"

She straightened up in her chair and squared her shoulders. "I'm positive, Dad. Oliver was set up, and he paid the price for Mason's greed."

Nathan stared at her for a few minutes before he hung his head. "You're marrying him in a week, Nicole. If you've changed your mind, you better have an exit strategy."

"I can...I can make one. Just as long as I know you're not worried about the company?"

"Screw the company. What do you need from me?"

"Miss?" The waiter said as he approached their table and then touched her arm. "There's a man here to see you. He says he's a friend of Chris."

Chris? She gave him a blank look, a bit of panic rising up inside, and then she remembered *Crisis...Chris. Oliver!* She smiled. "Oh yes. Can you show him to the table?"

"I'm afraid he's asked to speak with you alone."

Alone could mean it wasn't a friend, but Oliver himself, and he didn't want to be seen, not that anyone would recognize him the way he looked now. She kinda liked this new rugged version of Oliver...no, Chris.

Crisis.

"Nicole?"

Her father looked apprehensive but she squeezed his hand. "It's okay. They're from the caterer. I'll be right back."

He returned her smile, but he still looked worried.

She followed the waiter around the tables, past the lobby and coat check and into the bar lounge. She looked around, not recognizing anyone. "Where is he?"

The waiter looked behind her, nodded and stepped away. Nicole turned and looked into the off handsome face of a very tall, very red-headed elf. His hair was brushed back over his forehead and eyes above a long, straight nose. A van dyke the same color as his hair decorated his chin. He wore a nice tailored suit in black, and when he grinned she caught the faint points of fangs.

This was a vampire!

She opened her mouth, and he put his finger on his lips and winked. "Careful," he said in a pleasant tone. "Don't let the teeth give you some weird idea I want to bite you. I don't. And I *am* here on behalf of Crisis."

Oliver knew...*vampires?*

"I—"

"No," he shook his head and his hair fell over his eyes. "Let me do the talking. My name's Rick Lang, but everyone calls me Red. I've been following you ever since you met with Jericho and Crisis at the bridal shop. Ah, ah...let me finish. It's been for your protection. You're being followed by someone else who isn't me."

"You—who?"

"From their clothing and demeanor, I'd say occult investigators. When I spotted them outside, I ducked in to make sure you were safe, and decided I should—"

Nicole had been facing the bar and Red, the door. He trailed off as his gaze slid off her and something else behind her. His eyes widened and she started to turn to see what he was seeing. She managed a small turn just before he wrapped his arms around her and spun her to face him as if they were in an embrace, with his body now blocking her from anyone coming into the room. Nicole understood what he was doing, but it made her very, *very* uncomfortable.

Until she glanced at the door and saw a few very surly-looking characters walk through the lobby away from them. She followed them as long as she could with her eyes. "Red, are those the ones following me?"

"Yeah, but I don't know what they're doing in here. Normally they just follow, not engage. I knew something was up," he snapped his fingers. "Come on. Need to get you out of here."

He grabbed for her hand but she pulled it away. "I can't leave. My father's in there."

"That old guy's your dad, eh?" Red peeked around the corner. "Nicely preserved for a human."

She started to say he'd been human once, but that wasn't true. He'd once been an elf. "He's in great shape. If we leave we have to —"

Angry voices interrupted the hum of restaurant talk. Nicole saw heads turn, so she walked back to the entrance to the dining area to see the two men in front of their table, flashing badges.

"They've got badges! What're they doing with my father?" Normally, during any other time, no one could have heard Nicole. But the scene with the two men had quietened the nearby conversations, so that everyone heard her. All eyes turned to her and the red headed elf beside her.

"There she is!"

"Drek!" Red said and grabbed Nicole's hand. But she wasn't going quietly. At least, not until she saw one of them heading for her.

"Come *on*!" Red called out as they headed to the door.

Nicole ran into the back of him as he stopped. "What?" she hissed.

"There are two more on the street." He paused. "Come on." They headed back into the bar lounge again, past the crowd at the door who'd left their seats and the bar to see what was going on. Red pulled her behind the bar and then gestured for her to get under it.

"They'll see us under here," she said. "Or the bartender will. "

"No, they won't. Just be very quiet." He knelt beside her, closed his eyes and held out his hands. Light formed in each palm as he brought the two together into a single glowing orb. Once that happened the light reached out and engulfed him and Nicole. He grabbed the bar to steady himself as he knelt, and then got underneath with her.

"I saw them go in there!" said a voice.

Red put a finger to his lips again as they sat under the bar, very visible to anyone who stopped behind it.

Boots stomped on nearby marble, and Nicole held her breath. The squeak and scuff of leather and then, "Check behind the bar."

Her eyes widened at Red, panicked. *They'll see us!* But he just winked and kept making the *shh* gesture.

Nicole looked up—straight into the face of one of the men with badges. He stood at the bar's corner and looked under, then straightened. "Not here."

"Then they went out a back door. I'll get the father, you go after them. And shoot that red-headed freak."

Nicole would have bolted at the mention of her father, but Red reached out and held her still for a few more seconds, then he motioned her out and helped her stand. He put his finger to his lips again as he did this odd dance where he didn't touch anyone as they headed for the door again. Nicole followed his path as they reached the door and slipped out to the street. Red grabbed her hand and they started running away from the restaurant as her heart dropped in her chest.

Eventually they made it to a small park, where Red collapsed on the grass behind a copse of trees. At first she thought he was kidding, but when she saw his eyes were closed and he wasn't moving, she panicked. "Red?" She knelt beside him and then started shaking him. "Wake up!" she hissed. "What's wrong? What can I do?"

Red finally reached up and put a hand on her shoulder. "Please...stop shaking me before I throw up."

"Oh, damn..." She caught her breath and sat back. "What's wrong? Why are you white as a sheet now?"

"Invisibility spell..." he said in a whisper. "Improved, I might add. Damn...I didn't know it had such a kick. It's got a drain on it that sucked the life out of me. Literally." He grinned, his bone-white fangs really visible in the light from a nearby street light. "Sorry. I had to make sure they didn't see you."

"But they saw my dad!" She started to get up. "I have to go get him away from them."

"No...Nicole, please!" he hissed and stumbled, and then fell again as she started to move away again. "You can't. That's why they took him. They want you."

"Who?"

"My guess is it's Apollonius Turk. Nasty fucker. And you don't want him catching you."

She stopped and stared down at him. "Apollonius sent them after me and my dad?"

"Just you, I imagine. They've been following you. I can only guess something's happened, or they got the command to pounce. Sorry about your dad, though." He rolled over and lay on his back, arms out at his sides. "Oh...I feel like shit."

"You...you didn't have to do that."

"Yeah, I did," Red said as he pushed himself into a sitting position...sort of. "Pearl paid me. And you mean a lot to Crisis. You're also leverage, Nicole. Or you could be used as leverage. Against him. Especially if they realize that Crisis is your old lover."

"They told you?"

"Eh...I'm an information broker. I knows a lot." He put his hand to his mouth. "Uh...except how to recover nicely from a kick-ass spell. Did you see that? That guy looked right at us and never saw us."

"Yeah...that was impressive." She walked to him and offered him her hand. "So now what do we do?"

"I get you to Crisis and make sure you're safe. You can pretty much bet you'll be getting a call from Apollonius in a bit, asking you to turn yourself in to him and your father goes free." He batted her hand away and started a very not-elegant stand.

"This...this can't be happening. I mean I know he tortured Oliver, and he's got some issues—"

Red laughed as he made it up on two feet and then leaned on a nearby tree. "Issues? That's like saying the corps have a slight problem with obeying the law. Turk's a sicko. But he gets things done. And from what Pearl's told me, Crisis messed up a big project for him. So, let's go before they think to look here." He stood, tested his balance, and then wobbled past her.

"You need some help?" She said as she caught up to him.

"Nah. Remember when I said I didn't want to bite you? Well, that changed in the last few minutes. And I don't bite clients."

Nicole hung back just a little and followed the tall elf with his long coat into the evening.

CHAPTER 25

MIT&T
BOSTON
SATURDAY, NOVEMBER 9, 2975
EVENING

Going back up the stairs was nerve-wracking. I could hear the stomp of boots, hear voices shouting, but I didn't know what was happening beyond the confined silo of steps we kept spiraling up.

Chaz kept up at a good pace, even with Vertigo's body in his arms. I stayed in the back, keeping an eye on our rear. The wires hummed. Ready. Willing. And wanting. I wanted to kill someone for what they did to Vertigo. What they'd tried to do to those lynchpins we saved. And what they had done to me. I blamed Mason too, but I knew he wasn't the mastermind. He was a tool. Nothing more.

Once Variant and Loki reached the top, Pearl moved past them and put her hand on the door. A few seconds, and it popped open. She glanced back at Variant. "They know where we are."

"Shit." He pulled his weapon off his shoulder and readied it. I had my pistol for short range fighting, but I had plenty of ammo for my rifle and crossbow.

Lots of fun surprises.

Variant went out first for cover, followed by Loki. I knew she was using magic because I could see her hands moving, but I didn't know *what* she was doing. Pearl motioned for Chaz to proceed then paused with her hand on my chest.

"What?" I said in a horse whisper.

In answer I heard the first shot impact somewhere close and Variant's surprise yell. He and Loki came back in the door and crouched behind it. I peered out to see at least half a dozen drones flying in at a good clip. A few were already arriving and taking up positions along the media lab's roof.

My cybereyes focused as the HUD sync'd with my AR and the tags started pouring in. Seven drones, two distraction-specific; Horizon Flying Eyes both outfitted with a flash-pack and smoke grenade. One fly-spy, MCT, no weapon augmentation (someone just wanted to watch us die). Four illegally-armed and heavily-armored MCT-Nissan roto-drones. Two carried Ares Desert Strike rifles and two carried Crockett EBRs. Those last two worried me a little since the Crocketts were capable of burst strikes. I suspected there were support drones nearby for reload, but they were out of range.

The four MCT drones brought up my fight or flight response. I swore under my breath and went through my inventory. I didn't have anything for what I needed to do.

<*Loki, can you make a smoke screen?*> I asked.

<*A what?*>

<*He means like a fog. Can't you just shoot them?*> Variant messaged.

I answered, <*Nothing I have is going to stop them from firing on us if we take off across the roof to the cables.*> I gave him the list of specs I had. <*We have to be invisible. Their sensors could be scrambled by some kind of thick fog. They may look new and shiny, but I'll bet they're working off the same optics.*>

<*Unless they have thermal,*> Chaz piped up.

Variant said, <*Yeah and then one of us could fall off the roof because we couldn't see the edge. I don't buy it. We can take out the recons, blind the bastards a bit.*>

I pursed my lips as I kept track of their movements. Whoever was piloting them knew the area we were in pretty well. <*I agree. We've gotta be careful of the eyes as well. If those grenades or flash bombs go off, we'd be vulnerable.*>

I was out of options.

Then Chaz broke in. <*Loki, how's your invisibility? Basic or improved?*>

<*Improved. Yours?*>

<*As well. I can cover myself and Vertigo. Loki, can you cover Pearl?*>

Her persona frowned. <*I want to cover Crisis.*>

I smiled at her. "I know. But Variant and I are gonna run cover while you four get across the roof to the cables."

She looked put out, but agreed, and I put my hand on the top of her head. Her ears twitched and she grinned.

At that moment one of the MCTs dove in close and unloaded several rounds from its Desert Strike. Shrapnel flew everywhere. Loki turned and pounced on me, knocking me backward behind a row of chairs. Several panes from the Conference Room wall shattered and the rest of us scattered out of the way to find shelter.

Once the drone disappeared, probably to reload, I sat up and brushed the glass from my hair and Loki's snow white locks as she examined me. "We gotta take those fragging things out."

A movement behind me made me turn and raise my pistol as I pushed Loki behind me, but it was just Chaz. He'd sat Vertigo on the ground, propped up against one of the remaining glass wall supports.

"What're you doing?" Variant hissed as he and the others came close while crouching.

Chaz shook his head. "Vertigo is no longer with us. Taking her body is a burden. But like this, she can be a warning to the others that the Ancients are watching." He pulled his gun from his hip and checked the ammo.

"You'd leave her here?" I wasn't sure I liked this idea.

"Yes." Chaz nodded and put a hand on my shoulder. "But she will be avenged, will she not?"

I knew he meant avenged by me. That whatever I planned on doing with *Ghost-7* would be enough. I nodded, and he squeezed my shoulder before releasing it.

The blasting started then as two other MCTs moved in. One armed with the Crockett and the other with a Desert Strike. The smell of carbon scoring and seared plastic filled the space, as well as smoke. This time we didn't give either of them the opportunity to strike. Me, Chaz, and Variant fired at the two MCTs and destroyed them. Variant gestured at Chaz, Loki and Pearl. "Go, go, go!"

The three of them went invisible. Even my cybereyes couldn't pick up their signatures.

Variant held up his weapon. <*Sherry, you ready?*>

<*Yeah...but don't take too long. No one's really noticed me yet, but if they do, I can't stay. I can't afford no KE entanglements.*>

"Just hang tight," Variant said into his commlink.

I replaced my gun in my holster and retrieved my crossbow. I pulled a nice explosive headed bolt from the quiver on my hip, nocked it, and nodded at Variant.

"We're gonna have to make a run for those cables. You go, and I'll cover you."

"No," I watched the skies for the other two MCTs and that last Flying Eye. "You first. Make sure the others got down safe." I held up my free hand when he started to protest. "We got this."

After a slight hesitation, Variant ran out, firing at the next MCT to show itself. The other Desert Strike had returned. It fired back a few times, missed, and then exploded. I ran out behind him and aimed at the MCT fly-spy that'd been sheltering behind it, the skillwires singing as I targeted and released. I didn't wait for the boom before I ran for cover behind one of the food stands on the terrace and just missed being shot by the last MCT with the Crockett. The weapon laid waste to a swath of cement to my left, and I covered my head to try and protect my face. My eyes avoided damage as flying chunks of concrete battered the left side of my face. I hissed at the sting and risked a look-see.

<Hey you alive? That mother hit too close. You gotta watch them CBRs, Chris.>

And we'd just taken out the only fly-spy I'd seen. *<I'm alive. You know that can't be the only one they have.>*

<Probably not,> Variant replied. *<I'm sure they're gonna depend more on those Flying Eyes with the packs. Looks like they don't see the others. They're moving down the cables.>*

As a roto-drone with the Ares Desert Strike came tearing around the left side of the building, firing at Variant, he ran for cover as well behind a Stuffer Shack kiosk as one of the two Flying Eyes divebombed it. I looked away and squeezed my eyes closed as the whole structure exploded and the flash-pack went off. I shouted out to him, and he sent me a signal that he was fine just as his persona disappeared from my AR. His commlink must have been hit—I hoped—which meant he was offline from the rest of us.

I reported that to everyone as I aimed at the Ares Desert Strike, targeted, listened to the sing and hum of the wires, and released. Another explosion.

I only had two more explosive bolts, along with one shocker and one poison. The shocker would act like a tiny EMP blast and would bring the drone down without power. The only other three heads I had were feeds, which wasn't going to help much.

<*Jericho, you there?*>

<*Yes... Pearl, Loki, and Chaz have reached the sidewalk below. They're behind the screen right now, but Ames Street is crawling with KE. You two need to get out of there. They're gonna need cover.*>

<*What? Why are they visible?*>

<*Chaz got hit. He fell over the side just out of sight, but that made him and Pearl visible.*>

Damn it!

<*Can Loki cover Pearl? Variant's link is severed but he should be on his way down. I got two bogeys left and two shots. But only one's gonna take actually take out a drone.*>

Jericho said, <*I'll see if she can. I think the magic's taking its toll on her. Oliver, you need to get out of there now. KE's sending reinforcements.*>

Which meant more drones. Shit.

<*Jericho, when I loaded those drones before with looped feeds, did the drones also see the feed?*>

I caught a movement to my right, close to the terrace railing. Recognizing Variant's form, I waved for his attention and made hand signals for him to start down the cables. He nodded.

That's when my internal alarms went off in all directions. I'd let my guard down while checking on Variant. The last Flying Eye came careening down from the roof and arced in toward my location. The wires sang, and I lifted my crossbow to shoot it with my last shocker. But I never pulled the trigger as the Crockett-equipped MCT came from below and let loose the burst fire I'd worried about since the drones first arrived.

I screamed as bullets clipped across my right side and shoulder and dropped the crossbow. So much smoke, how did it find me so easy? Infra-red? Another fly-spy? It's shocking what goes through my head as I'm pumping out blood and crawl-rolling behind what was left of the kiosk Variant had taken shelter behind.

Agony brought me back to those first hours of awakening to this new life. The drive and desire to live, to survive, screamed at me above the ever-present pain. My right side and shoulder burned, and I couldn't move my right arm. I could hear the telltale hum of the drones as they circled around. The flash-pack didn't detonate. Whoever was piloting it wanted a good shot of me dying.

<*Oliver! Say something! Your icon's flickering. Answer me! Are you there?*>

It was Jericho filling up the text box in my AR HUD. Followed by another message—

<*Can you get to your crossbow?*> That was Variant.

<*I can't...hold it...*> I was getting dizzy fast, and making a bloody mess on the floor. I'd lost all feeling in my right hand and fingers and the wires screamed along my muscles. I narrowed my eyes, as if that could allow me to see through the haze and darkness. I caught a glint of metal and knew from the RFID tags on my cybereyes the crossbow was less than a meter to my left. <*Yes–but my wires are useless. It...took out my arm–*>

<*I know. I saw it. You're going to have to manually shoot the Flying Eye–*>

<*No! I have to take out the last MCT before it reloads.*>

<*Let me worry about that. Everyone else is with Sherry. That Horizon piece of drek is coming back for more. Take it out!*>

The only reason Variant would want that particular drone destroyed was because it was the last of its kind. Apparently KE hadn't brought more than the two, or the others hadn't seen anymore. Escaping without detection depended on getting rid of it. After that, escape would depend on Sherry's rigger ability. I had no illusions to my destiny. I was losing blood, and consciousness. I wasn't going to make it off this terrace.

The buzz grew louder. The sound spurned me forward as I belly crawled to my crossbow, pulling myself forward. Once I had my left hand on the handle I pulled it close, and had to pause as my vision blurred.

I closed my eyes, not trusting anything I could see, and thought back to the time I'd spent on a real shooting range. Yeah I had the wires, and the pirated skill-soft, but I also had something my dad used to talk about. Muscle memory.

I managed to get my hand on the trigger and stayed still long enough to "see" the drone in my mind by the sound of it, drowning out the shouts of people below and the clomp of footsteps approaching my position. KE would soon be on me. I couldn't fail the rest of the team.

I turned onto my left side, then on my back, pointed the crossbow at the pinpointed sound and fired. I was rewarded with a small explosion and the sound of raining shrapnel. I collapsed back and prepared to clumsily pass out.

The weapon was yanked out of my hand and I was unceremoniously pulled up and onto my feet. I had enough sense to know I was being slung over someone—or some*thing's*—shoulder. I made a feeble effort to fight.

"Stop that," Variant said in the surrounding chaos. "Just hold on."

After that it was better to keep my eyes closed as Variant moved beneath me. I know I blacked out because when I opened my eyes again, we were in Sherry's GMC. I was on the floor and Loki was treating my wounds. I felt the sting of a needle in my neck and looked into her face. I'd never seen her look so worried. "You all messed up, cub."

"I'll say." The pain was still there, but fading as whatever she'd given me took effect. I pushed myself into a sitting position and immediately wanted to throw up.

Variant came up behind Loki and reached over to help me prop myself up against the side of the rig. The painkiller faltered at that moment as a knife ripped along my right side and I realized my chest was wrapped tight and my arm firmly strapped to my front. I was shirtless and weaponless as the vehicle lurched to the right and then left. Sherry was in the driver's seat, cables extending from the dash into the jack in her temple, her hands on the controls. Jericho sat on her right, moving maps in the air and communicating with Sherry.

Chaz was manning a console across from where I sat and Pearl sat in a chair behind Jericho, her hands out, her eyes closed. I hoped she was okay.

Variant shook his head. "You look like shit."

"You shouldn't have saved me." From the speed we were going and the sound of squealing tires, it hadn't been as clean a getaway as we'd hoped. "We were spotted because you did that. Am I right?"

"Shut up," Variant pointed a meaty finger at me. "I got a lot invested in you, and I mean to get what I'm owed." He straightened up. "Loki got one of the bullets out, but you still got two in your chest. You're gonna need better medical help than we got."

"We were trying to get you there when two bogies showed up on our tail," Jericho said as he moved a map in front of him and tapped it to zoom in on a wire-frame set of streets. Even I could see the names from where I sat as my cybereyes linked with his AR.

There were three fast moving objects. A square in the lead, that was us. And two round dots with ??? identifiers over them right behind us.

I started to stand and Loki tried to keep me seated.

"Move, baby," Variant gently urged Loki aside and hoisted me up by my good arm and supported me as we moved to stand in the vacancy behind Sherry, to the left of Pearl.

I leaned heavily on Variant's right side as the van lurched again around a string of cars and through a red light. "How is this getting us out of here?"

A new screen came up on the van's front windshield, visible through the party VPN. It was a visual of our movement though Boston via an overhead camera. Variant nodded at it. "Got the Fly Spy up. Good work Chaz."

I glanced back at Chaz, wincing as the movement pulled at damaged muscles. The console was the van's RCC. "Drones?"

The van abruptly rocked to the left side as one of the pursuers fired on us. Variant kept himself and me upright, but Loki tumbled to the back.

"That was a direct hit," Jericho said. "And way too close to the fuel tank."

"Drek." Sherry increased our speed.

"How many drones?" I asked.

Chaz said, "Sherry's got sixteen standard rotos, pretty much throwaway fire—"

"Hey," Sherry interrupted. "That's still nuyen you're paying for, Chaz."

"—three with Remington 950s and two with—" He shook his head. "I don't know what's up with the Sikorsky-Bell Microskimmers."

"Those are my jewels. Each one has a grenade attached to it," Sherry laughed. "Get those things ready, Chaz. We got one for each of those assholes."

Jericho looked at her. "What are you gonna do?"

"She's gonna fly them under the vehicles and blow them up," I said. It seemed reasonable enough, but... "Sherry, the problem with those are their hackability. Using one might work, but won't they try and hack the other one once they know what they can do? Turn it on us?"

"Got that covered," Chaz said. "I'm running the software in the RCC and slaving the drones to it. The RCC's firewall should protect them."

"Let's hope so," Variant said. "Send out eight of the rotos for cover so you can get the first of the skimmers under the closest vehicle."

The van lurched hard to the left and nearly tilted over. This time Variant and I did hit the side and he fell on me. I screamed—couldn't help it. My entire right side was on fire. Loki was on me like cute on a puppy, kicking and pushing Variant off me.

"Sorry, Chris," Variant said as he stood back up and faced the other three. "Loki, give him something that'll knock out that pain."

"No," I said through clenched teeth. The only way to knock out this kind of pain would be to knock *me* out.

"First pursuer has engaged the drones," Chaz said. "Deploying skimmer one."

Loki hovered over me with a syringe in her hand. "Pup must sleep."

"No Loki...I can help."

<*No, you can't.*> That was Pearl. <*Let them do their job. The packet is safe.*>

<*Pearl! Are you all right? I thought that ICE had hurt you.*>

<*It did. But I'll mend. Your injuries are bad, Crisis. You must–*>

Something abruptly shoved the van forward a bit and I heard an explosion just as Loki stuck the needle in my neck.

Damn it!

<*You tricked me so she could do that.*>

<*Yes.*>

"Pursuer asshole one is blowed...up," Chaz said as he smiled.

"Do the same with the second one," Variant said. "And watch the softs...and hope that firewall holds."

The sedative was working fast, but I was fighting it. I had to. I couldn't just sleep while the others fought for our lives.

"They're behind us," Chaz said.

"What about the skimmer?"

"Almost there..."

A deafening sound, followed by a jolt to the van stopped everything for me. Time slowed as I started to move to the back of the van. Someone grabbed my ankles and held me tight as I watched in a haze as the back doors of the van vanished and Loki tumbled through them.

"Loki!" I screamed.

Another explosion. "Got you, you bastard!"

"Go, go, go!" Variant said.

"No...we gotta get Loki..." I told him. Or I thought I told him. I couldn't see anymore. And I couldn't think.

In fact, I couldn't do anything but mourn Loki in my dreams.

CHAPTER 26

MIT&T
SUNDAY, NOVEMBER 10, 2075
EARLY MORNING

Mason stood a couple safe meters behind Apollonius as he knelt over the elf's body. He'd already confirmed she was part of the Ancients. A shadowunner. And a thorn in Apollonius' side. They were in the basement of the Geisner Building, a level kept secret on a strict need-to-know protocol.

Apollonius stood and motioned for his people to remove the body. "Make sure no one knows she was here. There will be no vids on this, no news, no leakage she was ever here. And I want no trace of her found. And if you find anyone talking about this, dispose of them as well."

Two men in suits lifted the body and carted it away.

He'd already checked to make sure nothing was stolen. And as far as they could tell, the thieves had hacked into a single off-grid node with nothing of importance on it. Except... the backups from Nicole's home security system. Mason had stored them in the media lab's node farm, because he didn't know what else to do with the data, and because her security had recorded him doing a few things he'd rather not have made public, keeping it on one of the older nodes seemed a safe bet.

The fact that that was the only node hit and the black IC had been triggered was revealing—he just didn't know what the reveal was. At least, not yet. And he wasn't sure he wanted to share this information with Apollonius.

Once they were gone, Apollonius turned to Mason. "Did they get *SPECTRE*?"

Mason frowned. "I don't know. I wasn't in charge of the transfer of *SPECTRE* here." It was the truth, but it was also the wrong thing to say to Apollonius at that moment. The fixer launched himself at Mason, with both hands around his neck.

One of the remaining men in suits said, "Sir!"

That seemed to bring Apollonius out of his fit of anger. He released Mason and stood up, then backed away.

Whether the suited man knew they were about to have company or not as a reason for interrupting his boss' enjoyment in strangling Mason would ever elude the human CEO as three uniformed Knight Errant officers entered the room.

The one in the middle looked around. "Where is the body?"

Apollonius ran his fingers through his hair to move it from his face. "What body?"

"There is a report of a body discovered."

"I'm afraid you were misinformed." Apollonius frowned. "How did you get in here?"

The man stepped forward and Mason could see by the markings on the man's uniform he was a lieutenant. "We're with Knight Errant, sir. We're employed to know every nook and cranny...and secret room...in every building we patrol." He clasped his hands in front of him. "Now, again, where is the body?"

"If that's so, *Lieutenant*," Apollonius narrowed his eyes at the man and got in his face. "You know that I own this building, and I have the right to remain silent."

Mason pursed his lips. He wasn't sure that was the way things worked.

"We're not leaving, Mr. Turk. What we are going to do is ask you and Mr. Andreas to come to the station to give a full statement."

"For what?" Apollonius fired back. "Mason and I weren't even here. Why don't you and your jackass flunkies go out there and find out how these shadowrunners got into this building?"

"Are you telling us how to do our jobs?"

"No," came a voice behind them. "But I am, Lieutenant."

Everyone turned to see a formidable-looking troll in uniform squeeze through the door.

The look on the lieutenant's face was priceless as he saluted and came to attention. "Commander!"

"I suggest you do what Mr. Turk suggested you do. I'll handle the rest from here."

The lieutenant hesitated a second, glanced at Apollonius, then decided it was best to follow orders. But it was obvious to Mason the KE officer did not like Apollonius.

Not many people did.

"Thanks, Hugh," Apollonius looked relieved. "You'll take care of the body?"

"Of course. We don't want any damn elf gang making a statement at one of our greatest historic institutions. Now, how can we help you?"

Unbelievable! Mason tried not to shake his head. *The bastard has* KE *doing his bidding!*

"Mason, will you excuse us?"

He didn't have to be nudged out twice. Mason left the room and hurried back up the steps to Ames Street. There he took in the blasts to the building's outside, the dark, harsh marks of burning tires on the asphalt and concrete.

The question of what was so important in those particular files nagged at Mason. All along he'd sort of suspected if Oliver left anything behind, it would have been in something of his fiancée's...but in household recipe programs?

The BMP forensics team arrived and Apollonius emerged from the lower level. The KE Commander walked away, and Apollonius put his hand on Mason's shoulder. Mason couldn't help wincing and trying to pull away. "I'm not going to kill you. Not yet."

"What the hell for?" Mason heard himself say, and regretted it. A beat later, he didn't. "You took me off this project, remember? You said I wasn't competent enough. I didn't even know you'd moved *SPECTRE* yet."

"It hadn't been secured," Apollonius said. He gestured for Mason to follow him. "Come with me."

Mason hesitated, and watched as Apollonius strode across Ames Street to a black van parked on the other side. He finally followed when Apollonius stopped in the middle of the blocked off street and glared at him. The van was a surveillance van, set up with drones and a piggy-backed access to the media lab's security. Mason figured this out when he stepped inside and saw two Andreas Martin techs in chairs before sharp holo-vids.

Apollonius took a seat beside them. "Pull up the recordings from the drones."

Mason sat in one of the smaller chairs. "They said the drones had been hacked."

"Theirs were. And two of mine. But the others recorded some information."

Mason leaned forward as an action movie unraveled in front of him. There was a tall, leggy woman, a smaller animal-looking shapeshifter, a man with a crossbow, and a tall, imposing orc. They burst out of a door on top of the media lab roof, according to the info tag on the recording.

The orc ran out first, dodged a shot from a drone, and then ducked back through the door. Nothing happened as the other drones came into place and other images appeared the main view. Mason assumed the technician was adding in the different angles from other drones.

The door opened again as the ork came out firing, then the guy with the crossbow. The door remained opened a few more seconds before it closed, but no one else appeared. The camera focused on following the ork and human as they ran, and dodged fire on the building's terrace.

Apollonius said in a tone that sounded preoccupied, "Wait...go back to the clear shot of the orc."

The trid rewound, and then slowly inched forward to a very clear shot of the man's face. He was dark-skinned, with what might have been a handsome face if it weren't marred by the small tusks thrusting up from his lower jaw. There were markings on his shaved head, and he had several gold loops in each of his pointed ears.

"I know that face," Apollonius said before he pushed the tech out of the way with his chair. His fingers flew over the virtual keyboard until Mason recognized a personnel database. On one side he had the ork's face, on the other he streamed through a database of employees. Within seconds there was a match, and a clearer image appeared. Beneath the clear image, which looked like an ID photo, the name said *Orlando Variant Miles*.

"Is that a NeoNET database?"

"Yes. But he was never an employee," Apollonius said as he pulled up the entire file. There were other images. One of them of a very handsome human Orlando Miles. "He goblinized late in life. But his wife stayed with him. She truly loved him." A woman's picture appeared. Asian. Beautiful, and very delicate.

Mason scanned the information below the picture. A NeoNET employee record. "She worked for NeoNET."

"Yes." The image disappeared, but not before Mason saw two very important things. *Technomancer* as classification and *deceased* under position. "She died in a lab experiment. Orlando wouldn't accept it, and continued to harass us with lawsuits. Well, he harassed me with lawsuits. Accused me of lying. Even had the support of the technomancers on his side, feeding him lies that she was being held in the one of the towers here in Boston." Apollonius snorted. "And now here he is, all these years later with a new I.D., a new persona in which to torture me with. Crisis."

"You now think this Crisis is Orlando Miles and not Oliver Martin."

He glanced at Mason. "It wasn't Martin who was after me. It was someone from my own past. Oliver Martin is dead." He settled back. "But I'm not sure how Jericho McCleary and Nicole O'Neal figure in with Orlando Miles." He slapped his thighs. "No matter. I'm sure Maxine's procured Miss O'Neal by now."

Mason's heart thudded against his chest. "*Procured* Nicole?"

"You didn't think I was going to just wait on her to suddenly show up again, did you? I did enjoy the meal, though. The lobster was excellent."

"Nicole isn't part of this." Mason pointed to the image of Miles. "She doesn't even know who he is."

"Possibly. We'll soon be able to question her and see how all of this is coming together." Apollonius put his hand in the air and opened his AR. Mason couldn't read or really see what he saw, but he did watch the elf's expression go from relieved to bright red. Something was wrong.

Mason got up and moved to the door.

As if on cue, Apollonius wiped way his AR and then slammed his fist into the console in front of him. The technicians yelled and jumped back as Apollonius stood, grabbed the chair Mason had been sitting in, and used it to smash the instrument panel.

While Apollonius had his fit—and Mason didn't care why he was having it—he stepped out of the van and intercepted a KE officer holding a small package.

"Yes?" Mason said.

The officer looked past him to the van as it bounced from side to side and the two technicians ran out. "I uh...we found these scattered on the roof and around the body of the elf."

Mason glanced back at the rocking van and then held out his hand. "I'll give them to him if you'd like?"

The relief that washed across the officer's face was nearly laughable. He almost shoved the bag into Mason before hurrying off.

Mason examined the bag. Standard evidence gathering for Knight Errant. There was a name and date and place where the items were found. He opened it and looked inside. At first he wasn't sure what he was looking at. It looked like a bunch of odd metal stars. Using his handkerchief, he reached in and pulled one out. It wasn't a star at all, but an arrowhead, like the ones mounted on the ends of arrows. It was well-made, and appeared to be a lot more complex, with a spring mechanism inside the shaft where the wood or metal would go. He pulled out another one, and it was different than the first.

An idea came to him. The guy in the video with the crossbow. It might be possible to get a fingerprint off these and find out who he was. Find him, and he might lead Mason to this Miles person. Find Miles and maybe he could appease Apollonius and save Nicole from undergoing any of the bastard's interrogation methods. Mason heard the clap of a heel on asphalt and shoved the bag into the inside pocket of his suit jacket just as Apollonius stomped past him.

"Don't lag behind, Mason. Nicole got away. We haven't found her father. Yet."

Mason's heart skipped. He was relieved she got away, but feared what might have happened to Nathan. He hurried to catch up and devised a plan to get the arrowheads to a contact of his, someone who could get the fingerprints to him in a few hours. Maybe by that time he could find Miles Orlando and spare both Nicole *and* her father from Apollonius's wrath.

CHAPTER 27

TUESDAY, NOVEMBER 12, 2075

My first sight when waking was a blurred face with red hair. In fact, all I could see through the slightly steamed glass was the hair. I stared at it, trying to come up with a name for it.

Crimson.

Garish.

And when the face grinned, I saw the fangs.

"Easy," Variant said in my ears. His voice sounded canned, electronic.

I was in an auto-doc. The lid depressurized and opened. The outside air was cold against my bare skin, and I realized I was naked.

Butt naked.

"Nice abs, Legolas."

I reacted with the usual jerk of my arms to somehow cover myself from the leering vampire. But I couldn't move.

"Get back, you freak." Variant's girth pushed the vampire out of the way as he bent over me and unfastened a few clamps. They weren't restraints, per se, but stationary guides for the machine to inject healing needles of...whatever it was they used.

Once they were disengaged, I sat forward as a blanket was tossed over my head. I moved it down to cover myself and realized my right arm, side and shoulder were sore, but they didn't hurt. And I could move them.

I looked down to see the puncture wounds from the doc, as well as healing holes where the bullets went in. I twisted my torso to take a look around, hissing as a sharp pain lanced up my side.

I had hoped I was healed too soon.

"Careful," Pearl said as she came forward and offered me a glass of something green with a straw. I took it. "This auto-doc has its limitations."

I sipped the drink. It looked like toxic waste, but it tasted like melon. "How long?"

"About three days," Pearl answered. "It's Tuesday."

"Damn, that bad, huh? The doc couldn't heal me completely?"

"You stretched its limitations. You still gotta a bullet in you," Variant said. "It's too close to your spine and behind your lung."

I lowered the glass. "That's not a good place to leave something."

"Nope," Variant said. "But it'll have to do for now. The auto-doc's eighty-nine percent sure the bullet won't move, as long as you don't take a hit to that area."

That news wasn't reassuring. The kind of surgery would take to remove it was a bit more than what an auto-doc could do. I would need a better facility and no price on my head. So I would have to be careful because I didn't know what would happen if the bullet moved closer to either my lung or my spine. I finished up the drink. It gave me some energy and Variant didn't have to help me too much getting out of the doc.

We were back at The Slaughtered Donkey, so I took it slow back to my room, took a shower and changed. I did take a good look at my arm and chest before slipping on a t-shirt. There were scars. Would be scars. And I'd been hit more times than I realized. I counted six holes.

Jesus.

I ambled into the war room to find Variant, Pearl, and the vampire. For a shadowrunner, the idiot sure dressed conspicuously. Bright red suit matched his bright red hair and goatee. I hadn't noticed the facial hair before. He also had a smirk on his face I didn't like.

He moved to stand in front of me. "Red Lang. And you must be this Crisis these people told me about. Can't say I've heard of you outside of Boston."

"And I've never heard of you at all." I looked around. "Where's Nicole? That's who you were protecting, right?"

"Oh, wow. That's a look that'd melt a steel girder." Red gave me a crooked smile, which fit perfectly with his devil-may-care look. "She's with Jericho. Variant didn't want us all in the same place, and figured it was better for she and your friend to hide out together. We're still not sure where her father is, though. What we can say is that Apollonius Turk did not take him."

"Her father..." Part of my mind was avoiding asking about Loki, so it took me a few seconds to comprehend his words. "He tried to snatch Nathan, too?"

"First name basis. Nice." Red moved away and leaned against one of the other desks in the room, holding himself up with his hands against its edge. "I'm afraid Turk's henchtroll... woman...lost him in all the commotion. I was able to get Nicole out of there to safety."

Clarity brought anger with it. "You mean Turk actually tried to grab someone in broad daylight?"

"Night, actually. It was just after nine. Dark." Red nodded.

Pearl, sitting at Variant's terminal, activated three holovids. She studied the information that came across them, her face illuminated in the green and blue glow. "Interesting that the restaurant's security feed is blank for that time."

"Apollonius probably paid 'em off," Red said as he glanced back at Pearl. "What're you doing?"

Pearl said, her attention still on the screen, "Right now I'm looking for Liza."

That revelation caught my attention. Liza! I'd completely forgotten about her. She'd been with Chaz and Vertigo. "Where the hell did she go? Wasn't she supposed to stick with us?"

"Personal agenda. As in she had one. Vertigo wasn't sure what Liza was up to, but apparently it's got to do with the Ancients' own beef with NeoNET. And just like Var—" she glanced at me through the projections, "—they saw this an opportunity to strike at them."

"I don't give a shit about what the Ancients want," I said as I moved carefully past Red to stand beside Pearl and look at the screens.

I hesitated and she looked up at me. "We don't know, Chris. Reconnaissance didn't show a body, and no shifters have been reported at the scene. No database has her DNA in it for after cleanup."

"You think they have her?"

"That's what I'm looking for..." Pearl's voice trailed off as her eyes unfocused. All the hairs on my arms and the back of my neck stood on end. I stood close, ready to catch her if she fell.

"Don't worry about Pearl," Sherry said as she entered the war room and plopped down in front of Pearl's terminal. "She's doing her TM thing. If anyone can find your girlfriend, she can."

"Loki's not my girlfriend." Not that I really had anything against shapeshifters, I just... she felt more like a little sister. Well, a little sister who kept wanting to bathe me with her tongue. "She's just...very dear to me."

"And to Variant," Sherry said. "She's like his daughter. Or that was the impression I got."

I didn't want to be reminded of how Variant must be feeling at the moment.

The door to the room burst open and Nicole came running in, followed by Jericho. The two of them together gave me a heavy case of déjà vu. She stopped when she saw me—I was pretty sure I looked beat to hell.

I opened my mouth to say something, but she ran to me and threw her arms around my neck. I stood in stunned silence for a few seconds before I put my own arms around her and inhaled. She still smelled like jasmine and roses. "Oliver—"

I made shushing noises in her ear and held her close. I looked over at Red. "I don't know what your price is, but we need to find her father."

The vampire nodded. "Already on it."

Chimes went off, and I watched as Variant and Pearl produced weapons. A beat later Pearl put hers away and pointed to the door. It opened and standing in the center was Liza.

She stood in silence, her eye makeup smeared and her shoulders slumped. I assumed she was upset about Vertigo's death.

"You—" I released Nicole and started toward Liza, but Variant put his hand out. I looked at him and he shook his head.

Liza came into the room, followed by two more Ancients, both male elves with shaved heads. This made their ears look even bigger and pointier. Chaz brought up the rear. Liza held her hand out to me. "This is for you. It's all there."

I held my hand beneath hers, palm up, as she dropped something into it. When she moved her hand away, I held a chip, unmarked. "What is it?"

"George Spinoza left a back door they didn't know about." She smiled weakly. "He was a good friend to the Ancients."

That piece of information floored me. I never considered old George worked for a gang. "Spinoza...gave you information?"

"When he had it. And when he remembered." She flashed that smile again, and then looked solemn at Pearl. "I'm sorry about the black ice. I tripped it when I was going after George's file."

I heard Pearl gasp behind me. "Liza...we already pulled a packet of information from a KE node. You're saying he had more information on MIT&T's? Why are you giving it to Crisis?"

She swallowed. "It's a program called *SPECTRE*. I didn't make a copy of it. But I did leave the original on the node." She nodded to Variant and then averted her eyes as she was escorted from the room.

"Is she in trouble?" Red said from where he stood by the desk. "Cause those two beside her look like trouble."

"She indirectly caused the death of Vertigo," Pearl said. "They knew it, and I didn't. I thought it was my fault."

Red winced. "Vertigo. Yeah...she's in trouble."

I wasn't surprised he knew who that was. Red seemed to know everyone. And they all seemed to know him, too.

I stared at my hand. Was it really possible? That George left the Ancients access to AMAS's new version of *Ghost-7*? I handed the chip to Pearl, who immediately sat down at a console. She slipped the chip in a slot and her hands moved in the air as the screens all displayed different pieces of information.

And then I saw it. My original files. The ones I'd copied to the chip. "There it is. You mean George moved everything into a central location?"

"He probably recognized it for what it was and stole it before Nicole's information was transferred." Pearl retrieved the code, opened the file, and downloaded *Ghost-7* as well as *SPECTRE*. I finally had my baby and its progeny. "If Liza would have shared this, we could have avoided so much..."

I knew she meant we might have avoided Vertigo's death. But I had the feeling even Liza didn't know what she was going after.

"I'm looking through it." She tossed different windows to different screens. "And I think we have a way to right a few wrongs." She looked at me. "If you're ready to do some net work. You know, take a little time off from being a hero for a while."

Red joined them and shrugged. "So what does this mean?"

I felt Variant's hand on my shoulder. I said, "It means we can hit Apollonius Turk where it hurts most. And if you can give Jericho and I some time and find Loki, we can undo what's in the works now."

"Meaning?" Variant said.

"Meaning," Jericho said as he leaned in over Pearl's shoulder and looked at the floating screens. "By adding in the data Pearl got off the node, we can..." he pointed at a few lines of code, "...save lives and companies."

I saw what he was looking at. Three names. Three different companies. A slow grin pulled at the sides of my mouth. "Variant, how would you like to really become a thorn in Apollonius Turk's side?"

CHAPTER 28

FRIDAY, NOVEMBER 15, 2075

Two successful retrievals, one more to go. And this one would be the most difficult. Mostly due to the brash method Turks' Asset Management team was planning to use to eliminate the final target.

Shelley Prior was the CEO and mastermind behind Emporium Analyticum, the top competitor with AMAS. EA had been established three years before Oliver and Mason met, and had worked with megacorps such as Saeder-Krupp, Shiawase Corporation, Renraku Computer Systems, and most recently, Wuxing. It was rumored that Ms. Prior had connections with dragons.

But that wasn't proven, and was nothing I was worried about. My only focus was thwarting Black Hat's intentions and saving her life. But I also had a favor in mind. And if she died, that favor could never be realized.

I'd done my research on Ms. Prior. I knew she had three residences known to the public, but also had a private residence here in Boston that she shared with her wife, Taylor Finn, an elf with ties to Tír na nOg. Ms. Prior wasn't someone to mess with, and I was sure Turk knew that. Her death would start a cataclysmic downfall of Emporium Analyticum, which in turn could have repercussions that could influence the corporations she worked with that were in direct competition with NeoNET. And what a coup it would be for him to brag about being the mastermind behind such an event.

Well...that just wasn't going to happen.

Shelley Prior was as private as they come. She was rarely seen outside of security-enhanced meetings with her clients, or her doubly enforced dwellings. But tonight was a special night—the anniversary of hers and Taylor's wedding. And Taylor wanted sushi, and there was only one place she wanted to eat at.

The place where the two of them met.

Phinnagan's Feast on the harbor.

I did my usual reconnaissance, watching the AMs from Black Hat observe the restaurant. Pearl had done her magic on this hit as she had with the other two. She'd procured Miss Prior's schedule and listened in on her communications, as well as Black Hat's. She was amazed at how absolutely arrogant Apollonius Turk was. To have such a shrewd, devious mind and yet to be almost ignorant of what others could do to him.

"It's like he's daring anyone to take him down," she'd said earlier that day.

To which Variant had said, "Don't get cocky."

It was nearly showtime, and I was on my perch across the street. Black Hat's assassins, two elves with ties to a few of the less appreciated gangs in South Boston, had gotten jobs in the restaurant and their plan was to poison Shelley Prior. The restaurant would take the hit by serving her something she was allergic too, and their asset would be managed as well.

I didn't buy it. It was too easy. Var didn't want to hear it, but at least Jericho did. So he'd also gotten a job at the restaurant, bullshitting his way in to be a host for the evening and keep an eye out for me.

Yeah so, I had an unaccounted asset on the field. Sue me.

All of my "something's hinky" alarms were going off, just like they had outside the KE node. The two Black Hat employees were in their place. Pearl had eyes on them in the kitchen. Jericho was at his post at the host desk. The Black Hat getaway cycles were in the back alley, both watched by a few Ancients.

What made me sit up and take notice was the arrival of another Black Hat Asset Manager. I recognized him as he drove his Maserati up to the door and the valet came over to take it. An Asian man, young, formerly employed by Wuxing. I was sure he was still upset because his target from the last hit was still alive, and the window of opportunity to take them out had passed.

"This bastard's making sure tonight's hit doesn't fail," I muttered. I'd thought Loki was beside me and I would talk to her like I always had. Only, she wasn't there.

<*What're you talking about?*> Variant said.

Pearl answered. <*We got another player on the field. I see him, Chris.*>

Everyone's AR flipped so we could see cameras tracking the man as he went inside.

<*Oh great. Son-of-a-bitch's here for clean-up.*> Variant said. <*Chris, is this why you got Jericho in here?*>

Here? <*Variant, are you in the restaurant?*>

<*Of course he is,*> Pearl said. <*Went in the moment he saw Jericho. He's right, isn't he–head's up. One of the marks just took Miss Prior's order.*>

<*Did you see him do anything to it?*>

<*No.*>

Pearl's camera tracked the fake waiter as he approached the table. I tensed to move, ready to run to the restaurant just as Jericho appeared and scooped the plates out of the waiter's hand.

"Oh no, no, no. This goes to table five. Weren't you paying attention?"

<*Shit,*> Pearl said.

I smiled as I slid down the ladder I'd set up and ran to the alley. The AM's motorcycles were little more than pieces. The Ancients had already struck and got what they wanted. No one was taking those bikes anywhere.

Pearl adjusted the cameras as we watched the waiter grab Jericho's arm. The plates went to the floor, the china crashing against the marble. Patrons stopped talking and looked at the commotion as Ms. Prior stood. Her bodyguards came out of nowhere as the waiter was tripped by Jericho and sprawled on the floor.

"Oh, I'm so sorry!" Jericho said as he tried to help the man up.

I saw the other one duck out of the back kitchen and run to the bikes. He cussed and started running away. A few yards down the alley, he vanished. I doubted they'd find his body for some time, if ever.

<*That bastard's making his move!*>

I watched in shock and horror as the new arrival, still at the lobby, waiting to be seated, pulled out some kind of weapon and ran into the main dining area. Prior's bodyguards, two of them, ran toward him while another figure, a big one, blocked any attempt to get to Ms. Prior and her spouse.

I made sure I was in place in the back as the back door opened again. Variant proceeded them out, then urged them to come out. The two women stepped out and into the light of the alley. Luckily it was still dark enough that Variant's face and mine would be unreadable.

"What do you want?" Miss Prior demanded as they moved to the opposite side.

"Call your driver to get back here," Variant said. "I just want to make sure you survive."

That was my cue and I stepped out. I was pretty sure I looked less menacing. A human in a long coat, a crossbow, and a rifle. "Ms. Prior."

They both turned to look at me and I could hear both commotion inside and the screech of tires outside as a vehicle came down the alley. Variant was already gone.

I tossed a small box at them. Miss Finn caught it in mid-air.

"That chip has information on it you can use to bring down Apollonius Turk."

The expression on Ms. Prior's face was the one I'd been wanting. The one I'd hoped for. She knew who he was. "Don't move," she said.

The vehicle was coming closer and I could hear the sirens from the BMP. "Can't stay. The information is clean, and it's yours to do what you want with it. And it's all true." I nodded and blended back into the shadows.

A few minutes later I was at my secondary perch, watching as the BMP crowded around the back alley. Miss Prior and her wife were escorted away from the area as news drones moved in. I made sure they didn't see me.

Jericho sent me a missive. He was out and the remaining two asset managers were under arrest. How long they stayed in jail was anyone's guess. Whether or not Miss Prior used the information I'd just given her—I was taking a risk. But I wanted the truth out there. And I wanted that son of a bitch brought down. I felt Shelley Prior was the best way to do it.

Variant would be mad at first. But I didn't care.

I pretended Loki was beside me, wanting to get ice cream. And after the area calmed down, and the Ancients were on the move, I left.

And went home.

CHAPTER 29

THURSDAY, DECEMBER 5, 2075

Mason Andreas slammed his hand on his desk. He'd been doing that a lot these past few months. So much that his hand was bruised. But hitting his desk was so much less complicated than hitting a living thing. At least desks didn't threaten lawsuits.

After the very maligned death of Oliver Martin, along with the fabricated story of his sabotage of Andreas Martin Analysis Systems's software, and the public sympathy that came with the spin of a broken heart for one of Boston's most adored debutantes, Mason had been able to legally reinvent himself as the sole owner of the company.

But that didn't get rid of Apollonius Turk. No. Instead, the bastard had bought one of Nathan O'Neal's companies—his original business—and set up his own somewhat questionable business. He called it Black Hat Operations, and turned it into a temp office. Only Apollonius wasn't exactly hiring out jobs for temporary wageslaves.

Mason's marriage to Nicole O'Neal was a part of Apollonius's campaign to brighten NeoNET's public image, especially in the wake of accusations made in the Matrix, on trid and through public demonstrations, that the megacorp was kidnapping, holding, and killing technomancers. None of this had anything to do with AMAS, but the idea of them creating something that could give the ordinary citizen, the start-up, the underdog, a fighting chance in the market to start a business and see it succeed, was always good press. So a collaboration was made in the public arena that AMAS and MIT&T were working together to reconstruct the prototype stolen by Oliver Martin. Slap on a wedding, and all they needed was the cherry on top.

But as Mason sat in his office, the latest test results from MIT&T's reverse engineered version of Oliver's prototype, now named *SPECTRE*, displayed on his AR, his confidence in the product finally dwindled. They weren't creating something to help the little man. They were creating a means for those already in power to crush anyone in their way.

Of course, he'd originally seen this path for Oliver's *Ghost-7*, but with himself in complete control. He believed he could cull the use of the program by setting up a branch of AMAS that handled the reported lynchpin. By handled, Oliver's idea had been to reassign them or find them jobs elsewhere, then run *Ghost-7* again to make sure the problem was taken care of. Of course, the model always showed a new problem cropped up, surrounding that same employee. Destiny was apparently real, and it had been under Apollonius's guidance and suggestion that hits were put out on the positive lynchpins identified in subsequent tests, and not the negatives ones.

And then Oliver noticed. *Of course he would. Oli had always been the one with the conscience.*

But now Mason found himself wrestling with Apollonius's ideas to fix the new problems *SPECTRE* generated so the development and sale of this new software could proceed.

The future was filled with golden apples ready to pick from the trees, Apollonius had said. But Mason knew those apples were rotten beneath the gleam.

His office door opened, and Max and Maxine proceeded Apollonius into the room. The CEO's stride told Mason something was wrong, and the beautiful man planned to blame him.

"Apollonius." Mason waved away the reports and dismissed his AR. "What can I help—"

"Save it, Mason," Apollonius motioned to his bodyguards. They nodded and left the office, closing the door behind them.

Whatever was wrong, it wasn't something he wanted widespread. Mason immediately set the privacy screens up and put his elbows on his desk, his hands clasped in front of him. "What's wrong?"

Apollonius wore less than his usual uniform of fashionable suit. Today he sported a long-sleeved shirt, a vest and matching slacks, and leather shoes. No tie. And his hair was down instead of in a queue.

When he focused his ire on Mason, he did so with a gesture of putting his hands flat on Mason's desk. Apollonius's hair fell forward. "Crisis."

With a narrowed gaze, Mason chose his words carefully. "Crisis as in there is a crisis, or Crisis as in Orlando Miles?"

"Both," Apollonius pushed himself back and flipped his hair behind his shoulders. "Didn't you read the access reports?"

The access reports were those black documents Apollonius sent Mason about the successful kills on lynchpins. Reading them sickened him, so he kept them in a folder on the company's securest node. Not having read them... He braced himself for violence. "No, I haven't read them."

Apollonius glared at him, but instead of reaching across the desk and striking him, as was his usual action, the man put his hands on his hips. "Putting too much time into this damn wedding."

Mason felt relief wash over him, and he made a mask of his reaction, giving Apollonius his best ashamed expression. "I do apologize. But if something has happened—"

"*Nothing*, has happened. That's the problem." Apollonius gestured in the air between them. Mason's AR activated as the latest access report opened in front of him. He skimmed the contents, getting the general idea...

Oh no...

His expression must have alerted Apollonius. "You see it? That break-in at MIT&T *did* have a purpose. They stole *SPECTRE*."

"But...it's still there. It was accounted for. The Black Ice was triggered. There was a casualty."

Apollonius slowly shook his head. "Because that's what they wanted us to believe. Those shadowrunners found it, copied it, and left it exactly where it was." He narrowed his eyes on Martin. "Three test runs, each producing their usual targets for a hit ratio of three—all of them failed. Their targets still live."

Martin's mind raced for some other explanation. Anything but the idea that their security had been for nothing. "What... what asset managers did you hire? It had to be their fault." Asset manager was Apollonius's word for assassin. But no matter how you spun it, that's what they were.

"The same team I've *been* using. They've successfully eliminated all twelve targets since *SPECTRE* was brought online. And now, suddenly, they've failed three times." Apollonius pointed at Mason. "All three of those lynchpins were rescued. Someone prevented our assets from accomplishing their missions." He put his hand on Martin's desk. "The last fiasco was the worst. It was Crisis."

Mason made a face. "And you really believe this is Orlando Miles seeking revenge for his wife?"

"And you *don't*?" He emphasized this as if Mason was supposed to agree.

Unfortunately he didn't. "Apollonius—is this a shadowrunner? Maybe some vigilante trying to make some nuyen—"

Apollonius was on the desk in a flash, his fists grabbing Mason's collar. His eyes were wide, red-rimmed and bloodshot. His veins popped out along his usually smooth temples. He wasn't nearly as attractive like this. "You stupid piece of drek! It's *him*, Mason! He's *back*! He knows about *SPECTRE*. *He's* the only one who could break into this place and find those lynchpins! He's helping Miles destroy me! And he's using his game name! I was so blind not to see it, not to see the two of them were working together..."

Mason put his hand on Apollonius's wrists and tried to pull him off. The man was insane.

Just as abruptly as he'd lunged at Mason, Apollonius released him and pushed himself back from the desk. His face was still red and his eyes wild. His hair hung in tangles around his face, half-hiding it from the office's overhead lighting.

Mason pushed his chair back and stood, ready just in case the crazy bastard tried to tackle him again. Something had him very upset, this time. Apollonius wasn't just angry, he was... *afraid*.

Really afraid of something.

And that made Mason afraid, too. He straightened his suit and tie. "What the hell are you talking about? Who's helping Miles?"

"You really don't know," Apollonius said. "You fool."

Mason blinked. "Know *what*?"

"The truth. You believed it all. Probably the lies as well."

"Apollo—what the hell is wrong with you? Who are you talking about—" And then a thought came to Mason. It was a stupid idea. Just his mind working on what could frighten Apollonius Turk so deeply as to make him lose his composure.

Something the bastard said. Someone working with Orlando Miles.

Someone who could know how the lynchpins were assessed and find them before—

Game name.

"You see it now?" Apollonius said as he straightened his hair. "The lie wrapped in the truth? The danger he represents?"

He? Mason narrowed his eyes at Apollonius now.

The lie wrapped in truth.

No...the truth wrapped in a lie. Who else in the world knew about *SPECTRE*, or at least understood its algorithms? Understood its complexity?

Mason staggered back as if struck, harder than anything Apollonius could have physically given him. "You...you said he was dead." He pointed at the unkempt elf. "You said he was *dead*!"

"He was *supposed* to be."

"But—but I saw a body—"

"*A* body, you idiot." Apollonius turned and composed himself, raking his long fingers through his hair. "It didn't take much to pay off the right people and fool others. The bastard was shot in the chest when he tried to escape. There was no way he could survive."

"Maybe you need to tell me what really happened with Oliver Martin," Mason said and heard something in his voice he hadn't had in months. Confidence.

"There's no time." Apollonius faced him. "Crisis—*Oliver Martin*—is the only explanation for my managers' failures. He hacked into Black Hat's nodes and stole the latest reports. He made a copy of SPECTRE and used it to find our lynchpins. And he made sure they lived past their expiration day."

"That's not possible."

"*Anything* is possible, Mason. Never forget that. At two of the hit points, the targets were already gone. Instead there were daisies painted on the wall. *Daisies!* That is the signature of Crisis! And at the third one there were witnesses. Wageslaves who saw our assets attack an unarmed woman, the very lynchpin needed to be brought down to destroy one of AMAS's largest competitors. They saw an ork save her life. An ork! She's on the trideos, Mason. She's telling them AMAS sent assassins after her. The identities of our assets were traced back to Black Hat."

"I'm not seeing the problem here—no one's going to believe her."

"It's on vids, you asshole!" Apollonius's usually pale and flawless skin was blood-red as he spoke, spittle landing on Mason's suit jacket. "She's telling everyone about our software and how it works, how it targeted her. She provided the BMP with *proof*!"

Mason stood back as far as he could go behind his desk. "But you have sway with the BMP. Lone Star. Knight Errant. Can't they just arrest her for lying? There's no *real* proof!"

Apollonius paused and bent his head down a beat before he stood back and straightened up. "They have the same kind of proof you created to make Oliver Martin into a monster. They have missives, calls, security footage. They're investigating the other lynchpin deaths after seeing their names on the lists generated by SPECTRE, Mason. She had documentation of AMAS's reports on what SPECTRE does, and how she was targeted in order to bring down the company she works for. He set me up, Mason. That bastard *set me up*!"

Mason remained silent. What Apollonius said couldn't be the truth.

Oliver could still be alive? Mason had seen the pathologist report, he'd seen the body, he'd seen the DNA records, and had been sure Oliver Martin was dead. But it had all been faked because Apollonius hadn't found him. He's assumed Oliver was dead.

"What are you thinking? You've grown quiet." Apollonius watched him.

"If Oliver is alive and working against AMAS, then how would he even know of *SPECTRE*'s existence? We've been very careful keeping that under wraps, with only a few people with that knowledge."

"Give me a list of everyone that knows about *SPECTRE*, even if it's just peripherally, and I want it yesterday."

"What do you plan to do with it?" Mason felt a slight ping of apprehension.

"I plan on finding out if any of them have talked to Oliver... or Crisis, or whatever the hell he's calling himself now." Apollonius's calm demeanor had returned, his composure intact. "And I want to talk to Nicole."

"No. She's not a part of this. She doesn't even know about *SPECTRE*. Unlike Oliver, I haven't shared everything with her."

"But that's just it. She knew about *Ghost-7*, and don't think if he's still alive he won't try and contact her, Mason. They were engaged to be married, and you took everything away from him." He paused for a moment, and then glared at Mason. "Funny...how all these failed missions started happening after you announced your engagement."

He strode to the door. It opened before he got to it, pushed aside by Max. Apollonius paused and looked back at Mason. "I want Miss O'Neal."

"But, I don't know where she is. She disappeared after your people attacked her in that restaurant. She hasn't been back to her apartment, and her father's MIA."

"Then find her! Or I'll interrogate *you*."

Mason watched him leave, the door slamming behind him. He had to stop himself from shaking before he could return to his desk. He knew what it meant when Apollonius wanted to question someone. Oliver was the best example. He'd set his old friend up, then Oliver had disappeared, and then allegedly reappeared dead. But as to what Oliver had gone through at the hands of Apollonius, no one but he knew. Mason wasn't sure if he wanted to believe Oliver was really still alive. Seven months had passed since he'd destroyed his best friend's life. Seven months, and not one word.

Mason finally sat down and pulled out his encrypted decking unit. He logged into the Matrix to search for anything relating to someone named Crisis in South Boston and found several articles on a shadowy figure, an assassin and shadowrunner by that name. He was wanted by Lone Star, Knight Errant, and the BMP for the deaths of more than a dozen humans and metahumans, as well as various thefts.

No. That couldn't be Oliver. That was more Orlando Miles's style, wasn't it? Mason had to admit he didn't know this Miles person. Hadn't really cared. Apollonius was just paranoid. Heading down that road was a dead end. He needed to find out who had leaked information on *SPECTRE*, and if he had a traitor working at AMAS, or one at MIT&T. Let Apollonius follow his insanity all the way to hell if he wanted. Mason planned on looking closer to reality—and at those who still lived.

A name showed up in an old database. Someone he hadn't thought of in months.

George Spinoza.

He'd worked under Oliver, known the base work involved in creating *Ghost-7*, and he'd been the one Mason had used to start Oliver's decline. He'd disappeared right after Oliver did, after claiming he was afraid if Oliver knew what he'd done, he'd kill him. Of course, Mason knew then that Oliver wasn't capable of killing anyone. He was a boy scout, a do-gooder, and a man of conscience.

Mason had thought of getting rid of George himself because the metahuman knew too much. But after George disappeared and nothing surfaced, Mason really hadn't thought of him. Because he knew George had bought the story Mason had made up about Oliver, about the drugs, the weapons, and the shadowrunning.

And a very glaring fact that nagged at Mason was that George had left *before* the creation of *SPECTRE* even began.

Mason dug into the security footage to find any moles himself. SIN entries, exits, logs, every bit of data showing someone entering the building, and leaving it. *SPECTRE*'s node was off-grid at MIT&T, and only two people knew this: Mason and Apollonius. So the only way they'd known to hit MIT&T was if they'd gotten the information from the inside—which meant there'd been someone physically in this building.

At first he didn't see it, the missing time stamp in the long list of enters and exits. A gap of ten minutes. In the grand scheme of things, ten whole minutes of no in and out traffic into the building housing AMAS, a building with three other businesses, including a law firm, was suspicious.

The file had been altered.

Unfortunately, Mason didn't have the pay grade to know *how* it was altered. Code had never been his forte, but remembering faces, names, numbers—those were. So he went back to the logs of entries and exists on the cameras, especially the drones Apollonius had set up around the building. They hovered above the people, just out of sight, but they were there, ready to record or call on the BMP if needed.

And there she was, entering the building with a group of familiar faces. The one face he didn't recognize. Her SIN read as Delilah Sholes. She was beautiful, with soft, mocha cream skin, long hair, slender, pointed ears and a delicate face. An elf of remarkable beauty, and that was saying a lot, since most elves were beautiful. Her golden eyes actually looked up and into the drone camera in the lobby for a second before one of the employees touched her arm and they walked through the metal and plastic detector together. Flipping to the security readout, Miss Sholes had carried nothing suspicious. She had a standard jack installed, and various things in her purse. Lipstick, compact, and tissue box, but no commlink. Nothing data could be stored on.

Mason followed the path Miss Sholes took, his gaze straying to the lulling back and forth sway of her hips. She got off the lift on the second floor and walked into Johns and Remini, the law firm on the floor beneath them. Brasher was on the sixteenth floor.

After that, he had no access to the footage inside the firm, and no one entered the room with the secure node. Mason sat back. Everything inside of him said there was something peculiar about that elf. But even after screen capping her image, and running it through every criminal database he had hacked access too, he only found her ID as Delilah Sholes, elf, systems analyst and software technician.

Feeling defeated, he sat back and tried to think like a thief would. He wasn't sure he'd ever fully bought in to the idea that his best friend was still alive, but the fact was that whoever was acting as Crisis, whether solo or in tandem with a group, knew about SPECTRE. And knew which files to access to identify the lynchpins. The names didn't appear on the monitor or a AR. They were encoded into the results, and a decoding program had to decipher the names, SINs, and addresses.

So where to go now? He needed to get ahead of this before the sick bastard did something stupid that would jeopardize Mason's life as well as his own. He knew Apollonius still had the little shapeshifter. Had more than likely tortured her the same as he'd tortured Oliver. It'd been a few weeks, and the asshole hadn't mentioned her name. Not once. Mason wondered if she was still alive. He knew where she'd been, but was she still there? She had been part of the team that broke in. Dead or alive, knowing her name could bring Miles to him.

But if Oliver were alive...what name would bring him out of hiding? Nicole was in the wind. So was her father. The city still believed there was a wedding on the horizon. Not without the bride, there wasn't.

A name came to him. One he hadn't heard in some time. Mason started a search application. This was a name as close to Oliver as Nicole's.

The name of Jericho McCleary.

CHAPTER 30

SATURDAY, DECEMBER 7, 2075
EVENING

Jericho walked the quarter-mile from the closest Stuffer Shack to his home. Snow fell like powdered sugar, coating everything like a Solstice cake. He wore his usual long coat, fingerless gloves, matching hat and boots. He was warm enough, though being out in this weather much longer could be dangerous.

His step was lighter than it had been in months. He felt like he had a purpose again, something he'd always felt when he was with Oliver. Just knowing his best friend was still alive and was more like Crisis made him think that heroes did live among the wageslaves. Those with destinies that were larger than life.

Mulling over everything that'd happened to Oliver in less than a year made him think about how he'd have reacted to the situation.

No contest, he told himself. *I'd have died in jail from that beating. My XP would have dropped so low, no pots would revive me.*

But not Oliver. In the past week since meeting with Nicole, Oliver had brought Jericho into his world. One so much like *Dark City* that Jericho was afraid to comment on it. Not because he was embarrassed or wanted to dredge up Oliver's simpler past, but because the characters Oliver, known to them as Crisis or Chris, now ran with lived the life of that game every day. There was no logging out to return to a wageslave job and the 9 to 5 rut of the powerless. They were playing for real. Real stakes.

Real life.

Real death.

And until now, I'd only been an NPC.

After getting Nicole on board and making sure she and her father were safe in the Slaughtered Donkey and working behind the scenes, Oliver had spelled out to both of them the truth of what *Ghost-7*'s descendant, *SPECTRE*, was being used for. Jericho had known a little of this, having listened to Oliver's worries earlier. But knowing Mason Andreas and Apollonius Turk were setting up these secret deaths, in which the targets were named *assets* and the paid assassins were *asset managers*, made it real. And scary as hell. These people were psychopaths, especially Turk. But then, he'd always come off as a bit of a freak in the trideos Jericho watched, and in the information he'd found deep in the Matrix.

After that, he culled everything he could on what was now called *SPECTRE*, and the info packet George Spinoza had created to save his own skin. George had been brilliant to stuff communiques, missives, recordings, data, everything he could copy off the Andreas Martin Research Node, into that packet every night, up until the moment it was transferred to MIT&T.

The last job to save the lynchpins had gone off like a bomb, and the trideos were announcing the decline of Andreas Martin Analysis Systems. In fact, just that morning Lone Star, with the help of the UCAS Intelligence Agency, was launching a full investigation of Apollonius Turk and his relationship to Black Hat Operations.

The company stock was bottoming out. In a few days, AMAS would cease to exist and NEOnet would never have their miracle software because it didn't work. Or as far as public knowledge went, it didn't.

Oliver—Chris—had gone into great detail to let the whole team know what was at stake if those lynchpins—those people—were killed. The team understood it, but getting the targets to understand it had proven difficult. At least the first two had listened and taken Crisis's offered help to disappear, at least temporarily. The third though—she had refused and gone about her night, but in the end, she'd proven to be the best mouthpiece they could find.

It's one thing to tell someone their lives were in danger, but quite another when they were faced with that potential death.

Jericho smiled as he spotted his place a block down, the snow like powder under his boots. The last thing he expected to nearly run into was a drone. Jericho skidded to a halt before running into it. It hovered at eye level and beamed a line of light over his face, scanning him. A small, female voice came from its speakers. *"Name, Jericho Edward McCleary. Age, thirty-two years. Occupation, unknown. Family, killed during Crash 2.0–"*

"Hey!" Jericho called out and held up his hand to block the light scanning. "What the hell are you? And why are you reading out my life story?"

The drone turned off its scanner and rose into the air. Jericho watched it stop several feet up and hover.

Someone stepped out in front of Jericho just before he got to his apartment's front steps. They were big and solid and unmovable. He stepped back to get a better look and gasped when he found himself looking into the irritated, snow-dusted face of the largest troll he'd ever seen in person.

"Oh...sorry. I d-didn't see you there." Jericho tried to go around the troll. The guy might have been big, but he was fast, and caught Jericho's upper arm in a vice-like grip. He yelled and tried to twist free as the troll jabbed him with a needle.

Jericho's game training kicked in and he pulled back, feeling the needle break off in his neck. When the troll didn't let go, he balled up a fist and punched up, aiming at the brute's face. He heard a *crack*, and knew a moment later it wasn't the troll's nose, but his own knuckles. He felt a wave of dizziness spin the sidewalk underfoot, unsure if that was his body reacting from the drug or the sharp pain in his hand.

And then he was on his stomach on the snow. His hands were bound behind him and something was placed over his head. He tried to scream for help, but just drooled instead. His last experience was being picked up and unceremoniously thrown over someone's shoulder. But then the blood rushed to his head and the alley winked out.

CHAPTER 31

CAMBRIDGE, MASSACHUSETTS
SUNDAY, DECEMBER 8, 2075

Upon entering his Cambridge estate, the house AI greeted Mason through his AR, giving him the events of the day, reviewing his appointments for tomorrow, and usually his plans for the evening.

Mason pursed his lips as he handed his coat and gloves to his housekeeper, a well-muscled ork he trusted named Frederick. Fred, as he preferred to be called, asked if he wanted dinner started, and gave him three choices of menu.

"I'll have the lobster," Mason said as he started into the living room, wanting to get closer to the roaring fire and his beloved view of Boston harbor.

"Very good, sir. And will your guest be wanting the same?"

Guest?

Before Mason could ask Fred, another voice came from his favorite chair. The one in front of the fire. The one Mason liked to sip his brandy in.

The chair turned to reveal Apollonius Turk seated in it, a snifter in his hand. His hair was cut short, which made him look thinner than usual. He was dressed all in black, including gloves. So as not to leave a fingerprint. This did not bode well. "I'll have the steak. Rare."

"Very good, sir." Fred nodded both to them and left the room.

Mason didn't say anything for a few seconds. A full minute passed before he finally stepped into the room. He strode to his bar to the left of the fireplace and poured himself a drink. "Why are you here, Apollo?"

"I do so like that name. Don't you?" Apollonius stretched his legs out in front of him. "It gives one a sense of power. Strength."

Mason stood by the fire, inwardly glad Nicole wasn't home. "Again, Apollonius," he made sure to use the full name this time. "Why are you in my home?"

"Colleagues can't meet and discuss business at home, Mason?"

"You haven't been at the office since everything went to shit. This is my home. What do you want?"

Apollonius set his snifter on the side table and made a gesture in the air. "I want an explanation as to why you used one of my asset managers to find someone named Jericho McCleary."

Another image popped up, and Mason knew he was looking at a drone capture of Jericho. The images were just a tad grainy and dark, and the time stamp was Saturday night.

"Apollonius—"

Mason didn't see his boss move, just heard the *clink* when something struck Apollonius's snifter on the table, knocking it over. Apollonius was up and across the room, his hand at Mason's throat before the snifter bounced on the carpet. Mason dropped his own glass as he was shoved with bone-crushing force against the window and then pushed up against it until he was looking down at Apollonius Turk. Even if he wanted to answer, he couldn't. Because he couldn't breathe.

"YOU USED CLASSIFIED RESOURCES TO LOOK FOR SOME THIRD-RATE PROGRAMMER?!" Apollonius's voice boomed in the room. *"NO ONE GAVE YOU PERMISSION!"*

His view of Apollonius's enraged face blurred as he struggled to bring in air and couldn't. He made noises as his feet kicked against the glass at his back and grabbed Apollonius's wrists.

"Who the frag is he, Mason?"

When Mason proved he couldn't answer, and that death was eminent by making choking noises, Apollonius finally let him go. Mason landed on his hands and knees, gasping for air. He struggled to bring it into his lungs. His neck hurt and he drooled a bit onto the carpet before he could bring his breathing to some kind of recognizable pattern, but he didn't speak. Mason had no intention of telling that fucker anything useful.

"Who is he?" Apollonius said as he retrieved his snifter, didn't touch the brandy stain on the carpet and poured himself another drink.

Mason sat up and continued to work on breathing. He had no intention of answering Apollonius until he had his voice back. After a few tense minutes, he grabbed his glass and pulled himself up into a standing position by the fireplace, but he didn't approach the bar because Apollonius was still standing at it. He cleared his throat. "He...was an old friend of Oliver's. S-Someone—" he coughed. "Someone close."

"Really." It wasn't a question. "And you were hoping this friend could somehow collaborate my insistence that Oliver could be alive."

Mason kept his features flat. "I thought if—" *cough,* "—Oliver contacted anyone—" *cough,* "—it would be Jericho." And in all his searches, there had been no message, missive or otherwise from Oliver to Jericho.

"So, you do have him." Apollonius sipped his brandy, staring at Mason. "You kidnapped him."

Mason thought—even feared—that Apollonius would explode again, and braced himself for the physical and verbal onslaught. When none came, he continued. "Jericho McCleary is safely—" *cough,* "—in my custody."

Apollonius swirled the snifter. "Who do you plan to contact to trade for his life? That is why you had him kidnapped, isn't it?"

Mason took in a few breaths, deep and slow, and made sure he was a good distance away from Apollonius. This madman could and would kill him. "I needed to speak to you first."

"Me? Really? You wish to include me in on your clandestine affairs?" Apollonius continued swirling the snifter at a ridiculous speed.

Clearing his throat, Mason said, "I do have some knowledge and expertise in hiring the *right* people, Mr. Turk. Upon undergoing a bit of serum, Mr. McCleary did reveal a few key things."

Apollonius set the snifter down hard on the side table. The dark gold contents splashed on the surface. "What?"

"That the shapeshifter you've kept as a pet...is the adopted daughter of Orlando Miles."

The tall elf didn't say anything. He didn't move. But the lines creasing his face appeared to ease. "What about Oliver Martin?"

"He didn't give much on that subject. Just that he missed Oliver, but Oliver was dead. He'd never see that friend again." Mason swallowed. "Given that Mr. Cleary confessed to aiding the shadowrunners in the MIT&T break in and helped Miss Prior avoid her scheduled demise, he might be as valuable an asset to that team as the shapeshifter."

Apollonius slowly moved closer to Mason. Mason took as many steps back as he could. "You want to exchange them for Miles."

"I think, with the right incentive and a good bit of nuyen, it could be a fair trade."

To his relief, Apollonius moved away and looked outside at the darkening courtyard. The sky lit up a few seconds before distant thunder announced a coming storm. "And you did all of this with the use of *Black Hat*."

Mason hesitated. "Yes. I didn't want AMAS to be involved."

"The nuyen can come from Black Hat. I'll have it ready." He half-turned and glanced at Mason. "I want a physical meeting. Miles on sight. Public place. Very public. I plan on having Knight Errant there ready to take Orlando Variant Miles down to the ground. It will be the best public spectacle I can give him, for what he's put me through." He stared at the window again. "I'll bring you the shapeshifter."

"You don't have to—"

"I'll contact you later today to give you the specifics of how this meeting will go down. And you will deliver the message exactly as I give it to you." With that, he grabbed the brandy snifter and drained it. He pulled air between his teeth and threw the snifter into the fire. The shattering of glass made Mason wince. "I know you're contacting Nicole—or you'll attempt it. Just keep an eye on her. And I'll keep an eye on you."

And with that, he left.

Mason gave himself another few minutes before he allowed himself an attempt to breathe. He managed to get to his chair and collapsed into it. He stared at the fire so long it was Fred who roused him from his thinking, letting him know dinner was ready.

He had no appetite, but he wouldn't let lobster go to waste. No, he'd eat and drink and think more about what he'd say to

Nicole. He wasn't even sure she'd open a message from him, or believe it. Or that she actually had any contact with these people.

Either way, he was resigned to one thing as he stood and walked stonily to his dining room.

Apollonius Turk had no plans to allow any of those shadowrunners to live. He just had to figure out what the son of a bitch was planning.

CHAPTER 32

MONDAY, DECEMBER 9, 2075

I couldn't find Jericho. We were supposed to meet up in game on Sunday, and he never showed. All of my calls went unanswered, and there was no activity on any of his accounts. Yeah, it was just Monday, and anything could have happened.

But I wasn't so sure. Everything inside of me that made me who I am now warned that something was wrong.

I seemed to be the only worried about him. Variant was beside himself with happiness over the vid coverage of Apollonius Turk and AMAS, especially the parts where they were now under investigation. Nicole had even anonymously sent the UCAS Intelligence Agency the information we had about Oliver Martin's accounts, the alleged stolen SIN, and his disappearance. Just this morning a smiling anchorwoman announced there were plans to exhume his body.

I wasn't sure what they'd find, but it sure wasn't me. Apollonius had made a mistake burying anything. If you wanted someone to disappear like that, cremation would have been the right choice.

Jesus...listen to me.

Thinking about the proper way to destroy a body. Not to just anyone either.

But *me*.

We were all in the war room. Variant, Pearl, and me. Variant was enjoying himself. Reveling as the screens displayed news reporters accosting Mason Andreas as he left his office at AMAS. He looked old. Worn. Haggard. There'd been no news on his wedding, and yet no one had seen him with his fiancée in weeks. Was the wedding still on? Were they fighting? Was

Nicole having second thoughts? I watched my old partner and friend field off the people and the intrusive news drones as they hounded him into a limo.

Sighing, I glanced at the little chair Loki always filled and felt the weight of her absence on my shoulders. There had been no word on the street about a fox shapeshifter. No body. Nothing. That not knowing is what ramped my anxiety up with Jericho.

"If I'd have known all I'd had to do to get that bastard's attention was steal from him, we'd've have that come-to-Jesus meeting a long time ago."

Red Lang was still in Boston. Here with us at the Donkey for a while. He'd "found" Nathan O'Neal a week after I came out of the auto-doc. The man was careful, and a lot more knowledgeable—and savvy—to the lies of the corporate world. He'd already had people spying on Mason's orks and had an escape route in place. He'd also known Red Lang had been shadowing his daughter, and had contacted him and upped his payout. Damn bastard had been ahead of Mason and Apollonius every step.

And us.

Except when it came to Apollonius taking that company. He hadn't seen that coming, and it bothered the great Nathan O'Neal. So he was hellbent on taking him, and Mason, down. In essence, he was our new Mr. Johnson.

It looked like we'd done what we'd set out to do. Well, not what I'd set out to do, because in a sobering realization that'd taken me a few nights to process, it was evident I had no idea what it was I wanted. I had Nicole, and that made me happy. It looked as if Apollonius and Mason would go down under the pressure of the UCAS Intelligence Agency, though there had been no news about reneging on the merger with NEOnet.

And that bothered me.

And the fact I was in a sense, rudderless. Even if they cleared my old name, too much had happened to me. I'd killed humans and metahumans. A lot of them. And I'd broken more laws in the last nine months than I'd ever known in my forty-two years.

The door into the common room outside the war room opened and Sherry appeared. She'd been our rigger on the SPECTRE jobs, and proven to be one hell of an asset. Variant liked her. So did Pearl.

"What's wrong?" Pearl said as the laughter and talking ended.

Nicole came through the door at that moment and I could tell from the set of her shoulders and the look on her face that something was wrong.

Just as I'd suspected.

I stood up. "It's Jericho."

She looked at me but didn't say anything. Nicole summoned her AR and then after a few hand movements, swiped her fingers in the air. Pearl's hand came out and it looked like she caught something before all the projected holos in the room went blank, only to be replaced by the soft-skinned visage of Mason Andreas.

"Good evening, Nicole. I'm not sure if you'll even watch this, though I hope you do. For others' sake. First I apologize for Apollonius Turk's attempted acquisition of you during a dinner with your father. I am happy to confess that he was unsuccessful."

"Well, he's a cagey son of a bitch," Variant muttered.

Mason sat at his desk. I recognized the shelf behind him. I also recognized several of the company awards that once rested in my own office. Funny...I didn't really feel anything about that. *"Apollonius is aware of the interception of assets belonging to competitive entities, as well as the serious accusations hurled at him from one of those assets. He is also certain the information released was indeed manufactured by Orlando Miles, otherwise known as Crisis."*

That comment brought a guffaw from Variant. He slapped his knee. Even Pearl was smiling. She said, "Apparently, they don't believe Oliver Martin is still alive."

I nodded. Maybe this was a good thing. I just wanted him to get to his point.

"Because of the reports, the vid coverage, and the rise of AMAS competitors in the past month due to the failure of Turk's Asset Managers, I have offered to broker a deal."

"Here it comes," Red commented from his perch on the far side of the room.

"You might recall one of Oliver's friends, a Jericho McCleary. I've had several chats with him and he's been keeping a small shapeshifter company–"

I nearly jumped at the screen. "Loki!" I shouted, just as Variant did. Don't get me wrong, I cared about Jericho as well, but I'd truly believed Loki was dead.

"Wait," Pearl put up a hand. She'd paused the message until Variant and I calmed down, then restarted it.

"–and the two have gotten along quite well. Both are safe for now. What Turk wants is an exchange. The two of them for Orlando Miles, as well as any and all of the copied files of SPECTRE*, as well as* Ghost-7*. Mr. McCleary didn't give any information on the exact location of Oliver's old software–Andreas Martin Analysis System's software. If your friends agree, Nicole, then Apollonius wants a meeting at the AMAS building lobby. Friday. Eight o'clock p.m."*

Mason paused and looked down for a second, and in that instance, I thought I saw...regret? Worry? Something close to humanity?

But it was gone in the next instant before he said, *"The wedding date and venue are still reserved, in case you change your mind, Nicole. I truly do love you."*

Pearl cut off the message and we sat in silence for a few beats. Thinking.

"How much of that slippery asshole do you believe?" Red said, his right hand up in emphasis.

"He really doesn't like you, Var," Sherry said, her hands on her hips. "He's offering two of your people for just you."

"Apollonius doesn't like me. I don't think Mason Andreas gives a damn either way. He's just a puppet, nothing more." Variant turned to face me. "We have to get your friend and Loki back."

"We don't have any proof that either of them are alive." I hated to say it, but it was necessary. "This could all be a big trap."

"Then perhaps we get some of that proof?" Pearl pushed the chair back and stood. She pulled out the chip. "This thing had a tracer on it."

"It did?" Var and I looked at her and I felt my heart skip.

She twisted her lips into a smirk. "I spoofed the ID. My Sprite re-routed the ID back to AMAS. He'll just catch his own tail."

"Don't *do* that," Variant shook his head, looking visibly relieved.

I licked my lips. "You said back to AMAS."

"That's where this was message was created. He didn't try to hide the origination point."

"That's odd." Sherry looked at Pearl. "I mean, if I send a message, even a recorded one, I have subroutines that make it look like I recorded it in Japan."

They were right. And Mason understood secrecy. Protection. Why would he be that careless. "Unless..." I muttered before I went to a terminal and pulled up the public security grid for the building AMAS was in.

Everyone gathered behind me, looking at the large monitor above me.

"What're you thinking?" Variant said.

"That Mason *didn't* hide it," Nicole said as she put her hand on my shoulder. "Because he wanted you to know. Maybe he's sending a message?"

I knew the building AMAS was in like the back of my hand, hinging on the idea that nothing had been drastically changed in my absence. And since renovation permits moved like glaciers past the Boston city officials, I was pretty sure even any initiated renovations hadn't started yet.

The secure place to keep Loki and Jericho would be the basement where the nodes were housed. No windows. And three of the rooms that weren't part of the node farm only had one door each. I'd noticed them years ago and looked into each one. I'd found old desks and office furniture, but not much else. A few old filing cabinets, but whatever paperwork had been inside them was long gone.

I told everyone about those rooms. "Apollonius would keep the two of them down there, most likely in separate rooms. Maxine would be in charge of security. I'm not sure if Max would be there, or be by Apollonius' side. I'm assuming that means more trolls."

"That's kinda racist," Pearl said. "Just because they're trolls doesn't mean they just hire more trolls."

I shook my head. "No racism intended. I just know Apollonius. He likes trolls because they make him feel safe. He'll only approve more trolls. If there are any other races involved, I'll be surprised."

She seemed satisfied.

Variant stepped up to the layout grid of Andreas Martin Analysis Systems on the holoscreen. He pointed to the rooms. "So the rooms are in the basement of the building, but not actually part of AMAS property."

"Yep."

"Is there ductwork in here? I can't tell from these plans."

"I really don't remember," I said. "I'm not sure I ever noticed. I'm sure there is for the nodes. There is a back door into my old office."

Everyone pivoted and stared at me. Variant held out his hand. "You just telling us this now?"

"Because that's all it is. A door in the parking garage that leads up to straight to the office. Nowhere else."

"We can use it," Sherry said.

"And then have to go back down to get to the rooms," I said.

Nicole said, "The only reason I can come up with is...they're trying to make it a setup if we sneak in down there."

"How?" Variant asked.

Pearl had moved to the side and had her hands out, her eyes unfocused. She spoke up, "She's right. I just found three communications between the BMP and Mason's office."

"Encoded?"

"Yeah."

"What do they say?"

Pearl smiled. "There is an event that night in one of the large conference rooms on the first floor. Apparently they are expecting us to break into the building. They're making preparations for us. So I believe Nicole is right. This is a set up."

Now I was getting twitchy. "Event?"

"Yeah. There's a press conference scheduled at the same time. Apparently they're announcing something big with the company. But the communications with the BMP are warnings that their special guest might be in danger."

Nicole put a hand on my shoulder. "You don't think that's my father, do you? Turk's been trying for months to get my dad to sell what's left of the company to him."

I grimaced. "Oh, so he can make a bigger asset hit squad? No... there's something about that date..."

I did the most perfect, epic face palm ever. Friday was December thirteenth! "How could I have forgotten? You're right. They're doing the public signing Friday. The Acquisition. The special guest is probably some big name from NeoNET, not your dad."

"Then why in the hell would they arrange a hostage swap during this?"

"Easy," Variant said. "Because the software is the golden egg in all this. NeoNET wants it all under its wing."

"But we saved the assets," Sherry narrowed her eyes. "Doesn't that mean something?"

I nodded. "Yes, but economic indicators are usually months in advance. Sometimes two, sometimes six, or even one. I'm pretty sure the intel they have on the assets we saved to prevent them from taking down the companies in competition isn't something they've shared with NEOnet. They're still going through with the acquisition as planned." I looked at each of them. "They still have *SPECTRE*, remember? That's what NEOnet wants. They don't know that the key to cracking what *SPECTRE* can do is out there. The software is useless."

Pearl sighed. "They can't be that blind."

"Greed makes you very blind to the truth," Nicole said. She looked at me. "But still...to have a swap that night?"

I pointed to the map. "It's a trap. Not just for us, but for NeoNET. What if we arrive looking for Loki and Jericho? We're then surrounded by BMP or whoever they've got on the take. My name's already synonymous for causing them problems. We get arrested, accused of stealing the one thing NeoNET wants more than the brick and mortar the software was built on. The software itself. They lock us up, NeoNET is grateful to Turk for helping to catch us, and he's free to broker a deal to create new softs that will safeguard SPECTRE. He'll be safe within the very company he'd built the muscle under."

It sounded like a great plan. We take the fall for the hacked prototype, the one they've been promising since it disappeared off AMAS's node. But then it's gone, we show up, we're arrested and bam.

Nicole shook her head. "He's throwing Mason under the bus as well."

Variant nodded. "And I'm willing to bet Jericho and Loki aren't in AMAS at all."

A new grid appeared on the screens. The view shifted and changed until it stopped on the basement level of a new building. Why were these things always in the basement? "Nicole, how well do you know the Black Hat Operations?"

"You mean my father's company? Well enough to know his node farm is on lower basement two."

"He got any offline nodes?"

"I don't think Dad did, but I'm sure Turk's got something in there. Something to protect his assets from being found."

Variant pointed to the vids. "You think they're being held at Black Hat?"

I ran my fingers through my hair. None of this felt right. Nothing I could come up with made sense. "Honestly...I don't know. They could be in either one. And we don't have time to waste looking for them." We needed someone on the inside. Someone who would know exactly where Loki and Jericho were being held. Someone who would break if the right pressure were applied.

Someone who had just sent us a message that lead us right to intel that the meet up was a trap.

"Chris...you've got a really scary grin on your face." Pearl sounded worried.

"Because I have a plan. Variant, get ahold of the Ancients. I think we've got a way you and they can get your revenge. As well as a better plan to rescue Loki and Jericho."

I just hoped like hell I was right.

CHAPTER 33

BOSTON
WEDNESDAY, DECEMBER 11, 2075

Mason was checking his reflection in the mirror of his private bathroom at AMAS when he heard the office door open.

Assuming it was Apollonius, or perhaps one of the reporters from outside sneaking in, he remained where he was, still and quiet. He listened for a few seconds to see if he could pinpoint where the intruder was in his office, but there weren't any other sounds. Frowning, he peeked around the washroom door and saw a movement to the left. Because his bathroom was behind his desk, he had to move further out of the bathroom to get a full view of the room.

He saw someone's boots crossed on the top of his desk and knew someone was leaning back in his chair! How dare they! Yet before he could charge forward and order them out, another movement caught his eye. This one by the door.

Nicole stood there, dressed in tight-fitting leather. Her dark hair had been pulled back from her face and again he was taken by her beauty. Her pale skin, blue eyes, and red lips. There was nothing in this world more beautiful than her. He forgot the person on his chair for a moment. "Nicole—you saw my message."

"Hello, Mason. I'm sorry, but we won't be crashing the party in the lobby."

"We? Party?"

"The one where you and your boyfriend Apollonius were going to frame us for the disappearance of *SPECTRE*." This was a man's voice. And there was something oddly familiar about it.

Mason turned, and indeed there was someone sitting in his chair. Human. Maybe early forties, with short if not a bit spiked salt-and-pepper hair. A two-day shadow of beard accentuated his strong jaw, but it couldn't hide a long scar on his right cheek. It started just beneath his eye and slashed across to his ear. He wore leather as well, and a long leather coat that flared out as he jumped up from the chair. That's when Mason saw the crossbow and the rifle displayed on his desk, and knew who he was. "You're the one they call Crisis."

Crisis wore fingerless gloves and slowly clapped them together. "That's one of my names, Mason. But not the one you know me by."

"Know you?"

"Oh come on, *Mase*. Take a real good look at me. I haven't changed that much. It's only been what...nine months, maybe?" He stepped close. Too close. So close Mason could smell sweat, and oil, and leather. And when he looked into this shadowrunner's eyes...

No...

It's not possible...

Mason stumbled back until his back pressed against the wall.

"I think he remembers me now, Nicole."

"Oliver, stop. You're going to give him a heart attack."

Oliver...

OLIVER!

The mention of a heart attack made Mason put his hand against his chest. He thought of the panic in Apollonius's face when he'd insisted Oliver Martin was alive. At the time, Mason had thought the man raving mad, but...here he was. Standing in front of him.

Mason saw his shaking hand rise to point at Oliver. "You... You died."

"In a way I did, *omae*. Oliver died under the metal pipe and knife and syringe of Apollonius Turk. I still wake up from night terrors, remembering every single thing that bastard did to me."

Oliver came at Mason and slammed his hands on the walls to the sides of Mason's head. At that moment he was more afraid of the specter in front of him than Apollonius Turk.

"And *you* let him do it to me, Mase," Oliver snarled as he came within inches of Mason's face. "You and he set me up so well, fucked my life up so bad so fast, that Oliver Martin's never coming back!"

"Stop it, Oliver," Nicole chided. "We don't have much time, and we need his help."

Oliver's angry face filled Mason's world until his one-time best friend stepped back and strode to the door. There he turned with a swish of his coat and glared at Mason.

"I...I swear I didn't know." Mason put his hand to his chest when he could move again. "Apollonius said you escaped, and his hunter killed you."

"I killed *them*, Mase. I've killed a lot of people. And I'm going to kill you. But first, you're going to listen to Nicole. And if you do anything I don't like, I'll kill you right now."

Mason believed Oliver would do just that. Sweating along his upper lip and brow, Mason turned his attention to Nicole. "It wasn't my fault. I didn't know he was alive—"

"Can it, asshole," she said sharply. "You set him up. I know all about it. And I know your evidence against him was falsified. So stop your pleading right there."

She approached and activated her commlink. Mason's AR came up with a received message icon. He opened it. "It's a list of links."

"Links to all the stock reports, industry insider tips and worldwide trading feeds you and Apollonius pay attention to. And within an hour and ten minutes, there's going to be another serious drop for Andreas Martin Analysis Systems stock."

"No..." Mason laughed at the absurdness of the statement. "Apollonius said he had it all under control. He's going to discredit that whistleblower."

"No. He can't do that, short of killing her, but even at that, the evidence against AMAS is already out there in Matrix. That little acquisition ceremony you want us to walk into will be the last ditch effort of Apollonius to save what's left of the deal. He plans on framing us for it all, specifically Orlando Miles, claiming it was all revenge for the death of his wife. He'll have all that old evidence of Miles' harassing him all those years ago. He'll insist Miles hacked the software, making it useless."

Nicole stepped forward. "And then he'll sell you out as well, Mase. You'll take the brunt of the breach of contract NeoNET will use to nullify the acquisition." She smiled grimly. "That's the worst case scenario. There is also the possibility we'll all die, and he'll be able to spin whatever story he needs in order to continue his work and start over, with NeoNET's backing. Either way, Mase, your ass is in the same sling as ours."

Mason had never heard her use terms like that before. Honestly, he'd always thought of her as little more than an accessory, not someone with brains. "That's...that's ridiculous! NeoNET's getting exactly what it wants."

"Oh cut the crap, Mason," Oliver snarled and crossed the room again. Mason found himself backing away along the wall, so Oliver stopped. "You and Apollonius have no intention of giving NeoNET a tool that will make them God in the markets of the world. *He'd* prefer to be God, and have others bow down to *him*."

Mason looked at each of them. Whatever they were trying to say wasn't getting to him. "Look, I don't know what you're trying to do here. Great, Oliver, you scared the piss out of me. I thought you were dead. Now you're not. But don't think you can just come in here and take back what's mine—"

He didn't see the strike coming. In fact, he didn't see anything for a few seconds until he realized he was staring up at the ceiling and Nicole was scolding Oliver. "—no good if he dies right now. We have to keep him alive!"

Mason tried not to make a noise as he struggled to sit up, but failed. Oliver held out his hand, but Mason slapped it away. "I'm calling the guards, and you'll both be taken to jail."

"Wrong," Oliver said. "Your guards are taking a long nap. We want Jericho and Loki unharmed. *Now.* We're not going to be there for that bastard's little party."

"Wait," Mason held up his hand. "I don't know where they are."

"You," Oliver said. "Are a drek liar. Now, you're going to get your coat, and we're going to get our friends."

"Wait." Mason put his hand. "What is it you think he'll do to me?"

"No time, Mason."

"Goddamn it, Oliver, I've got time. You want to find Jericho and the little wolf girl? Then you answer my damn question!" It was the closest he'd come to an all-out yelling match with Oliver Martin. Ever. "Tell me what you suspect."

Oliver glanced at Nicole, who pointed to her chronometer. "It's possible he doesn't want to know, so he never saw it. He can't see it now."

"Know what?" Mason looked from Oliver to Nicole and back again. His heart sank. "Wait...Apollonius is planning to frame me as well, isn't he?"

"You know everything, Mase," Oliver said. "You know every move Apollonius ever made. For him to get out of this unscathed and keep his reputation and wealth and power, he'll have to do what he's always done."

Mason slowly shook his head. "You mean his job as a fixer."

"And now he'll want to fix what he sees as your mess."

"No, this all started because he wanted *Ghost-7*," Mason pointed at Oliver. "Which you stole."

"I never stole it, Mase. I downloaded it before I left with Nicole because of what I found. What I brought to your attention. I wanted to know who was using the application incorrectly." Oliver snorted. "Then you set your own plan in motion, the one where I was destroyed, my ID wiped, and then what was left of me had to be murdered."

"I had nothing to do with that!" Mason said as he boldly took a step toward Oliver. "Yes I wanted your name off the project. I got greedy, and then Apollonius got even greedier. But I trusted he knew what he was doing."

"You still don't get it, do you?" Oliver matched Mason's movement until they were less than an inch apart again. "You know about the Asset Managers. You know what his little teams was doing to the lynchpins. You know everything. You are the loose end here. Not me, or my team. He has no plans of ever letting Black Hat Operations go. That's his baby. That's the thing he's wanted to create since he made a name for him in this town. Even if *SPECTRE* never sees the light of day, he still has the program. He can still offer his team for hire, not just to remove lynchpins, but to eliminate anyone." He stared at Mason. "Even you."

The weight of what Oliver was saying struck Mason in the chest. He backed away. "No..."

"Yes," Nicole came over to stand by Oliver. "Apollonius has sunk over two million nuyen into BHO in the past three months. Node farms, security—but there's no staff. None. What he plans to do is terrible, Mason."

"In case you haven't figured it out," Oliver stepped in. "Your buddy plans on running an assassin's guild out of Cambridge. A place for companies to come to, find out what's wrong with their businesses. And depending on the price, Apollonius wants to run your precious *SPECTRE* to find the three nexus employees and get rid of them. It does matter that I cracked it, that we can cull the information from the software—no one will care if we're all dead. The information's in the Matrix, but no one knows how to use it.

"No one cares." Oliver turned away. "So I suggest you pick a side right now, *omae*, because Apollonius is going to watch you go down with the ship. You don't have *SPECTRE*, he does. And we're betting it's on his main node and ready for business just as soon as AMAS is destroyed."

Mason staggered to his chair and sat down hard. It all made sense when he looked at everything through Oliver's eyes. The odd requisitions for building permits, all the materials. He'd wondered why it was so important to fortify BHO and not AMAS. *But* SPECTRE... "There's nothing I can do to make up for what was done to you, Oliver."

"Tell us where Jericho and Loki are, Mason. Where inside of AMAS or BHO would he hide them?"

"They're not at either place." He swallowed. "They're at our home," he looked at Nicole. "In the lower rooms."

"You're lying," Oliver said.

"No. Apollonius didn't want them found, so he figured the last place you'd look would be my house."

Oliver quickly moved to Mason and grabbed his arm. "Then you're coming with us."

Mason allowed his old friend to manhandle him. He didn't have the strength or the inclination to fight. He felt weary. Bruised. And Oliver was so much stronger.

In truth, he'd always been the greater man.

"What about the press conference and the exchange?" Nicole said as Oliver half-dragged Mason down the hall to his old office and down the secret staircase. Something Mason had never bothered to tell Apollonius about.

"If we can get to Jericho and Loki, then they can have their big meet n'greet. Just not with us."

In the underground garage, a white van pulled up and the side door opened. A dark-skinned ork reached out and pulled

Mason inside. He was slammed against something very hard with sharp edges and yelled in pain.

"None of that," the ork said. "We're good, Sherry."

The van pulled away at a reasonable speed.

When he eyes adjusted to the dimmer light, Mason got a better look at the ork and assumed this was the infamous Miles Orlando, the ork in Apollonius's side. Another ork, female, drove the van as a gorgeous dark-skinned, white-haired elf sat in the passenger side.

"You got all that?" Oliver said as he clamped cuffs on Mason's wrists.

"Pearl's already investigating the residence," the female ork named Sherry said. "We should be there in about fifteen minutes."

Oliver reached out and squeezed the ork's upper arm. "If we don't find them, you get to kill Mason."

Mason swallowed hard at that, hoping Apollonius hadn't double-crossed him and not left the two in his basement. "They're there. If they're not, it's because Apollonius moved them, not me."

No one else spoke for the remainder of the drive.

Mason knew when they approached his home. His AR opened up on his commlink and asked for a code. "I have to enter the code."

Oliver removed the cuffs so he could input the correct string of numbers. The gates opened and they drove in. "Can you open your garage from here? Dismantle your cameras?"

"Yes but why? There's no one here."

"I'm finding seven individuals on the grounds," the elf said as her eyes remained unfocused. "Two are Jericho and Loki."

"You have staff?" Oliver asked Nicole.

"Yes." She slipped out of the van just before Oliver dragged Mason out. "But I don't know why they're not here."

Mason would have come willingly, he just had a very bad feeling and started to say something. Everyone should have been here.

Nicole's commlink buzzed and she paused to bring up her AR. Mason thought he saw Nathan's avatar on the superimposed screen.

Variant whistled. "Nice spread."

Mason led them through a hallway to the kitchen, then to a part of the wall that popped open when he pressed it. Variant went down first with his weapon drawn. Pearl had stayed in the van with Sherry. Oliver pushed Mason to the stairs just as Nicole caught up with them.

"What's wrong?" Oliver asked her.

Mason could see that whatever her father had called about was bad.

But it was Variant that yelled out from below, interrupting Nicole. "Hey—what the fuck happened down here! We got a bunch of dead bodies piled in the corner! They been shot!"

Mason felt the color drain from his face. No... "Are they in uniform?" he called down.

"Yeah...it's a mess."

"Oliver—" Nicole put her hand on his arm. "Dad was still monitoring the BHO and AMAS activity. AMAS delivered six crates to our house yesterday. They're downstairs."

"Six crates of what?"

"That's just it—there's no manifest to say what's in them. The order flagged at the delivery service but someone over rode the protocol and they were delivered down—"

Just then Mason's own AR activated and popped up with a message from Apollonius. *"Thank you for your service."* The image ended with the flashing icon of a bomb.

He turned to Nicole and Oliver. *"MOVE!"*

And then the world was on fire.

CHAPTER 34

BOSTON HARBOR
FRIDAY, FEBRUARY 14, 2076

Apollonius had done more than just set a bomb to detonate when we entered Mason's house. It was meant as a way to get rid of Mason Andreas, and any evidence of Apollonius's duplicity in the events at AMAS. He'd had it all delivered under a stack of explosives.

He hadn't counted on Mason actually leading us into the house. More bodies. And Nathan O'Neal's vengeance against Apollonius reached a fevered pitch after it. He had testified against Apollonius Turk with all the evidence we'd gathered, as well as some of his own.

The blond asshole had signed his own death warrant.

Mason, Nicole, and I survived because we were thrown through a wall. Survived is a relative term for Mason. He suffered serious head trauma, and is still breathing through a tube, two months later. Nicole's injuries were even worse, but because she was still physically there, even if the physicians told Nathan she would be a vegetable the rest of her life, he kept her on life support.

I came through it because of Variant's training. Variant ran into a side room when he heard Mason yell and was buried for a bit. He had broken bones, including a crushed leg, but he was already getting used to a few cyber upgrades. Loki had been able to shift into fox form, which made her small enough to get through with just a minor amount of damage. Pearl was shaken from the blast, but protected by the van.

Jericho didn't make it.

I didn't realize how much I still cared for Nicole until I climbed over the rubble to find half of her buried body.

As for Apollonius—the press conference announcing the acquisition was interrupted, just like Apollonius wanted it, just not by us. Everyone's ARs and PANS lit up after the explosion. All trideo drones and their reporters exited stage left in a mass exodus to get to the blast. I can't remember who was the first one to announce it was Mason Andreas's home, the CEO of Andreas Martin.

Apollonius explained the missing prototype away as a casualty of that explosion, that Mason insisted on keeping it on his home node. Funny how forensics never found a trace of that software on any of the surviving nodes in Mason's home. NeoNET retracted their offer, and sued Apollonius for breach of contract. Not quite what the power-hungry little prick wanted. They went after BHO and all its assets, which meant all of Apollonius's assets, since he'd pretty much sunk everything into his company.

And what made Variant and I happy was watching as the entire building was seized and Apollonius, wanted for various crimes such as fraud, and possible murder, disappeared. Pearl had made sure the records of all those assassinations, the ones we found on Black Hat's node, were sent to Apollonius's personal node from an anonymous source.

Andreas Martin Analysis Systems became an empty set of offices.

And Apollonius? I wondered where the bastard went. He disappeared very quickly and quietly after the explosion.

Until today.

Nathan had finally agreed to let Nicole go. He'd asked that I be there. We were all there. Pearl, me, Variant, Loki, a dozen of her personal friends I'd never met. We all said our goodbyes as the machine was turned off.

Everyone left but me.

I was there holding her hand when her heart stopped.

And then there was just silence.

The nurses ushered me out, and I went to the waiting room window and looked out over the harbor. The snow had stopped for a bit, and the world was white. Pristine for a moment, hiding the darkness underneath.

Nathan's visage appeared reflected in the window. I didn't turn. I didn't want him to see my face.

"Oliver—"

"It's not okay, Nathan. It'll never be okay."

"I know. I'm sorry any of this happened to you. If there is anything I can do—"

"You just lost your only child, Nathan. Remember Nicole. Go home to your wife. If I need you, I'll contact you."

I watched he nodded, turned, and strode down the hall to the elevator. I lowered my shoulders and pressed my forehead against the cold glass. Everyone left me alone as I let my pain roll over. I kept my anger in my gut, where I would hold it until I could exact my own revenge.

That time came a month later in March, not far from the very day I'd first woke up to the rain and cold, not knowing who I was.

Loki and I were walking through South Boston. We'd just had a meeting with the Ancients, going over territories and where we could help each other out. It was an odd alliance, if not frail in a lot of ways. But we were bound by tragedy. Vertigo had saved my life. And I owed her—and them—for that.

Loki and I had just strolled through a run-down area of mostly empty, half-rotted buildings when something about the place struck me as familiar. In fact, the déjà vu was so strong it nearly knocked me over.

"Pup?" Loki asked, and put her hand in mine.

But I was focused on the fence in front of a hollow building, at the torn piece of filthy cloth caught on a single metal barb. I walked to it and carefully pulled it off. It was a piece of a cotton shirt I'd worn a lifetime ago. The tatters of what had been left of me when I jumped this fence and caught its shirt on the wire. I'd finally found the building I'd been tortured in. Here. Close to Ancient territory.

Behind me, I heard the footfall of a familiar boot, and I was thrown back to that moment when I'd hidden inside that hole and watched as my pursuer's boots stood just inches away from me. It was the step of the assassin that had shot me. The one that got away.

"Someone's coming. He smells familiar," Loki sniffed the air as her ears perked up and twisted.

"Loki," I took her hands. "Run to the Donkey as fast as you can. Get Variant."

"I not leave you!"

"Do it, Loki. We'll get ice cream later."

"It's too cold."

"Chili?"

"With beans!"

I smiled. "With beans. Go!"

Loki gave me a peck on the cheek, twisted and shifted into her fox, and scampered into the shadows.

I straightened and turned in time to see that same pair of boots striding toward me. Stark black against the snow. And as I moved my gaze up the length of the dark coat and the sword in his hand, I wasn't surprised to see the face of Apollonius Turk at the top. Somehow knowing *he* was one of the assassins to come after me the day I escaped, that he was the one that left the others to die at my hands and never returned—filled me with a kind of symmetry. Apollonius was the last remnant of that dark, hollow moment in my life.

I turned to face him. Just the two of us in the snow, on an abandoned street. Though, with it this close to Ancient territory, I doubted we were really alone.

"Nice sword."

"You got away from me once. You won't do it again, Oliver Martin."

I held out my hands to my sides, thankful of my gloves as the wires in my muscles sang. The skillsoft loaded as my cybereyes started their prep before battle, weighing in speed, distance, weather, and a readout came up to my left. "You really believe there's still something between us?"

"You know there is."

"No, I don't. I was a means for your future. A future you failed to achieve. There's so much nuyen on your head, Turk, you're a fool to show yourself here."

"I will never go to prison, Oliver Martin. But I will kill you before I die."

Yeah, yeah. A few movements visible along the rooftops caught my attention. My eyes told me they were elves. Ancients? Or assassins? It would be just like Apollonius to cheat. "So...you plan on having me shot by someone else, or you want to try it yourself?"

"I am alone. Whomever is watching us—they are not on my side. But this is my fight."

Baka.

I reached behind me to retrieve the short sword I kept tucked beneath my crossbow and rifle. It wasn't as elegant as the long-ass blade Apollonius carried. But it was strong and we knew each other. Variant would be proud.

But then, it was just so damn cold out here.

I grabbed the rifle instead, brought it down, aimed, and fired. The bullet hit Apollonius right between the eyes. By the time he fell over, several Ancients came out of the shadows, open doors and windows and began scavenging.

Variant came running up, weapon in hand, and when he saw the group of Ancients he looked at me with confusion. "Loki said—"

"You better get over there and get a piece of Apollonius Turk before the elves take it all."

He pointed. "That's Apollonius?" And then he was gone, yelling at them to leave him something.

I watched as they devoured the last piece of my old life, stripping it of its earthly possessions. Knowing Turk had been that assassin in the shadows that day I awoke to this new life, the one who got away from me, drove home the realization that my old life was truly gone. Nicole would always be with me, in my heart. Mason and Turk had ripped away what could have been, but Variant and my team gave me what is, and what will be. A family.

I'll never be a wageslave again. Instead, I planned on surviving day to day, enjoying life the best I can, and shooting assholes like Turk.

Loki was standing on the corner, winded, and in her human form. I set my rifle back into its slot on my back and jogged to her. I picked her up and put her on my shoulder.

"Chili?" I asked as we walked.

"Pizza. Variant wants some, too."

"Pearl?"

"She's on a date."

"Who's Pearl dating?"

Loki shrugged. "Techiemancer. Some guy named Kazuma."

SNEAK PEEK:
STIRRED

BY RUSSELL ZIMMERMAN

COMING SOON!

NO PLACE FOR A HERO...

Jimmy Kincaid, burned-out mage, P. I., and the closest thing Puyallup's got to a hero, has a lot on his plate these days. Simmering gang wars, feuding mobsters, missing runaways, magical power only as reliable as his stubborn sorcerous patron, and–well above his usual pay grade–an encrypted data file that's already cost him friends, but that he can't even access. When the always-dangerous troubles of the Seattle sprawl deepen into a bloody conspiracy with ties to neighboring nations and inhuman powers, he knows he's on the job of his life. Facing the longest of long odds, Kincaid's all too aware that the house always wins.

Luckily, he's not alone. A man like Jimmy can't walk these shadowed streets without making enemies, but he's made allies, too. With the help of his bounty-hunting best friends, an up-and-coming shadowrunner team, a former Lone Star detective who's short in stature but big in style, and his loyal, albeit flighty ally spirit, Jimmy's stacked the deck in his favor. Maybe he's got a shot after all. Maybe he can make it all work. Maybe he can find the right balance, share the right truths, and make something good out of a whole lot of bad.

Of course, the problem with a house of cards is it just takes one good hit to bring it all tumbling down...

It was a cute little party, and Ariana just made it cuter. Silver and shining, hair and smile like platinum and white gold, eyes blue as amethysts, clapping and shaking her skinny, elven, booty in time to the birthday girl's sugary pop music; she loved it as much as the kids loved her. Jasmine was turning eleven—her being impossible was just around the corner, her ma worried—

and the fact "she'd" arranged for a real, live spirit at her party had to be doing her middle school street cred some favors.

Not that Ari minded. Heck, she was having a great time. Me? I was cycling through images and files in my headware, little pop-up boxes displaying themselves thanks to the tech-wizardry of my cyberoptics. While Ariana played, I brooded and worked. That's the life. That's the job.

Jasmine's mom, Sally, was from the neighborhood. I'd gone to school with her big brother and her ex-husband, known her and her family a long time. She waited tables down at this Korean/Tex-Mex fusion joint I swing by maybe once a week, so we kept in touch. I always left a good tip, just like my dad taught me, but I slipped her a few extra nuyen whenever I could.

Sally'd scrimped and saved for Jasmine's party all year—she always did—and it was turning out just fine. She and a few other worried moms, all wringing hands about their precious angels growing into makeup and skirts and AR avatars and today's awful music, hung out on one end of the room, and as far away from them as they could be, the girls sang terrible karaoke, giggled about giggle-worthy stuff, thumbed at their commlinks, and ate cake while swearing they'd only gotten seconds 'cause they'd skipped breakfast.

It *was* a cute little party, sure, but I had better things to do. My heart just wasn't in it. I had too many other cases, too many other problems, too many other projects I was juggling. Pinkerton'd understood when I said I needed the afternoon off in order to attend, and he'd understood why. It wasn't just a party to me. I wasn't just here for the cake and the shrieking, no, it was a work lunch for me. *Both* jobs.

Sally had me here working security, believe it or not, at this little rented conference room. The internals of this little Puyallup city building weren't covered by the Knight Errant contract past normal government hours. The cameras were on—the city had to worry about protecting its *stuff* 24/7, after all—but there was no security present. When the politicians and employees left, so did the cops.

So that was one job. The usual one. The one folks expected of me. Champion of the people, Mr. Puyallup, Jimmy Kincaid, wasting an afternoon by hanging around to get ogled by low-rent soccer moms while his ally spirit dances and puts on a light show for the kids and their karaokean caterwauling. The glamorous life of a Puyallup PI, all just to get paid with a tired smile, some cake to take home, and a little good karma around the neighborhood.

"Hey Sal," I jumped the gun and gave her a tired smile of my own, then nodded at the door. "I'm gonna jump outside, grab a smoke, yeah? You ladies have fun."

"And Ari," I raised my voice just enough, even though my ally spirit's psychic link meant she knew a conversation from an *order*, anyways. "You sit tight, doll. Have fun in here for a little bit, okay?"

It was an order. An *order*-order, magi to ally. She wouldn't come interfere. She couldn't. I wanted to work alone, but I didn't know if it was to keep Ariana from crossing a line, or to keep her from seeing me do it.

I left the women, girls, and female-gendered extramaterial entities to their party as I sauntered outside, flipping up my collar and ducking under my hat against a light drizzle. I fished out a crumpled pack of Targets from an inside coat pocket and lit one up while I waited. These front doors were the only ones left unlocked when Knight Errant pulled out at the end of their shift, so I was standing watch.

I thought about the little flask in my back pocket, but I left it there. Even out here, taking a breather from the party, I was on the job. I scoped out the parking lot, watched security cameras, cycled through my files to kill time.

Sure enough, three butts into the smoke break, the real reasons for my afternoon's employment pulled up.

I heard 'em coming before I saw 'em. The latest Fraggin' Unicorns tune was blaring outta an oversized set of speakers—three, four hundred nuyen a pop, the silly things—that looked especially incongruous compared to the rest of the run-down Toyota Talon, the sound system no doubt taking up most of the compact SUV's storage space. It was dirty and spotted with rust, but had fancy chrome rims, a gaudy undercarriage light system, and those damned speakers; Puyallup priorities, among a certain class of citizen. All flash, no substance.

Sally's ex, Jasmine's dad, was driving. He had a burly orkish buddy riding shotgun, and a bug-eyed guy with a shaved head was riding in the century-old shame spot of back-seat, middle. I gave Bug Eyes a long look, but he stayed put. I saw beer cans rattling around as Dad Of The Year climbed out, and my Sideways gene treatment helped me count exactly how many empty twelve-ouncers there were. The stereos did their work, and the FU's latest punk anthem played soundtrack while the other two sat in the SUV and bickered about something.

"That's far enough, Truck," I took a few steps away from the door, angled to put myself squarely in the way, as he approached. "This is as close as you're getting, *compadre.*"

"Frag off," Thomas "The Truck" Kowalski glowered and blustered, just like he had back in high school. He'd started out two years ahead of me, but we'd tied come graduation. Not one of Puyallup's great thinkers, Tommy, but he'd made a hell of a defensive end, once upon a time. Varsity squad for a record six years, in fact. He'd gone fleshy since then, gotten soft, but not lost the bulk, not lost the brutishness.

"She's my girl, Jimmy, you fraggin' keeb. My baby girl," he moved to sidestep, I did the same. "Ain't seen her in a while, and it's her birthday, an' I jus' wanna go give 'er...a..."

"Birthday present? Yeah." I shook my head. He wasn't carrying a damned thing. "If it's a nuyen transfer, you can do that remotely. Or, better yet, you could send some of that backed-up child support to Sally, couldn't you? I ain't letting you in there. You'd just wreck the good time anyway."

His piggish eyes went narrow, face went red, big hands curled into fists.

"Mind yer fraggin' business, Jimmy," he slurred.

"I am, Truck. Sal hired me on for the afternoon. I'm workin' the door. You don't have an invite, man. I'm not lettin' you in. You know why."

I sure knew why. I could reach into my headware commlink and call up the pics any time I wanted to, or just sift back through my memories from some of the lunches Sally'd served me over the years. She'd had to compound the footsore waitress routine with the shame of bruises, black eyes, missing teeth, a fat lip. "Truck" was a piece of work, all right. He hadn't grown out of that high school bully phase.

"You don't like girls yet, but someday you will." I looked him square in his idiot eyes, hearing my old man's voice from decades earlier. *"And when that happens, you treat them like queens, you hear me? It's what your mother would've wanted."*

I thought about my mom. I thought about my dad. I tried to give him one, good, chance to walk away.

"Just go home, Truck. Go be drunk somewhere else, and get around to paying her the money you owe, yeah? Do the smart thing. For once."

"Out of my way, Jimmy," he said, with the same tone he'd used decades earlier, suited up in helmets and pads, when he was looking to make his way past in a practice. He had the same tone, same body language, same ugliness around his bloodshot; not rushing a quarterback, but crashing a kid's birthday party, but just as cruel-looking about it.

Hell with that. I wasn't moving. I knew he'd try to move me.

He went for a shove—guys who have muscle and fat on you, they always shove, unless they start to turn away, in which case, I guaran-fraggin-tee it, they're gonna turn back your way with a haymaker—and I just rolled with it, then reached up to trap his hand against my chest. Then it was easy-peasy to bend forward to cock his wrist back, and adjust my grip to turn it into a lock.

I looked him right in his face as he cried out and went to his knees, one arm stiff, the other flailing ineffectually, looking up at me mad as nails but without knowing how to lash out about it properly. Old Lone Star pain compliance holds. They weren't as satisfying as cracking somebody in the face, but I had a feeling—yup, my cyberaudio picked up the clatter of empty beer cans, the thump of car doors slamming shut—I was about to get to punch some people, too.

The ork led the charge, my headware calculating his range and his increased speed, scuff of work boots on a sidewalk giving him away. I just twisted, wrenched on Truck's arm to lurch him into the way, and sidestepped. The pair of them went down in a heap, and I took two paces to pick up steam, then started kicking.

My wingtips are work shoes in disguise, with slip-resistant traction that handles my home's perpetual rainfall, and high-impact polymer toes that make 'em great for kicking. I didn't take either of these two assholes out of the fight with a few good stomps and a couple'a soccer kicks, but I made Bug Eyes go even buggier and think twice about diving in. Truck and his ork buddy were both slow to get up, and bleeding when they did. That, the booze, and their natural inclinations made 'em all mad and sloppy, that being the case. It made it easy.

I slipped a wild overhand right from the tusker and snuck in a kidney shot, then a shove to buy myself space for Truck to come in. Left jab, left jab, get the range, keep him off-balance with them. Another left jab, then a good right kick, sidelong, aimed right at that knee he'd blown out his second Senior year, when we'd made a run for the Metroplex Championship.

He went down, howling. The ork came back in, but he was nothing a quick jab, cross, uppercut couldn't smack down. Truck whimpered and crawled toward his Toyota Talon, slow, cursing as much as moving. The ork was down for the count, I'd clipped his chin just so—lots of practice helps—and that just left me and Bug Eyes.

He gawked. I pulled out a fresh smoke, and this time I lit it up the fancy way, the magical way. Adversary, my mentor spirit, was as good as his word; I had a little more sorcerous 'oomph' lately, and I used it. A little glare, a little whispered Enochian, a little focus, and the cherry blazed red.

"Fff...fuh...frag me," Bug Eyes swallowed. "You're a muh... muh...mage?"

"Mm-hmm." It felt good, that kind of fear. I took a long, slow drag, watching just over his shoulder as Kowalski kept crawling. Eyes was standing in a good spot, it'd help if he stayed there.

"You stay put."

I strode right past him—cutting across the pitiful lawn, the city fathers had my grass-walking on camera, I knew, but I took the shortcut to time my arrival just right—and got to the Talon just in time. Kowalksi'd gotten the door open and was reaching for something under the seat, like I thought he might. My foot slammed into the door, and the door slammed shut on his elbow. He wailed, but doggedly kept reaching.

I shouldered into it again, grinding it shut on him, until he got the hint and wrenched his arm out of there and fell onto his butt in the Puyallup gutter. I gave him a second, glaring down at him, hands on my hips, then I stooped and reached for whatever-it-was. My arm was longer—elven genes'll see to that nine times outta ten—but I also wasn't just a drunk fragging idiot with a bum leg and a concussion; I grabbed it more easily than he did.

Then I cursed and threw the Seattle Mariners minibat back into his dumb Toyota. The small aluminum club was dirty from rolling around under his filthy seat, but also brown with old blood. I knew some of it was Sally's. It fit the reports, and what she'd told me.

"You prick!"

I loomed over him, hands on my hips again, fists clenched, wanting to stomp the life right out of him, wanting to haul his head up to slam the door on a few times, wanting to go for my gun, or my knife, or to just rip the mana, the life-stuff, right out of him with my worst spells. I wanted to piss on him, to establish dominance completely.

He snatched the little club off the car floor with his good hand and held it in front of him like a wand, like a warding amulet, like a desperate talisman of protection.

"You stupid. Fraggin'. Prick. It wasn't even a piece you were goin' for? Huh? An Ares, a Browning, a fraggin' *Tiffani*? Something that might've actually given you a chance? It was that toy? You thought waving a fraggin' *novelty bat* at me was going to help?"

I fumed, blood up, mad at the whole world but especially this waste of flesh. Like I didn't have enough problems, like Sally didn't have it rough enough already, like Jasmine needed this piece of garbage back in her life...

"–you treat them like queens, you hear me?–"

"All you had to do was leave. I tried, Truck, I gave you that out. You know. You know about the restraining order, you know I know about it, you know who I am. You know what I do."

I waved an arm, lashed out with it, gestured at the city building like it was a backhanded slap. He flinched.

"I measured it, you stupid prick. Thirty-seven yards from where you parked to that door. Thirty-seven. You remember what a hundred yards looks like, Truck? Huh? Think back to your worthless goddamned glory days, and remember a football field. A hundred yards. That's how far away from her you stay. And you know it."

"That's how far." I leaned over him, he cringed back into the gutter.

"You *stay*," I growled, the back of his head squelched into the Puyallup muck. "*Away. From. Her.*" I jabbed him, just a stern little poke of the finger, with every word.

I straightened up again, looming over him like a titan.

"But now here you are. Recorded on city fraggin' cameras," and my cyberoptics. Sure, I kept 'em in black and white most of the time, but I was almost always recording. "Driving drunk, violating that restraining order, committin' battery, and then escalating a violent situation by goin' for a concealed weapon, which looks like it's, itself, evidence of prior crimes."

I let it all sink in for a second. It took longer than it should have, 'cause he's a damned idiot, but eventually he got it. This wasn't just idiot blustering. This wasn't him harmlessly crashing a party. This was him throwing a good chunk of his life away, making it—somehow—even more worthless.

I wanted to kick him. Stomp him a few more times. Choke the life right out of him. I didn't let myself. I didn't let Adversary make me do it.

"You think real hard over the next couple hours, Kowalksi. Harder'n you ever thought before in your idiot life. Sober up, clear your head, and do the right thing. Leave a note for your girl, do what you can to pay what you owe, and turn yourself in. Soon as this party's over, Truck, I'm makin' the call. You've got the rest of the afternoon to get your shit together and decide how it goes down. If you decide wrong—if you so much as think about running—you stupid bastard, I'll find you and kill you myself."

"And you," I turned, instead, letting my coat send Truck flinching into the slimy ash again. I stalked over to Bug Eyes, who was, at least, smart enough to be obedient. He'd stayed put. Good. At least one thing in my corner of the world was going right today.

"Your name is Alvin Sparetti, right?" It wasn't really a question. My headware'd done the trick already, optics suite synched up with facial recognition protocols synched up with criminal databases. I knew more about him than his friends probably did.

He nodded. His eyes went even wider when I stood in front of him, squarely, and my hand went into my coat. He hadn't noticed my Colt was holstered down on my hip, along with my wand, my knife; my deadliest stuff wasn't up high in a shoulder rig, but he didn't realize that. Clearly. 'Cause he wet himself.

Taking a half-step back, I shoved an old-fashioned paper envelope at his chest. His eyes nearly fell out of his head.

"These're for you. Legal docs, on behalf of Ms. Kimberly Hightower, Esquire. I think you know why. If you don't, read 'em and find out."

I thumbed over my shoulder to the same cameras I'd—roughly—pointed out to Truck.

"City government's seen me hand 'em over, no need to sign anything. You've got thirty days to answer the complaint, or fellas like me'll come and find you. Again."

"Congrats." I turned and started for the building again, stubbing out my Target in the ash-covered tray as I hauled the door open. Over my shoulder, a parting shot while I saw them gathering up their orkish buddy. "You've been served."

That had been my second job, the one that paid better than free cake and tired smiles. The one that really justified taking a break from my work with Pinkerton. The one Sally didn't know about, didn't *need* to know about. A favor for a lawyer, an up-and-comer in the shadow community who was providing legal counsel to skells, but also doing a fair amount of *pro bono* work that reminded me of an idiot paranormal investigator I knew. Gals like Hightower, they were nice to have handy. Trying to keep one foot on each side of the law, a fella could do worse than keeping on her good side.

Once I'd heard *this* moron ran with *that* moron, the jobs had been easy enough to line up. Two birds, one stone. Two favors, one afternoon. Two idiots, one beating.

I was a man of my word. I'd give Truck until the evening before calling in his litany of criminal idiocy. I wasn't going to stick around for the party, though, not really. I didn't have the time to burn. Pinkerton was waiting, and every minute I was away he was stuck working solo a cold case that we were worried was growing colder. I had more things to worry about. I had more work to do. I had bigger problems looming.

These days, "bigger problems" might as well've been my middle name.

The afternoon blurred into the evening at Pinkerton's side, hitting the streets and realizing he knew Downtown as well as I knew Puyallup. Then evening turned to night, and we gave it up again. I was tired. I was hungry. I was crabby. But I wasn't so tired I could miss these two new idiots.

They were waiting outside my place, standing in the long shadows and the drifting ash.

I was exhausted and frustrated. I was distracted enough I hadn't noticed their big Chevy parked out front, was too used to the street having plenty of cars parked on it. But just a few steps out of my own ugly Ford, I saw the pair of them, huddled into the Happy Thai-m doorway against the cold wind, their bulk and their suits and the garlic stink of one giving them away.

With a head full of chrome like mine, with the supercomputer, the eyes, the ears, with the bio-genetic Sideways treatment that sharpened my senses and aided in pattern recognition, I'd have to be dead not to see these two mooks. And I wasn't dead. Not yet.

"Are you two fraggin' serious?"

I stopped a couple meters away, just shook my head and sighed. I knew those stupid shoulders, that stink, those suits, I recognized the dull shine of their leather shoes. I knew the shape of these two, and the only reason they could be here. They were muscle, usually posted at Sunny Salvo's, across town. Enzo Gianelli's joint. They were his goons. His doormen. A couple of mobsters.

"You come for me here? Middle of the fraggin' night? I oughta shoot the both of you." My headware raced, Lone Star-implanted cyberaudio suite scanning, cybereyes darting, searching for any more of them.

"It ain't like that, Jimmy, nothin' rough," the little one said. He was a human, but had enough bulky slabs of implanted muscle that he looked more like an ork.

"Don't have to be rough," the bigger one agreed. He actually was an ork, but was so cartoonishly broad, so swollen from his own implants, that you'd swear he was trying to impress trolls.

One big, one huge. Neither one was the brains-of-the-outfit type. They both shuffled a bit, but didn't step all the way out of their little cubby. The harsh neon of the Happy Thai-m sign, a cartoonish clock, gave my light amplification software more than enough to see with, but they were both half-hidden enough I couldn't see their hands. I didn't like that.

Always watch the hands.

"That so? How is it, then?" I stayed where I was, down the sidewalk. I kept my stance casual, hands thrust deep in my longcoat's pockets, hat low on my head, collar up against the cold. Frag 'em. They wanted to talk to me, they could step out here into the wind and the drizzle, too. Where I could see their hands.

"Mr. Gianelli wants to talk, is all," Jumbo said.

"Yeah, Jimmy. Just talk," Economy-Size bobbed his little head.

I was acutely aware of my Colt on my hip, the weight of my wand and spare magazines balancing out my belt on the other side. Could there really only be two of them? God, what was Enzo even pissed about this time?

"He told us to fetch you." Another grunt, another shuffle like they weren't sure what to do. I knew what "fetch" could mean. I knew how many folks had been tossed in the back of that big Chevy and never been seen again.

"He told you that? Okay. Well, I'm tellin' you frag off and get away from my place. I'm going upstairs. I'm expecting a call. I'll talk to him tomorrow."

"Jimmy," Economy-Size was the dumber of the two, his naturally orkish bulk making him a little more confident. He stepped my way, backlit by the sign, ghostly shadow drawn out all down the dark street. His hands were empty, but his voice dropped to a low growl, "Boss wants you, boss gets you. You know the rules."

"Frag your rules," my Mentor spirit, Adversary, crowed through my mouth. "I don't owe Enzo money, and I don't owe him fear. I'm not just some skell you two can come collect for no damned reason. You tell him I said that. You tell him whatever you have to. But you ain't takin' me nowhere."

They started toward me, then, too-wide torsos balanced on top of natty leather shoes. Theirs were less scuffed than mine, carried less ash than my Oxfords, less mileage. They didn't walk anywhere. They drove, they picked up, they stood around outside Sunny Salvo's, and that was it. They didn't mingle much, didn't soak up the streets like a local had to. Puyallup was just a job to them. To me, it's home.

I scowled fiercely as they got close. I was still in a shit mood, and—truth was—I owed these pair a few licks for the last time we'd chatted, anyhow.

I watched their hands as they came my way. Both sets were empty. When Economy-Sized lifted his ork-big set of mitts and reached for my shoulder—putting hands on me, getting ready to grab me just like I knew they'd grabbed so many others before pitching them into the back of that big Chevy—I finally moved.

My left hand was empty, too. I launched a straight arm, elf-long reach trumping his muscles, my fingers flat, thumb out wide, web of my hand *thunking* right in below his warty chin, hitting his Adam's apple just right. He fell back, croaking, eyes wide.

My right hand wasn't empty when *it* came up. I slid back and to one side, angling a few steps, keeping both of them in front of me, and held my big Colt on Jumbo, the human one. His hands went up. Still empty. Maybe he was the smart one. It was easy to do the smart thing, looking down the mean end of a Colt Model 2061.

"Go home," was all I said.

My voice was as level as the Colt, unwavering, sights and smartlink targeting pip all lined up, pointed right at his nose. Nobody felt as big and strong looking down the barrel of a gun, least of all mine.

They glared. They grumbled. They exchanged a look, then they decided. Economy-Size coughed, spat a mouthful of Puyallup ash, coughed some more. They slunk away, kicked hounds with their tails between their legs, clambering into their big SUV, and as the engine purred to life Jumbo's driver-side window slid down.

"Mr. Gianelli ain't gonna like this, Jimmy," he said, voice low and certain. "He ain't gonna like this at all."

I holstered my Colt with a shrug.

"He can call me and tell me how much he don't like it. But he can fragging *call* me. Like a normal person. You two stay away from my place."

Ash kicked up as they drove away, as Puyallup's darkness took their taillights away.

"Boss?" There was a frantic edge to the new voice, a high pitch that gave away childish concern, genuine hurt, a little indignation. "Why didn't you call me?!"

It was Ariana. In the time it took me to spit and turn and reach for the side door, the one that opened into a row of mailboxes and a narrow hallway that fed into a staircase that'd take me home, in the time it took me just to brush off the ash and swipe my thumb to unlock it, she'd materialized right inside.

She lit the place up. Glowing, shining, an inhuman brightness to her, her body going from astral to real but still impossibly clean, magical, pure, all metals and jewels. Her light show at the party hadn't been fake, or forced, or just for the girls. She just glowed. I'd first summoned her from materials mostly found on the elemental metaplane of Earth, and it showed in her metallic gleam. Normally my cyberoptics suite showed me the world in black and white, old-timey, unreal, like everything I saw and did was an ancient movie. Ari, though, Ari always shone through. She was like gold in the dark.

"There was a fight, wasn't there?" For all her usual childlike wonder, all the naivety she had that I didn't, her current tone was petulant, almost maternal, instead of innocent. "There was a fight and you didn't let me help! Again!"

"You were busy, kiddo," I gave her a tired smile, started up the stairs. "And it wasn't much of a fight. Just some of Enzo's guys. They left."

"Mm-hmm. Likely story," she sulked, floated up the stairs behind me. "You didn't let me help earlier, *and* you didn't let me help now? You're supposed to let me help! It's what I'm *for*."

It was true. Ask any hermetic textbook, they'll tell you that security concerns are one of the chief reasons to summon yourself an ally spirit. An initiate willing to devote themselves to enough high-level arcane study to make such a ritualized summoning possible is, after all, a precious goddamned snowflake that shouldn't worry himself with the simple art of fisticuffs, don't ya know?

"I only ask you for help when I need it, doll." I swiped my thumb to unlock my office door, she just went semi-astral again, floated right through the wall. "And I didn't need it."

She crossed her arms, sulky and pouty, until I gave her a smile. She just wanted to feel needed. She had that part of me, too, that I'd long ago lost.

"There was only two of 'em, anyways, kiddo. What kinda jerk would I be, if I let you loose against just two guys, huh? If Enzo sends 'em back with a dozen buddies, then it'll be a fair fight."

It probably still wouldn't, actually. She *had* gotten loose against just two of his guys before, a couple years back. Her gorgeous, elf-perfect, nails could turn as sharp as flint or obsidian in an eyeblink. Her strength was the strength of mountains, her fury an avalanche, her heart as inhuman as it was beautiful. Odds're good she could physically tear a dozen of his guys to pieces without getting scratched, and that wasn't even taking into consideration her real power; the spells she could cast.

But then she flashed me that shining smile, all innocence and brightness again, and it was easy to forget all that. She held her hands out for my coat, jacket and hat and gave them all a quick once-over with her favorite little Fashion spell. Ash and grit sluiced off, colors melted and shifted, long coat turning a warm brown, suit coat and hat sliding to a light blue. The magic took no more effort from her than hanging them on the rack near the door did.

Ari had my old power, too. Not just my youth, my sense of wonder, the elf-pretty features I'd given up for decades of punches and hard living. Not just the fey-bright eyes I'd had replaced by cybernetic cameras, not just the kindness I did my best to fake most of the time. She had my raw talent, my magical strength. She'd been ritualized into existence when I'd been at the peak of my powers, before the vampire attack that had crippled me, and she still had all of it.

She was a firestorm, as beautiful as it was dangerous. I was a scratched and battered old Zippo, useful but half-empty.

I slumped into my squeaky office chair, synth-leather groaning almost as loud as I did.

"No luck with the kid's case today," I said, though the same empathic link that had drawn her back home meant she could surely read my disappointment. She frowned anyways, like the update was actually news.

"Did Mr. Pinkerton say anything?" She swayed a little, eyes down. I think my little girl's got a bit of a crush.

"He said to say hi." Probably. "And that we're gonna keep looking."

"Good!" She beamed, satisfied with both statements. Aside from her best friends—Skip and Trace, bounty hunting gals who she'd been off hanging out with most of the evening—Dexter Pinkerton was her new favorite, I think. He let Ariana play with the colors on his clothes more than I did, let her cast and recast Fashion spells with more dazzling displays. Pink liked stuff brighter than me, maybe that's why he fit in so well in Downtown.

We were working a runaway case, but from a weird angle. I'd heard from a—friend?—girl named Gem that her big brother'd run off, but heard it well after the fact. The kid, Danny Finn, had ditched their old man back in the CalFree Bay Area and hit the road about a year ago. She was sure he'd come to Seattle, so she'd run away, too, left behind their prick of a dad—I was probably gonna shoot him if I ever met him—and she'd made her own way up the coast, chasing her big brother. She was a good kid, Gem.

She'd helped me out, so I'd promised I'd ask around and try to find him. She and her brother were dwarven like Pinkerton, and Pink knew more people'n me outside of Puyallup, anyways, so I'd asked him to help out. We were trying, but it was hard. A runaway in Seattle wasn't even as easy as a needle in a haystack. It was a needle in a scrapyard. Runaways poured into Seattle all the time. Runaways went missing all the time, especially metahumans. Seattle ate kids like that, ate kids like Gem, ate plenty of dreams and tomorrows without skipping a beat or even making a headline. A kid who'd come to Seattle *trying* to disappear? I didn't have high hopes.

But hell if I was telling little Gem, or even bright-eyed Ariana, that.

I told myself it was keeping a promise. I told myself it was because every day mattered. I told myself I had to even the score with Gem, follow through like I'd said I would, get her and her brother back together. I told myself it was in my Adversarial nature to ignore the odds, and do the underdog's work.

Truth was, I'd maybe been focusing on the missing Danny Finn in order to ignore the other case looming over me. I was searching the whole stinking Emerald City for one little runaway because it meant doing PI work, it meant tackling a problem—even a difficult one—that I knew how to tackle. It meant doing my job, the way I knew to do it. The other job? The other problem? It was way out of my league, and it was the main reason for the shitty mood I'd taken out on idiots like Truck and Enzo's clowns.

I sighed and gave Ari a smile.

"Anyways. You head on back to Skip and Trace, kiddo. Have fun. Tell 'em the coast is clear, Enzo's guys took right off, so they don't worry. I gotta take a call." I waved Ari away, and she faded and flew off, dazzling me with a return smile first.

She could move as quick as thought when she wanted to, and I knew in just a few heartbeats she'd be halfway across town, going back to whatever "girl time" she got up to with the pair of bounty hunters.

I was pretty sure Enzo's muscle wasn't going to come back tonight. They'd probably called him just after pulling away from the curb. If he'd been high when they told him what had happened, I'd've heard from him by now. If not, he'd just brood, but I didn't expect any trouble from him tonight.

Which was lucky, 'cause I had trouble enough without him.

As I steepled my fingers and glared down at my desk, the little datachip case drew my eye. It was empty, the chip itself was with a...a friend? An employee, I guess, right now. I'd inherited the chip and the data from another friend, in his will. An old teacher of mine had been murdered, at least in part for whatever research he'd been doing, whatever files were on that little chip, whatever fantastic cosmic truths he'd dared to etch onto it. I'd read the synopsis, just the little preamble to his research, and scanned the file names, and they'd scared me to death. *Inhumans and the Cycle of Magic*, it called itself, a self-proclaimed sequel to some seminal Hermetic work that'd changed how our metaphysicists viewed time and nature and our place in it.

This little chip had gotten things rolling, turned my wreck of a life into straight-up chaos and madness, lately. Blood had been spilled, vampires had come dredging up from my nightmares, I'd sent myself skipping through the metaplanes, heads'd been cut off, hearts'd stopped, lives'd been cut short, and all of it was tangled up around what was on that datachip. A dead man's research had already killed so many more.

It was a harmless-looking little thing, but potentially more dangerous than my Colt, my wand, or any of the other weapons I carried around on the daily.

It was secrets. It was trouble. It was way over my usual pay grade. And it was locked tighter'n a dragon's claw.

Encrypted. Too hot to hack; I'd had friends try, friends who were good at it. We couldn't access the full data, so I didn't even *know* what exactly it was that'd put a bullseye on my back. I'd had to send the chip away, to the one place where maybe it could get decrypted. Sometimes you had to go back to the source with that stuff, so that's where the chip was headed. All I had right now was an empty chip case and—if she ever dialed me up—a call from a troll, Ms. Myth, who was supposed to tell me when they hit the road. I'd wrapped it up with Pinkerton and the missing kid because I was waiting on that call, waiting on an update, waiting on a departure time. I wanted to be here in Puyallup when they were leaving, not halfway across town, in case anything went wrong.

A quick thought pulled up my headware chronometer and I scowled. It wasn't like her to be late, but I tried to remind myself there was no need to be this tense. My Sideways gene-treatment made me antsy sometimes, my too-sharp senses made every blink of a time display feel like an eternity. I needed to take the edge off. I spat out my WhiteBrite betel gum and reached into a desk drawer for something to help, and for something to remind me the cost of the call I was waiting on.

I splashed a little twelve-year Presley Highland into a tumbler, drank down the peaty dram and immediately poured myself a second. The moonlight through my window lit up the amber whiskey, but it was a piece of gold on the table that had my real attention. It was a chain with a small amulet, the seal of the Hermetic Order of the Auric Aurora flawlessly laser-etched onto it. It wasn't the design that made it valuable, or even the gold, though.

It was a focus, an item imbued with magic. Some were straightforward, like my little too-sharp pocket knife, a tactical folder with a mono-edged blade. It was just sharp, just a weapon, just an impossibly strong blade that could hurt things mundane steel couldn't. Handy, but simple. The little wand I kept—a sliver of Voodoo-infused bone hidden in an anodized aluminum tube, a "whatever works" magical mishmash concealed to look scientific and hermetic—was a more potent focus item, one that channeled raw mana for me, that fed me power and bolstered the strength of my spells when I used it. Useful, undeniably so, but straightforward. It was a battery pack, lending extra oomph to whatever castings I tried.

Some focus items were more complicated, more specific. I fidgeted with my own new ring, a white gold piece with a ruby winking at me, as I looked down at the amulet. These two were similar in more ways than one. I'd gotten 'em from the same place, on the same night. Earned 'em the same way. They also held a similar trick. They could hold mojo for you, store a spell, hang onto it instead of making you work to hold it yourself;

once you did the heavy lifting of casting a spell into them, they maintained it for you, taking the weight off.

Foci were valuable. Foci were expensive. This particular focus, the amulet, was a big part of how I was paying for a job, and that particular job was what I was waiting for a call on.

I fidgeted with my ring, and scowled. It wasn't like Ms. Myth to be late. She was a sharp cookie, and not just for a troll. Knew her stuff. Appreciated both precision and improvisation. She was good.

The negotiations had gone well enough that I knew something was up. She and I had worked together before, and I knew enough about her to know that she'd let me off easy for some reason, hadn't driven up the price as high as she could've. It wasn't stinking of a double-cross, though—her rep was too solid for that, and so was her team's—but I knew she'd been a little too eager to take the job.

Still, I wasn't going to look a gift horse in the mouth. I was getting a hell of a deal. Her crew might not've been Seattle's shadow legends—not yet—but they were reliable, and reliable shadowrunners were normally much more expensive. This focus, the amulet that stored spells, was half of the payment; they'd get it on their return, and in the meantime it and the empty chip case were reminders, to me, of the gig I'd sent them on.

The other half of their payment had been up front, standard terms, cold, hard, nuyen. I'd earned it the hard way, leftover bounty cash, a windfall I hadn't really wanted. I'd doled out plenty of the UCAS bounty on the Infected—Human/Metahuman Vampiric Virus carriers, victims of the disease that had lost their minds to it and gone predator-feral—already, paying off the circus side-show of friends who'd helped me kill the stupid monsters in the first place. The rest of the payment had just cleared, though. The HMHVV bounty payout was a good pile of nuyen, but I was willing to invest, if it got me to the bottom of this mess.

The reason I needed a solid crew like Myth's folks—Sledge, Hardpoint, and Gentry, who I already knew, plus some spellslinger gal that I'm sure was about to decide she liked white gold necklaces that served as spell foci—was because the one thing we knew for sure about the encryption on the datachip, the only real advice I'd gotten from any of my jacked-in friends who'd taken a peek at it for me, was that the security on it was bad news.

The wall of data-locks and security protocols between us and the info was boldly branded as Willamette Compustat work. A Tír Tairngire company. *The* Tír Tairngire company, where Matrix security's concerned, my tech-geeks tell me. The Matrix provider that's trusted by paranoid elven princes to oversee their secrets. The Matrix provider on retainer to handle e-security for the whole nation. The Matrix provider sub-contracted—so a few quick searches told us—to handle sensitive research from the Tír's major universities; and Dr. Christopher Minirth, my departed friend whose chipful of data I had burning a hole in my life, had been neck-deep in just such research.

Which meant my best bet of cracking the file—Gentry, himself a Tír brat born and raised, assured me—was a trip down south, into a paranoid elven nation, where we could find hackers who were used to taking can openers to Compustat's work...and hell if *I* was going.

"There are *raé* down there that can crack this, bro, for sure! It's a magical country, bro." The decker had chimed in over Myth's shoulder, the first time I'd talked to them about the job. "I got people down there. You'll see. Ain't a file we can't open."

His exuberance wasn't the most reassuring thing in the world—he *was* the sort of overconfident dummy that liked to jump rooftops and free-run his way through Seattle like a crazy person—but his lead was the best bet I had. I was light on tech support. Trace had been the first to try to slice into it for me, and the first to notice the Willamette Compustat earmarks, no elf pun intended. Gentry'd confirmed it, but that was all he could do, solo. I would've loved to get an old shadow-buddy, Frostbyte, to take a peek—himself Tír-born, and Tír trained in Matrix work—but he'd run off with his Neo-Anarchist buddies, and I already owed him a favor, anyways. Gentry was the best I had, the best I had access to, and there's no point in surrounding yourself with experts if you ignore their advice.

So Compustat was our lead, the encryption protocols they supplied to Tír universities was our goal, and Gentry's connection back home was our best chance of reaching it. Enter Ms. Myth, Gentry's teammate and agent, and voila. The deal'd been brokered. The chip itself was slotted, secure, in one of the many dataports he sported. The kid was a professional courier when he wasn't running the shadows, I could've done a lot worse, in that regard. But they were supposed to be leaving, and they were supposed to be calling, and they were late doing both.

I flicked the little case around on my desktop, scowling at it as it slid one way, then the next. I knew a little bit of what it held, yeah. That introduction, the briefest report of it, had been enough. Heavy enough to believe folks might kill for it. *Inhumans and the Cycle of Magic* talked about mana cycles. It talked about the rise and fall of sorcerous tides, floated theories at the reader first proposed decades earlier, by an elf many claimed was honest-to-Buddha immortal. Chris Minirth had been there when this nutty professor, Ehran the Scribe, had first ruffled Hermetic feathers by giving his little talk, and he'd collaborated with Tír-based scholars for decades since, even after his transfer up here to Seattle, where he'd taught palookas like me at University of Washington.

Where he'd died.

A big part of me wanted to just flick the whole thing out of my life. Toss it. Burn it. Wipe the chip and call it a day. This was bigger than I liked, bigger than I was used to. A big part of me wanted to get back to the shadows I called home, wanted to focus on the problems that scaled to me and my friends better, wanted to throw my attention back on Puyallup and promises, to worrying about smaller problems, like keeping the Mafia and the Yakuza from tearing my neighborhood apart, like tracking down deadbeat parents and cheating spouses, like paying my rent. I won't lie. I liked my life easy. Black and white.

But the bigger part of me? Just a dog with a bone, plain and simple. Chris'd left it to me, he'd trusted me with it—not even the Hermetic Order of the Auric Aurora, but *me*—and that made it my responsibility. I wanted to read what was on it, wanted to see what had made it so important to him, but I also just didn't want to let him down. I wanted to buck the odds and handle it, see the thing through, finish the job, if not for him, then because it *was* supposed to be too big for me.

And besides, it was a case. Solving cases was my job, right?

LOOKING FOR MORE SHADOWRUN FICTION, CHUMMER?

WE'LL HOOK YOU UP!

Catalyst Game Labs brings you the very best in *Shadowrun* fiction, available at most ebook retailers, including Amazon, Apple Books, Kobo, Barnes & Noble, and more!

NOVELS

1. *Never Deal with a Dragon* (Secrets of Power #1) by Robert N. Charrette
2. *Choose Your Enemies Carefully* (Secrets of Power #2) by Robert N. Charrette
3. *Find Your Own Truth* (Secrets of Power #3) by Robert N. Charrette
4. *2XS* by Nigel Findley
5. *Changeling* by Chris Kubasik
6. *Never Trust an Elf* by Robert N. Charrette
7. *Shadowplay* by Nigel Findley
8. *Night's Pawn* by Tom Dowd
9. *Striper Assassin* by Nyx Smith
10. *Lone Wolf* by Nigel Findley
11. *Fade to Black* by Nyx Smith
12. *Burning Bright* by Tom Dowd
13. *Who Hunts the Hunter* by Nyx Smith
14. *House of the Sun* by Nigel Findley
15. *Worlds Without End* by Caroline Spector
16. *Just Compensation* by Robert N. Charrette
17. *Preying for Keeps* by Mel Odom
18. *Dead Air* by Jak Koke
19. *The Lucifer Deck* by Lisa Smedman
20. *Steel Rain* by Nyx Smith
21. *Shadowboxer* by Nicholas Pollotta
22. *Stranger Souls* (Dragon Heart Saga #1) by Jak Koke
23. *Headhunters* by Mel Odom
24. *Clockwork Asylum* (Dragon Heart Saga #2) by Jak Koke
25. *Blood Sport* by Lisa Smedman

26. *Beyond the Pale* (Dragon Heart Saga #3) by Jak Koke
27. *Technobabel* by Stephen Kenson
28. *The Terminus Experiment* by Jonathan E. Bond and Jak Koke
29. *Psychotrope* by Lisa Smedman
30. *Run Hard, Die Fast* by Mel Odom
31. *Crossroads* by Stephen Kenson
32. *The Forever Drug* by Lisa Smedman
33. *Ragnarock* by Stephen Kenson
34. *Tails You Lose* by Lisa Smedman
35. *The Burning Time* by Stephen Kenson
36. *Wolf and Raven* by Michael A. Stackpole
37. *Born to Run* (Kellen Colt Trilogy #1) by Stephen Kenson
38. *Poison Agendas* (Kellen Colt Trilogy #2) by Stephen Kenson
39. *Fallen Angels* (Kellen Colt Trilogy #3) by Stephen Kenson
40. *Drops of Corruption* by Jason M. Hardy
41. *Aftershocks* by Jean Rabe & John Helfers
42. *A Fistful of Data* by Stephen Dedman
43. *Fire and Frost* by Kai O'Connal
44. *Hell on Water* by Jason M. Hardy
45. *Dark Resonance* by Phaedra Weldon
46. *Crimson* by Kevin Czarnecki
47. *Shaken: No Job Too Small* by Russell Zimmerman
48. *Borrowed Time* by R.L. King
49. *Deniable Assets* by Mel Odom
50. *Undershadows* by Jason M. Hardy
51. *Shadows Down Under* by Jean Rabe
52. *Makeda Red* by Jennifer Brozek
53. *The Johnson Run* by Kai O'connal
54. *Shadow Dance* by Aaron Rosenberg
55. *Identity: Crisis* by Phaedra Weldon
56. *Veiled Extraction* by R.L. King

ANTHOLOGIES

1. *Spells & Chrome*, edited by John Helfers
2. *World of Shadows*, edited by John Helfers
3. *Drawing Destiny: A Sixth World Tarot Anthology*, edited by John Helfers
4. *Sprawl Stories, Vol. 1*, edited by John Helfers
5. *The Complete Frame Job*, edited by John Helfers

NOVELLAS

1. *Neat* by Russell Zimmerman
2. *The Vladivostok Gauntlet* by Olivier Gagnon
3. *Nothing Personal* by Olivier Gagnon
4. *Another Rainy Night* by Patrick Goodman
5. *Sail Away, Sweet Sister* by Patrick Goodman
6. *The Seattle Gambit* by Olivier Gagnon
7. *DocWagon 19* by Jennifer Brozek
8. *Wolf & Buffalo* by R.L. King
9. *Big Dreams* by R.L. King
10. *Blind Magic* by Dylan Birtolo
11. *The Frame Job, Part 1: Yu* by Dylan Birtolo
12. *The Frame Job, Part 2: Emu* by Brooke Chang
13. *The Frame Job, Part 3: Rude* by Bryan CP Steele
14. *The Frame Job, Part 4: Frostburn* by CZ Wright
15. *The Frame Job, Part 5: Zipfile* by Jason Schmetzer
16. *The Frame Job, Part 6: Retribution* by Jason M. Hardy
17. *Tower of the Scorpion* by Mel Odom
18. *A Kiss to Die For* by Jennifer Brozek

©2018 All Rights Reserved.
Catalyst Game Labs and the Catalyst Game Labs logo are trademarks or registered trademarks of InMediaRes Productions, LLC.

Made in the USA
Coppell, TX
18 July 2020